No Strange Fire

No Strange Fire

Ted Wojtasik

HERALD PRESS
Scottdale, Pennsylvania
Waterloo, Ontario

Library of Congress Cataloging-in-Publication Data
Wojtasik, Ted, date.
No strange fire / Ted Wojtasik.
p. cm.
ISBN 0-8361-9041-6 (alk. paper)
1. Barns—Fires and fire prevention—Fiction. 2. Young men—Pennsylvania—Fiction. 3. Amish—Pennsylvania—Fiction.
I. Title.
PS3573.0445N6 1996
813'.54—dc20 96-1197
CIP

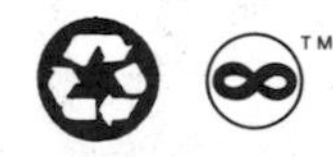

The paper used in this publication is recycled and meets the minimum requirements of American National Standard for Information Sciences—Permanence of Paper for Printed Library Materials, ANSI Z39.48-1984.

This is a work of fiction. Names, characters, places, and incidents are the product of the author's imagination or used fictitiously. Any resemblance to events or persons, living or dead, is entirely coincidental. See Author's Note on page 399. Scripture is adapted from the *King James Version of the Holy Bible.* Prayers from the early Swiss Anabaptist prayer book, *Die ernsthafte Christenpflicht*, are translated by Leonard Gross and used by permission of Herald Press, from *Prayer Book for Earnest Christians* (1996).

Library of Congress Catalog Number: 96-1197
International Standard Book Number: 0-8361-9041-6
Printed in the United States of America
Book design and cover illustration by Gwen M. Stamm

05 04 03 02 01 00 99 98 97 96 10 9 8 7 6 5 4 3 2 1

Dedicated to
the Nebraska Amish
and
my mother and father

CONTENTS

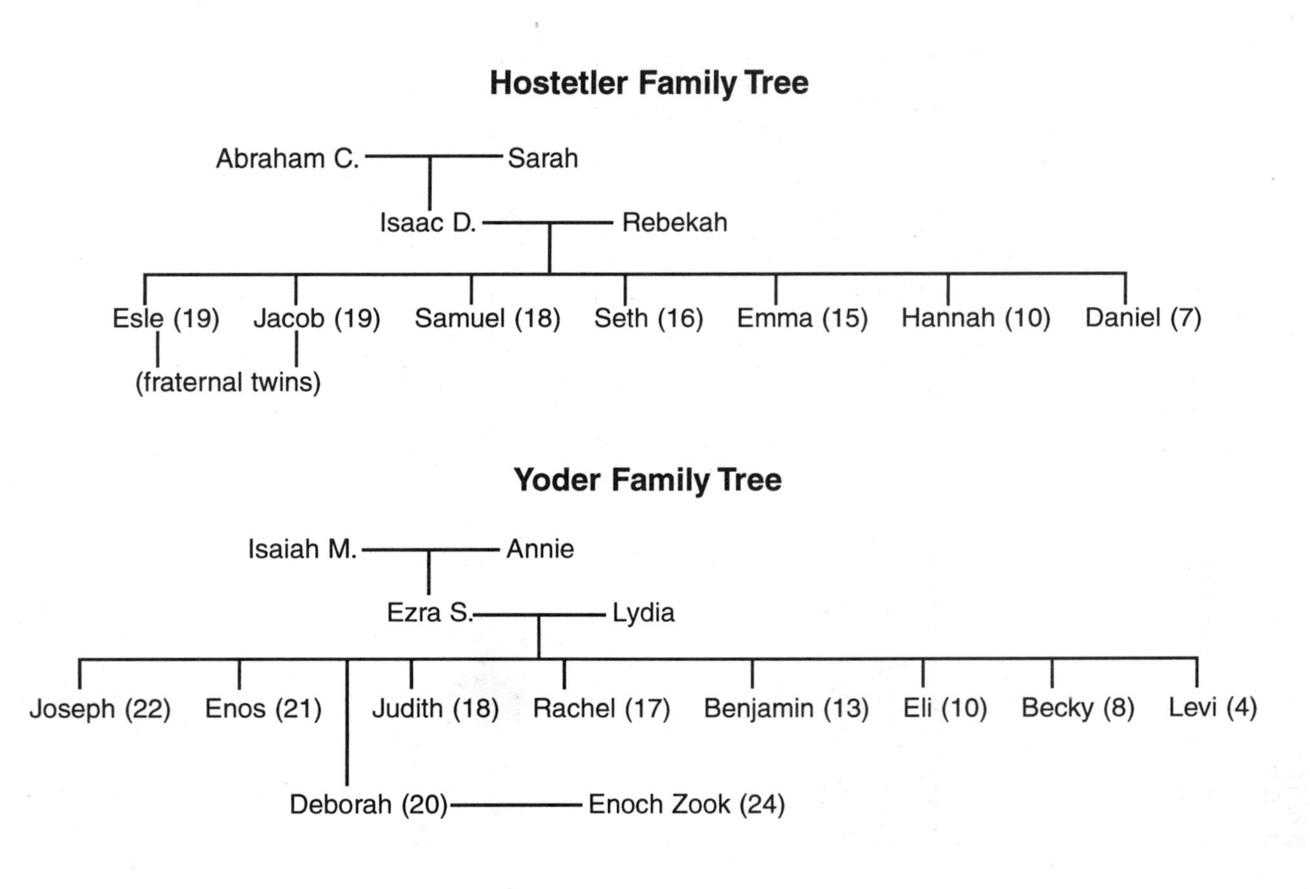
Hostetler Family Tree
Abraham C.
Sarah
Isaac D.
Rebekah
Esle (19)
Jacob (19)
(fraternal twins)
Samuel (18)
Seth (16)
Emma (15)
Hannah (10)
Daniel (7)
Yoder Family Tree
Isaiah M.
Annie
Ezra S.
Lydia
Joseph (22)
Enos (21)
Judith (18)
Rachel (17)
Benjamin (13)
Eli (10)
Becky (8)
Levi (4)
Deborah (20)
Enoch Zook (24)

ACKNOWLEDGMENTS

Esther Stuter is the person who supported me and believed in me unhesitatingly throughout this entire project. She introduced me to Big Valley and to the Amish, and she was the driving force most responsible for the success of this work. My gratitude is endless.

I am equally indebted and cannot extend greater appreciation to all the Amish who graciously worked with me. I also wish to thank the following people who helped me: Frances Barnes, Bob Bartlett, Beano, Mike Bratt, Patti Burke, Don Chapman, Major Terry Clemens, John Crownover, Clair Delong, Jim Felmee, Brandon Forsythe, Corporal Norman Gantz, Shawn Gonsar, Gary Gonsar, Bob Harris, Carrie Henry, David Kauffman, Elaine Mercer, Percy Renninger, Ollie Shipe, Eric Specht, Grace Straley, Karl Westover, Denny Woodward, Dennis Yohn, and anyone else whose name I might have overlooked. Without your help, this novel could not have been written.

Finally, I must submit my heartfelt thanks to S. David Garber and Herald Press for their support, encouragement, and faith in this novel.

—Ted Wojtasik

And Nadab and Abihu, the sons of Aaron, took either of them his censer, and put fire therein, and put incense thereon, and offered strange fire before the Lord, which he commanded them not.

—Leviticus 10:1

And Nadab and Abihu died before the Lord, when they offered strange fire before the Lord, in the wilderness of Sinai, and they had no children.

—Numbers 3:4

Beloved, think it not strange concerning the fiery trial which is to try you, as though some strange thing happened unto you: but rejoice, inasmuch as you are partakers of Christ's sufferings.

—1 Peter 4:12-13

For there may be no strange fire offered before God.

—Menno Simons, 1535

CHAPTER 1

The calves were crying. Ezra S., with dream-disturbed eyes, stepped onto the front porch. The north side of the barn, facing the farmhouse, exploded into a wall of fire as the smell of smoke filled the cold night air. Prince, one of his best Belgian draft horses, burst as in a vision from the barn of fire and smoke—the great mane flaming, the leonine head scorched, the eyes blinded—and galloped straight into a barbwire fence and crashed to the ground, tangled in the sharp barbs. Helplessly, Ezra S. watched while the horse whinnied and jerked, snorted, shuddered.

Then Eli, his ten-year-old son, shouting, "King! King!" dashed into the wall of fire to save his four-month-old colt. Ezra S. plunged into the burning barn after his son. The intense heat swarmed over him and stung his skin, his eyes, his tongue. His breath burned so that he thought he was swallowing fire. The colt darted past Ezra S. as his son charged toward him. A thick oak beam thundered through the floor of the hayloft, cracked Eli in the back, and knocked him down.

Ezra S. was rushing from the barn of fire and smoke with his son, unconscious, in his arms when he heard not the crying but the screaming of the calves, a shrill crescendo like a gruesome choir that could not hit the right notes. As he laid his son on the ground, blue-and-white lights flashed in his eyes. Lydia, his wife, knelt next to him and stared fearfully at her boy's limp body while the colt scampered about the barnyard, kicking up its spindly hind legs. A policeman marched over to Prince, still tangled in the barbwire fence, and shot him in the head.

The strident sound of distant sirens embraced the shrill screaming of the calves. Ezra S. stroked Eli's corn-blond hair. The horses kicked frenziedly in their stalls. The cows yanked their stanchion chains and mooed and kicked and then simply burst open. The methane gas in their stomachs from chewing cud combusted under the extreme heat and just split open their sides like milk pods. Never had he heard such a sound.

In his eyes red-and-white lights flashed as fire engines, horns blasting, screeched into the barnyard. A stream of water slammed into the side of the barn while the flames, as though alive, turned and twirled, jumped, twisted. A stream of water soaked the farmhouse. Men surrounded Eli with tubes and cylinders, metal boxes, and a stretcher. Over a walkie-talkie a metallic voice crackled. Then a helicopter lifted Eli into the dark sky. Ezra S. felt as though something had been ripped from his flesh. His mouth tasted of smoke and screams.

Ezra S. Yoder stood alone Sunday morning, facing the black pit that had been his barn. Over and over, images of the night before tumbled and turned in his mind. The square tips of his work shoes were at the edge of the blackened earth where the barn doors of the second level used to be, the entrance to the threshing floor and the haymows. He stood still, his eyes two stones of sorrow, and stared at the ruin of charred wood, chunks of concrete, and disfigured cows. His brain felt tight with knots: confusion, disbelief, and fatigue had tied his thoughts into a headache.

He gripped the crown of his straw hat—the thin white hatband tied around the base of the crown smudged with ashes—and pulled it from his head. A breeze lifted a few strands of his thin bangs which, with his receding hairline, emphasized his high forehead. His hair, the color of cinnamon, was in the traditional notched haircut: bangs trimmed straight an inch above the eyebrows and hair cut straight an inch below the ears. Slowly he wiped his brow with a sweat-stained white handkerchief and then fitted the straw hat back on his head.

The breeze swirled over the black pit, raising coils of soot and carrying the miserable stink of burned animal flesh into the bleak landscape. Across the two-mile span of farmland in Big Valley, above the distant mountain range on the first Sunday morning in December of 1992, the winter sun burned in a sky without clouds. He shifted his gaze to the pastures and the far fields and the distant sun: its cold light glittered in his eyes.

Big Valley, in the virtual center of Pennsylvania, is noted primarily as a community of Amish and Mennonite dairy farmers. Their ancestors were among the first settlers to plow the land. After the 1754 Albany Purchase, most of the Native Americans of the Delaware and Shawnee tribes moved out. Several Moravian converts stayed and helped the early Scotch-Irish settlers through early difficulties, and a peacemaking Shawnee chief, Kishacoquillas, left his name on the stream. By 1800 fifty Amish families were established there.

The valley itself is a thirty-five-mile stretch of fertile limestone fields between half-mile-high mountain ranges—Stone Mountain and Jacks Mountain—protecting this paradise of Christian simplicity. The eye is continually confronted and delighted by the sweep of fields and the mass of mountains because the landscape itself possesses a heartbreaking beauty. There are also moments difficult to describe: on a summer night, when flickering fireflies fill the humid fields of wheat; or on a winter twilight, when dark fields dusted with snow and silence seem to extend endlessly, a sudden stillness emerges that transforms the natural world into a dimension of spiritual purity. Those moments of sudden stillness seem eternal.

At the northern entrance to Big Valley, along Route 655, the main road that cuts through the center of the landscape, a pale-green sign painted with black letters pronounces:

> Every word of God is pure:
> He is a shield unto them
> That put their trust in Him.
> —*Proverbs 30:5*

A line of cars and trucks bumbled along the road. Most drivers paid little attention to the various road signs proclaiming the Word of God. But this morning their watchful eyes studied the words with apprehension because the night before, at midnight, six Amish barns were burning simultaneously. Each barn belonged to a family of Nebraska Amish, known locally as the White-Top Amish for the white tops of their buggies. They were the most conservative Amish in the valley and known as the most conservative group in the entire Amish family of churches.

By dawn, the barns, as well as the field equipment, the winter store of hay and grain, buggies, corncribs, wagons, milk cans, and all the livestock within—the heart of an Amish dairy farm—had been destroyed by fire. Dead were 162 holstein cows, 54 calves, 24 heifers, 21 Belgian draft horses (for fieldwork), 18 standardbred horses (for driving), 15 rabbits, 11 ponies, eight cats, five bulls, four colts, and two dogs. And young Eli Yoder, who had saved his four-month-old colt, was in critical condition at the Geisinger Clinic in Danville.

Ezra S. adjusted the brim of his straw hat. He picked up a crumpled kerosene lantern and studied its broken glass, its blackened shape, then cast it down in dismay. For an odd moment he gazed at the black smudge on the palm of his hand before wiping it on the leg of his dark-brown broadfall pants, trousers with a front fold of cloth fastened by waistline buttons, prescribed by his church district. In fact, the dark-brown color itself, the thin white hatband, the hooks and eyes on his vest jacket, and the bloused white shirt with a rounded collar—all these were distinctive sartorial features immediately identifying him as Nebraska Amish.

He examined the palm of his hand after wiping it on his pant leg. His hands were strong and coarse with thick, short fingers, sprinkled with tufts of hair the color of paprika. At six feet he was much taller than the average Amishman in the valley, and with his thick-bodied figure, he could have been a lineman for the Philadelphia Eagles. His untrimmed beard jumped in a wiry mass to the top of his chest, and a stubble of mustache hair itched his upper lip since he had gone three days now without shaving. Except for a few wrinkles at the corners of his eyes, his skin was smooth for a man forty-five years old. His blue eyes, the color of a summer twilight, were usually attentive and bright with wit, but this morning they were two dark stones.

He dragged his gaze from corner to corner of the black pit. Ezra S. had inherited this dairy farm twenty-five years ago from his father, who had inherited the farm from *his* father, who had inherited the farm from *his* father. The Yoder dairy farm on Stone Mountain Road had been established in 1889, nine years after the Nebraska Amish group formed. Indeed, his great-grandfather had been a close friend of bishop Yost H. Yoder, who in 1880 was responsible for founding the church with the strictest rules in the valley. The barn that had vanished in one night, in a rage of smoke and fire and disbelief, had stood in the valley for over one hundred years.

One entire century, Ezra S. thought as bitterness tightened his throat. *And the animals. And my son.* He coughed and spat. A car horn honked. For a distracted moment, he turned to scrutinize the various vehicles before returning his gaze to the black pit.

At 9:00 a.m. Stone Mountain Road was already thick with traffic. From rolled-down windows, faces gaped at the blackened remains of his barn. Just after dawn, as the final fire truck rumbled away up the farm lane, the cars, pickup trucks, and vans started to crawl along the mud-stained road, searching for the burned-down barns, snapping photographs of the fire-damaged farms, and wondering who in the world could have done such a thing.

From the line of vehicles on the road, Isaac D. Hostetler turned his horse and white-topped buggy into the rutted farm lane, gouged and battered by truck tires. Rebekah, his wife, sat at his left side. Esle, his nineteen-year-old son (one of the fraternal twins), sat crouched in back. While the horse bumped the buggy over the uneven surface, the three inside were jiggled and jolted. The iron-rimmed wooden wheels rattled noisily. Isaac D., grateful he had replaced the back spring in October, loosened the reins to let the horse pull the buggy at its own pace. Rebekah held the front post tightly and gazed with disbelief at the scene before her. Esle gripped the back of the seat.

The horse reached the corner of the weathered picket fence enclosing the front yard. "Whooaa," Isaac D. said firmly, pulling back lightly on the reins. "Whooaa, Pat."

Suddenly the front porch filled with people. Annie, the grandmother, a stout woman in her late sixties, stood on the front porch with her arms around four-year-old Levi and eight-year-old Becky. Rachel and Judith, teenagers, huddled together behind her. The women as well as little Becky all wore long, dark dresses, the color of blueberries, with multipleated skirts. Becky grabbed the edge of her grandmother's apron, the same dark blue as the dress. Placing her hand gently on the back of her granddaughter's head, Annie adjusted the back of her white cap.

Esle snapped open the white curtain at the back of the buggy and heaved himself out that way. As he stretched his back, he scanned the faces on the porch for Judith. Isaac D. tossed the black lap robe forward, stepped down heavily from the buggy, and held the horse while Rebekah climbed down. Loosely wrapping the tie rope to the hitching rail, he nodded at the grandmother as his gold wire-rimmed spectacles slipped down his nose. He pushed the bridge of his spectacles back up and directed his gaze at the lone figure on the edge of the black pit.

Rebekah, however, as she stepped down from the buggy, had not once removed her eyes from Ezra S. or the black pit. The thought of *something missing*—not the barn—stole into her mind. She pulled together the front of her *Mitzle*, a short, brown jacket, then stood with a straight back and stared steadily, almost defiantly, at the loss before her. A black scarf, tied tight around her head, accented the sharp features of her face and the intensity of her penetrating blue eyes.

She let the image in front of her settle into her mind before she shifted her gaze to the cow pasture. There she saw Enos and Joseph, the eldest Yoder boys, both in their early twenties, walking aimlessly along the fence line. She turned her head and saw Benjamin, the thirteen-year-old, with Isaiah M., the grandfather, in front of the chicken house, tossing feed to the chickens, the only farm animals that survived the fire. Then she saw a dead draft horse, tangled in a barbwire fence. Finally she saw the colt tied to a post in the pasture lane and shuddered.

Swiftly she returned her gaze to Ezra S. and scrutinized his solitary figure. That thought of *something missing* kicked about in her mind, something odd and disturbing about seeing him there alone, isolated, standing in front of what used to be his barn. Shortly it occurred to her that the *something missing* was his standing there *alone*, without Becky or Levi trailing along at his side, without Benjamin or Eli laughing and hopping about, without Enos or Joseph chattering and working methodically. She tried to remember if she had *ever* seen him without his children because the usual image of Ezra S. was that of a huge, bull-like, energetic man, bursting through the barn doors or stomping onto the front porch or jumping down from a hay wagon to be surrounded by children with uplifted faces and bright eyes. Here was a man who loved children. After all, Ezra S. and Lydia had five boys and four girls and one more on the way. Never had she seen her animated neighbor so subdued or so quiet or so still.

Adjusting the brim of his straw hat, Isaac D. started to walk across the farmyard toward Ezra S. Briefly, Rebekah watched her husband before turning to face the grandmother and the gathered children. Judith was just stepping down the wooden stairs to talk to Esle. She had a black scarf on her head and was slipping on a jacket against the chill.

"*Gut mya* (good morning)," Judith said softly to Rebekah as she passed her.

"*Gut mya*," Rebekah replied, just as softly, as though words murmured louder than a whisper could shatter the fragile morning.

With a faint smile, Esle greeted Judith before they moved down the lane toward the cow pasture. Rachel, the other teenaged girl, watched them apprehensively as she thought about Jacob, Esle's fraternal twin. Rebekah climbed the few steps to the front porch and stood before the grandmother, absorbed her gaze, and reached for her hands. For a moment, the grandmother held her hands and squeezed gently. Then the two women entered the warmth of the kitchen as Levi and Becky scampered after them. Rachel, looking down at the gray floorboards with as gray an expression on her face, followed.

Twice Isaac D. stopped walking. Shaking his head, he stared into the far distance between him and Ezra S., at the barn next door, also set on fire but saved, thanks to the watchful eyes of the two Speicher boys across the road. They alerted the firefighters, who dragged out three smoldering bales of hay. Isaac D.'s dairy farm, however, had been spared the arsonist's wrath. His barn, his livestock, his winter grain, just down the road, around the bend, a mere fifteen-minute walk away. No one yet knew why some barns had been burned and others not. The only facts clear on Sunday morning were that each barn torched belonged to a Nebraska Amish family, and that one barn had belonged to a minister. The rumors, too, about Isaac D.'s son Jacob had started circulating at dawn.

Focusing his attention on the barn next door, Isaac D. continued his slow pace toward Ezra S. Across the dormant vegetable garden and barnyard, he could see Gideon M. pointing at the burned bales of hay while Sergeant Stuter, a state police officer, nodded his bald head and scratched notes onto a notepad. The two men marched to the barn door and disappeared inside.

Isaac D. glanced at the black pit. He had been there the night before. He had watched the flames spin themselves around the barn like some gigantic cocoon until the barn collapsed with a trumpeting crash, releasing enormous wings of fire that seemed to beat the very sky itself. At 3:00 a.m., he left. There was nothing more he could do. At that point, he knew that the fire would not spread to the farmhouse or other buildings. Clasping his hands behind his back, he huffed up the final grade to the edge of the black pit where Ezra S. stood.

"*Wie geht's* (how're you)?" Isaac D. said, pushing the bridge of his spectacles against his nose.

In reply Ezra S. nodded his head once, sharply.

Isaac D. let his nearsighted gaze tumble into the black pit as his eyes filled with the sight of charred chunks of horses and cows, crumpled parts of farm equipment, and great slabs of concrete. After two hours of intense heat, the base of the concrete silo had cracked and pitched into the flames. The silage stored in the towering bin had acted like an accelerant.

Side by side, the two men stood in silence. Somewhere in that miserable mess was the Yoder dog, Jack, a friendly mutt, a harmless animal, who would never hurt anyone, not even a stranger slipping into the hayloft late at night.

"Who could do such a thing?" Ezra S. finally asked. "Who? And why? Why Amish?"

Isaac D. shook his head slowly. Rumors, gossip, wild accusations, and preposterous tales were already rumbling through the valley. And the subject of one outlandish allegation concerned his own son. For a moment, a certain sad absence floated before his eyes. To think of Jacob at all always pained him: *the undutiful son, the lost son.* But to think of him in connection with these terrible fires was beyond comprehension. Apparently Ezra S. had not yet heard the rumor about Jacob.

"I do not know who could have done such harm," Isaac D. replied stiffly.

"It's so strange," Ezra S. said, "because the harvest this year was good, and now all my hay, all my wheat, all my corn—gone. Gone." He raked his fingers through his thick beard. "And the barn. The barn was here since 1889. I still cannot believe it." He tugged his beard. "I still think I'm going to wake up soon from this nightmare, so I can milk the cows. I keep thinking to myself, *It must be time to milk the cows. It must be time to milk the cows.*"

Isaac D. nodded and remained silent.

Ezra S. exhaled heavily and stopped tugging his beard. A flush of sorrow crossed his face as he thought of the animals.

"The cows and horses were just burned alive!" Ezra S. groaned.

"Betty, my best milker, seven and a half gallons a day she was giving, just burned alive!"

The image of the terrified farm animals, kicking and crying, knocked Ezra S.'s heart across his chest. Each cow, each horse, each heifer, each calf had a name. Like true Amish, the family talked to their farm animals almost like cousins: they were not quite pets, but also not mere beasts to produce a profit.

"You cannot imagine," he exclaimed in a harsh whisper, "the sound of the calves crying, crying, screaming! Terrible!"

Isaac D. stared into the far distance.

Ezra S. started raking his beard again and said, as an iciness seized his heart, "And my son, Isaac. My ten-year-old boy is in the hospital in Danville. He saved his colt. He ran into the barn to save the colt." He delivered the last two sentences with a puzzled sense of pride. "It's just like Eli to do something foolhardy like that. He's hurt, but he is alive, thank the good Lord."

Isaac D. sensed his anguish and felt powerless. He could do nothing but pray for Ezra S. and his family and for Eli. He lifted his face to the sky with a prayer in his eyes, thinking dimly of Jacob, when he heard a voice calling Ezra S.

The two turned and saw Sergeant Stuter marching up the grade toward them, clutching a notepad in his hand. He had parked his cruiser behind Isaac D.'s horse and buggy. The sergeant appeared alert and rested, as though he had slept for ten hours; in fact, he had managed to sleep only one fitful hour in the front seat, just at dawn.

"The show," Ezra S. muttered to him, glancing at the traffic and gesturing at the black pit.

Sergeant Stuter nodded.

"Look there," Isaac D. said abruptly.

Two men with a camera had climbed over the fence into the stubble of the front cornfield. One man, crouched down on his knee, was snapping photographs while the other man seemed to instruct him.

"HEY!" Sergeant Stuter shouted, his face flushed red with anger. "You'ns! Get outta here! NOW! This is private property!"

Disdainfully, the men snapped one more photograph before they left the front field. Ezra S. shook his head sadly while Isaac D. gazed at the ground. The Amish do not willingly allow their photographs to be taken. In Exodus is the Lord's word: "Thou shalt not make unto thee any graven image." Spending their lives on Stone Mountain Road, Ezra S. and Isaac D. till now had little trouble with outsiders taking pictures, because no true tourism existed in Big Valley, unlike Lancaster County. Since 1791 the Amish in Big Valley managed to live simple Christian lives in relative obscurity, with little interference from the outside world—making it the ideal existence, the perfect place.

"Last night was the end of my barn," Ezra S. remarked, "and this morning is the end of my privacy, eh?"

"Only for a little while," Sergeant Stuter responded in Pennsylvania Dutch as he watched the intruders saunter back to their car. He stood, arms akimbo, in an imposing manner, an emblem of authority in his blue-and-gray uniform and dark-blue overcoat.

Sergeant Henry J. Stuter, a first-generation German-American, born and reared in Big Valley, had gone to public school with the Amish before they started their own private one-room schoolhouses in the midsixties. His father had been a county farm agent, so as a boy, he had also spent much time on Amish farms. His parents, both devout Lutherans, fearful of Hitler in 1937, had emigrated from Oberndorf, Germany, a small town in the Neckar River Valley, where people spoke the same German dialect as the Amish. In the states they joined relatives in Big Valley. Sergeant Stuter knew not only the Amish language but also their God-fearing ways. He respected their humble lives, and in turn the Amish respected him.

He was a tall, trim man in his midfifties who could boast that he wore the same size uniform in 1992 as he had in 1972; however, he could not boast the same way about his hair. Over the years, with mild regret, he had watched his thick, blond hair thin, gray, and disappear until only a few gray streaks lined the sides of his head. He wore silver-framed eyeglasses with large rectangular lenses that centered all the features of his face in his gray-eyed gaze. That gaze was direct and disciplined and discerning, the result of working in law enforcement for over thirty years. As soon as he finished a major in criminal justice at Penn State, he joined the Pennsylvania State Police force. He achieved a high success rate in cracking several perplexing cases and rapidly developed a formidable reputation for skill and efficiency in criminal investigation.

Sergeant Stuter turned his attention once again to the black ruin before him. Anger sharpened his gaze as he thought of Eli Yoder, critically injured in a barn fire that was deliberately set. "I'm very, very sorry about your son."

"He's in God's hands," Ezra S. declared solemnly.

"Is Lydia with him?"

"*Ya*, last night she went with him in the helicopter."

Sergeant Stuter nodded his head.

"I'm going to the hospital this morning," Ezra S. continued. "Irma should be here soon to take me."

"Well," Sergeant Stuter replied, "at least it won't take too long to get there."

A faint smile crossed Ezra S.'s face. Irma Keiser, who owned the Valley View Farm, a bed-and-breakfast just down the road, had a reputation for driving fast.

"But I'm afraid I have to ask you a few questions about the fire before you go."

Ezra S. nodded his head knowingly. "I feel as though I'm carrying a block of ice on my back" (thinking of the huge blocks of ice used in summer to cool the milk) "and have turned cold inside."

Isaac D. nodded sympathetically at this remark.

"Let's go inside, though," Ezra S. said, "and get out of this stink."

As Ezra S. headed toward the house, another photographer climbed the fence to take pictures. Sergeant Stuter began to shout at him, but Ezra S. waved his hand. "Let him. It's useless. For now."

As Isaac D. walked across the barnyard to talk to Ezra S., the grandmother led Rebekah into the kitchen, where she removed her *Mitzle* and black scarf and hung them on a wooden peg near the door, among other jackets and straw hats. The two small children scampered upstairs to watch their father and Isaac D. from an upstairs window while Rachel, still looking down, her face gray, glided over to help her sister.

Deborah, the eldest daughter, recently married, was cleaning a pot of oatmeal at the dry sink. A faint odor of ammonia lingered in the room with the strong smell of burning oak from the wood-burning cookstove at the far end of the kitchen.

The grandmother opened the door to the summer kitchen, a

room used for cooking during summer months and for storing food during winter months. She showed Rebekah all the moon pies, fruit-filled turnovers, each shaped like a half-moon. Annie, Lydia, and three other Amish women had baked all day Saturday in preparation for the noon meal on Sunday. The Yoders were to be the host family for church that day. Over three hundred moon pies, arranged on plates, serving dishes, and cookie sheets, all wrapped in Saran Wrap, covered the table and dry sink, benches, and seats of chairs. On a church Sunday (once every two weeks), the host family expected over two hundred members, men and women, boys and girls. Rebekah inhaled the cool scent of apples, cinnamon, allspice, baked dough.

"All day we rolled and cut and filled and baked." Annie sighed and shook her head. "Three big bowls of apple *Schnitz* (slices) we used. The crust, too, was just right."

The old woman sniffed with satisfaction, shook her head a few times, and shut the door. "Such a shame. Would you like one?"

"*Nay, danki* (no, thank you)," Rebekah replied.

As the two women moved toward the kitchen table, the sweet smell of moon pies blended with the scent of the burning oak.

"Maybe I could have Ben and Becky take a plateful to each family who was to be here for church this morning?" Annie suggested, pulling the corner of a dark blue cloth that covered the window and hooking it to the side. The Nebraska Amish cannot have curtains; they improvise with window-size pieces of dark cloth or brown paper bags. The morning light fell on the table top.

"Sit down, sit down," Annie invited. "Would you like some coffee or tea?"

"Tea," Rebekah said, sitting down.

"Rachel?"

Rachel nodded and placed a teakettle on the stove.

"And we have two big pots of bean soup in the washhouse," Annie continued, sitting down, her voice tightening, "and loaves and loaves of bread. Maybe we could sell the moon pies at the Wednesday auction?"

"Do not worry too much about the moon pies," Rebekah urged softly.

"*Ya*, you're right," Annie agreed. "The moon pies are not worth worrying about."

The old woman sighed heavily, sat back in the wooden chair, and gazed out the window through silver spectacles with small circular lenses. She had a full, round, plain face whose most distinctive feature was a mole on her chin with a single gray hair sprouting from its center. Rebekah, too, turned to the window and viewed the garden, the edge of the apple orchard, the cornfields, and the distant cluster of black walnut trees. Since the leaves were gone, the concrete silo of her farm, like a pillar of stone, stood visible in the distance. She could just discern the roof of her house.

"Can you see your farm?" Annie asked, squinting to see better.

"*Ya*," Rebekah answered. She did not want to say that last night she had seen this farm burning across the dark fields, as though a star had smashed into the valley. She still did not know what to say or how to console after such a tragedy.

For a long while, Annie let her gaze rest on the far horizon before she shifted in her seat and let her eyes travel over the narrow wooden benches stacked against one wall and a cardboard box filled with hymnals on the seat of a chair. The benches, about twenty-five in the kitchen and the living room, were supposed to have been used for church Sunday. Yesterday afternoon, the family had pulled them off the wagon and carried them into the house.

"I'm so sorry that you must miss church," Annie apologized, fiddling with a straight pin in her apron, near her waistline.

"Do not worry about church either," Rebekah said gently. The Yoders and Hostetlers were in the same church district. At this morning hour, they all would have been sitting on those wooden benches, singing a hymn, celebrating the glory of Jesus Christ.

"Lydia scrubbed down the walls twice." Annie had finished adjusting the pin on her apron. "You know how clean my daughter-in-law is on any given day, but a church day, well, she is very clean. 'It is only once a year, *Mamm*,' she says, dragging out the buckets and sponges." Annie then recounted the soap-and-ammonia commotion on Friday when all the women and girls in the Yoder family spent the entire day cleaning: scrubbing walls, washing windows, sweeping porches, wiping tables, dusting chairs, scouring wooden floors.

Continuing to study the distant fields surrounding her farm, Rebekah only half-listened. She wondered why their farm had been spared but was thankful that their barn still stood. At some point during Annie's recitation, Rachel placed a steaming cup of tea in front of Rebekah.

Suddenly, Annie stopped talking and stared at the top of the table. Rebekah stirred a spoonful of sugar into her tea.

"Everything has been turned upside down," Annie sighed. "I do not know what to think."

"Do *not* think, Annie," Rebekah counseled firmly. "Place your trust in God. Let your mind and heart fill with the love of Jesus."

Annie considered her words for a moment. "Have you heard about Eli?"

Rebekah bit her lower lip, nodding at this painful question.

"He was life-flighted to the Geisinger Clinic in Danville," Annie said in a thin voice. "It must be very bad."

The two women were silent.

"He is how old now?" Rebekah asked. "Nine?"

"Ten. He's ten now."

Rebekah nodded and sipped her tea. She thought of Daniel, her seven-year-old, and the normal distress that pricks the heart whenever a child is hurt—the cuts and scrapes, the stitches, the broken bones. But to have a child so badly hurt that he must be flown to the Geisinger Clinic was the type of heartache Rebekah hoped she would never have to experience. She bowed her head and prayed for his recovery. She also prayed again for the safety of Jacob, her errant son. Her anxiety had increased since his black car had been found that very morning in a cornfield off Route 655.

The pot of oatmeal spluttered on the stove. Annie began to chatter again. Rebekah sipped her tea and nodded but continued to contemplate Jacob with confused and painful emotions as she had done now for months, ever since he decided to leave the Amish. To lose a child to the world is a hard blow to an Amish parent. She had scrutinized the past for shortcomings in her child rearing and searched for a cause or a mistake she had made in forming his character. She and his father and his grandfather and, for that matter, the entire family had tried to reason with him, to badger him, to get him to return. But he did *not* return.

She was thankful he had left before his baptism. If he had not, he would have been shunned, and she could not have withstood such sorrow. At least this way, she could still see him and still hope for his return. But now, because the police had found his car in a field, that horrid rumor was circulating that he was responsible for the fires! Jacob could not do such a thing! As she felt her heart collapse, she wondered whether Annie or Ezra S. had heard that rumor.

The front door opened. The three men, smelling of cold and smoke, stepped into the kitchen with nods and murmurs of good morning. Ezra S. hung his straw hat on a wooden peg and stepped into the living room. Sergeant Stuter and Isaac D. followed him.

Wedged into the far corner of the living room stood a large oak desk with a calendar tacked on the white wall above it. The calendar, advertising Zook's Orchard, was the single wall hanging in the room. A kerosene lamp had been pushed to one corner of the desk, and a rolled-up copy of *Die Botschaft*, a weekly Amish newspaper, lay next to it. The rest of the desk, usually cluttered with papers and pens and farm pamphlets, had been put in order for church Sunday. Along the opposite wall were piled more wooden benches.

Ezra S. crossed over to the desk, pulled out a swivel desk chair, and slumped into it. Flipping through the pages of his notepad, Sergeant Stuter sat down in a plain wooden chair next to the desk. A short distance from them, Isaac D. settled on one of the benches, holding his straw hat in his hands and gazing out the window.

"I know you're tired, Ezra," Sergeant Stuter began, "and I'm tired, too. But I want you to try to remember as much as you can about the fire last night. I'm going to ask you some questions and then ask them again and again. But I have to do that. Is that okay?"

"*Ya, ya,*" Ezra S. said soberly, pulling on his beard. "I'm not a child. I know you must ask questions, even if it *is* Sunday. I am sure that Gideon M. answered your questions."

"He did," Sergeant Stuter replied, "but John S. and Seth D. would not."

"*Nay*, not today for *them*," Ezra S. declared. "Did Moses C.?"

Sergeant Stuter nodded.

"You're making your way up the valley then? Is Melvin A. next?"

Sergeant Stuter nodded again.

Esle and Judith lingered along the edge of the cow pasture. The breeze had shifted to the southeast, easing the stench of the dead animals. Deeply distressed, Esle did not speak except to express his concern about Eli and his prayers for a quick recovery. When he leaned against a fence post, she did not wish to disturb his thoughts or his silence and stood quietly next to him. Since she could not bear to look at the ruins of the barn, she gazed at the far fields.

Judith had burst into tears when she saw Prince, his mane on fire, gallop from the barn and crash to the ground tangled in the barbwire fence. She could not bear the cries or screams or the sound of horses kicking in their stalls. Clutching Levi and Becky to her sides, she stood sobbing in the orchard and watched the barn burn and her father stagger with Eli in his arms and the helicopter swishing into the sky.

Judith had been a tearful, willful child who had grown into a sensitive, tolerant, eighteen-year-old woman with brilliant, water-clear blue eyes and thick, dark eyelashes. Her brooding beauty came more from her sober demeanor than from the comeliness of her dark complexion, her auburn hair, or her graceful figure. For her slender size, however, she had large, clumsy hands. As a result, she preferred the large-gestured housework of cleaning or cooking or washing clothes, where she was skillful and confident, rather than the precise work of sewing or quilting, where she was awkward and easily distracted.

Although she did not wish to disturb Esle's thoughts or his silence, she sensed that she must speak first to help him find his voice.

"Do you want to talk about what you did last night?" she suggested softly, still gazing at the far fields.

He fixed his stern eyes upon her face and studied her profile.

"It is Jacob I want to talk about," he declared firmly. "Not us. I am deeply concerned about my brother."

Judith sighed at this rebuke and turned to face him. "You are concerned about his safety?"

"I'm concerned about everything." He was looking down. "Did you know his car was found in a field?"

"I knew a car was found," she answered. Near dawn she had overheard the police talking about a black car found near Tyler Road, in a field, with something broken. Her stomach tightened. "I did not know the car was his."

"The car swerved off the road."

"Do you think he's hurt?"

Esle said nothing and turned and stared at the black pit.

Judith also knew the police were *searching* for a black car seen leaving Melvin A.'s farm last night, the last barn to burn. But she thought the police had found that car. Later she heard that a black car had been found in a field.

"Isn't he at his place in the city?" she finally asked.

Esle continued to stare at the black pit but said nothing. Never would he forget the Sunday afternoon when he saw Jacob in a black car with some strange kind of name. He had not fully forgiven his brother for leaving his family, for leaving the Amish.

"Let's go back," he said.

Sergeant Stuter, after asking Ezra S. a few pertinent questions, stood on the front porch and studied the dismal scene. Esle and Judith, both faces dark and downcast, slowly trudged up the field lane toward the house. Horns honked. The sickening stench of burned meat assailed the nose. The fire marshal stood at the edge of the black pit and scratched notes onto a clipboard. At the base of the collapsed silo, the assistant fire marshal crouched to take photographs for the official report of the criminal investigation unit. Cars and trucks parked along the road. Interspersed with the motor vehicles were buggies with black, yellow, or white tops. Faces full of curiosity lined the front field. In the pasture lane, Isaiah M., the grandfather, his ancient face etched with painful resignation, stood staring fixedly at the phenomenon before him.

Studying the somber face of Isaiah M., Sergeant Stuter imagined his drive over to Melvin A.'s farm: the devastation, the perplexed pain in their faces, the repeated questions. "How could this happen? Why us? Who could do such evil?" He shook his head, bewildered. How *could* someone just set a barn on fire? How *could* someone knowingly burn cows and horses and calves? And not just one barn but six barns? And of all people to attack, these people, the Amish! Then his mind filled with the image of the black car, anchored in the field, its driveshaft snapped: what happened to Jacob Hostetler?

CHAPTER 2

Nine months earlier, under a cold, gray sky in late March, the entire Hostetler family of Stone Mountain Road—grandparents, parents, and children—climbed into three white-topped buggies and rattled up the farm lane on Sunday morning to attend church. The drive to Joni D. Yoder's farm, where church was being held, was over two miles away. They left at eight fifteen to assure themselves a good fifteen minutes for fellowship before the nine o'clock service.

Jacob drove the first buggy with Esle, his fraternal twin, sitting on his left, and Sam and Seth, the next oldest boys, sitting cross-legged in back. Sam pulled off his glove to inspect a small bruise on his hand caused by a slipped screwdriver. After the morning milking, he and Seth had gone through the ritual of unscrewing and removing the large orange triangles, the slow-moving vehicle signs, from the back of each buggy. Since it was church Sunday, no element of the outside world was allowed, in accord with a concession the Nebraska Amish extracted from the state of Pennsylvania years ago. Abraham C., the grandfather, drove the second buggy with his wife, Sarah. Isaac D., the father, drove the third buggy with his wife, Rebekah, in front and the younger children, Emma, Hannah, and Daniel, piled behind them in back, wrapped in dark woolen blankets.

As the buggies turned onto the road, a sharp wind rushed over the unsown fields and stung Jacob's face. He shivered, even though he was wearing his *Überrock*, a cape overcoat made of gray wool with large black buttons and a small circular cape, attached at the neckline and draped around the shoulders. He hitched the black lap robe higher on his body. All the men and boys wore cape overcoats and plain-crown black hats as well as white shirts and the usual brown pants and vests. Only the grandfather, being a bishop, wore a blue-gray suit. All the women and girls were clad in traditional dark-colored dresses and long gray capes, edged with black, called *Mantels*. Black scarves were wrapped around their heads, over the black caps of the unmarried girls and the white caps of the married women. The women tucked their bare hands under the blankets for warmth while the men wore gloves.

"Gid-dap, Tom-my!" Jacob called out once he was on the road, slackening the reins, clucking his tongue, and leaning forward as though he could get the buggy to move faster through his posture alone.

Behind him Abraham C. sat erect and drove his horse with gusto. He clearly did not like the cold, and the sooner he got to church the better. But his appearance avowed that if necessary he would ride through the frigid air for hours without question.

Isaac D. followed him, with hands tight on the reins and shoulders hunched up as though in a perpetual shrug. He squinted through his glasses at the haunches of the horse and concentrated on the rhythmic motion to avoid all thoughts of the cold.

"Oo-oo-oo, it is *cold*," Jacob moaned to Esle and added, in English, "cold as a witch's—"

"It is Sunday," Esle broke in sharply, rejecting such language.

"*Ya, ya*," Jacob grunted, knowing his brother's intent, and then continued, "it's *sooo* cold. It must be twenty below."

"It is cold for March," Esle said in a matter-of-fact tone, "but I doubt it's twenty below."

"And for winter weather, we should have a storm front."

Other Old Order Amish in the valley, Renno Amish with black-topped buggies and Byler Amish with yellow-topped ones, had storm fronts, the buggy version of a windshield, dashboard, and windows to protect against the cold. The Nebraska Amish still had open fronts. On each side, there were four supporting posts and two sets of roll-up curtains. In cold weather, curtains were rolled down; in hot weather, they were rolled up. The base of the buggy was brown, the top was white, and the running gear was black. The step plates were mounted at the crosspiece on the shafts rather than on the buggy itself. Thus, a person entered through the buggy front rather than the side to sit on the front seat.

"We should have windows and we should have storm fronts," Jacob declared, "just like the others."

"But we are not like the others," Esle replied in a calm and even voice.

"Maybe we should *be* like the others," Jacob countered, his face red with cold and annoyance.

Esle was silent for a moment and then stated simply, "Then we would not be who we are."

"*Ya, ya, ya*," Jacob replied, clucking his tongue and crying, "giddap, Tom-my!"

The horse clip-clopped along at a brisk pace. *Clip-clop, clip-clop.*

Once again Esle tried to dismantle the same complaints he had heard Jacob recite, day after day, for the past year. The brothers, being twins, confided in each other. Jacob would never utter such complaints in front of their father, unless in an offhand manner, and certainly not in front of their grandfather, who after all was a well-respected bishop. His gripes, though, had escalated over the course of the year from the realistic to the trivial: from plowing, milking, and the cold to clothes, animals, and using an outhouse. Now he even complained that he had to wear bangs.

Esle turned his head to gaze at the cold landscape. Here and there, under the dark shadows of a pine or a hemlock, he could still see scraps of snow. He studied the winter-hard fields and could not wait for the softening spring weather and the annual cultivation. Already he could picture himself sitting on the harrow with the April sun warm on his neck and back, snapping the reins of the draft horses, and watching the steel teeth bite into the earth. Already he could see the silent fields break out with that first green-gold whisper of color. Already he could smell the fresh-turned soil. How he loved the land, the animals, the farm. The muscular work and the sense of fatigue strengthened his spirit.

The winter months never bothered Esle because he knew the summer months would follow. He enjoyed the changes in the weather, the pace of the seasons, and the transformation of the valley from brown to green, to red and yellow, to white. He could not imagine himself in any other type of life than the life of an Amish dairy farmer. He never challenged the Amish way: he accepted it all. He never opposed the *Addning* (*Ordnung*), the rules and regulations of the church:

he simply obeyed. His habit was not to question but to listen. For nineteen years he had lived contentedly on Stone Mountain Road in Fairville, Pennsylvania. The language of the farm and the fields and the valley had long ago written itself into Esle.

As the horse and buggy passed the Ezra S. Yoder farm, his mind turned to Judith. He longed to see her that morning at church. In the front orchard the dark branches of the apple trees moved creakingly. From the farmhouse chimney, a line of white smoke curled upward and, buffeted by the wind, twitched, gyred, and scattered into the gray sky. Jack, their mutt, sat on the front porch and thumped his tail on the floorboards at the sound of the clip-clopping hooves and rattling wheels. The Yoder barn, one of the largest in the valley, well-weathered and built on a slight rise not far from the road, dominated the farmyard scene. Behind it towered the single concrete silo. On the lower level to the right and toward the back, next to the cow stable, extended the milk house. On the upper level to the left stood the buggy shed. All the buggies were gone. The Yoders had already left for church.

All these thoughts and images flitted through Esle's mind like bats at twilight, which he had often seen while hunting in the woods. He was an avid hunter. In every season since he was twelve, he hunted as much as possible. He steadied his dark blue eyes and saw in the pasture, next to a fence post, the upright figure of a groundhog. Esle pictured himself raising the barrel of his rifle. His nature registered the various details of the landscape into three broad categories: hunting, farm labor, and simple wonder at its beauty. From years of hunting, he had trained his eyesight to utmost acuity; from extensive farm labor, he had developed a strong body; and from simple wonder, he had created a presence of trusting innocence.

Esle was a man of sight and strength and virtue. He was also unusually hairy. Not only did he have hair the color of dark red clay, but he also had hair growing in abundance on the back of his neck and shoulders, on his chest and arms and the backs of his hands, on his legs. Already he had a thick, short, rust-colored beard. Nebraska Amish grew beards as soon as possible even though other Amish remained clean-shaven till baptism or marriage.

Whenever Esle entered the kitchen, his mother had the fuzzy image of a great bear crashing through the woods and foraging for food.

He ate immensely. Now, although he had just eaten a huge breakfast, he was already thinking about the white bean soup and the moon pies that would be served for the noon meal after church. The groundhog abruptly disappeared.

He turned toward Jacob. "Sam and I have to harrow the back field as soon as it gets warm."

"Is that so?" Jacob replied.

"We're sowing oats there this year." He called to the back, "Aren't we, Sam?"

"What's that?" Sam asked.

"Sowing oats in the back field!"

"*Ya, ya*, in a few weeks."

"How many acres?" Jacob asked, listlessly.

"A good ten acres," Esle muttered. He sensed Jacob's indifference and fell silent.

Esle, Sam, and Seth always worked in the fields. Jacob, however, worked in the fields only sporadically since he had a job at the Harrisville Planing Mill four days a week. He preferred carpentry more than fieldwork.

"It is so-oo *cold*." Jacob slackened the reins as the horse picked up its pace. "I wish we'd be there already."

"Not much longer," Esle answered.

"Why does church have to be at his farm anyway?" Jacob complained. "It's so far away for cold weather."

Esle remained silent and simply stared at the road.

When they had passed the Yoder farm, Jacob had also glanced at the buildings while dubious thoughts of Rachel filled his mind. How strange it would be if both he and Esle were interested in the two sisters! Jacob had to admit that the seventeen-year-old Rachel was an unquestionably beautiful girl, but he resisted too much involvement with her because his mind was preoccupied with matters other than romance. He stared intently at the dark leather harness of the trotting horse and listened to the monotonous clip-clop sound of the hooves. The clip-clop sound soon started to echo in his mind like the tick-tock sound of the windup alarm clock in his bedroom. *Clip-clop, click-clock.*

Jacob pressed his lips together and brooded over the weather. The cold possessed his mind as much as it stung his face. He thought his entire head was a block of ice. His thoughts drifted to his *englisch* (non-Amish) friend Gary and the warm interior of his van last Saturday night. How it disturbed him that on a cold morning he could not have the simple pleasure of warmth because the *Ordnung* forbade it! Often he had used logic to analyze rules that never made complete sense to him, despite continuous talk about separation from the world, plain living, tradition, history, the value of a Christian community.

All of a sudden, the horse snorted and jerked its head, shaking the harness.

"Ooo-oo, Tom-my, easy," Jacob soothed him.

The horse twitched both ears, snorted again, and without breaking stride, maintained its energetic pace. Plumes of white air surrounded its face. *Clip-clop, click-clock.* Jacob studied the harness and decided that the bridle must be too tight. The blinders now were a bit crooked. Then it occurred to him that he, too, wore a harness, complete with blinders, reins, and a bit—*the harness of Amish society.* He just wanted to be *warm* on a cold morning. *Is that so bad? So disobedient? So unchristian?* He did not think so. He envied the Amish groups who could at least have a storm front on their buggies to stop the icy wind from blasting into their faces.

Jacob glanced at Esle and the stoical resolve, the cold composure, stamped on his face. *He's such a perfect Amishman,* he thought mordantly. As much as Esle had accepted the way of the Amish, Jacob had questioned it—inwardly at first, then tentatively with Esle, and then more and more openly with his Amish and *englisch* friends. Nature had not only constructed Esle and Jacob differently in body, but also in emotion, intellect, and spirit.

Jacob had the same dark blue eyes as his brother, but his eyelids were more full and thick, giving his face a slanted look and a more intense expression. The hair on his head was the light brown color of a pear, but he had no body hair. His beard was so thin and scraggly that it looked as though he had pasted it on his chin that very morning. His face, however, was long and lean and handsome. As much as Esle liked to plow the open fields and hunt and farm, Jacob liked to saw wood in the shop and read and think.

Nannie Zook, an Amish schoolteacher who had taught the twins, had been amazed at Jacob's interest in books and reading. Above all he enjoyed reading storybooks and history books. In all her years of teaching, among all her many scholars, Jacob had been the pupil who had learned the German and English languages with the most ease and in the least amount of time. Just this past winter, when he had driven over to the schoolhouse to pick up his younger brother and sister, she had even suggested that he might want to become a schoolteacher. But since few men were teachers, he had dismissed the idea and taken the job of a carpenter at the planing mill.

Now at nineteen, Jacob still liked to read storybooks. Ever since he left school fours years ago, he went with his father to the auction, a large farmers' market and livestock sale held every Wednesday in downtown Fairville. By habit, he would stroll over to the public library sometime in the morning to return a book and to check out a new one, or two books during winter months. The Amish put no restriction on how much someone could read. They were encouraged to read the Bible, the writings of Menno Simons, the *Martyrs Mirror*, Dirk Philip's *Enchiridion* (handbook of Christian teaching), *Die Botschaft* (weekly newspaper), and the many letters written to one another.

However, Jacob knew that he had to be careful about *what* he was reading because the others might try to set him straight on the subject matter. If there was a book he knew would be considered "too worldly," he would check out another book as well and keep the questionable book hidden to read in private. He read as much as possible and always with two paperback dictionaries next to him: *Cassell's German-English English-German Dictionary* and *Webster's New World Dictionary*.

How these fictional worlds filled Jacob's imagination! How surprised he was while reading *O Pioneers!* It was a novel about life on a midwest farm, describing various buildings, vast cornfields, and a tragic love affair. But what impressed him most was the choice of words, the power of sentences to create an image in his mind. He checked out another book by this same author, *The Song of the Lark*, not about a bird or a farm but about a young woman who struggled to make a career of singing and who eventually became an opera star in New York City. It was odd for Jacob to think that someone could have a job singing, but the story, her struggle, and the description of places called Chicago and New York City thrilled him.

The more familiar idea of having a job as a schoolteacher had actually stuck in his mind for a day or two, like a burr on his pant leg, but he eventually plucked it off to take a job at the planing mill. In the morning and late afternoon, Jacob still helped to milk the cows but did not have to deal with any of the other farmwork (the point of having the mill job, as far as he was concerned) except on days when he was home. The family, however, benefited from the additional income, the angle he used when he had initially presented the outside-job idea to his parents. By custom, an Amish boy turned over all his earnings to his father until his twenty-first birthday. Shortly after he started work, he began to resent that practice as well.

The start of his complaints coincided with the start of his job at the planing mill. Not that the mill itself exerted a bad influence, since most of the employees were Amish anyway. The simple fact of being away from the immediacy of the farm let his mind race with ideas and possibilities. He even savored the short van ride to and from work each day. Mr. Sherman, the owner of the mill, provided transportation for the Amish who lived too far away to walk or drive a buggy. On frigid mornings, he relished the climb into the van with the heat whistling around the interior and then watched, in head-shaking disbelief, the Nebraska Amish buggies on the road and the farmers' faces red with cold. When he considered his own grandfather, he often marveled that for over fifty years he had been driving an open buggy every winter of his life and, as much as possible, even refused to ride in cars or vans on occasions that other Amish would consider reasonable. But, after all, his grandfather was *the* Bishop Abraham Hostetler, the true Amish patriarch.

Finally, at eight forty-five, Jacob reached Joni D.'s place, pulled on the reins to slow the horse to a walk, and turned into the farm lane to drive up the slight incline to the farmhouse.

CHAPTER 3

Early Sunday evening, Sergeant Stuter drove down Route 655 with Special Agent Michael Tate next to him in the passenger seat. All Sunday morning, telephones rang and buzzed and faxed among the local, state, and federal governments. At the urging of the governor and a local congressman, the FBI joined the investigation for possible civil-rights violations. Hence, Agent Tate, who worked in a branch office for the FBI in State College, had been assigned to the case that afternoon.

Sergeant Stuter always welcomed help in any criminal investigation and had worked well with the FBI in past cases. But he did not yet know this man or his experience or his methods. After Agent Tate briefly reviewed the material gathered that day, he decided to interview Jessica Smith, Jacob's girlfriend, that very night. "That's the place to start," he declared. Sergeant Stuter murmured something about it being Sunday but grudgingly agreed.

On the drive into Big Valley, Agent Tate asked numerous questions about the locale and the Amish, with almost boyish fascination, staring out the window at the passing dark fields. In his dark blue suit, he was tall and slender, and his face was lean and narrow with a pointed nose, a sharp jaw, and a cleft chin he seemed consciously to jut forward when he asked someone a question or listened to an answer. His thin brown hair was meticulously parted on the side of his head and combed across his forehead. His eyes, dark and crafty, were in constant motion. Just like a fox, Sergeant Stuter concluded. At one point they drove a short distance behind a yellow-topped buggy before they passed it.

"Why can't they drive cars?" Agent Tate asked. "If they can *ride* in them, why can't they *drive* them?"

"It's a compromise with the outside world, a way of getting along without getting involved in it. With anything new or different, they always ask one basic question: How will this affect the Amish way of life?"

"And the Amish way of life is their religion?"

"Correct. Their religious belief *is* their life, and their life *is* their belief, and their belief is *maintained* through a small, rural, close-knit community. Anything that threatens that community threatens that belief."

"And cars threaten that community?"

"In their eyes, anyway. You have to look at the issue from a historical perspective. Up until the Great War, really, *everyone* drove buggies and carts and wagons. *All* farmers, Amish or not, were basically working the same way. But when tractors and cars started to appear, as well as electricity and other technology, the Amish stopped and wondered whether those things would affect a rural community."

"And decided they would."

"Correct. The Amish reasoned that the car could tear apart their life. A person could become too independent, traveling with ease over long distances, moving away. They feared the car would separate members in a family and disrupt the stability of simple farm life and face-to-face visiting. The car became a symbol, in a way, of the outside world, and the Amish did not want to have anything to do with that."

As Agent Tate considered this information, Sergeant Stuter pulled off Route 655 onto a side road and then onto another road.

"Here we are," he announced, turning the police cruiser into the driveway of a white ranch house.

When Jessica opened the front door, she stared at the two men. "Hi, Sarge."

"Hello, Jessica," he said. "Do you have a moment?"

Her voice drooped. "Look, I already tole that other cop this afternoon, I don't know where he is. I just don't know."

"That's fine, Jessica, but we have a few more questions. Can we come in for a moment?"

"Well, sure, I guess."

"Are your parents home?"

She shook her head. "Nah, they went over to Auntie Kate's for dinner. Julie too. I'm 'home alone.' " She laughed at her own wit.

Sergeant Stuter smiled. "Jessica, this is Special Agent Michael Tate of the FBI. He's been assigned by the federal government to investigate possible civil-rights violations."

Jessica narrowed her eyes as she shut the door.

"We can sit in here." Sergeant Stuter indicated the dining room. "Is that okay?"

"Fer sure."

When Sergeant Stuter sat down, he placed a yellow legal pad on the table, clicked a ballpoint pen, and scratched down a few notes. Agent Tate sat down opposite Jessica and simply folded his hands together on the tabletop.

"I want to thank you for meeting with us, Ms. Smith," Agent Tate said pleasantly.

Jessica leaned back in her chair and stared uncertainly at the two men. She sipped a can of Pepsi. Her hazel eyes, flecked with green and gold, were pinched tight with suspicion. She was short and solid, roughly built, with long legs, square shoulders, and thick black, perm-wavy hair pulled back into a bushy ponytail dangling between her shoulder blades. Tied-back hair accentuated her narrow face and her hard features. Her chin was sharp, her ears were pointy, and her lips, painted a dark red, looked slightly cruel. She wore two silver studs in her left ear lobe and a plain silver ring on the little finger of her right hand. Just above the ring was a tiny tattoo, a green-and-red rose. She was wearing dark-blue sweatpants and a plain white T-shirt.

"This won't take long." Agent Tate asked her a few preliminary questions about her age, her place of employment, her job title: eighteen, Fullertown Planing Mill, accounting assistant.

As she answered, her voice thinned with tension. She crossed her legs. Sergeant Stuter jotted down notes on his legal pad, kept glancing at Agent Tate's folded and manicured hands, and wondered why he did not take notes.

"Jacob Hostetler hasn't tried to call you or reach you in any way?"

She shook her head no, ponytail twitching from side to side.

Agent Tate paused a moment, unfolded his hands, adjusted the knot of his blue-and-green tie, and concentrated his gaze. "You haven't seen him or talked to him since last night?"

Again she shook her head no, sipped her Pepsi, and recrossed her legs.

"Now isn't that odd?"

"Whaddaya mean?"

"That he hasn't tried to call you?"

"Not really."

"But I thought he was your boyfriend?"

"I'm *seeing* him," she said strongly. "I wouldn't really call him my *boyfriend* or anything like that. We go out and do things, y'know, but if I want to go out with someone else, I could. I'm not gonna tie myself down when I'm young."

Agent Tate nodded once or twice. "Well then, how long have you been *seeing* him?"

"Since May . . . the beginning of May."

"And where did you meet him?"

"In Lewistown. He moved into the front room, just up the hall from my brother's pad."

"And that's on Basil Street?"

"Uh-huh, 9 Basil Street." Jessica produced a pack of Marlboro Reds from somewhere in her sweatpants. She lit a cigarette and dropped the match into the Pepsi can.

"So you don't find it odd that Jacob hasn't tried to call you?"

"Nope. Not odd at all. It's only been a *day*."

"But it's been *quite* a day, wouldn't you say?"

She took a drag on her cigarette, inhaling the smoke greedily. "Yeah."

"Have *you* tried to call him?"

She hesitated. "Sure."

Agent Tate persisted. "Did you or did you not try to call him?"

"Yeah, I tried to call him," she replied quickly, "this morning."

"And?"

"He wasn't there."

"How many times did you try to call him?"

"I don't know. Once or twice."

"And he was never there?"

"Nope."

"The night of the fires, what did you do?"

"When they were burning?"

"No. Before that. Could you just tell us what you and Jacob did that night?"

Jessica took another drag on her cigarette, carefully tipped the ashes into the soda can, and said in a careful voice, "Well, we didn't really do much at all. There's not much to do around here, especially in the winter. Jake picked me up—"

"Jake?" Agent Tate interrupted.

"Jacob. I always called him Jake, y'know. That's how he introduced himself to me, and that's what I always called him. That's his English name, I guess. It was kinda like gettin' more away from the Amish, changing his name a bit."

Agent Tate nodded.

"Well, as I was sayin', Jake picked me up at seven or so."

"Here?"

"Yeah."

"What was he driving?"

"That big, old black Grand Prix. He bought it back in August for nine hundred bucks. It's really a piece of crap, but he never owned a car before, being Amish and all, so it was a really big deal for him. He *loves* to drive. One of the first things he did when he left was go get a driver's manual."

"Did you notice anything unusual about the car that night?"

"No-o, not really." Her voice was noncommittal, her eyes narrow, studying his expression, as though facing a trap. "He might've cleaned it up a bit, that's all."

Agent Tate nodded his head again.

"Well, anyhow, we drove down to the Original to meet Jimmy and Lil."

"The Original?"

"Johnnie's OIP, the Original Italian Pizza, next to the Uni-Mart on Center Street. It's a pizza chain around here."

"And Jimmy's your brother?"

"Uh-huh, him and Lil. That's his girl, Lillian Leach."

"What time was that?"

"Around seven, seven-ten, somewhere around there. I didn't really pay much attention to the time. We had a pizza and soda and left, oh, around eight, I guess, and drove over to State College to see if anything was happening. Jimmy and Lil went in his car. Me and Jake went in his."

"What kind of car does your brother drive?"

"A black Camaro." She took a final drag on her cigarette and dropped the stub into the Pepsi can. The cigarette hissed as it went out. "Nothin' was really going on, so we just walked around a bit and had some pie and coffee in Carrie's, that's on Atherton Street, and then me and Jake drove home. Jimmy and Lil stayed there and went to Hobart's; that's a bar on East College Avenue. Me and Jake are underage, so we can't get in. I got home around ten-thirty."

"Were your parents up?"

Her eyes flattened. "I don't know. I doubt it. They go to bed early."

"Did Jacob come in with you?"

"Nope. He left right after that."

"That's odd," Agent Tate said slowly.

"What's odd?"

"I don't know. But when I was a teenager, eighteen, nineteen years old, I certainly didn't want to be home at ten-thirty on a Saturday night."

Jessica shrugged her shoulders, dismissing his comment.

"Did Jacob say where he was going?"

"I guess he was going home. I mean, I just figured he went back to his place."

"Did you notice anything unusual about Jacob that night? The way he talked, the way he dressed, the way he acted?"

Jessica shook her head no, and then added in a confidential tone, "Well, he was a little nervous, I think, about being in the Original. That's where he used to hang out when he was Amish. He was afraid he'd run into some of them, I guess. Other than that, nothing really."

"And you haven't heard from him since?"

"I already tole you no."

"Do you have any idea where he might be?"

"Nope."

"Friends he has in Fairville?"

"Nope. I only knew him from Lewistown. I don't know who he used to hang out with before that."

"What was he wearing?"

Jessica looked up at the ceiling. "Well, jeans and a blue shirt, I think. And he had on a jean jacket."

"Did he wear a hat or anything?"

"Oh, yeah, his KOOL baseball cap. He always wore that." She laughed. "I guess since he's Amish, he has to have something on his head."

Agent Tate stood up. "Thank you, Ms. Smith."

"Is that it?"

"That's it," he said, smiling. "That wasn't too bad, was it?"

Jessica shook her ponytail from side to side.

As they drove south along Route 655, Agent Tate pulled out a handheld Sony tape recorder from his briefcase, clicked it on, and started talking into it. Sergeant Stuter watched this. So that's why he doesn't take notes. As he concentrated on his driving and listened to the murmur of this FBI agent next to him, he pieced his own impression of Jessica Smith into what he already knew of her family history. He would have to tell Agent Tate about that soon. Approaching Lewistown, Agent Tate clicked off his tape recorder and flatly stated, "She's a liar, you know."

CHAPTER 4

On that cold March morning, the Hostetler family arrived at the farm in plenty of time for morning services. As Jacob steered the rig into the farm lane, he gazed at the horse's chestnut-colored coat, dark with sweat, and the steam that floated from its body like an aura. He lifted his eyes to the line of white smoke climbing into the sky from the cinder-block chimney. The scent of burning oak and morning silence embraced the farm, and he could not wait to get inside to be warm.

He drove past the farmhouse to a line of at least twenty buggies parked by the barn and stopped there. Sons in the host family, acting as hostlers, greeted the arriving church friends and unhitched the horses to walk them into the stable for hay and water. Abraham C. and Isaac D. both stopped their buggies next to the front porch to let the women and children out before driving to the barn.

The four Hostetler boys followed the two oldest Yoder boys, one leading their horse. A few men stood inside, talking softly. Unbuttoning the black buttons of his *Überrock*, Jacob was content just to stand inside the barn out of the cold, always curiously amazed at how warm stables could be since the only source of heat arose from the body heat of cows and horses. During winter months, since there were no closets in an Amish house and not enough pegs in the kitchen or living room to hold all the winter coats, men left their coats draped over the front seats of their buggies or in the barn. Women left their capes in the summer kitchen or the washhouse. The four Hostetler boys hung their cape overcoats on hooks, along with the harnesses, and then dashed across the barnyard to the house.

Standing in the kitchen, Esle searched through the multitude of faces for Judith. Jacob stood next to him. The kitchen was a field of black hats, white caps, and the black caps which unmarried women and girls wore on church days only. The distinct odor of human bodies mingled with the smell of burning wood. The twins, murmuring greetings in subdued voices, moved slowly through the crowd and shook hands.

"Esle! Esle!"

Esle looked down and saw Eli Yoder, with bright blue eyes and corn-blond hair.

"Are you going for a gobbler this spring?" Eli asked.

"That's not for another month." Esle chuckled.

"May I go with you?" he pleaded.

"That's for your father to say."

"But is it okay with you?"

"We'll see, we'll see. Where's your sister?"

"Which one?"

Esle smiled. "Judith."

"She was last with *Mamm*." Eli abruptly disappeared into the crowd.

Esle craned his neck toward the living room. The Yoders had removed the double doors leading from the kitchen to the living room as well as the double doors leading from the living room to the *Kammer*, the parents' bedroom. This opened the entire first floor as much as possible for church. It was standard (not just Nebraska) Amish practice to have wide doors with removable partitions built into their homes. The result was an airy open space, so the voice and vision of the preachers could reach the church members. Rows of backless benches were lined up in the *Kammer*, the living room, and part of the kitchen. Centered in the living room stood four plain ladder-back chairs, reserved for the bishop, the deacon, and the two preachers. Esle did not see Judith till the last moment, and then it was time to take seats as the crowd shifted positions in the kitchen area.

A standard method of joining the assembly, determined by age and sex, controlled the seating arrangements. When church began, grandmothers and married women just sat down, mainly in the *Kammer*, clutching their infants and toddlers next to them. The ordained men then entered, followed by grandfathers, unmarried girls, unmarried boys, and lastly, married men. The men and boys sat in separate rows and areas from the women and girls. The oldest men, to help support their backs through the three-hour service, usually settled on benches set against the walls. Sam D. Zook, nicknamed Old Man Sam for his seventy-nine years, lowered his frail body into a rocking chair set along the wall just for him. Filing to their seats, Esle and Jacob each glanced unobtrusively at the opposite side of the living room, where Judith and Rachel sat next to each other.

As Jacob edged along the bench, a complaining expression abruptly crossed his face as he thought of the hardness and the discomfort of the wood on which he would have to sit for three hours. *No comfort outside and no comfort inside,* he thought peevishly before he sat down. *Why must everything be difficult and tiresome?* He leaned forward with his elbows on his thighs, his back curved, and his shoulders slack.

Esle sat down, shifted about a few seconds, straightened his back, and squared his shoulders, at attention. Again and again, he had told Jacob that if he would only sit with a straight back, he would be more comfortable in the long run.

After everyone was seated, the deacon passed out some thirty copies of the *Ausbund* to be shared in the assembly. Most of the older members knew the hymns by heart and did not need a book. This official hymnbook of the Amish was a small, thick, palm-sized black book. Its earliest hymns were composed from 1535 to 1540 by Anabaptists imprisoned in dungeons of the great castle of Passau, Bavaria. The lyrics protested wicked tyrants, embraced loneliness and sorrow but not despair, and celebrated firm conviction in a God who would not forsake his people, leading them on to everlasting life and joy.

Jacob sat slouched. Holding the *Ausbund* tight in his hands, Esle sat straight.

The deacon returned to the preachers' row, and silence seized the room. It was time for the service to begin.

"Two sixty-five," announced Moses J., a married man sitting a few rows behind Esle and Jacob.

When the *Vorsinger* (song leader) gave out the hymn number, all the men and boys in one deft movement removed their black hats and placed them on the floor under the benches. People turned to page 265 of the *Ausbund* for *Lied* (hymn) number 47.

After a short pause, Moses J. sang the first high-pitched syllable, and then the entire assembly joined in thunderous unison. All singing was in German, entirely a cappella, and quite slow. The Nebraska Amish sang decidedly slower than other Amish groups. As everyone sang, the ordained men stood up and filed out of the room. The four climbed the stairs to the second floor and held *Abrot* (counsel) in an upstairs bedroom, where they prayed before deciding who would preach the sermons for that day.

When the assembly finished singing the first hymn, a long period of silence followed. After the forceful singing, the silence itself seemed intense. A baby gurgled. Old Man Sam coughed.

"Seven seventy," Moses J. then announced.

The second hymn for the Nebraska Amish as well as for all Amish is always the "Loblied (praise hymn)," hymn number 131, on page 770 of the *Ausbund*. Everyone sang the words to this hymn with deep solemnity:

O Gott Vater, wir loben dich,
Und deine Güte preisen,
Die du, O Herr, so gnädiglich,
An uns neu hast bewiesen,
Und hast uns, Herr, zusammen g'führt,
Uns zu ermahnen durch dein Wort.
Gib uns Genad zu diesem!

(O God and Father, you we bless,
Your love and goodness praise,
Which you, O Lord, so graciously
Have shown to us always,
And have assembled us, O Lord,
To warn and guide us through your Word.
Give us your grace and blessing!)

Both Esle and Jacob had rich, vibrant voices with good pitch. Jacob, though, squirmed in his seat as he sang these ponderous words. He enjoyed singing, but his mind kept drifting back to Saturday night a week ago, to the rock song "Nothing Else Matters." For most of that night, he had ridden around with his *englisch* friend Gary Schippe, a local Fairville boy, in his metallic-green van, drinking beer, smoking cigarettes, listening to rock music. When he had a chance, he listened to the raucous music of Metallica, Guns n' Roses, or AC/DC. He never forgot the first music book he saw, tossed in the back of the van when Gary had decided to learn to play the electric guitar. All those lines and black circles looked like a barbwire fence with tadpoles on it! But the *Ausbund* was filled only with words; the music was learned by rote from the elders. That was the tradition. That was the Amish way.

Esle sang with the same attentiveness in his voice as in his posture. While singing, though, he was aware of Judith's presence across the room and tried to catch a furtive glimpse of her whenever he could. He listened, through the roar of voices, to distinguish hers and fancied that he could pick out her melodious tone from the blend of sounds across the room. Unintentionally, he fell into a muse about Judith. When she sang, she lifted her face, her throat long and smooth. He considered her handsome but not beautiful like Rachel. At first, diminished by the stunning beauty of Rachel, she appeared to be the plain Yoder daughter, until one noticed her features one by one: a smooth complexion, shimmering blue eyes, a strong chin, well-formed lips, finely arched eyebrows. The *new* Judith pieced herself together in his daydreams over months, like a picture puzzle, until one day he had a sudden, altered, handsome image before his eyes that settled itself decisively in his mind.

Judith also enjoyed farmwork: her strong, rough, and clumsy hands were a testimony to that. The fact that she liked physical labor impressed him. He would never forget that one afternoon last summer when he saw her sitting on a rusted cultivator, snapping the reins, and driving the huge Belgian draft horses through rows of corn. Her forearms were red and beaded with perspiration, the traditional flat scoop straw hat enclosed her face, and her strong legs were outlined in her dark-blue skirt. He admired the way she weeded the corn, driving the horses and working the cultivator. "*Ya, meine* Judith (yes, my Judith)," Ezra S. said once to him. "She can do as much work as Enos or Joe." Again he glanced at her and could not wait for the singing later that night to talk with her.

After the assembly finished singing the *Loblied*, another long period of silence prevailed.

"Three forty-eight," Moses J. called out.

During this third hymn, the four ordained men returned and resumed their seats in the center of the room. Jacob wondered idly if his grandfather would preach the main sermon this Sunday (no one ever knew what they would decide). The singing stopped at the end of the verse.

Daniel S. Zook, the youngest preacher, a short man in his mid-forties with a thick copper-colored beard that reached to the middle of his chest, rose to deliver the *Aafang* (introductory sermon), lasting only half an hour. A certain self-consciousness marked his demeanor since he had been a preacher for just a year and still felt awkward fulfilling his duties. Folding his hands beneath his beard, he mumbled in a low tone as he tentatively moved toward a confident, steady, distinct, and rhythmic flow of words. In that half hour, Daniel S. reminded the assembly that they were called together once again for the holy purpose of listening to the Word of God, obeying God's commandments, and seeking their own personal salvation.

"Wherefore, my beloved," he quoted from Philippians 2:12, "as you have always obeyed, not as in my presence only, but now much more in my absence, work out your own salvation with fear and trembling."

Esle and quite a few others nodded in emphatic agreement.

Jacob gave Esle a sidelong glance, then looked past Daniel S., who was emphasizing the need for trust in God and the importance of prayer. Across the room, his gaze settled on Rachel, just seventeen years old. She did not glance at him or at anybody, but kept her eyes fixed on her hands folded in her lap, as though she had just caught a tiny sparrow and was holding it tenderly in the cage of her fingers. Her solemn countenance aroused his interest. In the Yoder family, she was known as the energetic, lively, and beautiful daughter. Tall and slender, her eyes shone with the color of well-polished mahogany.

Because Rachel loved bright colors and intricate patterns, she always seemed to be piecing, marking, stitching, or sewing a quilt with her nimble fingers, much more useful for the precision of quilting than the rough labor of farm work. She would certainly help milk cows and feed chickens, but rarely would she toil in the fields or in the barn. She laughed easily in a high-pitched, delightful trill, tossing her head back and shaping her mouth into an expressive O. But on church Sundays, Rachel assumed a sober and sedate manner befitting the solemnity of the day. Jacob studied the delicate curve of her face and the thick, shining blonde hair visible beneath her black cap.

Daniel S. finally brought the *Aafang* to a close with an acknowledgment of his own weakness and preparation for Bishop Abraham C. Hostetler, who would deliver the main sermon this Sunday. Jacob winced. Daniel S. coughed slightly and then quoted another verse from Psalm 95: "O come, let us worship and bow down: let us kneel before the Lord our maker. For he *is* our God; and we *are* the people of his pasture, and the sheep of his hand."

Daniel S. coughed again.

"If you are all agreed," Daniel S. concluded, "let us pray."

The assembly knelt for a period of silent prayer. When Daniel S. felt that an appropriate amount of time had passed, he stood. The sound of his rising from his knees, the movement of his clothes, the scraping of his shoes against the floor—these signaled the church to end the silent prayer and stand.

John D. Yoder, the deacon, read Scripture from Matthew 13.

Jacob regarded his figure and wondered how long he had been deacon. John D., in his midsixties, was thin, short but rather long-armed, with red-circled eyes behind wire-rimmed spectacles and an expression of perpetual fatigue molded into his face. He stood. His thin shoulders slouched as he extended the German Bible before him and read the entire chapter in a slow, methodical, chantlike fashion. "Thus far extends the Scripture," he said curtly, after the final verse, and closed the book. The entire assembly sat down.

Bishop Abraham C. then stood to deliver *es schwere Deel* (the main sermon). "Grace be with you and peace from God our Father. We have been admonished many times this morning by the brother."

Thus, the sermon began. Jacob tilted his head and studied his grandfather. Abraham C., a short, compact man in his late sixties, was a forceful member of the church and an imposing figure in his family: the model Amishman, the ideal bishop, the paradigmatic pilgrim. His white hair and silver beard cowled his head like the mane of an ancient lion. His pale blue eyes, patient and piercing, translated the world into prayer. In conversation, he had a habit of tilting his head back and peering intently at one through his gold wire-rimmed spectacles.

At thirty-seven, Abraham C. had been ordained a bishop, and for thirty years he had carried out his duties with resolve, responsibility, and zeal. He had studied the Bible with great care to strengthen his knowledge, his belief, and his spirit in order to cultivate an ability to shepherd his flock through sharing that knowledge, belief, and spirit. By reputation he was a stern but compassionate man, who emerged as the quintessential father-figure in his church district: humane, august, settled in his faith. Amish and *Englischer* alike respected and revered him as a conservative, strict, and unquestioning elder. His faith in God was absolute. As a young man, he had earned himself the nickname Father of Faith, which then evolved into Grandfather of Faith when the grandchildren sprouted up around him. At sixty, he retired from dairy farming as soon as he knew that his son and his grandsons could manage the farm and opened a small harness shop behind the barn to occupy his time outside his duties as an Amish bishop.

"Every man and every woman and every child must be obedient to the Bible," Abraham C. pronounced soundly, his compact figure swelling with the words as he preached. For such a diminutive man, his voice was powerful and resonant, mountainous. "And all sons and all daughters must be obedient to their parents. And all good Christians must be obedient to their vow of baptism."

At that word, Jacob frowned and lowered his head. Esle brightened and lifted his face to his grandfather. *Baptism!* The word knifed through Jacob's conscience. *Baptism* is perhaps the single most important word for a young man or woman in an Amish family. To take the vow of baptism meant to accept the Amish way of life. In just four weeks would be a day of decision, at spring communion. While the assembly sang, all the young people who wished to join the church would follow the preachers as they left the assembly to climb the stairs and hold *Abrot*. Upstairs, each young person would individually declare a desire *die Gemee nooch geh* (to follow the church). Then on church Sundays for the rest of the summer, the young people would gather in a separate room during the early part of the service, while the congregation was singing. There the ministers would prepare them for the fall baptismal ceremony, instructing them from the 1632 Dordrecht Confession of Faith.

Jacob knew that Esle was ready to join the church because they had been talking about it for the past few months. Esle had been pressing Jacob to join as well and claimed that as soon as he was baptized, all those stinging doubts and endless complaints would vanish with the solemnity of the occasion. Baptism would bring the *supreme* obligation to God and church, and entry into the adult world of responsibility. Jacob did not think that would happen. He dreaded baptism. Indecision seized him. A shrieking numbness coursed through his body. Jacob feared that ill-timed, improper, and irreligious behavior could end in excommunication—being shunned. He was not ready for baptism and wondered if he ever *would* be: he liked to drink beer, smoke cigarettes, listen to rock music. His father, vaguely aware of these activities, did not approve of them but also did not realize their extent. He merely hoped that Jacob was going through the usual stage of resistance and independence, sowing the proverbial wild oats.

Jacob heard the word *baptism* again and grimaced. How he dreaded baptism! Once a year, in the fall, men and women entered fully into the meaning of the word *Amish* through the vow of baptism. In one distinctive act of will on that single Sunday morning, a person truly began the Amish life, joined the Amish community, accepted the Amish church. To be baptized signified total belief in and absolute commitment to the religious and ethical ends of the church. In that single moment, the spinning world stopped turning, the past and the future gathered into one still point, the old world and the new world were made explicit. The baptismal water dissolved the turning and the past and the future and the world into one moment of eternity. In that moment the resolution to be Amish was achieved.

The vow of baptism was unconditional. The preachers, elders, and parents all warned applicants about the difficulty of "the straight and narrow way" and stressed that it was better not to take a vow than to take a vow and break it. Jacob thought that to be good advice, indeed. Since their grandfather was a bishop, Esle and Jacob were under more pressure than others to join the church. Although Abraham C. did not directly address the issue, they knew his concern that they were nineteen years old and not yet baptized.

Jacob sensed that Judith, too, planned to join. He speculated that she and Esle, once baptized, might marry in November, but they were still too young. In a year or two, certainly, if Esle remained deeply serious about her. His sudden interest in Judith, rather intense and fiery, astonished Jacob, as though he had just seen her for the first time this past month. Jacob liked Judith well enough and could recognize her dark good looks, but he sometimes felt that she tried too hard to appear devout, just like her mother.

The sermon continued. Jacob shifted his weight, stretched his neck, and listened, not to the words, but to the sound of the sermon. The mountainous voice of his grandfather surged upward with each phrase to a magnificent high pitch and then, on the final word, dropped abruptly, only to rise again and then drop again, then rise again in the traditional style of an Amish sermon, a singsong pattern like a chant. The rise and fall of his grandfather's voice reminded Jacob of the clip and clop of a horse's hooves, a steady, monotonous rhythm.

The room was now stuffy and warm. Without interrupting the resonant recitation of his sermon, Abraham C. pulled a white handkerchief from the pocket of his broadfall pants to dab the perspiration from his forehead. Jacob again shifted his weight on the hard bench. From the corner of his eye, he could see Esle's lifted face and upright figure. In the front row, he noticed little Emma Zook squirming and fussing until her mother placed an arm around her and nestled her close to her body. Old Man Sam fell asleep in his rocking chair, his head fallen forward, pillowed, as it were, in his beard.

The sermon continued. His grandfather traced the Old Testament story from Adam to Abraham, then followed New Testament accounts from John the Baptist to the missionary journeys of Paul. He spent considerable time on the suffering that Jesus Christ endured because the following church Sunday would present the crucifixion and after that, for Easter, the resurrection. He implored each church member to learn from the patient suffering of the only-begotten Son of God.

Halfway through the sermon, Jacob watched Lavina, the wife of Joni D., a tall woman in her midforties, quietly stand and leave the room. In a moment, she returned with a dish of Ritz crackers and handed it to Sara and her four-year-old son. The boy grabbed a couple of crackers. Sara passed the dish down the row, so all the children could have a snack. Lavina then passed a tall glass of water. After all, the main sermon alone could last up to two hours, and the young ones were required to remain as quiet as possible. Jacob's stomach tightened, and he wished that he had a couple of crackers.

After an hour and a half, Abraham C. concluded his sermon by reading John 15. "I am the true vine, and my Father is the husbandman," he began, holding a small black Bible before him and peering down at the pages. "Every branch in me that bears not fruit, he takes away: and every branch that bears fruit, he purges it, that it may bring forth more fruit."

When his grandfather finished reading that verse, Jacob thought he glanced pointedly at him and Esle before he began his commentary, as though to make them think, *Am I not one of his branches? And is not baptism the desired fruit?*

After the final verse, Abraham C. sank heavily into his chair. He then asked the other ordained men to give *Zeugnis* (testimony) to his sermon: to bring forward any point that should have been made or to correct any mistakes that might have been made. Without standing, Daniel S., Stephen D., and John D. each made succinct remarks, not to correct but to underscore certain aspects of his sermon. When their brief testimonies were completed, his grandfather again stood to make a few closing statements.

Thank goodness, Jacob thought, fiddling with his sleeve. He was impatient to stand, stretch his back, and eat the noon meal.

"I'm grateful," Abraham C. declared, "that my sermon can be received as the word of God. You must praise God and praise God only—not man, never man, but God alone. If you wish to enter a life of everlasting purity and goodness, then praise God only. Praise the works of God only."

He thanked everyone for their quiet attention and then asked the assembly to kneel for the closing prayer. Everyone knelt on the hardwood floor while Abraham C. read in that distinct chanting fashion from the three-hundred-year-old prayer book *Die ernsthafte Christenpflicht* (the earnest Christian's duty). Then the assembly stood for the benediction.

"Finally, brethren, farewell." Abraham C. recited from 2 Corinthians 13: "Be perfect, be of good comfort, be of one mind, live in peace; and the God of love and peace shall be with you. Greet one another with an holy kiss. All the saints greet you." He let his eyes roam over the assembly. "So I submit myself, with you, to God and his gracious hand, that he may please to keep us in the saving faith, to strengthen us in it, to guide and lead us until a blessed end; and all this through Jesus Christ. Amen."

At the mention of Christ, the assembly bent their knees to show absolute obedience and reverence. Then everyone sat again as John D. announced where church would be in two weeks. One final hymn was sung, slowly and movingly, and then the assembly was dismissed.

The children filed out first, followed separately by the women and the men. While waiting, Jacob twisted his back from side to side. His stomach rumbled as he walked out of the room. In one corner of the kitchen, Esle stood, discussing spring crops and the sermon with a couple of serious-minded friends. In another corner of the kitchen, Jacob stood, surrounded by Shem, Jonas, and Gideon, whispering about the cold weather and the singing that night. Still talking, Jacob gazed across the room at a circle of chattering young women, black caps bobbing up and down, and watched Rachel cast off that solemn church face that she wore all morning to don the cheerful smile that enlivened her eyes. Then she and Judith excused themselves to join some other women to serve the noon meal.

Several men quickly rearranged benches in the living room and kitchen, pushing pairs of benches together to form low "tables," and lining benches on either side for seats. The women moved from table to table, covering each one with a white tablecloth and setting down spoons, knives, water pitchers, bowls, and glasses. The noon meal for the Nebraska Amish on a church Sunday never varied: white bean soup, homemade bread, butter, apple butter, white or green pickles, moon pies filled only with apple *Schnitz*, coffee, tea, and water.

Since he was so hungry, Jacob watched the preparations for the noon meal with impatience. Tables were set for the preachers, older women, older men, girls, and boys. The ordained men were always the first to sit down. Eating had to be done in shifts, as quickly as possible, so there was little or no conversation at the table. As soon as one group finished, another group sat down. Young women and girls strolled from table to table to serve bean soup and replenish plates of bread and moon pies.

Finally, Jacob sat down and thought the silent grace extraordinarily long. He then leaned forward to eat from the bowl of bean soup in the middle of the table. Jacob, the man on his left, and the two men facing them ate directly from one large bowl. Each bowl served four to six persons. Jacob helped himself to a chunk of white bread, spreading a great gob of apple butter on it, and devoured four moon pies. He drank two glasses of milk and two cups of coffee. He didn't like pickles. Once he finished eating, he reflected on the food and thought how much he disliked bean soup with its white, watery taste. He did enjoy the bread, however, and liked the moon pies, though he felt the crust was not quite as light as his mother's.

After the meal, Jacob and his friends stood huddled near the kitchen door. From a short distance, Esle watched him, his face pinched with disappointment. He knew Jacob was in the middle of some scheme whenever he surrounded himself with Gideon Hostetler and Shem and Jonas Zook.

"Will Gary come through?" Shem asked.

"'No-o probe-lem,'" Jacob replied, in English, imitating Gary's voice.

The boys all chuckled.

"Does he have the money?"

Jacob nodded.

Just then Old Man Sam and Preacher Daniel S. Zook wandered near the boys, and their voices dropped to a whisper. At one point, Jacob noticed that Rachel, just before setting a new plate of moon pies on a table, was staring at him and his little group with a frown on her face. That frown nettled him.

By three o'clock Jacob and most of his family were climbing back into their buggies to drive home for the evening chores, mostly just to milk the cows. A silver sun had emerged in the overcast sky and cast a metallic brightness on the bleak landscape. The wind had dropped. The afternoon had become surprisingly mild, as though spring were finally loosening winter's hold on the valley. As Esle and Jacob were hitching the horse to their buggy, Eli dashed over to them, holding a hand on the crown of his black hat to keep it from flying off.

"My father said it was okay!" Eli gasped, breathless.

"Now, what's that?" Esle asked.

"He said it was okay if I went with you for a gobbler!" Eli explained in an excited voice.

"Did he now?"

Eli nodded his head rapidly.

"We-ell," Esle replied, drawing out his words, "if he says it's okay, then I guess it *is* okay."

A smile filled the boy's face and he dashed away again, his hand on his black hat.

"That Eli," Esle said, smiling.

Just then, Shem and Jonas Zook bounced past them in their horse and buggy.

"See yew later," Jacob called, in English.

Shem gave him a short wave.

"I hope you're not going to be foolish tonight." Esle's smile was gone.

Jacob disliked that tone of voice. He was still nettled by Rachel's reproving frown and now was more nettled at Esle's judgmental comment.

"What do you mean?" Jacob asked curtly, placing the wooden shafts of the buggy into the tugs, sturdy leather loops near the ribs of the horse.

"You know what I mean."

Jacob tightened the bellyband and ran his hand along the neck of the horse while Esle straightened the reins. Sam and Seth sauntered over and climbed into the buggy through the back flap.

"Gid-dap!" Jacob commanded sharply.

The horse jerked the buggy forward and ambled down the farm lane toward the macadam road. Irritated at Esle's remark, Jacob listened to the crunching sound the hooves and the iron-rimmed wheels made on the gravel and felt the sound crunch in his head.

CHAPTER 5

Pressing the channel button with his short arthritic forefinger, Dennis stood in the front parlor on Sunday night, flipping through the channels of a small color TV, set on the second shelf of a highly polished oak hutch.

"Oh, for goodness' sake, Dennis," Lizzy snapped, "just turn on channel 10 and be done with it."

Dennis grunted. He pressed the button till he reached CBS, adjusted the volume, and sat next to Irma on the floral-patterned sofa.

"I can hardly distinguish the words," Lizzy declared, leaning forward in the matching armchair. "I'm sure Irma can't catch them either."

They had invited Irma over for supper. Then, at 6:00, all three retired to the front parlor to watch the *CBS Evening News* because Lizzy had been interviewed for the broadcast that night. She had earned the distinction of being the first person to call 911 to report a barn fire the night before. Dennis and Lizzy Foster, both in their seventies and retired schoolteachers from the Philadelphia suburbs, lived next door to Irma. They had just celebrated their fiftieth wedding anniversary this past spring. Dennis and Lizzy and Irma were the only *Englischer* (non-Amish) in the immediate area on Stone Mountain Road.

Dennis Foster, a retired U.S. history teacher, was a short, brusque, and stocky man with gunmetal gray hair who reveled in political facts and argument. Each day he read three newspapers, in detail. Every morning at the breakfast table, with grunts and exclamations, he shook and rattled the pages of *The Philadelphia Inquirer* and the *Centre Daily Times*; every evening at the dinner table, he rattled and shook the afternoon *Sentinel*. Nothing mattered more to him than talking politics, and he defended every single Democratic president with impassioned and heated words, even Jimmy Carter.

On the other hand, Lizzy, a retired English teacher, was a lithe, sensitive, and quixotic woman who had tried for over forty years to plant the love of English literature in resistant teenagers. Beside their house, she had an elaborate herb-and-flower garden, where she spent endless hours working among the tarragon and rosemary, peonies, snapdragons, and large-faced red roses. She once claimed she had in her garden all the flowers named in Ophelia's mad speech in *Hamlet*. Wherever she walked, she seemed to drag the sweet scent of flowers and herbs behind her like a bridal train.

Irma Keiser, born and reared in Fairville, a widow and a member of the Maple Grove Mennonite Church, was a short, compact woman in her midsixties who expressed her thoughts and feelings with candor and directness. Twice daily, in the early morning and the late afternoon, she walked the back roads of the valley with Kirby, her English sheepdog. She had square shoulders and strong calves and walked at a breakneck pace, swinging her arms like a soldier on parade. There was a joke in her family that she walked the same way she drove a car: fast.

She had long, thin, pearl-gray hair worn in a tight bun at the back of her head; one niece claimed Irma could sit on her hair when it was hanging down. Her bold blue eyes, pert and animated, envisioned Big Valley as the setting for an ongoing drama. Not much happened in the valley without some observation from her, either noted just to herself or expressed to a neighbor. On too many occasions, however, she found herself embroiled on stage in the action rather than uninvolved in the audience.

After her husband died, Irma renovated the upstairs floor of her farmhouse and opened a bed-and-breakfast called the Valley View Farm. The front porch of her farmhouse, built high on the slope of Stone Mountain, where fields gave way to trees, offered a spectacular view of the valley as well as the Hostetler farm and fields. For her entire life, she lived there in harmony with her Amish neighbors.

The Hostetler and Yoder families both made regular use of Irma's telephone. Each time that included a short exchange about goings-on among the Amish. But in 1982, after Dennis and Lizzy bought the small white modernized Amish farmhouse next door, the Yoder family started to use their telephone instead. Though that house was farther down the mountain slope, the front porch, enclosed now with thermal glass for the winter, still afforded a good view of the valley and the neighboring Yoder farm and fields.

Late last night, as had been her habit for years, Lizzy was sitting on the front porch reading when the north side of the Yoder barn burst into fire. She dropped *The Narrative of Arthur Gordon Pym of Nantucket* on the floor, rushed into the kitchen, and at 11:38 p.m. (she had looked at her digital wristwatch) called 911 to report a barn fire. Then she woke Dennis. Eventually they both wandered down to the edge of their front lawn and with distress watched great flames reaching into the night and the comings and goings of fire trucks. At first, they could not account for the bright glow in the distant sky over Harrisville nor, in the opposite direction, over Greenville. Irma soon joined them, her bold blue eyes wide open with the alarming news of barn fires burning all across the valley.

Early Sunday afternoon journalists from both *The Sentinel* and *The Patriot* knocked on the Foster door, asking questions. A rather harried, middle-aged man from the *Centre Daily Times* knocked in the midafternoon. Lizzy was receiving that minor attention for having called in the Yoder barn fire. This journalist actually took a photograph of their front parlor as well as a view of the Yoder farm from their front porch.

When he stepped outside to take another photograph of the Yoder farm from their driveway, Dennis and Lizzy gazed at the traffic. All day long they had watched, fascinated by the endless line of cars, vans, pickup trucks, buggies, even a motorcycle, creeping along Stone Mountain Road.

"I dee-clare," Lizzy said, "I've never seen such traffic on this old road. The Amish fires are getting quite a bit of attention, aren't they?"

"This is just the beginning," the journalist assured her. "Trust me. Wait till the big papers pick this one up!"

Then Lizzy spotted the bright-yellow TV van, working its way through distant traffic on Reigle Creek Road. She ran inside to fix her hair.

"Would you *please* turn up the volume?" Lizzy pleaded.

Dennis grunted again, stood up, and raised the volume.

"Thank you so much. That's much better."

Dennis grunted once more.

"Isn't that better, Irma?"

Irma sipped her tea. Dennis sat down, fussing with the antimacassar.

"The White Tops were supposed to have church today, weren't they?" Lizzy asked, suddenly remembering something.

"Mm-hmm," Irma replied. "But church was canceled. Why?"

"I just remembered something about last—"

"Headlights," Irma said, squinting at the TV screen, as though peering down a road. Headlights appeared in a Honda commercial, and she began to remember something that put her on stage again.

"Pardon me?"

"We-ell, I missed my afternoon walk, working all day for that retirement luncheon, so I took Kirby for a short walk late last night and saw a black car parked near the stop sign."

"Oh, Irma!" Lizzy exclaimed. "When?"

"That must have been eleven fifteen or so."

"You have to tell Sergeant Stuter," Lizzy declared, in the voice of a detective, thinking of Dashiell Hammett. "That must have been the car the firebug drove to set the fires."

"Oh, that's not all—," Irma started to say, searching her memory for other details of that night.

"Sh-sh-sh!" Lizzy alerted them when the local evening news on CBS began.

All three turned their attention to the TV set. Donald Peterson, the local newscaster, led the broadcast that night with a report on the barn fires.

"The Amish community in Big Valley of central Pennsylvania has suffered untold tragedy. In the barn fires last night, six Amish barns were set on fire and destroyed in the space of six hours. A young Amish boy lost his life when he tried to save his four-month-old colt from being burned alive."

Lizzy sat up straight and clutched the front of her sweater.

"Eli Yoder, ten years old, of Fairville, died this afternoon at 3:30 p.m. in the Geisinger Clinic in Danville from internal bleeding and a damaged spine."

The TV screen filled with the image of Life Star, the emergency medical helicopter, descending on the roof of the hospital.

"When local rescue workers at the site determined that Eli Yoder needed special medical treatment, a dramatic attempt was made to save him as Life Star flew to the Amish dairy farm on Stone Mountain Road shortly after midnight. Doctors at the Geisinger Clinic worked on the boy all morning but could not save him."

Then the TV screen filled with the image of a burning barn and the flashing lights of fire trucks.

"Not only did Ezra S. and Lydia Yoder lose their barn and their livestock in one of the most incomprehensible cases of arson in recent memory, but they also lost a son."

Dennis and Lizzy and Irma sat perfectly still, staring at the TV screen. Donald Peterson continued his coverage of the story, showing more exclusive film footage of the Yoder barn fire and stating again that six barns and over 250 head of livestock had been destroyed. The local state police reported that they did have several suspects at that time but could not release any further information.

The TV screen then showed a too-close image of Lizzy.

"I was reading," she said in a nervous voice, touching her hair, "as I always do at night. I can't remember what I was reading—oh, yes, *The Narrative of Arthur Gordon Pym of Nantucket,* by Edgar Allan Poe—when a bright burst of light filled my front porch, and I saw the barn burning and called 911."

The TV cut abruptly to the image of George Dobson, the Fairville fire chief.

"I've been with the fire department now for twenty-seven years," he stated, "and I can't *ever* remember such a confusing and chaotic night. There's never been nothing like it before, and I sure hope there's nothing like it again."

Many people in Big Valley, however, were still worried. There was an interview with a local German farmer, not Amish.

"Haw do ve know it von't happen again?" he asked. "I'm sleepin' in my barn tonight, that's fur shure."

The newscaster went on to state that Congressman Mike Beale and Senator Harris Wofford were pushing for a federal investigation into this heinous crime, citing possible violations of civil rights under the newly established hate crime bill.

"Why would someone attack the Amish?" Mr. Peterson asked. "This religious community, known for its pacifism, has lived peacefully, harmoniously, and largely unnoticed in Big Valley for over two hundred years without incident until last night when an arson attack, in one terrifying night of barn fires, shattered their plain and simple life . . . perhaps forever."

A commercial came on.

Lizzy, still clutching her sweater, had lost all pleasure of having been on TV. Her voice was low and intense: "Oh my dear, my dear! Little Eli *died!* How awful!"

Dennis did not say anything. Irma stared at her empty teacup.

"Poor Lydia!" Lizzy's voice had a catch in it, her eyes welling with tears. She removed her eyeglasses and wiped her eyes with a tissue from her sweater sleeve.

Dennis stood up and snapped off the TV set.

"He was only ten years old!" Lizzy exclaimed.

"It's sad," Dennis muttered, "but they do have other children."

"Oh-h, Dennis," Lizzy moaned, "how can you be so cruel? Each life is precious and unique and wonderful. And Eli was a *good boy*. He's the one who helped us clean up the back woods in October, don't you remember?"

"I know that, Lizzy," Dennis said in a hurt voice. Any discussion of death upset him since his mild heart attack two years ago.

"Oh, that poor, poor family," Lizzy murmured softly, still weeping.

And then all three sank into silence. Irma set her empty teacup on the side table. The cup rattled in its saucer.

CHAPTER 6

Silence settled in the buggy as they rode home from church that Sunday in March. Esle kept a stern face turned to the road, his hands folded under the lap robe. Driving the horse as hard as he could, Jacob stared at the harness again with renewed contempt and listened intently to the steady clip-clop of the hooves. No longer troubled by the cold but vexed now by Esle and Rachel, his thoughts clip-clopped ahead to his whiskey rendezvous at six that night.

Jacob had made plans for Gary Schippe to buy four pints of whiskey. He would meet Gary at the Original to pick them up. Gary always managed to round up booze even though he was underage. Jacob was bothered that he had to drive into downtown Fairville to meet him, a good fifteen-minute ride, before driving back out to the farm for the singing. At that hour, the sun would be setting, and the air would be cold again.

He snapped the reins and urged the horse to go faster and faster. Any minute he expected Esle to criticize his driving, but his twin said not a word. At one point, though, Seth shouted to slow down because he and Sam were bouncing around in back like sacks of potatoes. Just as he turned the horse and buggy into their farm lane, he asked Esle, "Are you going with Judith to the singing?"

"I'm taking Judith, Deborah, and Rachel to the singing."

"Enoch is not taking Deborah?"

"He'll meet her there," Esle replied, looking out at the fields. "The drive is so long, and it's going to be cold again tonight."

Jacob shook his head at the thought of the cold, but he was relieved that Esle was driving the girls because he would not have to drive with him. It made sneaking into Fairville much easier. Jacob pulled back on the reins to stop the horse in front of the buggy shed. Sam and Seth climbed out the back and ran into the house.

"Maybe you should drive Rachel," Esle suggested.

"Why?" Jacob asked, feigning indifference. He had not said a word yet to Esle about his interest in Rachel.

"Oooo, just to be good neighbors."

Jacob shrugged and went about unharnessing the horse.

That night, Jacob was late for the singing. He had planned to meet Gary at six to pick up the booze and drive the forty minutes back to Joni D.'s farm. That way, he would have a good half hour of drinking with his buddies in the horse stable before the singing began at seven thirty. But Gary was not at the Original at six. Jacob sat at a table, staring out the plateglass window at the parking lot, drinking a Pepsi and smoking cigarettes. Finally, at six twenty, Gary shuffled through the door but did not have the booze. Ken Heller had it. Jacob then had to wait *another* twenty minutes till Ken arrived.

The moment Ken handed him the brown paper bag, he jogged to his buggy, lit the lanterns, and unhitched the horse. Just before he snapped the reins, he swallowed a mouthful of whiskey. He had four pint bottles of Four Roses whiskey, one each for him and his three buddies. But now he was late! Shem would be furious. But it's not my fault, Jacob reasoned, swallowing another mouthful of whiskey. It was Gary's fault, and Ken's fault. All this trouble for a little booze!

By the time Jacob drove back on Route 655, the sun had already set and the sky, an incandescent lapis lazuli, was fading to black. The night air was dark, cold, and sharp. A waning moon faced him. Musing on the shape of the moon, he thought it looked just like a sickle or as though the night had been sliced open to expose an intense light behind it. He pulled the lap robe tighter around him. The cold air stung his face as he leaned forward in the seat. Bright headlights roared toward him and vivid taillights roared past him. At one point, a black Camaro swerved past him, blowing its shrill horn.

For night driving, by law, the Amish had to have some kind of warning light. The other Amish, Renno (Black Tops) and Byler (Yellow Tops), had flashing red lights in back and flashing yellow lights in front, to warn motorists that a rig was on the road. But the Nebraska Amish had grudgingly agreed only to allow a kerosene lantern attached on each side to the front posts. The lights were so dim that they were almost worthless. Even in matters of safety, Jacob thought, they resist and disagree. He drank more whiskey.

As soon as he turned off Route 655, he slackened the reins and let the horse trot along as fast as it could on the back roads, about fifteen miles an hour. He listened once again to the monotonous sound of the hooves, reflected on the Amish harness of rules, and drank more whiskey. Twilight abruptly vanished and thick darkness reigned. He turned on his flashlight and adjusted the high-powered beam on the road just in front of the horse's head, to show the way.

When Jacob turned the final bend in the road, he saw that all the windows on the first floor of the farmhouse were bright with light. He tossed the empty pint bottle into a ditch near the milk stand. As the buggy rumbled up the farm lane, he could hear muffled sounds of singing through tightly closed windows (on a summer night, the voices drifted over the valley like a soft wind).

"Ooo-OOO-oooooooo," he howled.

The singing, held at the same farm as the church services of the day, was a major social event for young people. Most adolescents could not wait for their sixteenth birthdays, so they could attend the singings to relax and visit, form friendships, and most of all, establish the foundation for romantic liaisons. Between six and seven o'clock, teenagers gathered at the farmhouse to socialize until the singing actually began. Most Amish youth loved to sing and would sing for close to two hours. The teenagers sang hymns from the *Ausbund*, again a cappella, but usually in a faster tempo than in church.

Ten minutes after the singing started, Jacob stumbled noisily through the kitchen door, chewing a great wad of gum. The girls sat on a backless bench or stood on one side of a long table in the living room. On the opposite side were the boys. All the forty Amish youth in the room looked through the doorway at him.

Lavina, the hostess for that Sunday, was standing in the kitchen in front of a hutch, replacing flatware into a drawer. Holding a handful of knives, she simply nodded a greeting but eyed him suspiciously. She had heard stories about this Jacob Hostetler but had not entertained them for too long. Then she caught a whiff of alcohol and clucked her tongue, dropping the knives with a clatter into the drawer.

When he stepped into the living room, Shem, Jonas, and Gideon all fixed their disgruntled eyes on him. Esle glared at him, a stern frown furrowing his face. Judith glanced at him, then looked down. Rachel scowled.

Still chewing gum, he sauntered to the boys' side of the table, his glassy eyes wandering over each girl's face. At the last singing, Jacob had talked to Rachel for the first time with decided attention and had resolved that if he *were* to see a girl, that girl would be Rachel. Leah, the only other girl he had taken home from singings more than once, stood in a far corner. She had explained to him last summer that she thought she was too young, being only sixteen, to start seeing someone. At the time, since he was only eighteen, he did not perceive that to be such a great problem. Only weeks later did he realize her refusal had been a polite way to tell him that she didn't really like him that much. Hurt and troubled, searching for his shortcomings that summer, he finally concluded that he had talked too much about books and had tried too quickly to touch her. Leah must have thought I was just too forward, he told himself. That summer he had also discovered the pleasure of Coors Light.

He sat down next to Shem at the singers' table and turned his eyes toward Rachel. I wonder what Rachel thinks of me.

Rachel, still scowling, looked at the pages of the *Ausbund* in her hands. Her shining eyes dimmed with disappointment.

Jacob turned to Shem, whose wide face was tight with impatience and displeasure. Jacob's mouth curled into an impish smile. Shem, Jonas, and Gideon exchanged glances of complicity. Now the question was how to slip out without too much notice, belt down a few shots in the horse stalls, and come back in. If they couldn't slip away without arousing too much suspicion among the adults, they would just have to wait and drink before driving home for the night. It was too cold to meet at the Curve, a roadside party spot known to the Amish boys, partway up the mountain on Mountain Climb Road.

Shem, visibly upset, had planned on drinking booze *before* the singing. He gave Jacob an I'm-fed-up look. Jacob raised his eyebrows in an it's-not-my-fault expression. Esle watched his eyebrows lift. Rachel, too, had pulled her eyes from the *Ausbund* just in time to observe Jacob's sign language. A scornful smile quivered on her lips.

CHAPTER 7

Early Sunday night, under a heavy winter sky that seemed to press against the earth itself, a blue van rumbled down the Yoder farm lane and parked next to the horse and buggy tied at the hitching rail. The downstairs windows of the farmhouse were bright with white light. Isaac D. and Esle, Isaiah M. and Annie (the grandparents), and the rest of the Yoder family stood on the front porch, an uneven silhouette of age against the background of light.

Out of the driver's seat climbed Clay Warner, a pudgy man with wide-set eyes and black hair slicked straight back on his head, always dressed in a black suit, always with lips slightly parted. He was one of the undertakers for the Amish in Big Valley. For the Nebraska Amish, though, he had little more to do than sign papers and burial permits since they did not embalm the body and conducted all the services themselves. He nodded to Isaac D. and stepped to the back of the van. A slight grimace creased his face as he smelled the rank odor of burned animal flesh beginning to rot after a day in the sun. Isaac D. murmured to Isaiah M. and carefully stepped down the porch steps.

The passenger door opened as Ezra S. slowly unfolded from the side of the van. He slammed the door shut and trudged to the center of the barnyard, where he stopped and stared at the black pit. The night was clear and mild. The moon, just risen in the sky, bathed his figure in a strong, radiant light. He lifted his face to the sky and the stars and the moon.

When Clay opened the back doors, an overhead light lit the interior with a dingy color. Isaac D. saw Lydia inside, propped in a seat against the back of the driver's seat, her face pale and without expression, her hands clutching a brown paper bag on her lap. Her eyes were hard, flat, and empty of meaning. Next to her, on a gurney, in a black body bag, lay her son.

Clay moved to the side of the van and slid the side door open. When he leaned inside, he spoke softly, "Lydia, may I help you?" He extended his hand.

For a moment she stared at his hand, yellowish in the overhead light, as if it were some unknown, puzzling object. Then she gripped his fingers. Awkwardly, still clutching the paper bag, she stepped down from the van. She turned to gaze at the black pit and her husband, unmoving in the center of the barnyard, his face lifted to the moon.

"Okay, Isaac." Clay tugged on the gurney to roll it out, and the two men carried it into the farmhouse. Judith stood absolutely still, tears streaming down her face. Little Becky clutched the hand of four-year-old Levi, who had a dazed expression on his face, as though he were just waking up. Joseph, the eldest Yoder boy, untied the Hostetler horse and drove over to see Hosea M. Zook, the coffin maker.

Esle followed his father and the undertaker as they maneuvered the gurney into the *Kammer*. On the bureau, a kerosene lamp illuminated the room with liquid incandescence. The room had been cleared of chairs and clothes and work shoes. The double bed had been dismantled. In its place stood two backless benches pushed together.

The men placed their burden on the benches. Isaac D. straightened himself, looked down at the black body bag, and felt his heart drain to emptiness.

"It's such a loss," Clay said in a constricted voice. "A terrible, terrible loss."

Isaac D. nodded but did not remove his eyes from the body bag.

"Is there anything else I can do?"

Isaac D. shook his head no, and Clay turned to go.

"Help him with that," Isaac D. told Esle.

Esle helped Clay push the gurney from the room and put it back into the van. Esle watched the red taillights disappear in the darkness. Ezra S. and Lydia were still standing in the barnyard, rooted to the earth in sorrow. Ezra S. stood straight, his face still lifted to the moon. Lydia stood straight, too, still clutching the paper bag and gazing through steel-rimmed spectacles at the black pit for the first time. She had been in the hospital continuously since the night of the fires.

Lydia was a strong, sober woman in her midforties who helped to run the farm as efficiently as did her husband: milking and gardening, cooking, washing, working in the fields when necessary. She had a finely etched face, a delicate mouth, and eyes as blue as chicory blossoms along the back mountain roads. From years of childbearing, she had gained a little weight and once again was six months pregnant. To see her face was to see faith itself. A profound Christian belief marked her every feature, her every motion, her every word.

During her baptism, she had actually fainted, overcome with emotional and spiritual conviction. Whenever she had a free moment, she read the Bible, always within easy reach on the top hutch shelf in the kitchen. She had even memorized entire chapters of both the Old and New Testaments. Often she repeated verses to herself through the day but would rarely quote biblical verses to other people for fear of being thought prideful. Her father, after all, had been an Amish bishop, Samuel Zook, a stern, unyielding, and unforgiving man, both as father and as bishop.

At first, with the black pit before her and with the stink in her nose, she closed her eyes briefly and did not know what to do. She did not know how to act, how to feel. How much more must she endure? Her brother, then her sister, and now her own son. How much more? She clutched the paper bag tighter and thanked God and her Savior Jesus Christ that her husband was safe. She thanked God that the rest of her children were safe. She thanked God that the farmhouse had not burned to the ground as well.

So much of that malevolent night was lost to her. But the barn fire was not the result of combusted hay in a haymow, not the violence of the sky that stabs the earth with lightning, not a human accident. Some person, with purpose and will and decision, set the fire in their barn and torched other barns to cause destruction and pain and death. With utmost difficulty she tried to comprehend such an act and knew that her faith demanded that she forgive the evildoer.

"If any man's work shall be burned, he shall suffer loss," she murmured from 1 Corinthians 3, "but he himself shall be saved; yet so as by fire."

Her son had passed on to eternal life. He was now in the hands of the Lord. As she recalled Eli's faint last words, she lifted her face to the moon. Then she turned to the farmhouse.

"It's good you're here," she told Esle as she approached him.

"My father is inside."

Lydia nodded. Esle followed her into the house and unobtrusively withdrew to the *Kammer*. When Levi and Becky heard the kitchen door open, they rushed to its sound, to their mother, to her attention. They did not speak or cry out, understanding in their young minds that silence was necessary. Becky sniffled, though. Levi clutched the folds of his mother's dress. Benjamin hovered in the doorway of the living room. Judith and Rachel stood quietly near the hutch. Enos sat hunched at the table with his grandparents. With one hand Lydia caressed the back of Levi's head and with the other hand held the paper bag as she let her maternal presence center her dislocated family.

With the sudden physical immediacy of her children—her other children—conviction filtered into her face and certainty enlivened her eyes. She moved with renewed determination toward the kitchen table, pulling Levi, still clutching her dress, along with her. She set the paper bag down on the table, untied the black scarf that she had fastened about her head, and adjusted her white cap.

When Annie reached for the paper bag to move it, Lydia spoke. "It's Eli's clothes. I'll take care of them."

Annie let her hands drop to her sides.

"There's nothing else for you to do tonight," she continued. "You must all go to sleep. You must pray for forgiveness. Father and I will attend to everything."

The kitchen door opened and closed. Ezra S. stood there. His sudden presence was monumental. At first he did not move. His eyes still seemed to glisten with moonlight as he let his gaze sweep swiftly over the faces of his children.

"Where's Joseph?" he demanded.

"He's gone to see Hosea M.," Lydia replied, "with Isaac's buggy."

Levi and Becky longed to rush to their father, to be near him, to touch his pants legs, to smell his earthy odor. Benjamin wanted that hefty hand clapped on his shoulder. Enos and Judith needed reassuring words. Rachel wanted his smile. But restraint had entered each face and each body and altered each impulse. They stared at him with sad, frightened faces.

"Father and I must attend to Eli," Lydia said firmly as she took off her *Mitzle* and placed it, along with her black scarf, on a peg near the front door. "Judith, help me with Levi and Becky."

Ezra S. removed his black hat. Rachel whispered to Benjamin. Isaiah M. and Annie shuffled across the floor. After the family was settled upstairs, Lydia descended the stairs. Only Enos remained in the kitchen, his huge arms propped on the table, drinking a cup of black coffee. She walked to the *Kammer*, where Isaac D. and Esle would prepare the body for the viewing tomorrow morning.

Just before she reached the room, her breath became ragged; she paused and shut her eyes tight. She stood in the doorway then and looked in. Isaac D. and Esle stood to one side. At the other side stood Ezra S., his head lowered, his eyes dark. On the two benches pushed together, still dressed in the pale-blue hospital gown, Eli lay as though asleep. The black body bag was crumpled in one corner like a discarded cocoon. Lydia studied this scene for a moment, a flickering moment, before reality pressed itself upon her.

"I'll get what you need." She left to find a basin, the cloths, the plastic bottles of rubbing alcohol. When she returned, bearing the items used to prepare the body, she strode into the room and stood before her son.

"I'll make the clothing now," she declared.

Isaac D. nodded and took the white basin filled with the plastic bottles and cloths. Ezra S. still stood at one side of the body.

Lydia turned and left. She moved mechanically around the living room. In one corner, she thrust two small logs of hickory through the side loading door of the woodburning stove. In the other corner, she lighted a kerosene lamp, set it on the large oak desk, and pulled open the bottom drawer to remove a roll of white fabric she used to make shirts. Crossing the living room floor, she paused again and glanced into the *Kammer*. Isaac D. was pouring rubbing alcohol into the basin.

Ezra S. lumbered into the living room, sat down heavily on a bench, and leaned forward, his forearms resting on his thighs, staring down past his folded hands at the cracks in the hardwood floor.

Eventually Lydia settled herself in front of her Singer Sewing Machine, set directly in front of a window for sunlight during the day. She withdrew a pair of scissors from the top drawer, pulled an arm's length of white fabric from the roll, and cut it. Next she removed the spool and bobbin of blue thread and rethreaded the machine with white. She cut more fabric. Her right hand gave the wheel a spin to start the needle moving up and down. She continued by pumping her foot on the treadle as she guided the fabric under the needle's sharpness. Her experience and long, nimble fingers made her an excellent seamstress and quilter. With hyperconcentration, her eyes narrowed as she methodically pumped the treadle by foot and maneuvered the white material under the needle.

At one point her foot-pumping seemed to synchronize with her beating heart, as though she were one with the machine. With solemn attention she contemplated the dip and rise of the needle. Her heart felt stiff. Her eyes, like quartz, stared. *Have Eli come back. Keep my son from rushing into the barn. Do not even have the barn burn.* With each sharp dip, she felt the needle pierce her own heart. Her Savior must have felt the same sharpness from his own crown of thorns, pricking his scalp and forehead and temples, and the spikes driven through his hands. Then sudden pain spiked her own heart. She stopped. She threw back her head, her throat rigid, her hands clenched into fists, and let out a muffled cry of broken love: "Oh, Eli!" The tears that did not appear in the helicopter, in the emergency room, in the intensive care unit, in the van, or in the farmyard, now appeared in anguished necessity. "Oh, Eli!"

Ezra S. placed his hands on her shoulders as she sobbed.

"We have lost him!" she cried. "We have lost him!"

Lydia rubbed her eyes with the backs of her hands and stared at the black windowpanes, seeing ghosts of herself and her husband reflected in the glass.

"We must entrust his eternal care to God now," she murmured, sniffling, regaining her composure.

Ezra S. kept his hands firmly on her shoulders.

"That is the will of God," he said quietly.

Lydia nodded in acquiescence. Her breath settled as she wiped her eyes with a handkerchief. Ezra S. returned to the bench along the wall and sat down again, staring at the floor and listening once again to the steady trundling noise of the sewing machine, like the noise within his heart.

In the *Kammer*, Isaac D. removed the hospital gown. Kneeling on one knee, he dipped the cloth into the basin and sloshed it around in the clear liquid. Esle stood at the foot of the benches. The sharp smell of rubbing alcohol, like the palpable smell of death, pricked his nose as he gazed mournfully at Eli's corn-blond hair and tender face. The lamplight flickered. The house was still but for the sound of the sewing machine and the slosh of the rubbing alcohol. Isaac D. squeezed the cloth and ran it along the boy's slender arm.

Esle, his forehead creased as though puzzling over a parable, contemplated the dead body. Already the skin was ashen. He examined the arm and then let his eyes slide over the slim shoulders and narrow chest, the nipples like two dark dimes. He surveyed the long legs, tight and sinewy from summers of running and climbing and working, and the feet unusually big for his age. Then he studied the ugly cut, the incision the doctors had made in an attempt to stop life from slipping out of his body. The gash went from the center of his chest past the side of his navel to his pelvis, an unsightly line of invasion sewn up with black stitches in the hope that Eli would recover. But there was no recovery. No healing. No return to life. Only eternal life now.

Isaac D. again dipped the cloth into the basin of rubbing alcohol. He wiped the neck and shoulders, the chest. After he finished cleansing the body, he and Esle stretched a sheet over him and waited patiently.

Aware of a sudden change in the room, Esle realized that the sound of the sewing machine had stopped. He turned and saw Lydia, standing near him, holding a white shirt and a pair of white pants, with an inscrutable expression sewn into her face. Esle took the clothes from her, not able to look into her eyes, and she left the room.

Isaac D. and Esle dressed Eli in the white shirt and pants. Isaac D. fitted a pair of white socks on his feet. Esle gently folded his arms across his chest and combed his corn-blond hair, arranging the bangs evenly across his forehead.

After a moment, as though sensing that Eli had been dressed, Ezra S. and Lydia entered the room and stood at the end of the benches. Then the floorboards in the living room creaked. When Joseph stepped into the room, Ezra S. could smell the black night on him.

"Did you see Hosea M.?"

"*Ya*," Joseph muttered, his face grave, staring at the white-clad figure. "He'll bring the coffin tomorrow morning."

Ezra S. nodded and pulled at his beard.

"I put your horse in Gideon's stable," Joseph murmured to Isaac

D., since Isaac D. and Esle were going to sit up all night with Eli.

Isaac D. nodded. Everyone stood in awkward silence.

"We must sleep," Ezra S. finally said. "We are done for now."

Joseph left the room first. His big, heavy feet clomped up the stairs. For a suffering moment, Ezra S. and Lydia stood still and contemplated their son, dressed in white, prepared for burial. How he looks as though he were just sleeping, Ezra S. thought. How he looks as though he could be gently shaken to wake up, wake up, it's time to milk the cows! It's time to milk the cows!

The night returned to him with sudden violence. The fear he felt when Eli ran into the burning barn to free King. The heat, the smoke, the flames. The oak beam cracking him in the back, knocking him to the ground. The screaming of the calves. Pulling him, dragging him, carrying him. If he had yelled sooner. If he had kept the boy from the barn. If he had followed quicker. If, if, if . . .

Eli was dead. He had been borne into the heavens in a whirlwind of fire. The loss of his barn, his livestock, and his winter grain hardly mattered to him now. How light it seemed compared to the life of this ten-year-old child—dead, gone, lost to this world! Winter grain will be donated, livestock will be bought, a barn will be raised. But Ezra S. could not raise his son. Only on the day of resurrection would the Lord raise Eli.

"He is now white like the moon," Ezra S. murmured. "He is now like an angel."

Lydia nodded. "The moon is like an angel."

"What is that?" Esle asked, turning to Lydia.

"In the hospital he kept saying the moon was like an angel, like an angel," Lydia replied, smiling faintly. "You know his imagination."

"*Ya*, I do." Esle's eyes were wet, looking at Eli, remembering how he had asked him this past summer to tell him what the moon was like. "How I'm going to miss him."

"We all will miss him," Lydia responded softly. "But now he is in heaven—with God."

With that, Isaac D. and Esle left the *Kammer* and found chairs in the living room, where they would spend the night watching over Eli.

"Come to sleep," Ezra S. gently told his wife. "There is nothing more to do."

Lydia nodded.

Ezra S. waited a moment longer, then turned and climbed the stairs to the spare bedroom, where he and Lydia would sleep that night.

Lydia listened to the stairs creak and the ceiling overhead groan as she continued to gaze at her son. Gently she placed one hand over her abdomen, swelling with new life. And then a certain, distinct, true calm descended. To replace the great pain, a formal feeling finally came. She inhaled deeply, as though this calm feeling entered her being through breath alone: the reassurance of the will of God, the supremacy of eternal life, the necessity of suffering on this earth. *We are here at his insistence, and we are recalled at his desire.*

She leaned over and kissed Eli gently on the forehead, tasting the rubbing alcohol and the cold skin. She stepped over to the kerosene lamp on the bureau and turned the flame down. In the kitchen she removed the brown paper bag from the kitchen table and carried it into the wash house. She paused for a few seconds in the doorway of the living room, looked at her good neighbors, and said simply, *"Danki."* Then, with a steady step, she climbed the stairs to sleep.

CHAPTER 8

At sunset on the first Saturday in April, Jacob drove his horse and buggy into downtown Fairville to join his buddies at the Original. That evening a dark cloud carried the sun away, but above the ridge of Stone Mountain, the colors still lingered, in tangerine and reddish tiers, brilliant and blurred. He was pleased with the rapid change in weather, which had turned springlike over the course of the week. Winter, at last, had lost its tight grip, and the strong spring sun was starting to warm the valley.

In the meadows and along the banks of the Reigle and Kishacoquillas creeks, shoots of daffodils flourished. Tiny heads of crocuses shouldered their way through the cold earth and adorned the edges of homes with dots of color. The evening air was cool but comfortable. Not only was driving a horse and buggy more pleasant now, but drinking beer made better sense. Jacob preferred to drink beer rather than wine or hard liquor. Since Shem felt Jacob had botched up the boozing last Sunday night at the singing, Shem insisted on making all the arrangements for this night, even though the scheme still involved Gary Schippe and Ken Heller. They were the only two local boys who could supply them with alcohol.

Since there was no church the following morning, young people could go out Saturday night to socialize with friends, go hunting, visit family, or go courting. There were no curfews, but most Amish teenagers were expected to have their buggies back in the shed by dawn to avoid "talk." The two nights most desired by Amish youth were on alternating weekends: church Sunday nights for the singings, and Saturday nights when there was no church the next day.

At seven Jacob pulled into the parking lot and drove past the Getty gas pumps to the hitching rail at the far end. Shem and Jonas had already tied their horse and buggy there. Gary had parked his metallic-green van in front of the plateglass window of the Original. Jacob smiled. The four Amish boys—Jacob, Shem and Jonas (the Zook brothers), and Gideon—had acquired a reputation as a "bad crowd" because they smoked cigarettes, drank alcohol, and ran around with *englisch* teenagers. Their rebelliousness had become all too well-known since last summer.

After Jacob tied his horse, he strutted across the parking lot into the Uni-Mart to buy a pack of cigarettes. In the convenience store, behind the counter, he saw a row of white baseball caps, strung along a metal wire like clothes on a clothesline, with a KOOL insignia inscribed on each one.

"How much are those caps?"

Marianne, the only attendant on duty, screwed up her face when she turned to him. She was as skinny as a cornstalk. Her thin nose twitched as though she smelled some rank odor. She did not like the Amish, especially the Nebraska Amish.

"Them thair?"

"Ye-ah." Jacob caught himself before he said the proverbial *ya*.

"Three forty-five plus tax."

"I'll take one of them caps then and two packs of Kools."

Slowly she rose from her seat on the stool, as though overburdened with having to stand, took one tiny step, and loosened a cap from its catch along the wire. She tossed it on the counter, dumped two packs of Kool cigarettes into it, and asked in a sour voice, "Anything else?"

Jacob shook his head no as he paid from his allowance money.

When Jacob appeared in the pizzeria, he had the KOOL cap clapped on his head and his hair pushed back behind his ears. He held his straw hat behind him.

Jacob swaggered toward the table where Shem, Jonas, and Gary sat. "How do yew like my new *englisch* hat?"

"KOOL!" Gary laughed.

"*Ya*, it *is* cool," Shem and Jonas echoed, both laughing as well.

Jacob simply smiled, tossed his straw hat on the table, and sat down next to Jonas.

"Hey-hey," Johnnie called from behind the counter, "wheredja get that kooool cap?" Johnnie Panunzio, the owner of the pizzeria, a middle-aged Italian-American with curly crow-black hair, laughed a big belly laugh and leaned his elbows on the counter. "Hey, yous gonna order that large pizza now or what?"

The boys sat drinking Mountain Dew.

"Not yet," Gary answered tersely. "We're gonna order a large pepperoni as soon as Ken gets here."

"I thought you said when Jacob got here."

"Jacob *and* Ken."

"Oh-oh-oh." Johnnie turned back to watch the TV, suspended near the cash register, just as Vanna White turned another letter on the *Wheel of Fortune*.

Elmer, a lanky sixteen-year-old who worked part-time, banged pots and pans around in the back kitchen.

"Hey-hey-HEY!" Johnnie yelled. "Whaddaya doin' back there, tearin' down the place or just cleanin' it? I can't hear the *TV*."

The banging stopped. Gary shook his head and rolled his eyes knowingly (he had worked for Johnnie last summer). Jacob rapped a pack of Kool cigarettes ceremoniously against the heel of his hand.

"I still don't know how you smoke them menthol cigarettes," Gary remarked as he lit a Marlboro Red and started tapping his cigarette lighter on the tabletop.

Jacob lit a cigarette and exhaled a stream of smoke in response.

"Where's Gideon?" Gary wondered.

"Don't know," Jonas replied. "Supposed to be here at six thirty."

"Ven is Ken supposed to get here?" Shem asked Gary.

"I thought yew made the arrangements," Jacob needled Shem.

"I did," Shem defended himself, "but Gary's part of them tew."

Jacob commented sarcastically, "Oh!"

"Ken said seven thirty," Gary repeated, tapping his cigarette lighter louder and louder against the table. "I told you *four* times already."

"And he'll have three twelve-packs, right?" Shem quizzed him.

"Yeah, yeah, yeah," he replied testily, "three twelve-packs of Coors Light."

Gary took an annoyed drag on his cigarette. Although he liked the Amish and certainly had quite a few Amish friends, he felt that they sure could be pushy at times: when they want something, they want something. He was a senior at Big Valley High School. As soon as he graduated, he planned on going to a trade school for auto mechanics because he loved to fiddle and fuss with any kind of engine on any kind of vehicle. Indeed, he always had a habit of fiddling and fussing, squirming in his seat, twisting his van keys, shaking his leg up and down, as though he had an overabundance of nervous energy. He was a wiry eighteen-year-old with curly coffee-colored hair, cut short without any style.

"So where are we going tonight?" Jacob wondered.

Shem shrugged his bony shoulders.

"I thought yew had plans."

"I dew, I dew." Shem glanced at the wall clock. "I chust hope Ken gets here soon."

"He will," Gary assured them emphatically. "He said seven thirty. It's only quarter past."

The Zook brothers were both tall and thin, though Shem was a few inches taller and a bit heavier than Jonas. They both, however, spoke with an equally thick German accent. Jacob had virtually mastered both languages with only a trace of an accent on a few English words. He was always surprised that the Zooks could not pronounce certain English words properly.

Holding his cigarette cupped in his hand, Jacob walked over to the glass-fronted refrigerator to get a can of Mountain Dew. If he wanted to smoke a cigarette or horse around in the pizzeria, he always had to be painstakingly attentive because so many Amish frequented the Uni-Mart next door to buy potato chips, soda, or ice cream. He kept a keen eye on the parking lot for any Amish driving into it, so he could hide his cigarette or slam the straw hat back on his head.

When he sat back down, snapping the soda cap open, he asked Gary, "Will yew let me practice tonight?"

"Maybe," Gary replied, jangling his van keys against the plastic ashtray.

"Yew know I'm careful."

"I know you are."

"So?"

"So-o . . . maybe yes, maybe no." Gary dragged on his cigarette.

Two months ago Gary had made the mistake, as he now regarded it, of letting Jacob drive his van around a parking lot in Harrisville, teaching him how to steer and how to use the foot pedals. At first, with the lurching of the van and the delighted laughter of Jacob, Gary had enjoyed showing him how to drive, as though he had given him some toy. Since then, however, Jacob had pestered him to "practice" every time he saw him. After all, he wasn't a driving instructor.

"Maybe later," Gary suggested, "but not if you're drunk."

"What about now?"

"Now?"

"*Ya*, while waiting fur Ken."

"I'm not going to drive all the way over to Harrisville and back so—"

"Oo nooo, here, around this parking lot."

"Here?" Gary exclaimed. Jacob was so worried about the Amish seeing him smoke a cigarette that the idea of someone seeing him behind the steering wheel of a van seemed outrageous. "What if someone sees you?"

"With my cap on, no one will know. Only fur a minute, down back and up around front. It's dark. No one's around."

Gary hesitated, crushed his cigarette in the ashtray, and as he stood declared emphatically, "This will be the only time tonight."

"*Ya*, just fur now," Jacob said excitedly. "I won't bother yew the rest of the night."

Gary knew he would keep his word. Jacob would drive the van around the parking lot with great satisfaction, be in a good mood for the rest of the night, and not bother him till next time. Shem and Jonas plodded outside after Jacob and Gary. But as soon as Jacob climbed into the driver's seat, a white-topped horse and buggy rattled into the parking lot. Jacob ducked into the back. Still standing next to the van, Gary shut the passenger door.

"It's chust Gideon," Shem assured him.

Gideon waved to them as he drove his buggy over to the hitching rail. Jacob popped his head up between the seats as Gary opened the door to tell him that it was Gideon.

"He-ey, vaat's goin' awn?" Gideon called while hitching his horse.

Gideon, short and stocky, with eyes that yawned in his round face, trudged over to the van. Jacob was once again in the driver's seat, beaming at the dashboard. Gary jumped into the passenger side.

"Yew're gonna trust him with that?" Gideon asked Gary, laughing. "He can't even drive a horse all that well."

Shem and Jonas snorted at that remark.

"*Ya*, well, I'll show yew how to drive a hundred and *fifty* horses," Jacob bragged good-naturedly.

Turning the key in the ignition, he started the engine and then pushed a cassette into the tape deck. AC/DC caterwauled from the eight speakers. Gary pulled on his seat belt.

"*Ya*, that's right," Gideon shouted, "yew better 'buckle up fur safety.' "

With great dexterity and show, Jacob braked while he shifted the automatic transmission to reverse. Slowly he backed out and then with short jerks drove down the alley from the parking lot. Shem, Jonas, and Gideon were watching the van disappear around the corner and did not notice that Esle had pulled into the parking lot. As Esle drove past them to the hitching rail, the boys glanced at each other with wide-eyed looks. While Esle tied his horse, the three boys stood shuffling their feet in front of the pizzeria.

Esle nodded to them as he walked over. "Is Jacob inside?"

The boys hesitated.

"*Nay*," Shem said, finally.

"Is he in the store?"

Shem shook his head no. The metallic-green van lurched around the corner and crept into the parking lot. Heading straight for them, with its tinted windshield and yellow headlights, the front of the van looked like the fantastic face of some oversized insect.

Esle turned to the van just as it jerked to a stop directly in front of them. Gary clambered out of the passenger's seat as Jacob climbed out of the driver's seat. Esle's mouth quivered, for a moment, and then settled into a rigid line. Jacob pulled off the KOOL baseball cap as he slammed the door shut.

"So," Esle said in a hard voice, "you're driving now, too."

"Just around the parking lot, that's all," Jacob replied in a too-hurried voice. He added, in English, "It's no big deal."

"It's a 'big deal' when we're planning to apply for baptism at the end of this month," Esle declared with irritation. "You act as though you live in Lancaster, not Big Valley."

Impassively, Jacob studied his brother's face.

Esle assumed that after spring communion, they both were going to request instruction for baptism. He felt that as soon as Jacob started his religious studies, he would cast off all this *worldly* foolishness: the cigarette smoking, the beer drinking, the late-night carousing. Now Esle found Jacob driving a van! If only he would be more serious about his life, his family, and his eternal soul. *Anyone* could have seen him doing that! What would their grandfather have said!

Finally Jacob asked, "What are you doing here?"

"Getting some chips and ice cream to go see—," Esle hesitated and then continued, "—the Yoders." He did not want to say Judith's name in front of the others. Most romances, especially in an early stage, were kept as secretive as possible.

"Oh," Jacob responded.

"And you?" Esle demanded. "What are you doing? Would you like to come over as well?"

Esle hoped that Jacob would take a more active interest in Rachel. He believed that there was nothing more sobering for a young man than to take an interest in a young woman: the interest would turn into a desire for marriage and then into a devotion to family. An interest in Rachel, he reasoned, would be far preferable to hanging out with this crowd.

"Nay," Jacob responded.

"What are you going to do then?"

"Well, we're going to have a pizza, and then later on, we're going to spot deer."

Gary had a powerful spotlight, which he could plug into the cigarette lighter socket, throwing close to a hundred candles of light to illuminate astonished deer feeding in the fields or woods.

Esle nodded his head. The image of deer briefly aroused his attention. All he could hunt now were opossums, skunks, and weasels, which were not that much fun to kill. Starting in May, though, he could hunt his single spring gobbler: hunters are allowed one wild turkey per season.

"Well," Esle said, "I have to go."

He stepped over to the Uni-Mart and vanished inside. Jacob and the others pushed back into the Original and tramped to their table.

"He is so-o serious," Jonas remarked.

Jacob nodded, put the KOOL cap back on his head, and adjusted the visor.

"Yous want that pizza now?" Johnnie asked.

"Not till *Ken* gets here," Gary answered in a hounded voice, glancing at the wall clock. It was seven thirty-five.

For an instant, Johnnie glared at Gary. Then he turned his attention back to the TV set and *Jeopardy*. The telephone rang. He snatched up the handset and scratched down an order for two strombolis to go.

"It's seven thirty-five," Shem announced, staring at the wall clock.

"I know what time it is," Gary sighed as his foot started tapping the linoleum floor. "Give him a minute, for goodness' sake."

Jacob lit another cigarette and inhaled deeply. Seeing his brother upset him. Esle had never actually *seen* Jacob drink or smoke or *do* anything before, though he did *know* about it. But he could hardly believe that, of all things, Esle had to see him driving a van—a considerable transgression! Not driving a car was a major rule of the *Ordnung*. Esle was so strict in loyalty to the Amish way that Jacob felt small and selfish and ashamed.

Just then Ken Heller, wearing a white shirt and a white windbreaker, coasted into the pizzeria with a wad of Skoal Wintergreen in the corner of his mouth. He had a dark, rough, disheveled handsomeness, much like a model in a Guess jeans advertisement: lean face, tousled hair, sneering smile that advertised a do-no-wrong attitude, and a slender swimmer's build since he worked as a lifeguard every summer. Ken wore a silver loop earring in one ear, and a silver St. Christopher medal dangled from a chain around his neck. He was a junior at Penn State at Altoona, commuting daily from Harrisville, and easily looked much older than twenty. Hence, he never had trouble getting served in bars or being carded at liquor stores.

Everyone at the table turned to him. Even Johnnie faced him.

"Yeah, yeah," Gary called out, looking at Johnnie, "you can make the pizza now."

"Hey-hey, give thanks to Mary and Joseph!" Johnnie exclaimed as he grabbed a lump of dough.

"So, dudes, what *is* the action tonight?" Ken began as he sat down.

"Dew yew have the booze?" Shem asked.

"I'm fine, thank you," Ken said. "Yes, I *have* the booze. Three twelve-packs of Coors Light."

Shem nodded his head up and down slowly a half dozen times.

"So, thirty dollars?" Shem asked.

"Thirty dollars," Ken repeated, winking at Gary.

Both Ken and Gary knew how insistent and impatient these Amish boys could be on a Saturday night.

"Where is it?"

Ken laughed and looked inside his windbreaker. "Not here. I must've forgotten it."

Shem frowned.

"It's in the car on ice."

In the trunk of his Chevy Cavalier, he had an Igloo cooler and a large black garbage bag, both filled with ice and beer.

Shem nodded his head again another half dozen times and looked with triumph at Jacob.

"Are you done with that Mountain Dew?" Ken asked Shem.

"*Ya.*"

Ken grabbed the soda can, lifted it to his mouth, and spat tobacco juice into it. "So what *are* we doing tonight?"

"First, we eat a pizza," Gary replied. "Then we go somewhere to party, I guess."

Shem and Jonas both nodded seriously.

"Where though?" Jacob wondered.

The boys looked at each other.

"Not the Curve," Shem decided. "Tew cold."

The boys murmured assent. The Curve was an extended shoulder on the first sharp curve going up Mountain Climb Road, where spring water poured out of a pipe. Local Amish boys met there on Saturday nights to drink.

"What about Woodward Lane then?" Jacob suggested.

"*Nay*," Shem replied, "Big Man has been cruising through there."

Big Man was Corporal Carrie, one of the county police officers, notorious for giving young people a hard time, Amish or non-Amish.

"What about the Freedman cabin?" Jacob proposed. "That's a decent place."

"Where's that?" Ken asked. He spat more tobacco juice into the soda can.

"Off Peachey Lane in Harrisville," Jacob told him.

Ken creased his forehead in question.

"Off Stone Mountain Road."

"Oh, sure, up past the cemetery."

"Ye-ah, that's it." Jacob nodded. "Nice place, good view of the valley."

"But the road *up* to the cabin is pretty nasty," Gary grumbled, a touch of concern about his van in his voice.

"It wasn't all that bad when we went up there last time," Jacob said.

"That's because we were in Lucy's Escort," Gary explained. "An Escort is not a van."

"Yew don't think the van can make it?" Shem asked, fretful about the turn in the conversation, as if not going to the Freedman cabin meant not going anywhere at all.

"It might not," Gary answered. "It's narrow and rough up there."

"Of course it will," Jacob said brightly. "The road's not that bad."

Gary tapped his van keys against the table top.

Johnnie soon set a large pepperoni pizza in the center of the table. When Gideon bit into his first piece, a long string of hot mozzarella dripped onto his chin. He cried out and dropped the slice of pizza, face down, on the table. Everyone had a good laugh at that.

After they finished eating, the Amish boys untied their horses and drove their rigs to the back of the building, where they had constructed a makeshift hitching rail. Johnnie had given them the space, provided that the buggies never blocked the service entrance and that they cleaned up the horse dung. All four boys returned hatless, toting rumpled brown paper bags. In each bag was a pair of sneakers, a pair of jeans, and a shirt. In the back of Gary's van, the boys changed into their *englisch* clothes. Only Jacob had a jean jacket; the other boys kept on their Amish vest jackets for warmth.

"Vell, I have to keep an eye awn the booze." Shem climbed out the side door to ride with Ken.

When the van reached the entrance to the dirt road off Peachey Lane, Jacob had to pull aside a large branch that had fallen across it.

"Great start," Gary commented as Jacob climbed back into the passenger seat.

"Don't worry."

"I *do* worry," Gary griped. "This isn't a buggy, my friend."

Jacob didn't say a word as Gary maneuvered the van up the bumpy dirt road. Branches and bushes scratched at the sides. The headlights bounced up and down. Often, the lights caught the eyes of some night creature, quick flashes of glowing coins. The mountain is filled with eyes, Jacob thought. I wonder why their eyes shine like that? Raccoons, possums, deer, skunks. Tiny bright disks of light in the dark, but dark themselves unless exposed to light—like the mind—like faith—

"Stop!" Jacob shouted.

Gary slammed on the brakes and bounced over a rut, scraping the bottom of the van.

"What?"

"Did yew see that?"

The other boys crowded their heads between the front seats.

"See what?"

"A big cat."

"A big *cat*?"

"Like a small dog," Jacob said quickly.

"Oh-h, great!" Gary groaned. "I ruin my muffler because you see a cat."

"*Nay*, not a house cat. Bigger than that!"

"A panther?" Gideon suggested.

"Could be," Jacob replied thoughtfully.

"A panther?" Gary scoffed. "Like in the jungle?"

"Ye-ah."

"There aren't any panthers up here." He started driving again.

"*Ya*, there *are*," Gideon and Jonas chimed in.

"Yew call them something different then," Jacob suggested.

Gary creased his forehead. "Oh. You mean, like, mountain lions or bobcats?"

The boys nodded their heads.

"Well, there aren't any mountain lions or bobcats up here either."

"There could be."

"Not now, not anymore," Gary declared to end the conversation. "It probably *was* a small dog or just a raccoon."

Jacob sat silent, trying to recapture within his memory the quick golden flash he saw, like a piece of a dream.

Finally, Gary pulled his van into a clearing and parked. Ken parked his car next to the van. At the edge of this open area stood a small cabin with a flat roof and, on two sides, a deck. Trees and thick bushes surrounded the entire cabin with just enough clearance on one side to use the stairs to the deck. Ken pulled the Igloo ice chest out of his trunk and handed it to Shem, who took it with an air of importance, while Gideon and Jonas carried the black garbage bag holding ice and beer. Gary clicked on a flashlight and turned its beam on the ground, slicing a bright way through the darkness.

"It wasn't so dark last time," Jacob remarked.

"There's no moon tonight," Gary observed. "It's wicked dark up here without a moon."

After they climbed the stairs to the deck, Jacob moved to the railing to look out over the valley. Some tree branches strayed down to him, bent to him. The night seemed to clutch and cling. In the dark distance, a scattering of lights from farm windows could be seen in the valley.

"Hey, Jacob, c'mere," Gary called. "Hold the light."

He handed the flashlight to Jacob, who turned the beam on the door while Gary, holding the doorknob in both hands, jerked it quickly to the right. The lock popped open.

"Cheap lock," Gary said as he opened the cabin door.

Jonas and Gideon dragged the black garbage bag inside. The cabin smelled musty, with a faint odor of burned firewood. There was one large near-empty room with a woodstove in one corner, a kitchenette with a kerosene stove, and a small bedroom—the bare necessities of a hunter's cabin. Gary shone the light around until he found the kerosene lamp.

"Just like the Amish," he commented, lighting it and setting it down on an apple crate that served as a coffee table.

"Dew yew think we should light a light?" Shem asked nervously, looking around.

"Way up here?" Gary countered. "There's no one around for miles."

Ken sat down on the lumpy sofa along one wall.

"Whose cabin is this, anyway?" Shem continued.

"Martin Freedman," Gary explained, "Lucy Freedman's uncle. That's how she knew about it. He built it five or six years ago for deer hunting and used it all the time the first year, as a getaway place, and then used it less the second year, and even less the third year. This year he had to go to Philadelphia on business, which means that it won't be used at all, except by us."

Shem looked at him suspiciously.

"Ask Lucy if you don't believe me," Gary said. "But you have nothing to worry about. Ken, hand me a beer."

Ken tossed him a beer.

"Where's Jacob?" Gary wondered.

Jacob was still outside on the deck, staring into the darkness.

"He's looking for his panther," Gary laughed. "I should tell you about the time Lucy and me came up here. Now *that* was a good time."

Shem reached into the black garbage bag, grabbed a beer, and tried to relax.

"Hey, Jacob," Gary called, "join the party."

Jacob joined the party.

CHAPTER 9

In the dawn darkness on Monday morning, Hosea M. Zook, a middle-aged dairy farmer with squinty eyes and gnarled hands, trundled down the rutted farm lane driving a spring wagon carrying a newly made pine coffin. He had a side business making coffins for his own Nebraska Amish. With each jolt the empty coffin trembled. Ezra S. and Hosea M. carried the five-by-two-foot coffin into the washhouse and set it in one corner. Eli would not be placed in the coffin until Tuesday morning, just before the funeral.

The two men removed the bureau from the *Kammer*, arranged benches in front of the body, and stood in silence staring at Eli's white-clad figure. Shortly Hosea M. left the room and entered the kitchen, where Lydia, her face clouded with fatigue, stood stirring oatmeal in a black pot with a long wooden spoon. She asked him to sit down for breakfast. Judith stood next to her, frying eggs. Joseph and Enos, unsure what to do, sat at the kitchen table; at this hour, they usually would be in the barn milking the cows, feeding the horses, tending to the calves. Ben and Becky came down the back stairs, rubbing their sleepy eyes with the heels of their hands. Levi was still upstairs sleeping as Rachel set flatware and green plastic bowls on the table.

Ezra S. appeared in the doorway. Everyone sat down. At the head of the table, Ezra S. bowed his head for a long moment of silence. Then Lydia and Judith served breakfast. They ate without speaking. After the morning prayer, everyone stood up except Hosea M., who sat hunched over with his gnarly hands on his knees.

The entire family—silent, somber, tight with grief—followed their father to the *Kammer*. A kerosene lamp, hanging from a hook in the center of the ceiling, illuminated the room. Behind the body, windowpanes were still black with the predawn. The air seemed pinched. Ezra S. and Lydia stepped over and looked down at their son, dressed in white, his hair nicely combed, his hands folded across his chest. His small face was dull with death and slightly shrunken. The rest of the family stood in a sorrow-stricken line, gazing at their brother. Judith and Rachel started to cry, then Becky. Joseph and Enos tried not to cry, but tears stung their eyes as their lower lips trembled. Ben sniffled. Then the family knelt down in front of a bench and lowered their heads to its surface while Ezra S. recited a prayer aloud. Afterward, Ezra S. and the children left the room. Lydia, sitting on the front bench, remained with Eli.

Judith and Rachel cleared the table, washed the dishes, and swept the floors in the kitchen and living room. Ezra S. stepped outside on the front porch to watch the dark sky fill with a dull, drab light as dawn, wrapped in low gray clouds, tumbled over the top of the mountain. He saw Isaac D. driving down the farm lane. After their night's vigil, Isaac D. and Esle had gone home for the morning milking. Isaac D. tied his horse next to the spring wagon. He had come back to supervise cleanup activities and the burial of the animals. Ezra S. would try to help whenever he could during the day, but his main responsibility was to attend to the details of his son's viewing and burial.

The two men talked briefly. Isaac D. explained that local construction companies in Big Valley and Lewistown were providing equipment to move the rubble and the dead animals and that a huge pit would have to be dug in the back pasture. As Isaac D. went inside to view the body, Ezra S. turned to gaze at the back fields.

While Ezra S. gazed at the back fields, Nannie Zook unlocked the front door to the Nebraska Amish one-room schoolhouse on Stone Mountain Road to fire up the coal-burning stove and to prepare lessons for the day. After she closed the door, she stepped through the entranceway and surveyed the interior of the schoolroom: the wood floors, white walls, rows of wood-topped desks, soft blue trim along the windows. The schoolhouse in the morning, before the fuss and racket of the children, was a peaceful place where she could enjoy the silence. She stood flushed from her vigorous walk down the mountain lane. There had been nothing unusual in her customary morning walk except a faint smell of smoke and burned, rotting animal flesh clinging to the air to remind her of the barn fires on Saturday night.

For over twenty-five years, Nannie had been an Amish schoolteacher; she was the first and only teacher hired for this particular school, which had opened in 1967. She was a thickset woman in her midsixties with wide shoulders and an open face. Silver-rimmed spectacles accentuated the perceptive gaze of her blue-gray eyes.

Nannie untied her black scarf, removed her *Mantel*, and hung both items on a peg near the entrance, in an alcove that stored coats and boots and had shelves for lunch buckets. She smoothed the front of her dark-blue dress, aligned a straight pin in her apron, and adjusted her white cap. In the entryway, firewood was neatly stacked; she picked up a handful of kindling and a small log. The schoolroom was chilly because the fire had burned out over the weekend. During the week, a bucket of coal at day's end would burn all night and the room would be warm the following morning.

In the back corner stood a stove. She opened the loading door, thrust the kindling and log into the firebox, splashed in a few drops of kerosene, and carefully lighted the fire. Watching the flames sizzle and snap, her thoughts returned to the barn fires and Eli Yoder's death. Nannie shivered. She stood straight and looked at the stovepipe, then dumped a bucket of coal onto the fire and closed the door.

Nannie walked down the center aisle of desks, the old-fashioned type having double-desk wood tops attached to black wrought-iron frames with wooden seats. The teacher's desk stood centered at the front of the room. Behind that, in three attached sections, a green chalkboard ran along the entire length of the wall. Along the top of the board was the English alphabet in cursive letters, small and capital. An alarm clock dangled from a nail next to the letter *M*. Nannie set the correct time and wound it up.

She sat at her desk. Briefly, before shuffling through some papers to review what lessons had to be taught that morning, she listened intently to the ticking of the clock. Then she stood at the chalkboard, stretching her arm up high, and wrote in the far right-hand corner: Today is Monday, December 7, 1992. On the wall calendar, she drew an *X* through the blocks for Saturday and Sunday and circled the day's date in red. Since arithmetic was the first subject taught every day, she wrote the assignments for each grade on the chalkboard.

When Nannie stepped over to the tall wood cabinet to get some scrap paper, she paused and gazed out the window at the front field at the horse stable used by the children who drove horses and buggies to school. This morning there will be only be two horses instead of three, she thought sadly. She returned to her desk and stared out another window at the back field, a worn winter brown, where the children played during recess. Her eyes fastened on that turf and then followed a boy racing across the back field. He slammed shut the door to the outhouse. That Dan Speicher, she thought with a smile, must have had five glasses of water before he left home. At twelve years old, he still hasn't learned!

The front door burst open as Barbara and Franny Speicher bustled into the room. They removed their coats, set their lunch buckets on a shelf, and chattering, sat down at a back desk. The two girls said, "*Gut mya,*" to Nannie, who nodded and smiled in return. Rudi, their thirteen-year-old brother, was putting the horse in the stable. Dan then barged into the room, fussing with the button on his trousers. He slammed his lunch bucket onto a shelf and ran back outside to run around the field with some other boys. In twos and threes and fours, her scholars banged through the front door.

As each face appeared, Nannie felt her heart lift. She was a born teacher who enjoyed watching each child learn the daily lessons—even that squirmy Dan, who resisted each assignment but invariably took great pleasure in having accomplished it. For Nannie, most of her God-given maternal love had descended upon her scholars since she never had a child. For two years she and her husband, Sol J., had tried without success to start a family. Finally, they had consulted Dr. Wallace, who told them that Sol J. was sterile because of a bad case of boyhood mumps. For a week Nannie had grieved, with severe depression. Then she realized that she must transform her suffering into something useful, charitable, and Christian; so she decided to become a schoolteacher.

Ruth, Abe, and Gideon stomped into the schoolhouse. Gideon's eyes were tear-swollen and red, his mouth clamped tight. Nannie called Ruth to her desk and asked what was wrong. Ruth said that he wanted to stay at the farm to watch the *englisch* machines bury the dead animals. As Ruth returned to her seat, Hannah and Daniel, Isaac

D.'s children, entered the schoolroom.

Finally, at nine, Nannie rose and walked to the front door with the school bell, which she rang vigorously a few times. Immediately, the boys stopped playing and scrambled inside the schoolhouse. She walked back to her desk and waited for them to settle, then lightly tapped the desk bell. The children fell silent.

"Goot morning, boys and girls," Nannie greeted them in English.

"Goot morn-ing, Nan-nie," they all replied.

Nannie scanned the room, the youngest children sitting close to her and the oldest ones sitting toward the back. Everyone was there except Ben and Becky Yoder, who were at home that morning for Eli's viewing—and Eli. She opened her record book to mark Ben and Becky absent for the day, and then paused at Eli's name. The sharp pencil point hovered over the block for his name without marking it. She closed the record book. She felt tears in her eyes.

She stood and opened the Bible. As she read from 1 Corinthians that morning, she felt the biblical words return command to her feelings. After the Scripture reading, the children stood and bowed their heads to recite the Lord's Prayer. They sang a hymn. During the hymn, Nannie heard a noise, turned to cast one of her stern glances at the errant child, and saw that Sarah, who usually sat near Eli, was crying. The ten-year-old girl stood facing the empty seat with her head bowed, sniffling, tears dropping from her eyes. She started bawling. The singing voices stumbled and stopped. Ruth, Sarah's older sister, stepped down the aisle and simply embraced her little sister.

The children stood silent. The lower lips of the younger children started to tremble. Nannie stared at the empty seat and felt the emptiness curl around her heart.

As Ruth embraced Sarah in the schoolhouse, a backhoe maneuvered its long arm over a gouge in the back pasture of the Yoder farm. Karl Eckard, owner of Eckard Construction Company, a tall man with a horseshoe of iron-gray hair on his bald head, stood next to Isaac D., watching the powerful scoop dip into the land and lift bucket after bucket of earth. A huge pile of red dirt formed next to a bulldozer.

"Just like an ice-cream scoop, isn't it?" Karl shouted.

Both men stood near the edge of the hole the backhoe was digging. Three construction companies had donated manpower and equipment to help the Nebraska Amish bury the dead farm animals. The sky was thick with low, lumpy clouds that obscured even the top edge of the distant mountain range. The air seemed pale and ashen.

"At least it's not too cold to work this morning," Karl said.

"*Ya*, not tew bad," Isaac D. replied, adjusting his spectacles.

"Bad, though, for the smell."

Isaac D. nodded.

The burned-flesh odor Sunday morning had been appalling. The stench Monday morning with the temperature a balmy forty-eight degrees was unbearable. All day Sunday the carcasses, soaked in water, had festered in the sun.

Karl turned and glanced at the Yoder farmhouse and the line of white-topped buggies.

"I feel awful we have to do this today," Karl went on, referring to the viewing, "but there was nothing we could do to delay it. The state said to bury those dead animals immediately."

The diesel-powered backhoe sputtered and churned. With boyish pride Karl turned back to the machine. Although he had grown up on a Mennonite dairy farm, he had managed to build one of the largest construction companies in Mifflin County. He was also chairman of the Mennonite Disaster Service and responsible for coordinating the cleanup effort that week. Hundreds of volunteers were there to help. Amish and non-Amish from the valley itself were there. Amish from other communities—Lancaster, Centre, Perry, and Dauphin counties—arrived by vans and busloads. In one united effort, men and women, Amish and non-Amish, boys and girls, worked to clean up the miserable mess: to shovel ashes, to toss debris into trucks, to haul burned field equipment, to rake the grounds, to work the bulldozers and dump trucks and backhoes.

Isaac D. turned to the farmhouse and declared, "Never have I seen so many people."

Once again the traffic started to inch along the road. Since there were so many people helping the Amish, it was impossible to separate workers from strangers who simply wanted to gawk. People swarmed over the farm. Reporters, not only from the local papers but also from *The New York Times*, *The Philadelphia Inquirer*, and *The Altoona Mirror*, milled about the farm, chatting with people, asking questions, taking pictures. Journalists from *Life* and *People* magazines were also wheeling through the grounds. The CBS van drove down the farm lane and parked in the back pasture. The camera crew lolled around, waiting patiently for the dead cows and horses to be buried. The reporters, photographers, and newscasters had all been briefed to respect the Amish wish not to be photographed and to take pictures only of the dead animals, the land, the ruins of the barn, or other buildings.

Isaac D. noticed in the distance that Esle and a few others were snipping barbwire to untangle a dead draft horse caught in it. "I must go help Esle."

Walking at a diagonal through the back pasture, Isaac D. crossed over and helped Esle and the others drag the dead horse into the open. That rust-colored beard. Those strong arms. Working, toiling, helping. He watched as Esle stood straight and clapped his hands together to shake dirt and ash from his soiled work gloves. Then in Isaac D.'s mind, Jacob clapped to the surface again: *His baseball cap was found near the farm. He was missing. His black car was found in a field. He might be responsible for the fires.* Isaac D. refused to believe that a member of his family could possibly commit such an act of destruction. He reasoned that if he did not *believe* it was possible, then it *must not be* possible. Still, doubts lingered, strange facts and inexplicable evidence remained. What happened to my son in that city? What happened to him in the outside world? How Isaac D. wished he had the spiritual strength of his own father.

After the other men moved over to a pile of charred debris, Isaac D., trying to convince himself, said to Esle, "Jacob did not burn down this barn."

Esle, with soot smeared on his cheek, just gazed at his father before he turned and walked over to a group of men tossing debris into the back of a pickup truck. Isaac D. followed him with his eyes.

A woman from *People* magazine approached Isaac D. "Excuse me, excuse me, please. But do you mind if I ask you a question?"

Isaac D. eyed the woman and shook his head no.

"What do you do when someone tries to take your picture?"

"We turn our head so they can't."

"But why can't the Amish have their pictures taken?"

Isaac D. pushed his spectacles up on the bridge of his nose and in a firm voice stated, "My father never did, and neither will I."

Just then the payloader roared. Everyone turned to watch. Isaac D. was fascinated by the huge yellow machine: the gigantic tires, the hissing levers, the rumbling engine, the colossal scoop. The massive machine moved forward as the iron teeth rammed into the debris of the barn, raising a black jagged scoop of charred timber and rotting cows. He thought he heard bones crack. He heard the odd whirring sound, like summer locusts, of cameras taking pictures. He heard the piercing meep-meep-meep sound as the payloader reversed its position. It dropped the dripping mess into the back of a dump truck.

The payloader slammed its scoop once more into the foul black pile as Isaac D. let his eyes wander across the farm, looking for his family. Daniel and Hannah were at school. Esle was still busy throwing debris into the back of the pickup. Sam and Seth were in the back pasture. Rebekah stood in the front yard with Emma, serving the workers coffee and moon pies that had been baked for church Sunday. He saw Ezra S., his eyes dull and his face hard, standing in the front yard.

A police cruiser turned into the lane and parked beside the apple orchard. Sergeant Stuter climbed out of the driver's side as another man, dressed in a dark suit and a dark overcoat, emerged from the passenger side. The two men strode directly toward the farmhouse.

Ezra S. regarded the stranger with suspicion.

"Ezra," Sergeant Stuter began, "I'd like to introduce you to Michael Tate of the FBI. He's been assigned by the government to help investigate the fires."

Agent Tate extended his hand, but Ezra S. merely nodded his head. Agent Tate managed to let his hand drift back to his side with little embarrassment, as though he had been in numerous situations where a person had refused to shake hands with him.

Sergeant Stuter noticed this awkward moment and said sharply in Pennsylvania German, "He's here to help you."

"God will help me," Ezra S. retorted, as sharply.

"How do you know God did not send him here to help you?" Sergeant Stuter replied without hesitation.

Ezra S. considered this. Just then the payloader edged its iron teeth under the dead draft horse in the open and dropped it into the dump truck. Using English, Ezra S. declared, in a severe tone, "Whoever did this should be punished!"

"That's why I'm here," Agent Tate assured him. "I'm here to help you. I am very sorry, and I am deeply concerned about what has happened here. I have two boys. A twelve-year-old and a nine-year-old."

Ezra S. regarded his face again. "My Eli was ten."

Agent Tate said nothing. He pressed his thin lips together and nodded his head.

Sergeant Stuter watched this exchange with relief. He knew that Ezra S. could be stubborn and difficult, but that he was also intelligent and sensible. He admired Agent Tate's technique: quiet, patient, deferential, speaking at the proper point: mentioning his two boys was a perfect gambit to establish empathy.

"If you don't want to talk now—," Sergeant Stuter began, glancing at the farmhouse.

"I can talk now," Ezra S. interrupted. "A little."

"I want to have a word with Isaac D.," Sergeant Stuter said. "Is he here?"

"Over there. By that big machine."

Sergeant Stuter crossed the barnyard.

"Could you show me your farm?" Agent Tate asked.

"Yew mean what's left of it."

Agent Tate nodded.

"Those are not goot shoes fur a farm," Ezra S. remarked, looking down at Agent Tate's black wing-tip shoes.

"Next time I'll wear work boots."

Ezra S. and Agent Tate walked into the swirling activity of the cleanup, toward what used to be Ezra S.'s barn. Tate carefully asked questions that further established trust, to gain information that might be useful for his investigation: what contact Ezra S. had had with people that week and that day; if there had been any type of misunderstanding or disagreement; if he could remember any odd remark or unusual incident that had occurred. Agent Tate was a master of the interview. Armed with a prodigious memory, he could dispense with the usual pad and pen or tape recorder and create an impression of simply carrying on a conversation rather than a detailed interview. Immediately afterward, however, he would record pertinent details into a hand-held Sony tape recorder.

Agent Tate's credentials and training were impeccable. At St. Augustine's parochial School in Cambridge, he had been inducted into the National Honor Society. Boston College had awarded him a degree magna cum laude with a double major in computer science and psychology. He had graduated at the top of his class at the FBI academy in Quantico, Virginia.

"There's no specific incident during the week where you might have upset someone or someone might have upset you?"

Ezra S. shook his head no.

"How well do you know Jacob Hostetler?"

"I knew him as well as my own sons."

"Do you know he's missing?"

"That's been said."

"Do you have any idea where he might be?"

"Nooo."

"Could an Amish family be hiding him in their house?"

"Can't say," Ezra S. replied, thoughtfully. "Could be."

Sergeant Stuter returned from his talk with Isaac D. and Esle. Agent Tate thanked Ezra S., and the two officers walked back up the farm lane to their car. Ezra S. watched as two more buggies drove past them. All morning, a steady stream of Amish neighbors and relatives had been coming to pay their respects. The death of his son had touched off a great wave of sympathy in the valley. He turned to face the back pasture. The air smelled of earth and ash and cloud.

"He always said Gideon M. or Seth D.—why does he use both name and initial?" Agent Tate asked.

"The same names are used so much that they need initials for identification."

"To avoid confusion."

"Correct."

"He kept using the word *englisch*, too. Why?"

"That's the German word for *English.* The Amish refer to anything not Amish as *englisch,* and non-Amish people as *Englischer.*"

"And he also kept saying that yesterday was a church Sunday."

"The Amish only have church services every other Sunday."

"And on different farms?"

"Correct. The service rotates from farm to farm. One family hosts, oh, every ten months or so."

"Why do they rotate? Why not just build a church?"

"Tradition. Custom. Sharing duties. That's the way it's always been. In the sixteenth century, the early Anabaptists were severely persecuted by the Catholics *and* the Protestants. Back then, there were *Täuferjäger,* hunters who spied on Anabaptists and arrested them."

"Like a medieval FBI," Agent Tate remarked mischievously.

"Kind of," Sergeant Stuter agreed, with a faint smile. "The Anabaptists were thrown into prison, tortured, kept from their families, and in many cases, killed, drowned, or burned at the stake. To avoid being caught by the hunters, they kept moving services from place to place. Not having a meetinghouse also reminds them that their faith is not restricted to a *place.* It's part of their entire fabric of being. The *people* are the church, not a building."

"And the thing that upset the Catholics and Protestants was that they didn't believe in infant baptism?"

"That's the main one. The word *Anabaptist* means 'rebaptizer.' They believed in adult baptism on confession of faith. But the state churches considered it heresy to rebaptize someone already baptized as a baby."

Sergeant Stuter pulled open the door to his cruiser. He started the car, adjusted the heat, and turned the car around. They were driving from farm to farm that morning.

"Ezra S. did not like talking about Jacob," Agent Tate observed.

"Well, Jacob was practically part of his family."

"How many children *are* there in the Yoder family?"

"Eight children. Seven now."

"That's still quite a few kids."

"That's about average for an Amish family. Many hands needed to work a farm. All that milking is done by hand, remember, and all the fieldwork with horses."

"And they don't like to talk about Jacob since he left the Amish?"

"Well, yes. But remember, he left before he really became Amish, before he was baptized."

"So that means he's not shunned."

"Not in a strict sense. Since he left *before* baptism, shunning doesn't really apply. Esle, though, acts as though Jacob *is* shunned. Stubbornly silent. Something's bothering him, but I can't make out what it is."

"Does he know about the car?"

Sergeant Stuter nodded. "I think everyone knows about the car at this point."

"And?"

"Nothing really."

"What about Isaac D.?"

"The same."

"But do they still want him back?"

"Of course they do."

"Maybe Esle's hiding him somewhere, in a barn or a shed."

"Possibly. Esle's hiding *something*."

"Well, we can't have his car and not have *him*. He has to be somewhere."

"My men are searching a three-mile radius from the car scene. Could be he's hurt. Passed out."

"When was the car found anyway?"

"Six thirty or so, Sunday morning. In that cornfield, with the driveshaft snapped. With all that pandemonium Saturday night, no one noticed a thing till the sun came up."

"What about that Amish boy in the field, smelling of kerosene?"

"Jeptha Swarey. A dead end. Courting night for the Yellow Tops. He was visiting his girl when he heard the sirens, saw the lights, and rushed over to see the fire. He was just filling a kerosene lamp when he heard the siren and spilled it."

"Then there's that entire White-Top family who left the Amish two years ago."

"Correct. The John A. Zook family. Very bitter situation."

"What are they doing here?"

"John A. works for a construction company now in Youngstown, Ohio. The family joined a Mennonite church over there. Apparently, he and his family were driving down to Lancaster on some business and stopped in the valley to rest and try to visit some friends."

"Do you think a family man could do something like that?"

Sergeant Stuter shrugged. "Have to check it out. Their name came up. Plus the name of another Amish boy who left this year—Daniel Yoder, a White Topper."

There was a moment of silence before Agent Tate said, "Well, what *do* we have to explain this mess?"

"First, the fires were all called in between 11:38 and 11:55 p.m., except for the one in Harrisville, which was at 12:40 a.m. That means all the fires had to be started between 11:00 p.m. and 12:30 a.m."

"Which means there had to be a motor vehicle."

"Correct. At least *one*. No one could set that string of fires and get away quick enough on foot or with a horse."

"Torching one barn and getting to the next and then the next. But do you think just one car?"

"Can't say at this point. We're talking close to thirty miles, mostly back roads. I guess one car or van could do it if it were really moving."

"All in an hour and a half? Stop the car, run to a barn, start a fire, run back to the car, and drive to the next one? The first five barns were burning within five or ten minutes of each other, and they were miles apart. Seems that person was in two or three places at the same time."

Sergeant Stuter nodded. "It *is* puzzling."

"And the order the barn fires were called in is not necessarily the order in which they were set."

"Correct. No way to know at this point. If it *were* one car, then he either started them in Wilton and worked his way north or started them in Fairville and worked his way south, saving the farm in Harrisville for last."

"So where does that leave us?"

"We have a black car in a cornfield that belongs to a nonmember Amish boy who left his family eight months ago, but we don't know where he is." He held up a sealed evidence bag. "We have this white baseball cap I found along the road, down a piece from the Yoder farm. Plus tire tracks."

He handed the plastic bag to Agent Tate, who read the word *KOOL* on the cap. "And the tire tracks?"

"We're photographing some tracks found at Levi M.'s farm this morning and some at that stop sign near the Yoder farm."

CHAPTER 10

Three panthers were leaping in a dark wood, hideous night creatures springing back and forth over a path, blocking his way. At four in the morning, Jacob woke to the night-filled dawn. In his chest, his tight heart throbbed. He closed his eyes and turned and turned again, trying to sink back into sleep, but could not. Instead, he sank into a stubborn wakefulness. He turned over on his back, opened his eyes, and stared at the darkness. From the night table, he heard the distinct ticking of his timepiece, a chrome-plated pocket watch with a chrome-plated fob. The ticking sound seemed to claw at the room as his mind returned to the rhythmic clip-clopping of the hooves and the metaphor of the Amish harness.

As though he were inhaling the night-filled dawn itself, he descended further into a place of dark disaffection. Intently he listened to the deep, cadenced breathing of Esle in the other bed and compared it to his own shallow, ragged breathing. Ever since the spring communion, two weeks ago, he had been restless, agitated, and distracted. How had he reached such a spiritual wilderness?

The first instruction class for baptism would be this weekend, the first Sunday in May. At church on spring communion, he and Esle, along with other applicants, declared their intention to join the church, *die Gemee nooch geh*. Before doing so, however, the brothers had quarreled heatedly over the issue until, finally, Jacob capitulated. "It's time," Esle kept repeating, "it's time for both of us." Since they were twins, Esle believed resolutely that they should be baptized at the same time. As Esle pointed out, he had been ready for baptism last year but postponed it because Jacob was so set against it.

Stubbornly awake, listening to his brother's steady breathing and the ticking of his pocket watch, he lay in bed and stared at the dark panes of glass. There was a single window in their room that faced the barn and the distant end of Stone Mountain to the northwest.

The darkness dimmed. The night-filled air faded. The window turned into a rectangle of luminous milk-blue light. Then, at five, the sun climbed into the stars as light edged into the room, investing it with form: the single night table between the two single beds, the kerosene lamp, the two bureaus. Along one wall were wood pegs hung with straw hats, black hats, jackets, broadfall pants, and white shirts. Muddy boots and soiled, crumpled white socks lay on the floor. An unloaded shotgun leaned upright in one corner.

Jacob kept his eyes fixed on the window. As the panes of glass filled with light, his mind filled with despair. Song birds trilled. The rooster crowed his elongated note. *Wednesday.* The routine of Wednesday: cows, breakfast, auction, lunch, fieldwork, supper, cows again, fieldwork again, sleep. He was usually keen, though, for this one day, the one day he did not work at the planing mill, because it included his weekly excursion to the local public library. But this morning the immediate dread of the first instruction class for baptism cramped his mind; in the far distance loomed the greater and more significant dread of actual baptism.

He pushed the white sheets, the blue blanket, and the quilt down to his waist. The air was cool and liquid on his chest. He wanted to stay in bed, to lie there forever without having to get up or get dressed or make any type of decision, to float in some kind of eternal suspension in the twittering light of dawn. But he knew he would have to get up, pull on his socks and shirt and pants and shoes, and stumble down to the barn to milk the cows. He scratched his armpit.

Jacob heard Esle stir. His twin brother had an internal clock that was invariably on time. At five each morning, Esle opened his eyes, stared straight up at the ceiling for a moment, and then swung his hairy legs over the side of the bed to get up. Jacob usually woke up from his brother's loud, clumsy movements as he dressed. Esle started each day, just as he entered the world at birth, a few minutes before Jacob. Once Esle clomped out of the room, Jacob sat up.

When Jacob finally entered the cow stable, Esle was already pushing a wheelbarrow, heaped with oats, from stall to stall and using a Maxwell House Coffee can to toss a canful into each trough. Two kerosene lanterns, one hanging at each end of a beam covered with cobwebs, fought off the darkness with a honey-colored glow. The barn smelled of old hay and shadows. Jacob climbed a ladder to the haymow and pitched down loose hay.

Sam, rubbing sleep from his eyes, stumbled in. He was a lanky eighteen-year-old with a flat face, watery eyes, the mere whisper of a beard on an almost nonexistent chin, and clothes that always seemed baggy on his slouched figure. Pushing up the brim of his straw hat and at the same time lifting his eyebrows, as though to see better, he picked up an armful of hay. Mechanically, he stepped from stall to stall, tossing a handful into each trough. Isaac D. shuffled in and turned up the light on one lantern, near where he would milk his first cow. He cast a glance through the stables and then removed his thick eyeglasses to wipe the lenses with a white handkerchief. Swiftly Emma glided into the barn with a strainer from the milk house.

Jacob climbed down the ladder, helped distribute the rest of the hay, and trudged outside to the feeding pen. He leaned against the wood rails of the fence and studied the cows, all holsteins, crowded together, coats wet with dew, legs caked with mud, udders swollen. A few cows stretched their necks and mooed impatiently. Seth, too, stood outside, leaning against the bright orange-painted metal gate, gazing languidly at the black-and-white faces. He had just turned sixteen but had the sturdy physique of a man, hands more strong than large, and a face still hairless and strikingly good-looking, clearly the most handsome boy in the Hostetler family.

Seth was shy and kept to himself, but his father considered him a good worker, quietly doing his chores in a methodical, businesslike, and unfailing manner. His one shortcoming was that he was extraordinarily slow to wake up in the morning. Rebekah always had a cup of instant coffee made for him when he first lumbered down the stairs; he was the only family member who needed coffee before the morning milking. As he sleepily sipped his coffee, she would regard him with a quiet comfort mingled with flashes of anxiety that he would marry too soon, enticed by some calculating Amish girl who could not resist his good looks: he had already caused a stir at the singings.

Isaac D. finally hollered from the walkway. Seth untied the gate and swung it open while Jacob stood on the muddied ground nearby to guide the cows in. They bumped and slipped into each other as they hurried into the stable, each one clumping and clopping to her assigned stall: Peggy, Esther, Minnie, Nancy, and then Josie, and so on. Each cow had its own name. An Amish dairy farm in the valley, in general, had fourteen or fifteen cows to milk, but the Hostetler farm had twenty-six head and each day averaged close to 125 gallons or a thousand pounds of raw milk that filled twelve or thirteen ten-gallon milk cans.

Sam stepped from head to head to tie each cow in its stall by looping a chain around its neck. Once the stanchioned cows were munching on hay and grain, Seth plodded from cow to cow with a handful of cut twine and tied the cows' tails to their right legs to prevent them from switching and striking the milkers in their faces. Not every cow had its tail tied, only the ones known to be strong switchers. Rebekah was switched in the face once and her cornea scratched; she had to wear a patch over her eye for three days.

While Seth was tying Bessie's tail to her leg, Jacob set a squat three-legged stool and a stainless steel pail next to her. Then he stepped across the aisle to pick up a plastic bucket of water near his father, already crouched next to a cow and milking. He positioned himself on his milking stool, pushing his straw hat up a bit. He pulled a rag from the water, wrung it out, leaned forward, reached under, and grabbed a teat to clean it. He sensed the cow's initial resistance to the wet rag. After he washed the four teats thoroughly, he gave the bucket to Emma.

The entire family gathered at dawn to help milk the cows. Isaac D. and the boys arrived first and then, after starting breakfast, Rebekah and the girls. At some point, Abraham C. appeared to milk a single cow. Daniel, the youngest child at seven, wandered about and helped however he could: carrying the bucket of water back and forth, tossing more hay in the troughs, pouring milk from the pails into milk cans. Too often, however, for the past couple of weeks, four kittens in a cardboard box sidetracked him until a shout from his father sent him scurrying to a new task. With eight family members in the stables, at eight to ten minutes per cow, the morning milking was usually finished by six forty-five.

Between his knees Jacob wedged the stainless steel pail at an angle below the udder. He reached both hands under, gripped two teats, and started to squeeze and pull to release jets of milk. With his face almost against the side of the cow, he sat on his stool and listened to the distinct pish-pish-pish sound against the bottom of the empty pail and the change in its tone as the pail filled slowly with foamy milk. His thoughts, inevitably, drifted back to the issue of baptism and the commitment to the church, to the Amish way of life, to the severe and strict existence that stretched before him like an endless field to be plowed.

Bessie fussed and jerked her hind leg, and Jacob grunted a few harsh words for her benefit. The cow next to Bessie lifted its tail. The plopping sound was soon followed by the pungent odor of the dropped dung. Jacob crinkled his nose. *Every single day. Do I have to do this the rest of my life? Milk cows, plow fields, pick corn? Work in the planing mill? Freeze in a buggy? No car. No music. No booze. No cigarettes. The straw hat and the bangs?* Back and forth, as though plowing that endless field, he kept turning these thoughts over and over as he monotonously and automatically milked cows. When he poured a pail of creamy milk through a strainer into a milk can, his dislike for farm work reached a sudden, feverish pitch.

While Esle and Seth hitched two Belgian draft horses to a flatbed wagon, Jacob helped Sam roll the milk cans to the milk house. Seth maneuvered the wagon into place next to the milk house door, and Esle tied the team to a post. The other boys turned the cows out to pasture. Then the men tramped to the farmhouse for breakfast. Before they entered the kitchen, each wiped his work shoes on a burlap bag tossed on the porch for a mat. They hung their straw hats on the wall. At the metal sink, they scrubbed hands and forearms with a bar of soap and numbingly cold mountain water. That sink was the only type of plumbing allowed in a Nebraska Amish household—cold water only, gravity-fed.

A white tablecloth covered the kitchen table. At each setting, ten-year-old Hannah had placed flatware, a plastic soup bowl, and a tall glass. In the center of the table were three bowls: one heaped with dark apple butter, one stacked with squarish mounds of yellow butter, and one filled with a mixture of white and brown sugar. A clear cut-glass dish held pickled green cucumbers.

Daniel and Hannah, eager for breakfast, plunked down first in their assigned chairs at opposite sides of the table. Standing at the wood-burning stove, Rebekah and Emma fussed with pots and pans and plates. Emma, fifteen years old and quiet by nature, worked for her mother with studied diligence. She wanted to learn as much as possible about domestic duties: cooking and canning, sewing and quilting, gardening, laundering, housecleaning.

The men seated themselves. Rebekah placed a large platter of pan-fried eggs and a bowl of deep-fried mush in the center of the table and then took her seat. Emma set down a basket of homemade bread and sat down as well.

Like other Amish, the family had a distinct seating arrangement. The father sat at the head of the table with the mother at his immediate left. To the left of the mother sat the youngest girl, next to her the next-older girl, and so on, to the eldest. To the right of the father sat the youngest boy, next to him the next-older boy, and so on, to the eldest boy, Esle, who sat at the foot of the table. The entire family bowed their heads in silence for grace, which lasted for at least a minute, until Isaac D. sat up straight with a sigh or a short cough or some audible movement. This was the signal that prayer was over, heads could be raised, and breakfast begun.

Isaac D. lifted the bowl of deep-fried mush, rectangular-shaped cakes of cornmeal the size of a deck of cards, and with his fork dropped two cakes into his bowl. He passed the bowl to his wife, who served herself one cake, and passed it on to Hannah. Next Isaac D. lifted the platter of pan-fried eggs and scooped two eggs on top of his mush. Using his spoon he mashed the mush and eggs together and lifted a yolk-dripping spoonful to his lips.

"They say it should be good weather the rest of the week," Esle said.

"That's good for planting the corn," Rebekah added.

Jacob, whose favorite meal was breakfast, carefully watched the food being passed. Impatiently, he watched Emma, who seemed to search for the one perfect fried egg before she took one. When the food finally reached him, his face opened with pleasure as he dropped four cakes of mush and three eggs into his bowl. He buttered a slice of bread.

"That last field is plowed," Esle reported, munching a mouthful of mush, "so we can plant the corn later this afternoon and finish it tomorrow."

"Gut," Isaac D. affirmed forcefully as he used a slice of bread to

sop up the yolk in his bowl.

Esle did not want to admit that he planned to spend Friday morning hunting for a wild turkey. He always managed to balance his passion for hunting with the demands of farmwork by applying himself extra hard in the fields, so he could steal a morning here or an afternoon there to hunt. The gobbler season had opened the first of May, but he had not yet found a morning free. He was determined to have the corn planted by Thursday night, so he could spend Friday morning in the woods.

"Then we'll hope for some rain next week," Rebekah said.

"I think we need to buy a few bags of oats, too," Esle suggested. "The bin's low."

Isaac D. nodded.

After the eggs and mush were finished, Rebekah and Emma both stood up. Emma carried the bowl and platter to the dry sink. Rebekah handed her husband a pot of oatmeal, while Emma placed a plastic container (a large ice-cream tub) filled with raw milk next to her father. Isaac D. spooned some oatmeal into his bowl, ladled raw milk onto it, and sprinkled it with the mixture of white and brown sugar.

"I'll take the spring wagon to the auction," Esle declared, spooning a mound of oatmeal into his bowl, "so I can buy the oats and leave early to get back for the corn."

"*Ya*, fine," his father replied. "That's fine."

"It should be pretty busy with the good weather," Esle added.

The auction, Fairville Livestock Market, was held every Wednesday downtown. It was not only an opportunity for the Amish to buy goods and farm animals but also a choice opportunity to socialize with Amish and *Englischer* alike.

"Also, *Daadi*, that dead limb on the walnut tree fell last night and broke the fence."

Isaac D., scraping his bowl with his spoon, directed, "Jacob, you go with Seth this morning and fix the fence. Just move the branch to the side of the lane for now."

Jacob and Seth nodded.

While the family waited patiently, Daniel fussed and scraped and finally finished his oatmeal. As soon as he placed his spoon in his empty bowl, the entire family bowed their heads again for silent prayer. After heads were raised, everyone knelt on the floor, rested their arms on their chair seats, and bowed their heads. In a deep voice, Isaac D. called upon God with the morning prayer:

> O Herr, allmächtiger Gott und himmlischer Vater, der Du uns Menschen nicht allein erschaffen, gemacht, und das Leben gegeben, und in diese Welt gestellet hast, das wir uns mit Kummer und Arbeit ernähren sollen, bis das wir wiederum zur Erden werden davon wir genommen sind, sondern Du hast uns auch eine Zeit gesezt unseres Lebens, auf das wir Dich fürchten und lieben, und von ganzem Herzen anhangen sollen. . . .
>
> (O Lord, Almighty God and heavenly Father, you have created us as human beings, formed us and given us life, and placed us into this world to obtain our sustenance with grief and toil until we again return to the earth, from which we were taken. You have also set for us a time for our life, so we may fear and love you, and be wholeheartedly loyal to you. . . .)

Isaac D. intoned the memorized words in chantlike fashion, repeating the entire four-minute prayer from the first pages of *Die ernsthafte Christenpflicht,* the early Swiss Anabaptist prayer book. Afterward, the family rose to finish their morning chores. Isaac D. retired to his desk in the living room to look over some bills and papers. Rebekah and Emma washed the dishes in the dry sink.

Sam marched into the stables to clean the manure gutters. Esle rummaged through the storage shed behind the farmhouse for a roll of barbwire, a jar of staples, a fence splicer, and a hammer. Jacob helped Seth load the milk cans onto the flatbed wagon, six from the evening before and seven from the morning. The evening milk cans were kept cool in two stone troughs flowing with cold spring-fed water. From the front porch, Daniel and Hannah, watching their older brothers, wished they could ride to the milk stand, but they had to get ready for school instead.

After Esle slapped the tools and the roll of barbwire on the wagon bed, he walked back to the barn to feed the calves and heifers. Seth, standing at the front of the wagon with the reins in his hands, clucked his tongue and urged the two draft horses forward: the milk cans had to be at the milk stand by 7:45, when the milk truck stopped to make its pickup. He always enjoyed the slow ten-minute drive, even on winter mornings (except when there was a strong wind), because he had a short spell to relax and admire the landscape. The dew-moistened fields fanned out before him. Already the alfalfa field was covered with a thin emerald veil of sprouts. In the side pasture, near a grove of black walnut trees, where a ragged patch of morning mist still lingered, the cows were grazing, their heads dipped into the ragged patch as if chewing the mist itself. The trees shimmered green with new leaves. Yellowthroats dipped and darted, perched in trees to trill their song. To Seth the morning air tasted of dew and green colors and high-pitched notes.

Jacob, on the other hand, preoccupied with the trip downtown and with himself, stood rigid and stared impatiently at the plowed fields. He turned his eyes to the east and to the northern end of Jacks Mountain, where the range crumbled into three smaller mounds, still shrouded in the valley mist, descending into the city of Lewistown.

When the horses pulled the wagon over the first rise, the two brothers saw the dead tree limb, lying half in the lane and tangled in the barbwire fence. Seth pulled out his pocket watch, hooked inside the front of his broadfall pants, and saw that it was seven thirty.

"We'll just move the branch now," Seth said, "and fix the fence on the way back."

Jacob nodded. He felt bitter as he looked at the tree limb, the damaged fence, the extra chore. It's always something, he thought, always something breaking or cracking or falling apart on this broken-down farm. Day in, day out, fix this, fix that.

"Whoa," Seth called, pulling back on the reins.

The brothers jumped down and tugged and pulled to free the tree limb from the fence, its branches and twigs like fingers clutching the tangled barbwire. With one final tug, they jerked it loose and dragged it to the side of the lane.

"We can cut that up and use it for firewood," Seth remarked, hopping back up on the wagon.

At the end of the lane, the brothers unloaded the milk cans onto the milk stand, a squat platform of weathered wood next to the mailbox. Because Seth wanted to fix the fence and get cleaned up to go downtown, he didn't wait to get the empties from the milk truck; he would go back later. As they repaired the damaged fence, Jacob cut his hand on one of the barbs and cursed under his breath, in English. Back at the farm, Jacob clomped into the kitchen, turned on the faucet, and thrust his hand under the running water. Rebekah, putting a moon pie into each of the two lunch pails, turned to him.

"What is it?"

"The wire slipped and cut my hand."

She took his hand in hers to examine the wound, a cut at the base of his forefinger.

"Ach," she soothed as she clucked her tongue, "it's nothing."

She led him to the kitchen table, where she sat him down, dabbed some iodine on the cut, and taped a Band-Aid over it.

"There, that's that. Goot as new," she declared in English.

"*Ya, danki, danki.*" He examined the Band-Aid.

She regarded her son with affectionate concern. "I wish I could put one on your heart."

"*Was* (what)?" He raised a troubled gaze from the Band-Aid to her sharp blue eyes.

"Over your heart," she explained, patting her own chest. "To heal your sadness."

He lowered his eyes to his hand, to the Band-Aid, and said nothing.

"What *is* it, Jacob?" she implored. "What's bothering you?"

"I'm okay."

"*Nay, nay,* you're not okay. I'm your mother. I know. I can see it in your face, in your movements, in your words."

He just shook his head slightly and touched the Band-Aid with his other forefinger.

"Do you fear baptism that much?"

Astonished at the directness of the question, he answered as directly, without hesitation, "I fear what follows baptism."

Rebekah stared at her son. For a brief moment, her heart trembled like the leaves of a tree in a sudden high wind. At least he's honest. Although she always tried to nurture each of her children with equal attention, to love them wholly, to scold them fairly, and to support them fully, Jacob was still her favorite son. But she must whirl him around and lead him back the right way, to the straight path and proper journey. She must say something decisive.

Emma and Hannah, black scarves wrapped around their heads,

giggled as they ran down the stairs into the kitchen. Daniel dashed after them.

"We're ready to go now, *Mamm*," Daniel declared, peering into a lunch pail.

"That's *my* lunch pail," Hannah asserted, pushing him to the side.

"Hannah!" Rebekah rebuked her sternly, standing up.

Hannah pouted and looked down at the floor.

Rebekah's eyes flicked back and forth from Hannah to Jacob. With extreme reluctance, she pulled herself from the kitchen table and from the conversation that had scarcely started.

"Are you going to the auction today?" she asked him, putting the box of Band-Aids and the iodine back in the top drawer of the hutch.

"*Ya*, in a little while," Jacob replied. "With Esle."

"What happened to your hand?" Daniel asked.

"I cut it on the barbwire fence."

"Is it a big cut?"

"Not big."

"Emma and I will be there as soon as we drop the children off at school," Rebekah said as she wrapped a black scarf around her head.

"How big?"

"Let's go, let's go," Rebekah urged impatiently.

Jacob studied the Band-Aid on his hand a moment longer, his mother's words swimming through his mind. Then he climbed the stairs to change his clothes and get the library book he had to return.

Every Wednesday morning buggies and cars clogged Route 655 and the narrow side streets downtown. The Fairville Livestock Market was a weekly event for the Amish and also for the local townspeople. Cars and pickup trucks parked along the sides of the streets and in a large open field, while horses with their buggies were tied to hitching posts along one side street and in one corner of the field.

The centerpiece of the auction was the livestock market itself, which started at 1:00 sharp in the livestock building and continued all afternoon, sometimes well into the night, until all the animals were sold: dairy cows and beef cattle, bulls, lambs, hogs and calves, rabbits, ducks, chickens and roosters and other farm animals. In another section of this building, men sold bales of hay and bags of grain, wheat, oats, flour, and corn. In another building, an auctioneer sold cheese and eggs, vegetables and fruit; in this same building were tight rows of stands loaded with baked goods, fruit, nuts, vegetables, knickknacks for sale: everything from moon pies to pecans, asparagus to Amish dolls and clay figurines. Old-fashioned cash registers rang and clanged.

In an open macadamized half-acre lot, tents and folding tables and huge bright table umbrellas sprawled haphazardly in odd geometrical patterns as sellers sold more vegetables, more fruit, more goods: tattered *National Geographics*, PENN STATE T-shirts, iceberg lettuce, steel-toed black work shoes, and straw hats. Small trailers sold hot dogs, french fries, pizza, sausage, soda, and what the Amish enjoy most of all: ice cream. The sometime tourists tried not to stare at the Amish, at the curious contrast of straw hats and baseball caps.

The twins went to the auction in the spring wagon, a light vehicle with a bench seat above its box. When Esle turned the rig into the field, Jacob saw the usual line of Amish buggies, white and black and yellow; the horses were tied along the edges of the area. In the first buggy sat Mahlon T. Speicher and his wife, Elizabeth, each licking a soft ice-cream cone. They waved to Esle and Jacob.

Esle stepped down and led the horse to the hitching rail. Jacob stood to the side and thought with a grim sense of the absurd that the Amish, who love to eat ice cream, couldn't have it at home because they couldn't have refrigerators; those two-bit, diesel-powered, mechanical coolers couldn't keep the ice cream hard. Just one more thing. The Amish have to wait for Wednesday, make it themselves, or drive to the IGA to buy a five-quart tub and drive it straight home to be consumed immediately by family and visitors.

"I'm leaving at eleven," Esle announced. He walked toward the livestock barn, where he would buy oats and examine the animals corralled in the back pens, waiting to be auctioned off.

Jacob moved into the milling crowd, carrying the library book in a plastic IGA grocery bag. He nodded and smiled from stand to stand, dragging his feet, glancing listlessly at the goods for sale. At one stand, however, he stopped to buy a raisin moon pie.

Rachel turned her head in a may-I-help-you manner before her shining eyes filled with recognition and pleasure.

"Jacob!" she exclaimed. "*Wie geht's?*"

He smiled clumsily in response. How pretty she looks this morning. The sun seemed to fill her face: her skin glowed, her eyes shone, her voice sparkled. Every Wednesday she worked at this baked-goods stand with the Zook family.

"Could I have a raisin one?" he asked.

"*Ya,* I think you can have that," she said with the slight catch of a giggle. She handed him the moon pie, wrapped in Saran Wrap. "But they're not as good as the ones I make at home."

"I'm sure of that," he agreed, dropping two quarters into her palm, "but I'm not in your kitchen, am I?"

"It's too busy to talk right now." She smiled broadly. "Come back later." She settled her attention on an Old Order Mennonite woman standing behind him.

Jacob turned from the stand, unwrapped the moon pie, and bit into it. He started through the crowd and made his way to the far edge of the marketplace, then crossed the road and walked around the block.

He pushed open the door to the Fairville Library, a small, one-room structure attached to the community hall. Mrs. Dwan, the librarian, was a heavy-set woman with dark-gray hair pinned in a lopsided pile on the top of her head. She sat at her desk next to the front window, peering through half-glasses at a few words penciled on the bottom of a reference card. Looking up, she let her half-glasses drop down to dangle from eyeglass holders against her full bosom. She had been a public high school English teacher in the Juniata County school system for forty years until her retirement five years ago. Then she enrolled in sufficient course work to qualify as a librarian, so she could be useful, she claimed, in her old age.

"Well, well, good morning, Jacob," Mrs. Dwan wheezed, smiling, her head slightly tilted, as though trying to balance her lopsided hair.

"Good morning, Mrs. Dwan."

He placed the library book in the box marked RETURNS.

"Did you hurt yourself?" she asked.

"*Ya,* cut my hand fixing a fence. It's nothing much."

Mrs. Dwan lifted her eyebrows and glanced at the book. "Well?"

"It didn't take tew long to read."

Mrs. Dwan chuckled. "Yes, that's true, but did you enjoy it?"

"*Ya*, somewhat," Jacob responded, slowly, watching her face for her reaction. "I liked the old man. I liked that he was so determined and so full of hope even though he didn't have any luck, as the other fishermen said. And I liked the descriptions of the boat and the fishing and the sea, though I've never seen the sea. I don't know what that must be like. All that water."

He fell silent, once again aware of how little he knew of the outside world. Mrs. Dwan nodded her head sympathetically.

"But the old man is supposed to be Jesus Christ, isn't he?"

She straightened her head. "Now why do you say that?"

"Well, I wondered a little bit when he went out to sea all alone and started having all these questions: about his luck, doubting himself, praying—searching, really—so that the sea seemed to me like a wilderness. And the old man struggled in the sea like Jesus in the wilderness. But then one thing really made me think. . . ." Jacob picked up the book, flipped through the pages, and read a passage to her:

> "*Ay*," he said aloud. There is no translation for this word and perhaps it is just a noise such as a man might make, involuntarily, feeling the nail go through his hands and into the wood.

Holding the book open in his hand, he explained, "When I read that section, the part about the nail and the hands and the wood, I naturally thought of Jesus. Then the rest of the story seemed to make *more* sense if you compared the old man to Jesus. A Christ figure, like you said once. Is that wrong?"

"Oh, *no*," Mrs. Dwan replied strongly. "Not at all. Not at all. That is a wonderful insight, Jacob, a wonderful connection, a wonderful interpretation."

With that compliment, Jacob's face opened up like the book he held in his hand. He listened intently to her short impromptu lecture on *The Old Man and the Sea*, occasionally nodding his head and muttering a *ya*. Then he would ask questions, offer his own opinion, present his interpretation. Jacob always enjoyed these discussions because he learned a great deal about what he read and about how to read. He often felt as though he were back in Nannie Byler's classroom, but this was so much better and so much more interesting. He had been an avid learner and had turned into a careful, reflective, insightful reader.

After their discussion ended, he asked, "Do yew have a recommendation for this week?"

"No, not this week. This week you choose."

Now and then she would just let Jacob wander through the shelves and choose a book at random. When she compared the motivation and intelligence of Jacob to students she had taught in the past, only a handful surpassed him. He would have been an excellent student and clearly placed on the college-bound track. Though she had utmost respect for the Amish and their ways, she often pondered the true loss of Jacob stopping his formal education at the eighth-grade level. She thought this not even in a practical sense of higher education but in a purely abstract sense of learning, since he had such a retentive, curious, and active mind; he could easily have learned any subject taught at the high-school level. Nannie Byler often talked to her about Jacob, how well he learned in school, how easily he helped younger scholars with their school work, how smart he was.

As Jacob moved up the aisle, his eyes searching through the various shelves and book titles, it was as though he were searching through the thoughts of Mrs. Dwan. How he enjoyed reading books! He knew, as she told him once, that he had read some of the best books ever written because she had introduced him, over the past five years, to American and English classics. As he considered that accomplishment, a certain humility surged through him, swiftly followed by resentment at how he had to struggle, at first, to read those books but would not have had to struggle at all had he been allowed to go on in school. But school had to end. No Amish go to high school. No Amish go to college. Who needs all that education to be a dairy farmer devoted to Christ?

The Amish had repeated that question year after year, again and again, fine upon fine, arrest after arrest of parents who refused to send their children to public high schools. That question was answered definitively in 1972 with the Supreme Court decision of *Wisconsin* v. *Yoder*, which ruled in favor of the Amish: compulsory education had to be weighed against the legitimate claims of the free exercise of religion. Secular topics considered detrimental to the Amish way of life were being taught in the public schools, but Amish wanted the entire emphasis to be vocational. As a result, Amish children did not have to attend school past the eighth grade.

Jacob moved to another shelf of books, running his eyes over the brightly colored spines. He removed one book and glanced through it. What would he have to do today? Bump back to the farm in the spring wagon, lug the bags of grain into the barn, plant the field, eat supper, milk the cows, and return to the fields to work in the last, final, pale light because Esle was determined to have all the corn planted by Thursday evening. He would be dead tired and crawl into sleep with not a moment to read. Then the next day: milk the cows, work at the planing mill, milk the cows, work in the fields. On and on and on and on. Then the first instruction class in baptism. Then baptism itself. He returned the book to the shelf.

"Have a good day, Mrs. Dwan."

She looked up from a reference card. "You're leaving?"

"*Ya.*"

"Without a book?"

"Too much fieldwork this week," he answered as he stepped through the front door.

The door banged shut. She stared at the door, surprised, expecting him to walk back in, thinking how odd that he did not take out a book. No matter what the season or the farmwork, Jacob always took out a book.

Jacob hurried around the block to the Uni-Mart, where he bought *The Sentinel*, the local newspaper, and bustled into the Original next door to buy a soda.

"He-ey, where's that KO-OOL hat this morning?" Johnnie laughed.

"It's home. In the barn."

Jacob sat in the front booth and flipped through the pages to the classified section. While he studied the ads, Johnnie eyed him curiously since he rarely saw anyone in the restaurant on a Wednesday morning. He was about to step around the counter to chat with him and see what section of the paper he was reading so closely, but the telephone rang.

"The Oh-riginal E-talian Piz-za," he sang into the receiver. Then his voice changed to an impatient tone: "*Si, si, quale è tuo problema* (yes, yes, what's your problem)?"

With the newspaper folded to the width of a column, Jacob walked outside and dropped a coin into the public telephone fastened to the brick wall between the Original and the Uni-Mart. Johnnie, who always liked to know what was going on, did not keep his mind on the conversation with his wife. Through the corner of the plateglass window, his eyes followed Jacob. Now what's he doing out there? Calling some number in the paper? But then his wife mentioned something about money, and he abruptly turned his eyes to the ceiling and started shouting into the receiver.

CHAPTER 11

At two o'clock Monday afternoon, Jimmy, Jessica's brother, was pumping gas when he saw the police cruiser slip into the parking lot next to the Exxon station. His stomach bumped his heart, and a sour taste coated his tongue. He narrowed his eyes. Jimmy had hated cops ever since he was arrested for a DUI, driving drunk when he was seventeen, and he had lost his driver's license for a year, the most miserable year of his life. When he was eighteen, he was almost arrested for growing a patch of marijuana near Jacks Mountain; the evidence was circumstantial, and they had to let him go.

As Jimmy finished pumping the gas, he watched Sergeant Stuter and Agent Tate climb out of the cruiser, cross the parking lot to the front office, and stand near a soda dispenser. He collected the money from the woman and sauntered over to them with a jaunty step.

"I guess you wanna talk about Jake Hostetler, right?"

"Something like that," Agent Tate responded dryly.

"G'dafternoon, Sarge."

Sergeant Stuter nodded.

Looking up at the sky, Jimmy commented, "Can you believe it's gonna snow? It's not that cold out, but that's what it said on the news last night. I mean, it was just Thanksgiving."

Sergeant Stuter and Agent Tate both glanced up. The sky was low with bright silver clouds.

"Just a dusting, if anything," Sergeant Stuter remarked.

"Sure, if anything."

"Do you have a moment?" Agent Tate asked.

"Do I have much choice?"

Inside, Jimmy banged open the cash register on the front counter.

Behind him were the usual sports-car posters and racks of cigarettes and chewing tobacco.

Jimmy turned to a side door and yelled into the bay, "Hey, Monkey!"

A moment later, a grease-spattered man with long arms and a wrinkled brow appeared in the doorway. "Whut?"

"Watch the pumps for a bit. The Ef-Bee-Eye is here to talk about Jake."

"Oh, okay, Jimmy, no problem," he squeaked and disappeared.

"Looks like a monkey, right?" Jimmy asked.

Sergeant Stuter and Agent Tate did not respond as Jimmy placed his dirty paws on the counter and stared at the two men for an uncomfortable moment. "To begin with—" He removed a cigarette from a box of Marlboro Reds. "I don't know nothin' about any fires, and I don't *want* to know nothin' about any fires." He lit the cigarette and with a gasp inhaled the smoke.

"Just a few questions, Mr. Smith," Agent Tate said. "That's all."

"That might be too much."

Jimmy Smith had been twenty-one years old for ten whole months and was happy that he could finally walk into a bar and order a beer without worrying that the bouncer would kick him out. Now he could slap down a ten-dollar bill in a package store and order a six-pack without worrying whether or not the clerk would accept his fake ID. Before turning twenty-one, the happiest day in his life had been his sixteenth birthday, when he strutted out of the motor vehicle department with his driver's license.

He had a great mane of thick black hair, long and shaggy, that fell in layers to his shoulders, and a pencil-thin mustache that accentuated his thick upper lip, turning his mouth into a sneer. His eyes were small, dark, and wide-set, and he had a habit of squinting and blinking: in high school someone once started calling him Blinky until he hauled off and cracked the kid in the mouth, loosening two teeth. That very weekend, he and his best buddy drove over the mountain to have a picture of the grim reaper tattooed on his left shoulder blade.

"Do you know where Jacob is?" Agent Tate asked.

"No, sir, I do not," Jimmy replied firmly, squinting, his voice dropping to the back of his throat and coming out like a threatening growl.

"Do you have any idea where he might be?"

"No, sir."

"At a friend's?"

"I have absolutely no idea."

"But you knew him pretty well. You lived next door to him, your sister dated him, and you partied with him."

Jimmy shook his head, dragged on his cigarette, and replied thoughtfully, "No one knew Jake that good. He was a tough guy to figure out."

"What do you mean by that?"

"He was quiet." Jimmy examined one of his grease-stained fingernails. "All that Amish stuff, I guess. I can't say I really *knew* Jake. We hung out together, sure, and partied some, but I never knew what was going on inside his head. About a month ago, he started to read a lot."

"To read a lot?"

"Yup," Jimmy declared, as if this were key information.

"I don't follow."

"It was weird that he started to read, cuz he used to watch TV all the time before that. And he wanted to go to the movies all the time, too. Like he couldn't get enuf of it."

"And then he started reading?"

"Yup."

"What kind of books?"

"Liberry books, some. And he used to buy books at that place on East Broad Street, the one that closed down a coupla weeks ago—"

"Downtown Books," Sergeant Stuter offered.

"Yeah, Downtown Books. He used to buy books there, but I don't know what kind, really. I know he had a Bible. I remember picking it up one day and thinking that the Amish just can't get away from all that stuff. And I remember he had another book called *Fear and Trembling,* cuz I liked the title and thought it was some kind of Stephen King book, y'know, a horror story, but it was all this religion stuff. I couldn't make head or tail of it. It was so weird."

"The book?"

"No, no, that was weird, sure, but just that Jake started *reading* after watching TV all the time since he never had one in dinosaur land."

"Dinosaur land?"

"The Amish. Y'know, like dinosaurs. Primitive. Living fossils."

Agent Tate glanced at Sergeant Stuter.

"I think he was gettin' a little weird after he started reading the Bible again, if you ask me."

"Weird in what way?"

"I don't know, just acting different. Nervous, high-strung, kinda depressed. I think he was goin' a little soft in the head."

"Now, specifically, on Saturday night, did you notice anything unusual about him?"

He hesitated. "Not really. He was pretty quiet."

"He and Jessica having any problems?"

"Did she say that?"

"I'm asking *you*."

"Nah. They have their ups and downs, like anyone."

"Were they having a fight that night?"

"Not that I saw. We, that's me an' Lil, Lillian Leach, my woman, we weren't with them all that much 'cept at the Original." He licked his upper lip and stubbed out his cigarette. "We walked around a bit at State College and had some coffee at Carrie's, that's on Atherton Street, but then me an' Lil went to Hobart's, and they couldn't get in. I don't know if they had some kind of fight on the way home or not. Couldn't tell you."

Agent Tate studied Jimmy's expression. "Okay, Mr. Smith, let's go through Saturday night from start to finish. In detail. Tell me what you did, where, with whom, everything you can remember."

"I picked up Lil about six thirty—"

"You drive a Camaro?"

"Sure, a 1990 black Camaro."

Afterward, as Sergeant Stuter maneuvered through the narrow city streets, Agent Tate, once again, talked into his tape recorder, gazing out the side window at the houses and buildings. When Sergeant Stuter pulled onto East Broad Street, a line of fast-food joints jumped into view. Agent Tate clicked off his tape recorder.

" 'Dinosaur land'?" Agent Tate raised his eyebrows. "He's hiding something."

"I should tell you about their family background."

"Their family?"

"Well, their father, really."

Agent Tate frowned slightly, as though solving a puzzle should not be made easy. "Let's finish the interview with his girlfriend first."

Sergeant Stuter nodded.

"What did he mean, though, when he said that Jacob was quiet?" Agent Tate asked. "Did he mean shy?"

"No. Nonassertive, I would think. Humble."

"Which is important to the Amish?"

"Humility and obedience are at the core of Amish life," Sergeant Stuter explained. "Pride is the ultimate form of egoism that they try to stamp out. The Amish stress the entire social fabric over the individual stitch. They encourage cooperation rather than competition and teach their children to surrender independence for the greater good of family, church, and community."

"Basically, they encourage teamwork."

"Correct. Personal goals are set aside for the greater goal of the community. Personal fulfillment for the Amish is not to be found in the individual, but in the group. No one functions alone. Alone is meaningless."

Sergeant Stuter turned into the parking lot of a Sheetz convenience store and drove to the front of the building. "That's Lil there, behind the counter."

As Agent Tate opened his door, he said, "And we have to look through Jacob's room as soon as possible."

"I can arrange that," Sergeant Stuter replied. "Tomorrow."

CHAPTER 12

Across an open field, a cloud of wild turkeys strutted with tail feathers fanned and blue heads tossed back in full-throated gobbles. Esle woke at five o'clock to a dawn buried in dark clouds. He sat up in bed, rubbed the dream of wild turkeys from his eyes, and stared across the room at his shotgun, leaning upright in the far corner. As soon as he milked the cows and had breakfast, he planned to go hunting.

During the spring season, hunters could hunt for only one turkey and only from sunrise to noon. He stood up, stretched his hands toward the ceiling, and thought about the new shotgun he planned to buy this summer for two hundred dollars. His mother had been selling quilts and had set aside a fund for each of the twins.

Jacob sat on the side of his bed, staring straight down at the hardwood floor.

"Are you feeling okay?" Esle asked, pulling on his broadfall pants.

Jacob shrugged to indicate that he was fine. Buttoning the waist buttons of his pants, Esle regarded his brother's figure with slight concern.

"You're turning into another Seth," Esle remarked, sensing that Jacob thought waking up each morning was a burden instead of a chance to start the day.

After he finished dressing, he left the room with Jacob still sitting on the side of his bed and staring at the hardwood floor. Rebekah was opening a jar of instant coffee at the kitchen table when Esle stamped down the stairs. He nodded to her, drank a glass of cold water at the sink, and slapped his straw hat on his head.

The Friday morning was gray and still and cool, the air heavy with moisture, and the far fields folded in thick tiers of morning mist. He gazed at the overcast sky, a slate-colored expanse, and hoped the sun would soon crack open the ceiling of dark clouds. Along the edge of one fence, clumps of daffodils cluttered the bank. The cows stood in a bulging line near the gate, staring at him as he crossed the barnyard. Guinea hens scurried and clucked. Ducks quacked. The rooster crowed.

As Esle lit the lantern, he hoped Jacob would not be too long waking up this morning. Sometimes he had all the grain in the troughs before Jacob even entered the barn. Today, however, while Esle was still filling the wheelbarrow with grain, Jacob appeared and started to climb the ladder to the haymow. But he slipped on the first rung and stumbled backward into a stanchion.

"You okay?"

"*Ya, ya,*" Jacob grumbled and returned to the ladder.

With solicitude Esle watched Jacob's climbing figure as his head and arms, his body and legs disappeared into the dark square hole. Although they were fraternal twins, Esle always thought of himself as an older brother, or even a father. Loose hay tumbled down.

At breakfast, after Emma handed him a bowl of mush, Esle announced his intention to go hunting that morning for a gobbler.

"*This* morning?" Isaac D. asked, his eyebrows rising.

"*Ya*, after breakfast, till noon."

"And all the corn is planted?" Isaac D. continued in a serious voice, his eyes bright behind his spectacles.

"I finished last night," Esle said quickly.

"Even for Gideon M.?"

"Gideon M.?"

"*Ya*, I promised him last week that you would help him and Solomon plant his corn this morning."

"*Was?*" Esle's face was stunned with surprise until he realized suddenly that his father was kidding around and that he had been snared by a practical joke. Rebekah had a broad smile on her face. Daniel and Hannah burst into squeals of laughter.

"I'll have to bring home a big gobbler," Esle responded, "so everyone can help pluck out *his* feathers instead of *mine!*"

The family laughed again. Even Jacob smiled. After morning prayer, the family dispersed to their various chores.

"*Mamm*, could I speak with you?" Jacob asked impulsively.

Alarmed, Rebekah studied his face, sensing danger, and nodded.

"In here," Jacob murmured, turning to the living room.

Rebekah wiped her hands slowly on a dish towel before she followed him.

Standing at the front of the flatbed wagon, Seth was pulling out his pocket watch to check the time when Jacob rushed from the farmhouse with his aluminum lunch pail, ready for a day's work at the planing mill. Clambering up next to Seth, he said, "All set."

"We have to wait for Esle this morning."

Jacob checked his own pocket watch impatiently.

When Esle galloped out the front door, wearing a bright orange vest and an orange band tied around the crown of his straw hat, he did not notice that his mother sat staring out the living room window. With his shotgun in one hand, he jumped up on the wagon.

Seth clucked his tongue, called out, "Gid-dap," and the two draft horses lumbered forward.

Esle and Jacob both had intense expressions on their faces. Esle gripped his shotgun and stared at the side of the mountain the entire time. At one point, Jacob snapped open his lunch pail and glanced furtively at the bulky brown envelope pressed alongside his sandwich and a bag of Hartley's Potato Chips. As soon as Seth pulled the horses to a stop at the milk stand, Esle jumped off and strode across the road. Jacob helped Seth unload the milk cans and peered down the road every few seconds for the blue van.

As Esle started up the side of the road, he saw Irma Keiser and her black-and-white English sheepdog bearing down on him. Wearing a gray sweatshirt and loose dungarees, Irma swung along at her usual breakneck pace in her black Reebok walking sneakers. Kirby, trotting a few yards in front of her, barked at crows flapping across the field pasture. When Kirby reached him, Esle patted the dog on the head.

"Morning, Esle," Irma called as she approached him.

"Having a long walk this morning?"

Kirby barked.

Depending on how much time she had, Irma took what she called a short walk, about a mile, or a long walk, about three miles.

"That's correct. No guests till later tonight." She stopped. Her bold blue eyes studied his shotgun. "Looks like you're taking a long walk this morning, too."

"*Ya*, the corn's all planted."

"Are you going up here or down at Reigle Creek?"

"Up here. At the pipeline."

A car roared around the bend.

"Kirby! Car!" she shouted. "Here, boy!"

Kirby stood barking at the side of the road until the car zoomed past. Irma squinted at the license plate.

"Did yew get that number?" Esle challenged, knowing that Irma had a habit of reporting the license plate numbers of speeding cars to the local police.

"You bet I did: 229 61C. Man alive! People walk along this road! It's one thing to drive fast, and it's another thing to *speed*." Then, changing the subject, she asked, "How're your mother's strawberry plants, by the way?"

"I suppose goot."

"Mine don't look too healthy," she declared. "We need another few days of good rain."

"Well, you might get that this afternoon."

Irma gazed up at the gray sky and pursed her lips, "We-ell, we might get a good gully-washer this *morning*."

"Could be."

"Hope you get a big one." Then she was off.

"I hope so tew," Esle called after her.

He walked a few more minutes, admiring the forsythia in bloom, great dazzling clumps of yellow along the edge of the pasture, until he reached the clearing for the pipeline. Here, the construction of a buried pipeline for natural gas had pulled down trees and shrubs in an even twenty-yard-wide path, as though some Amishman had driven a giant mower straight up the side of the mountain. The path rose on a gentle slope to the flat, the first ridge of the mountain, about a quarter mile from the valley floor, and then past that, more and more steeply, to the half-mile-high top.

He climbed over the barbwire fence at the edge of the road and stood in a great patch of bramble and huckleberry bushes. As he moved through the shrubbery, the thorns scratched and clawed at his pant legs as his thoughts turned to Jacob. He had been so shocked when he saw him driving that green van. How could he do something like that? What was going through his mind? Esle had faith that as soon as Jacob started his first baptismal class this Sunday, he would follow the *Addning*. At least, he hoped Jacob would just settle down. He was being too restless, taking too many risks. The cigarette smoking was annoying, and the drinking pretty bad. But to drive a car! That was much too much. He needed simple guidance. He needed to mature into the Amish way of life. He needed instruction for baptism.

As he climbed through the final reach of bramble, he saw before him a fat copperhead coiled on a flat stone. He stepped around the snake and entered the terrain, grassy and fern-laden, that stretched to the first rise before the flat. His mind drifted from Jacob to the simple wonder of forest colors. The white of rue anemones. The pale blue of hepatica. The shimmering new leaves of the oak, of the chestnut, of the beech. The dark leathery green of the mountain laurel. He knew the difference between an elm and a locust, a rhododendron and a forsythia, wild sarsaparilla and baneberry. He could identify the call of a cardinal, a yellow-throated warbler, a flycatcher. Unlike Jacob, who read anything, Esle only enjoyed reading books on the various fauna and flora of their native state.

He kept climbing the grassy slope. Just before he reached the flat, he turned to his right to enter the woods. His work shoes moved surefootedly along the uneven forest floor. Abruptly he stopped to peer uphill, searching for the cave. If he had not known the cave existed, he would not have seen it. Esle would never forget that summer afternoon when his father took him and Jacob to the cave for the first time. Their father did not say what he was going to show them, but he carried a flashlight and said it was something special.

Tree trunks obscured the entrance of the cave so it appeared as a dark shadow in a sheer cliff of ragged rock. When their father first pointed to that dark shadow, the boys bobbed their heads, squinted, and didn't know what he was pointing at. "That's the mouth of the cave," he told them. As they approached the darkness, it altered and changed, deepening into a narrow opening, the perfect size for an eight-year-old boy to enter, but a squatting stoop for a man. Legend has it, their father reported, that this was the sole entrance to a vast underground structure with over ten miles of tunnels, chambers, and streamways threaded through the mountain.

Esle heard a twig snap and turned his attention to the deeper woods; thoughts of wild turkeys supplanted his boyhood memory. Maneuvering easily through shrubbery and branches, rocks and trees, he tramped along to one of his special hunting places, a half-acre clearing along a stream. As a safety precaution, he wrapped an orange florescent band around the tree trunk to alert other hunters to his presence—not that he expected to see any other hunters on this part of the mountain, but the law was the law. He loaded his shotgun and sat down, his back against the tree trunk, his gun held loosely between his knees. From the pocket of his vest jacket, he pulled the Turkey Scratch, a small gadget for making a female turkey sound.

He sat a moment and then fingered the Turkey Scratch, which vibrated with a loud whining sound like the call of a hen, but cut it short to stop the sound. He could wait. He pulled out his pocket watch and saw that it was only eight forty-five. He had until noon, so he relaxed. The oak tree was solid and comfortable against his back. The tranquillity of the forest settled his mind and eased his spirit. Esle always enjoyed these solitary excursions to hunt because he had an opportunity to stop, to relax, to reflect. Something serene about the bright leaves and the mountain air and the quiet morning touched his face. His eyelids drooped. He had worked excessively hard this past week and deserved this brief respite. His mind filled with satisfaction as he considered the acres upon acres of fields, planted with corn and sown with oats. The alfalfa fields were already veiled with that brilliant emerald green. The field was the world, and the closer he was to the field, to the soil, and to the earth, the closer he felt to God.

In the distance the shrubbery rustled. He gripped his shotgun and raised it to a firing position. The rustling sound faded away. Probably a squirrel. How he enjoyed the feel of a shotgun in his rough hands. He was an expert marksman, unlike Jacob, who did not even like the sound of a gun. If he could hunt to earn a living, then Esle would probably have hunted; however, he managed to find much more time to hunt than most other dairy farmers in the valley. He could farm and he could hunt: what more could he want?

His blood stirred when he thought of Judith. How odd that he could have spent so much time at the Yoder farm near Judith, around Judith, with Judith, and never truly noticed her before. He had always thought of her more as a sister than as anything else. But she recently turned eighteen and over the winter matured into a handsome woman, leaving behind the last remnants of adolescence. He was not sure *how* it began, only that it *had* begun—that odd stumbling emotion of desire and passion. She was the type of woman who would make a wonderful wife, an admirable mother, a good housekeeper. Then his mind drifted in fantasy toward the fall baptism and the marriage month of November. Might it be possible to marry Judith this fall? Too soon, much too soon. His eyelids drooped again, and his head fell forward as he slipped into a light sleep.

All of a sudden his sleep snapped and he woke instantly. Hearing a *gobble-gobble*, he gripped his shotgun and repositioned himself. He fingered the Turkey Scratch. Immediately, a wild turkey answered. Then with a sudden rush, it burst through the mountain laurel down the slope and stopped in the clearing. It tilted its naked head, a faded blue-gray with intense red wattles, and listened intently. The wild turkey then spread its fan-shaped tail and strutted boldly, its long beard dangling.

Esle aimed at the dark-feathered body, just under the wing, and fired. The bird jumped in what seemed to be a final attempt at flight, wings spread in stunned stiffness, and then crumpled to the forest floor. From habit, he kept his shotgun aimed after firing while that thrill jolted his body at the moment of kill: the simple pleasure of the direct aim, the fire, the explosive crack of the shot, the thud of impact. He crossed the clearing. The wild turkey lay twisted, feathers spattered with blood, beady eyes black with emptiness. He had a clean shot; the bird died instantly. That gobbler must be a good ten pounds, he estimated, pulling at his rust-colored beard. He could already see it roasted and on the kitchen table.

The light in the forest was now dull. The trees were full of wind. Esle checked his pocket watch and saw that it was close to ten thirty. He must have fallen asleep. He looked up past the switching branches at the sky, a dark background for the bright green leaves. A gullywasher! Irma was right. As usual.

As he started to tie the bird's legs together, he heard an eerie shriek, harsh and lonely, rising with the wind. He stopped and tilted his head to listen. A screech owl? Another gobbler? Wounded? Then he heard only the wind, slipping through the leaves. He finished binding the legs and slung the heavy body over his shoulder.

Back home, Esle dropped the dead bird with a thud on the front porch. The sky was black and creaking with rain. When he trudged into the kitchen, the dark sky lurched in with him. The smell of spicy onions mingled with the smell of rain. Emma stood at the stove, stirring vegetable and beef soup in a big black pot. Rebekah was setting the table. Isaac D. sat staring at the white tablecloth, mechanically pulling at his beard.

"I killed a good ten-pounder," Esle announced, holding his shotgun.

Isaac D. turned a stricken face to him. "Jacob is gone!"

Esle stared at his father's face, at his thick spectacles, at his dark brown eyes magnified with confused sorrow. At first, he did not comprehend the meaning of his father's words until he let his eyes travel to his mother's pale face. He stood rigid, still holding his shotgun, his fingers stained with blood. He had never entertained the idea that Jacob would actually *leave*. He never thought that. Not once. So certain was he of being Amish that he never considered that the temptations and troubles racking Jacob could result in his leaving. Not his twin brother! Yet now, with the full force of his absence, he realized how obvious it had been all along and how dumb he had been not to have recognized it.

"He did not stay at work," Isaac D. explained. "Charlie said that after he dropped everyone off, he went inside the front office to have a cup of coffee. He saw Jacob come out of the mill, dressed like an *Englischer*, and climb into a car. When he asked what was going on, someone told him that Jacob just quit his job and asked for his week's wages."

"Didn't Charlie say or do anything to—"

"Jacob was gone before Charlie realized what was going on. He drove straight over here to tell me."

"Where did he go?"

"To Lewistown," Rebekah answered.

"Are you sure?"

Rebekah nodded.

"How do you know that?"

"He told me."

Esle stared disbelievingly at his mother's somber face and could not reply for a full minute. "He told you?"

She nodded again. "This morning. Before he left for work."

Esle turned his eyes to the floor, not knowing how to respond to this information.

"I knew," she began. "I knew deep inside long before he told me." She sat heavily in a chair and let her gaze drop to the empty bowl before her. "I knew he was more and more restless this past year. Impatient. Unhappy. He didn't have to speak it. I just knew. Inside. He was always sensitive. He found our way too difficult. I could tell by that long face he had after fieldwork and the weary tone in his voice. I prayed to God every day that he would find some consolation, some hope—." She broke off with a sudden painful intake of breath, eyes closed.

After a moment Esle asked, "But why didn't you say something when you knew he was leaving? To me or to *Daadi*?"

"What good would that have done?" Her voice was plaintive, accusing. "What could you have done? Stopped him from leaving?"

"At least I could have talked to him."

"If you had heard his voice, Esle, if you had heard the firmness in his voice, you would know there was nothing anyone could do."

"I could have said *something*. He is my brother."

"He is my son."

"He is gone," Isaac D. stated in a stern voice. "He is gone, and that is what we must first recognize. If he had such serious problems, he knew that he could have talked to any *one* of us. But he chose *not* to discuss them."

"But what did he say to you?" Esle asked.

"He said he did not want me to worry," she replied in a soft voice.

Esle still had not moved. As though realizing that fact for the first time, he stepped to the side, routinely checked his shotgun to make sure it was unloaded, and leaned it in the corner. He removed his straw hat and the safety hunting vest.

"Then he asked for the money," Isaac D. reported wearily, removing his thick spectacles and rubbing his eyes.

"Money?" Esle queried.

"He needed money," Rebekah replied simply. Her sharp-featured face seemed sharper as she gazed more intently at the empty bowl. "He needed money for the place in the city."

"I thought he got his final wages from work."

"He needed more money than that."

"How much more money?"

"I gave him four hundred dollars from my quilt money." Her voice was toneless.

Esle blinked his eyes a few times. An unknown sensation gripped his entire chest. His head pounded. "Including the two hundred dollars for my new shotgun?"

Rebekah nodded. "He said he'd pay it back."

Esle could not believe what had happened: not only was Jacob gone, but he took the money promised for the new shotgun. He knew it had taken a good year for his mother to set aside the money, little by little, quilt by quilt, and now in one morning all that money was gone—used to help his twin brother leave the family, leave the farm, leave the Amish. A black point of resentment marked his heart.

He turned to the metal sink and twisted the faucet. Esle splashed cold water on his face and neck and grabbed the bar of soap, vigorously washing his hands and forearms and face. With the towel in his hands, he gazed out the window at the black sky. The room grew black as the storm hit the valley with thunderous cracks. The rain fell straight, solid, unendingly, draining the sky of darkness.

Sam and Seth, holding their straw hats on their heads, darted in from the barn. In the kitchen they were grim and sullen as they washed for dinner. Emma noisily pushed the soup pot to the side of the cookstove. Dinner was tense and miserable. The family ate in silence. The wind turned and switched and howled through the fields. Rain pelted the windows. At one point, Isaac D. saw his father's ancient figure struggling against the storm. Abraham C. slogged through the muddy barnyard to his harness shop. There would be no fieldwork that afternoon. Dinner ended with an extra-long silent prayer.

Every Monday and Friday, Rebekah washed clothes. In the washhouse she walked to the kettle stove built in the far corner to look at the water in the two huge black cast-iron kettles. Staring at the pile of shirts, dresses, and pants on a folding table, she wished the rain would stop so she could hang the clothes outside to dry on the porch rather than inside the washhouse. She pulled out one of Jacob's white shirts and clutched it in her hands as her face tightened and her eyes burned. She put the shirt down and mechanically separated the clothes into various heaps of color: whites, browns, dark blues, dark purples. Emma, her eyes dim and her face faded, entered the washhouse and without saying a word helped her mother separate the clothes.

"Check the water now."

Emma peered into the kettles, as though checking soup. "The water's ready."

Rebekah nodded. Emma dipped a pot into the kettle and dumped the steaming water into the tub of the white Maytag wringer washer. Rebekah poured in a capful from the Wisk bottle and pushed in an armload of white shirts. Emma dumped in another pot of steaming water.

"May I?" Emma asked.

With a faint smile, Rebekah nodded again.

Emma enjoyed starting the small gas motor attached to the washer. She squatted, checked the fuel by unscrewing the cap then replacing it, and with a quick motion pulled the cord. The cord snapped back as the motor vibrated in a disturbingly loud hum. Emma gave a squeal of delight as the agitator started to turn and twist and swirl the hot water and clothes. As Rebekah poked and moved the clothes around a bit, Emma got another pot of hot water. For a moment, Emma had forgotten about Jacob, but as she dumped more water into the tub, that faded expression returned to her face. Both mother and daughter stood motionless, watching the sudsy water and swirling clothes.

When had he changed? Rebekah asked herself. How long ago? When he was a schoolboy and Nannie said he was skipping far ahead with his reading? When he took that job at the planing mill last summer? She did not know. And now he was gone. She knew that when a young man left the church to go into the world, he would likely never return. And she helped him leave, gave him the four hundred dollars, pulled it from the bottom drawer of the desk. Was it wrong to have given him the money? Her husband had not said so but had indicated his displeasure with the simple but stern reprimand: "Some of that money was promised to Esle."

For too long she had known how unhappy Jacob was because he questioned so much, too much, wondering, reading, thinking. He had a sharp mind. He would have been a good preacher or even a bishop if God had seen to that. If only he could have found happiness in studying the Bible. If only he could have taken more of an interest in the running of the farm. If only he could have worked with Ezra S. on the milk co-op. Nannie even said he could have been a teacher. *Anything* to interest that mind. But he chose to work at the planing mill instead. Now she saw that working there, for Jacob, was a small but sure step in leaving the farm.

After ten minutes, Emma turned on the switch to start the wringer. Rebekah, careful not to let her fingers get pinched, inserted the collar and shoulders of a shirt into the rubber-coated rollers. As the rollers pulled the shirt through, Emma guided the shirt on the other side into a tub of rinse water. Rebekah fed another shirt into the rollers.

"*Mamm*, why did Jacob leave?"

"I don't know."

"Doesn't he like us anymore?"

"Oh, that's not it, Emma. He likes us. He loves us. He's just not sure he wants to be an Amish farmer."

"But what does he want to be then?"

"Happy." Then she added, "Or at least not unhappy."

"He wasn't happy here?"

"I guess not."

"Will he be punished for leaving?"

"Only by himself."

She lifted Jacob's white shirt and gazed at its clean, empty shape.

Isaac D. stepped into the harness shop and escaped the rain that pounded the barnyard with such force that it seemed to be smothered in thick smoke. His father sat on a stool with his back to the door, bent over his work counter, reading *The Budget*, a weekly Old Order Amish and Mennonite newspaper. Isaac D. coughed and hung his straw hat on a peg. He watched the rain drip from the brim. He wiped his spectacles.

A window showed the hard rain outside and framed his father's bent figure. The building was small, low-ceilinged, crowded with stools and tables and shelves. Peterman shoes and boots lined one wall. Different types of Cooper horse nails were prominently displayed. Various bridles, blinders, reins, collars, halters, cruppers, and rings dangled from the ceiling and walls. His work table was cluttered with nails, hammers, cutters, rope, and strips of dark leather. The strong smell of leather mixed with the strong smell of rain. Isaac D. sat on a stool at the front counter. Abraham C. flipped another page of the newspaper. The rain drummed against the roof.

"Anything of interest in the paper?" Isaac D. finally asked.

Abraham C. turned slowly to face his son. His pale blue eyes smoldered behind his gold wire-rimmed spectacles. His face was tight as he asked in a forceful voice, "How could you have let Jacob leave?"

"I did not let him leave."

"Where is he then?"

Isaac D. pressed his lips together.

"Where is he then?"

"*I* did not let him leave," Isaac D. declared firmly. "*He* is the one who left."

"You are his father!" Abraham C. roared, his face flushed with sudden and surprising anger. "You are supposed to control your sons, discipline your children, guide your family in the ways of the church. He entered his name for baptism with all the dignity that request requires and then left before he even began the first class. How could he *do* something like that? How could my own grandson inflict such mockery, not only on the Amish church and the rite of baptism, but on his grandfather and his family as well? I am *deeply ashamed* of Jacob."

Isaac D. did not know how to respond to this blast of indignation. He rarely heard his father speak in anger.

"I, too, am hurt and ashamed."

Father and son gazed at each other in a heartfelt, protracted pause.

"Did you not see this coming?" Abraham C. questioned, his voice now soft, his smoldering eyes again that patient pale blue. He had struggled in the past moment to lift his earthbound anger into the realm of forgiveness. Jacob's decision ultimately fell into the hand of God and not into the hand of man.

"Nay."

"It is nothing sudden. The change does not just happen. The seeds of discontent are planted and grow and then all at once bloom. How could you not have seen that discontented plant growing? As soon as that first green shoot appeared, that weed should have been ripped from the soil."

Isaac D. felt that he was being lectured to on the sorrow of losing a child to the world, not only by his father but also by his bishop. In the rainy light, he studied his father's face. The white hair and silver beard seemed strikingly white and strikingly silver. When his father was a young man, his eyes had been a hard blue, but over the years, as he studied the Bible, contemplated the Amish, and grew to understand the world, that hardness evolved into a soft, patient, pale blue. It was as if a certain mystery had altered his outlook on the world, as if decades of faith and thought and discipline and wisdom were concentrated in his sight.

Isaac D. looked at his father's face with deep wonder as Abraham C. continued to speak about the temptation of the world and the loss of Amish children. Isaac D. dipped back into his own childhood and the love and fear that gripped him in his father's presence. He remembered the painful moments, not too many, when his father dragged him to the back shed with a hickory stick. "Spare the rod, spoil the child." He had grown to be an obedient and respectful son. But Isaac D. had *not* spared the rod on Jacob either, and look what happened. Where had he gone wrong? He reassured himself about Esle, who was an obedient son and a good Amishman. Yet how could they face their neighbors? He would never forget the forlorn expression on Josiah M.'s face when his son left the Amish two years ago.

A sudden gust of wind drove the dark rain against the building. Abraham C. stopped talking and turned to the window. The harness shop shook. The rain slapped the windowpanes and thundered on the roof.

"Quite a gully-washer, isn't it?" Abraham C. remarked.

"Ya," Isaac D. answered, gazing out the window.

Abraham C. sighed deeply, folding his arms and placing his hands under his armpits, a characteristic pose. Intently he listened to the sound of the rain.

" 'For who has known the mind of the Lord? or who has been his counselor?' " Abraham C. recited after a long moment. "We must get Jacob back."

"How?"

"We must pray," Abraham C. stated decidedly. He did not once remove his eyes from the window, from the rain.

On the threshing floor of the barn, Esle hammered the final nail into a plank of wood with one, two, three decisive strokes. He stood up and brushed the dust from his knees. The rain slammed against the tin roof of the barn, and he lifted his head, staring past the rafters at the roof. What a booming sound a hard rain made in the hayloft, like a thousand hammers hitting the roof all at once. He smiled at that image and thought Jacob would have liked such a comparison. Then his face darkened into a frown. But Jacob was gone. Gone with his two hundred dollars. The two hundred that was to buy his new Winchester 12-gauge shotgun. He set the hammer on one of the support beams in the wall and climbed into the haymow to lie down. He gazed at the rafters, covered with dusty cobwebs. The barn smelled of old hay and a summer storm.

Gone! Jacob gone. Two hundred dollars gone. Shotgun gone. Again and again he searched through the morning in his mind. Jacob sat on the side of the bed, staring down, and Esle had wondered if something was wrong. But Jacob said nothing. All I cared about was killing a gobbler. He could scarcely remember the drive up the farm lane with Seth and Jacob. Maybe if I hadn't jumped off the wagon so quick, he would have said something to me.

Esle closed his eyes and called up the image of the wild turkey being shot, but all that pleasure had disappeared when he stepped into the gloomy kitchen. His own twin brother gone! As much as he tried not to think about the money and the shotgun, he could not shake it from his mind; it stuck there against his brain like a burr. Sorrow raged against resentful anger. As he wondered what his father was going to do, another gust of wind and rain hammered against the barn.

CHAPTER 13

Lil was cleaning the counter with short, circular hand movements when Sergeant Stuter and Agent Tate came in. When she looked up, she tightened her grip on the bunched ball of paper towels. Sergeant Stuter introduced Agent Tate, who asked, "Could we have a word with you, please?"

"Hey, Mike," she called. "Can you keep an eye on thangs?"

A tall teenage boy with black greasy hair nodded his head. She led them to a closet-sized back room, where employees could eat a snack or smoke a cigarette. A small table and a few folding chairs were shoved in one corner next to a pile of cardboard boxes. The odor of cigarette smoke and cold cuts lingered in the air.

"It's a little cramped," she apologized as she sat down.

"This is perfectly fine, Ms. Leach," Agent Tate remarked.

Sergeant Stuter sat down opposite her with his yellow legal pad.

Lil looked from one to the other. She stared vacantly at the yellow pad before she lit a cigarette and flicked on a wall switch. The room hummed with the drone of an exhaust fan.

"That's not too loud, is it?"

Agent Tate shook his head.

"We have to turn it on if we smoke." She held her cigarette stiffly; the exhaust fan pulled a thin line of smoke from the burning tip like the unreeling filament from the body of a spider. Her inch-long fingernails were unpainted. Tucked and pinned under a red beret, she had a head of preposterous blond hair, like the hair color on a Barbie doll. It was unmistakably dyed, with dark roots visible at the break in her hair where bangs drooped to her thin eyebrows. She wore a short-sleeved red jacket, a red skirt, and a white blouse—the Sheetz store uniform.

Her lips were painted red, and her dark brown eyes were a mask of makeup: thick mascara, black eyeliner, smudges of blue eye shadow.

"Well," she started, in a tight voice, "Jimmy said you'd probably stop by." She smiled excessively, a broad smile that stretched her upper lip to reveal her gums and small pointed teeth.

"I hope this isn't inconvenient," Agent Tate remarked.

"Nope, good a time as any." Her smile turned into a suppressed yawn.

"Tired?"

"Nope," she replied speedily and smiled again. "Didn't get my second cup of coffee this afternoon." Her eyes looked tired, watery, and dull, as though she had just squeezed a few drops of Visine into them.

"Is that the right time?" Agent Tate asked, looking from his wristwatch to the wall clock. "Is it already three fifteen?"

Sergeant Stuter glanced at his wristwatch. "I have three ten."

"It's five minutes fast," Lil explained, "so we don't linger back here."

"You have three ten, too?"

"I wear bracelets," Lil laughed, "not watches." She shook two plain gold-colored plastic bracelets on her wrist. "But everyone knows it's five minutes fast."

Agent Tate smiled. "About Jacob Hostetler."

Lil nodded her head and seemed to wilt.

"Did you know him well?"

"Not really. Me and Jimmy partied with him on weekends sometimes. Quiet though. That's probably from being Amish—" Abruptly she stopped. "I'm not gonna get in trouble cuz I partied with an underage kid, am I?"

Agent Tate shook his head. "No. Not at all. We're interested in any information you might have about his present whereabouts and what you did this past Saturday night."

Lil nodded her head, but her eyes seemed to crouch in her face, cornered.

"Was that the last time you saw him? Saturday night?"

"For sure." Then, in a strained voice, she added, "We were at State College. We walked around and had some pie and coffee at Carrie's, that's on Atherton Street, and then me and Jimmy went to

Hobart's, that's a bar on East College Avenue, but Jake and Jessica went home cuz they couldn't get in, being underage and all."

Sergeant Stuter scratched some notes on his pad. Agent Tate listened closely to this tense recitation. "So then Jake and Jessica drove home?"

Lil nodded.

"And what time was that?"

"Nine thirty."

"How did you know that?"

"I'm sorry?"

"How did you know it was nine thirty if you don't wear a wristwatch?"

Her eyes jumped, and she dropped her cigarette. "Damn!" Her inch-long fingernails scratched at the table. "Sorry." She picked it up and crushed it out in the ashtray.

Agent Tate sat quietly.

"I'm sorry."

"You said Jake and Jessica left State College at nine thirty. Why nine thirty?"

"Well, it just must have been," she answered, concentrating, "cuz we left the Original at eight or so and it takes around forty-five minutes to get there, to State College, and we walked around for half an hour before they left."

Sergeant Stuter looked from Lil to Agent Tate, knowing that he was reading the silent language of her body: the small gesture or absence of gesture that clarifies meaning, exposes a lie, or displays corroboration. He wondered if Agent Tate had purposely asked about the time, earlier, to lead her into this confused moment.

"So it *must* have been nine thirty," Agent Tate repeated her words slowly, his eyes locked on her face.

Lil nodded, her lips pressed together.

"And he was driving his black Grand Prix?"

Lil nodded again.

"And that was the last time you saw him?"

"Yup." She was lighting another cigarette. "And I haven't seen him since."

"You have no idea where he is?"

Lil shook her head slowly side to side. "None at all."

"Do you know where he *might* be?"

Again, she shook her head slowly.

"At a friend's place?"

"I really don't know. I don't know all the people he hung out with."

"Okay. That's fine, Ms. Leach." Agent Tate paused. "Let's talk about what he was wearing that night. Can you remember that?"

"Well, he always wore that baseball cap, that white one with the KOOL logo on the front. That's cuz he always smoked Kools. And a jean jacket, a thick one. Jeans. I can't remember his shirt. Just a shirt."

As Sergeant Stuter wrote this down, she watched him.

"Did you notice anything unusual about him that night?"

She shook her head.

"Did he seem angry? Upset about anything?"

She shook her head again.

"Was anything bothering him?"

"No-o, not really. Like I said, he was always pretty quiet. He never said too much."

Agent Tate gave her a reassuring smile. "Okay, Ms. Leach, you're doing just fine. Now I'd like you tell me everything you did Saturday night, from start to finish."

She tightened her lips as her eyes dimmed.

"Do you think you can do that?"

"Well. I'll do the best I can, I guess."

"That's all we expect."

Sergeant Stuter and Agent Tate sat and listened as Lil repeated the same basic story that Jimmy and Jessica had told them earlier. However, according to her, they ordered a pepperoni and mushroom pizza at the Original instead of just pepperoni.

CHAPTER 14

Restless clouds smothered the sky. Dressed in jeans and a wrinkled plaid shirt, Jacob sat in the backseat of the taxi and stared at the swiftly passing fields and farms. His aluminum lunch pail and a crumpled IGA grocery bag, folded at the top, were beside him.

"Is that 10 Basil Street?" Karen, the driver, asked in an annoyed voice.

"*Nay*—I mean, no." He pulled a torn scrap of newspaper from his shirt pocket and read it. "It's 9 Basil Street."

"Smack downtown," she remarked, glancing at him in the rear-view mirror, at his KOOL baseball cap, at his beard.

Karen was a wrinkled old woman with wild white hair. When she turned off Route 655 onto the four-lane highway, the taxi merged into the flow of cars and trucks as if it were a boat gliding smoothly into the stronger current of a river. Ten minutes later she veered onto the exit for Lewistown.

At the end of the ramp, she paused at a stoplight. Jacob rolled down his window. He felt adrift. Unfamiliar sights and sounds pricked his eyes and ears. He stared at a frightful picture on a billboard, advertising the movie *Sleepwalkers*. Brakes shrieked, tires moaned, music cried from boom boxes. On the far corner two men clad in bright red shirts cursed each other in Spanish.

"You don't belong here," Karen declared stoutly.

Jacob turned his eyes to her. She stared at him in the rearview mirror.

"You're Amish, aren't you?"

Jacob nodded.

"And you're running away?"

Jacob nodded again.

"Why?" she demanded. "The Amish are a good people. Good Christian souls. You don't want to live in the city."

"But it's a hard life," Jacob said uneasily.

"And you think it's easy *here*?" Karen laughed, her dark eyes glowing like coals. "It's hard here, too. Probably harder."

The light changed, and Karen dipped into the slow-moving stream of traffic. Turning his eyes back to the buildings, Jacob studied the two- and three-story houses, walls pushed against each other. Parked cars and pickup trucks lined both sides of the streets. People sat on stoops with blank expressions or rushed along the narrow sidewalks with dour faces. In the dim morning light, they looked like moving shadows. The air smelled sour, dark, grim.

"We're almost there," Karen muttered, turning down an alley.

When she slammed on the brakes in front of a brown-shingled two-story structure, a sudden fear tightened Jacob's body. A gust of wind splashed the taxi. He gazed at the apartment building, his new home, and listened to the sounds of the city as his tight fear flamed into abrupt excitement.

"This is 9 Basil Street," Karen announced.

Mr. Teeter, the landlord, wheezed, snorted, grabbed the banister, and pulled his bulk up each step of the narrow stairway. He was not necessarily overweight but certainly not trim.

"I really have to give up smokin', I tell ya." Mr. Teeter coughed. His fingers were red and swollen from years of smoking. "Wrecks your health, ruins your lungs, destroys your ticker."

He wore a pair of cheap, baggy, black pants with a pink short-sleeved shirt. His black hair, slicked straight back on his sizable head, distinctly displayed the lines of the comb. His lips, thick and liver-colored, constantly twitched. His small, round eyes were a dark, indeterminate color. At the top of the stairs, he lit a cigarette. "Do you smoke?"

"*Ya*, yes," Jacob replied, "I dew."

Mr. Teeter smiled approvingly in a cloud of smoke. Holding the cigarette, he waved his plump hand in jerky movements about his head as though he were batting away mosquitoes or gnats. Then he pointed to a corner desk-chair with a black telephone that had an extremely long, twisted cord.

"That's yer phone," Mr. Teeter explained, "but everyone here shares it. The price of the phone is included in yer rent, but any long-distance is paid separately. You just mark yer calls when I pass the bill around."

Jacob looked at the telephone, scarcely believing that he would have one to use just down the hall. It was a luxury he had not even thought about. Till now, if he wanted to use a telephone, he had to walk over to Irma's house or drive to a pay phone at the IGA.

"Down here's the bathroom." Mr. Teeter guided him down the hallway toward the back of the building.

Jacob's eyes moved slowly over the toilet bowl, the sink, and the huge bathtub with a makeshift shower, as his mind drifted back to the outhouse and the galvanized tubs he had to use on the farm. When they turned to leave, Jacob closed the bathroom door, and the doorknob fell off in his hand. With a startled expression, fearful that he had already broken something, he held the doorknob before him.

"Ah-h, don't worry about that. That always happens. I'll fix it tomorrow."

Greatly relieved, Jacob handed the doorknob to Mr. Teeter, who jammed it back into the door.

"Now, you have to remember, the bathroom is shared." Mr. Teeter waved his cigarette. "There're three other tenants: Rick lives there at the end of the hall; Mark lives right next to him, that door there; and this here's Jimmy. He works downtown as an auto mechanic. They're good guys, quiet as mice. But you all have to share the bathroom, so you gotta be mindful of each other and pick up after yerself. And leave the door open when you're finished so they'll know it's free."

Jacob vaguely wondered about the other lodgers.

"And over here," Mr. Teeter said, squeezing past Jacob and plodding toward the front of the building, "is yer room."

Just before he unlocked the door to Jacob's room, Mr. Teeter puffed on his cigarette and batted at those invisible insects. When Jacob saw the dark wood-paneled room, he thought it was the size of a horse stall crammed with furniture: a double bed, a lopsided easy chair, a narrow desk and chair, a desk lamp, a bureau with an attached mirror, a standing fan, and a TV set with cable on a low table. Next to the door stood a small kitchen sink, a mirrored cabinet, a small brown refrigerator (half the size of a bale of hay), and a toaster oven. A brown-and-orange shag rug covered the floor like worn hay.

"I never had any complaints about this room," Mr. Teeter reported defensively, puffing on his cigarette. "It's a little small, I'll grant you that, but you have them there two windows overlooking the street, so you get lots of afternoon light." He stepped over to a window and looked down on the street, as though showing how to use it. "And you have fresh sheets," he added, pointing with his cigarette to a folded pile of white sheets in the center of the stripped mattress. Two flat pillows, like deflated dreams, were arranged at the head of the mattress.

"And it's $175 a month?" Jacob asked.

"Yup, $175, plus $14 for cable, plus that $100 security deposit I tole you about when you called."

Jacob set his lunch pail on the bureau, removed the envelope inside, and counted out $289. Fingering each bill like an American Ebenezer Scrooge, Mr. Teeter counted through the money three times before he stuffed the wad of cash into his pants pocket. "Now remember, no loud thumping on the floor because you're right over my living room."

Jacob closed the door, stepped over to the TV set, and pressed the power button. The screen crackled as it filled with electricity. For over two hours he sat on the edge of the bed, smoking cigarettes and leaning forward to change the channel and leaning back to watch for a few minutes before leaning forward again. He sat hypnotized by the bright colors and the talking images. He flipped to each station in turn, not believing all the different programs he could get. He had seen TV before, a program here and there while waiting for pizza at the Original, but Johnnie did not have cable. The smoke thickened.

Then the sky rumbled and the room darkened. The storm unraveled his interest in the TV, and he turned to the windows. Next to one window, wedged in the corner, was the lopsided easy chair. Sinking into the soft gray cushions, he saw that one of the back legs was propped up with two books. He wondered idly what the books were as he stared out the window at the street below. MTV flashed and shrieked.

He could not believe the strength of the storm, the dark sky falling and slamming into the street and sidewalks with such force it seemed as if steam were rising from the ground, or mist, or smoke. All was rain and confusion and wind. The rain fell in great sweeping sheets over the one-way street, parked cars, cars waiting for the traffic light at the intersection. Windshield wipers flicked back and forth.

A woman with a newspaper held over her head dashed up the sidewalk and took refuge in the doorway of a building. She glared at her wet red shoes. He noticed that the woman stood in the doorway of a fire station: Hook and Ladder Company Number 14. At the first lull in the downpour, she set the newspaper over her head again and dashed up the sidewalk. The traffic light changed, and the cars eased forward. A horn blared. Brakes screeched. Never had he seen so many cars before except at the auction. Then, as he thought about a driver's license, his eyes brightened.

The rain swirled along the street and blew against the windows. He watched the water course down the glass, then looked at the crumpled grocery bag on the rug. He picked it up and dumped his shirt and pants, straw hat and work shoes on the bed. On Thursday night Gary had taken that grocery bag, stuffed with his *englisch* clothes, over to the planing mill and set it by a particular pile of lumber out back. For a long moment, he stared at the clothes and then tentatively picked up his white shirt, shook it out, and held it before him, a clean, white, empty shape. He remembered his mother's tear-dimmed eyes, her tragic expression when he said he was leaving. Tossing the shirt down on top of the straw hat, he gathered the clothes up in a great ball, stuffed them back into the bag, and pushed it to the back of the top shelf in the corner closet.

As he slammed shut the door to the closet, his stomach growled. He opened his lunch pail on the bureau and ate the bag of Hartley's Potato Chips and the chocolate whoopie pie. Then he drank a glass of cold water. Turning on the hot-water faucet, he watched the steaming water flow into the sink: hot water all the time! Other Amish groups had hot water, he thought, but not the White Tops. No. Of course not. Just one more example of their foolish rule-bound existence.

He looked up and stared at his reflection in the mirror. When he removed the baseball cap, his bangs were plastered against his forehead. He studied the contours of his face and his thin, short beard, a tawny color like sawdust. He pulled it. How he disliked that beard! He pulled at it again, then walked downstairs to Mr. Teeter's apartment to ask for a pair of scissors and a razor.

In front of the mirror, Jacob stood staring one last time at his beard, a distinct Amish symbol; then he took a pair of scissors and clipped and clipped until it was mere stubble. He lathered his face with shaving cream, shaved off the stubble, and washed his face. Slowly he moved his eyes and his fingertips over the smoothness of his jaw and chin and cheek. He had not seen nor felt his facial skin for over two years. Peering at his image as if seeing himself for the first time, he was astonished at how dramatically not having a beard altered his face. His lips seemed more sharply defined, thicker. His entire face seemed longer, more angular. He held his bangs up off his forehead.

Downstairs, he knocked quietly on Mr. Teeter's door again. The door opened wide as Mr. Teeter, a cigarette dangling from his thick lips, appeared.

"Where can I get a haircut?" Jacob asked. "And I want to get a driver's license, tew."

"A what?"

"I want to get my hair cut." Jacob lifted the visor of his baseball cap.

"Oh, go to Homer's place. It's over past Monument Square on the left-hand side. Center Street Barbershop."

Jacob appeared puzzled.

Mr. Teeter sighed. "Do you know where Monument Square is?"

Jacob shook his head no. Inside his living room, Mr. Teeter sketched a crude map of the downtown area on a piece of scrap paper, marking the barbershop and the Lewistown Municipal Building.

"Here, take this," Mr. Teeter grunted, handing him a gray umbrella. "Just be sure to bring it back, okay?"

"*Ya*, I mean, ye-ah, I will," Jacob replied. He *had* to stop using giveaway German (not that it mattered to Mr. Teeter) if he was going to hide the fact that he was Amish or, as he repeated firmly to himself, *used to be* Amish.

Outside, the dark rain fell in vertical lines, steadily, heavily, but without the great sweeping swirls. Jacob walked slowly toward the intersection, chilled by the rain, enveloped in unreality. I am in the city, he thought, actually in the city walking on the sidewalk. And I have left the Amish. He passed a clothing store and scanned the manikins dressed in bright shirts, creased pants, and colorful dresses, realizing that he would have to buy more clothes. Reflected in other storefront windows, he caught startled glimpses of his clean-shaven face. In a drugstore window, he saw a display of Timex wristwatches and marched in to buy one. He strapped the watch on as he kept walking. Under an awning in front of Downtown Books, he admired the volumes displayed in the front window. He promised himself to go back there, but first he had to get information about applying for a driver's license and get his hair cut.

When he left the Lewistown Municipal Building, he had a manila envelope of forms and booklets under his arm. Opening the umbrella, he walked into the dark rain with a determined step, his face bright with the thought of easily having filled out the various forms, blackening in slots and circles, signing this, marking that. The imminent reality of having a driver's license in a few weeks quickened his pace. Intently, he watched each car drive past him. At Monument Square, more of a rectangle than a square, with a tall central column and cannons and statues commemorating the Civil War, Jacob turned down Center Street to search for the barbershop. In the distance he saw a glowing sign.

A clap of thunder startled him. For a moment he stared hard at the sky before stepping into the barbershop, awkwardly closing the umbrella and almost dropping the brown mailing envelope. Homer, the barber, was sweeping the floor. He gripped a broom like an ancient sword and turned to see who had come in. Holding the dripping umbrella, Jacob smiled slightly.

"Come on in," Homer said. "New around here?"

"*Ya*, ye-ah," Jacob replied, still fiddling with the umbrella.

"You can stick that over there." Homer pointed to an umbrella stand in the corner. "Still raining pretty hard?"

Jacob nodded.

"My name's Homer."

"Jacob."

"Well, sit down, Jacob, and warm up a bit. I'll be done in a second."

Jacob sat down in a chair with the mailing envelope on his lap and watched the barber step and stretch to sweep the cut hair together on the linoleum floor. He was a short, stocky man with calm eyes, dark skin, and silver hair cropped close to his head. His expression, neither content nor discontented, was curiously passive. A moment later, the door banged open as a tall man in his early twenties entered, closing and shaking a black umbrella as though it were some type of shield. He wore a pair of loose jeans and a baggy gray sweatshirt.

"Hey, Paul, through with school *already*?" Homer asked, still sweeping.

"No," he answered, "finals next week." He walked over to the umbrella stand with a well-balanced step. "I came home to study this weekend so I could avoid the parties." He folded his tall figure into one of the chairs opposite Jacob and selected a magazine from the rack on the wall.

"Grades good?"

"Pretty good."

"I bet they are!" Homer looked at Jacob and pointed the broomstick at Paul. "He's our regular scholar 'round here."

Paul smiled briefly at Jacob, turned his eyes upward to indicate that he had heard this many times before, and dropped his attention to the magazine. His eyes were chocolate-brown, weighted with curiosity. Paul had been class valedictorian at the prestigious Knox Academy in Philadelphia, had won the State Opens in Wrestling two years in a row, and had received a full scholarship to Penn State. He was just finishing his freshman year. Despite his loose, baggy clothes, he had a firm, solid body. His face was sharp, lean, and clean-shaven.

"Okay," Homer said. "You're up."

Setting the mailing envelope on a magazine table, Jacob slowly stood. With trepidation he approached the barber chair. He kept touching his chin. Homer shot a glance at Paul when he noticed some hesitation on Jacob's part. Paul, too, watched him curiously.

Jacob stopped before the barber chair and blinked. "I guess I want a regular haircut, like his." He gestured toward Paul.

"I don't know if this is a regular haircut," Paul chuckled, combing his fingers through his dark, wavy hair. "I call it Friday morning mess. I don't even think I combed it."

"Well, I'll see what I can do," promised Homer. "It depends on your hair, though. The way it grows. How thick it is. Sit down and I'll have a look."

Jacob sank uneasily into the barber chair, glancing at all the combs and brushes and scissors and electric clippers, before staring into the mirror at his KOOL baseball cap. His eyes seemed unusually large for some reason.

Homer stood behind the barber chair, watching him strangely. "Well, you might want to take that cap off unless you just want your sideburns trimmed." He laughed a good-humored but nervous laugh.

Jacob flipped off his baseball cap. Homer cut short his laugh.

"You're Amish?" Paul exclaimed, leaning forward, his eyes fixed on Jacob with intense curiosity.

"I was until this morning," Jacob admitted slowly.

"Does that mean you're not Amish anymore?" Paul asked.

Jacob briefly considered this. "Ye-ah, that means I'm not Amish anymore."

Paul now stood next to Homer, gazing at Jacob's reflection. Homer stood staring, unsure whether or not to wrap the plastic cape around him. Jacob frowned at his own reflection, embarrassed, feeling the tourist eyes, the finger-pointing curiosity, the amazed faces of people in cars.

"My hair's clean," Jacob said defensively. He had taken a bath the night before and knew the *Englischer* often unreasonably accused the Amish of not being clean enough. With contempt, he thought of Marianne in the Uni-Mart.

"Oh, no, it's not that," Homer responded. "But are you sure you want to cut your hair? I mean, since you just left. Are you sure?"

Jacob nodded vigorously. "The *decision* to leave happened months ago. The *act* of leaving happened this morning. I already shaved off my beard. I want my hair cut."

At the sound of that resolute voice, Homer flipped the plastic cape over him and snapped it tight around his neck.

"Are you a Yellow Top?" Paul asked.

Jacob realized that at his age and without his beard, he did not look like a Nebraska Amish.

"No, a White Top. Nebraska Amish."

"Are you married?" Homer asked, lifting his hair here and there, delicately, as if it were some fragile object.

"*Nay*, I mean no, I'm not married."

"But I thought the Amish only grew beards once they got married," Homer said. "Y'know, like a wedding ring being put on."

"That's down in Lancaster County. Not up here. The Black Tops and Yellow Tops grow beards once they're baptized, but we start growing beards as soon as we can."

"Why?"

"That's just how we do it."

Homer removed a comb from the sterilizing jar and picked up a spritzer. He sprayed his hair to wet it down, then combed it.

"Well, my name's Paul Virgilia," Paul introduced himself politely. "Probably the only Italian family in the neighborhood."

Jacob nodded. "My name is Jacob Hostetler."

"Jacob Hostetler," Paul repeated. "Well, welcome to Lewistown, Jacob."

Jacob smiled faintly.

Homer continued to spray and comb his hair.

"But why did you leave?" Paul asked.

Jacob hesitated. I'm talking too much to strangers, to *Englischer* who cannot possibly understand.

"Rules," Jacob stated slowly. "Too many man-made rules. And farm life is hard. And the Amish make it harder."

Homer nodded his head. "That's true. I couldn't live without electricity. Or a car. I don't know how you do it." He set down the spritzer and picked up a pair of scissors.

"Do you know Danny Yoder?" Paul asked.

Jacob had heard about him. Daniel A. Yoder left the Amish about seven months ago. He was a Black Top. "Not really. I used to see him at the auction once in a while. Why?"

"He lives here in town," Paul said. "Over near the McDonald's on Westbrook Drive. Maybe you'd like to meet him."

Homer lifted a combful of hair. "Are you absolutely sure now?"

Jacob scanned the hair held aloft and the scissors poised in the air like a line from the prophet Isaiah. "I'm sure."

Homer snipped, and a bunch of long hair fell to the floor.

"Do you know Daniel?" Jacob asked Paul as Homer clipped and combed and snipped.

"Danny-boy? Let's say I met him. He was at a few parties here in town. He's something of a celebrity, in a way, having been Amish and all that. I could probably get in touch with him if I had to. I've seen him on the Block sometimes, too."

"The Block?"

"Yeah," Paul laughed. "The Block. You'll learn. All the kids in town hang out in the parking lots and along the street downtown—it's a Lewistown tradition."

"And not a good tradition," Homer snorted, clipping the hair at the back of Jacob's head. "What with all that beer and all. It's not good, not good at all."

Paul ignored his comment. "So, do you think you'd like to meet him? He might be able to help you to adjust and all."

That did seem like a good idea. The thought of Daniel A. Yoder *had* crossed his mind, briefly, when the taxi circled and plunged into Lewistown—that somewhere in this city of shadow and concrete lived another Amishman who had left the church. He had known others who had left. The most dramatic instance was two years ago: the entire John A. Zook family, the father and mother and five children, one morning packed their belongings into a hired truck and just drove away to join a Mennonite church near Pittsburgh. At the time, he had secretly admired them but with others had grimly subscribed to the shock, the loss, the disappointment, the excommunication.

He knew the decision to leave the Amish must be resolute and must be acted upon without hesitation; otherwise, the risk of being persuaded or coerced back into the church was high. He knew the Yoder family was still trying to get Daniel to come back: all Amish families want their children back. With sudden, muddled alarm he wondered how his family would try to get *him* back. He knew he had to be firm and strong; he was fearful that he would falter and stumble and scuttle back to the family and to the farm. How did Daniel withstand such pressure?

"I *would* like to meet him," he said with sudden enthusiasm.

"I'll see what I can do."

Homer swiveled him around to study his face. He lifted a combful of bangs and then snipped and clipped as the bangs fell to the floor. Homer stepped back to eye his handiwork.

"Maybe more around the temples," Paul suggested, "and thin it out for spring."

Homer trimmed more hair. "Lower your head, please."

Jacob did. Gazing down at the cut pieces of hair on the cape, he felt himself being swiveled again. Homer turned on an electric razor and shaved his neck, the buzzing sensation prickling his skin and skimming along his spine. He felt that the electricity itself was surging through him, as though he were *becoming* electricity. The buzzing stopped.

When Jacob lifted his head to the mirror, his face registered surprise. He stared at his new haircut—the sides cropped close, shaped around his ears, short on top. But the features of his face looked so different: his forehead more prominent, his jawline longer and leaner, his dark blue eyes larger and wider, his ears jutting from the sides of his head like cup handles. He touched one ear. His ears had always been covered. And though he had never thought about it, he realized that the long hair and the bangs and the beard had worked to conceal his face, hiding it. But now his face had unfolded, as it were, or blossomed. His eyes especially dominated his face: deep, vibrant, and clear.

As Jacob turned his head from side to side, a faint smile formed on his lips. Now he looked like any *Englischer* swinging along the sidewalks of downtown Lewistown. Another significant but exterior symbol—the Amish haircut—had been removed. The interior, he thought heavily, will be much more difficult to change.

Homer smiled. "So you like it?" He took great pleasure in cutting hair and knew he had a good reputation.

Jacob turned his head again and said, "I like it."

"Good. So, that'll be four dollars."

As Homer was sweeping the hair on the floor into a pile, Paul wrote his telephone number on a piece of paper. "Now call me whenever you want. I'll be here this weekend but gone next week. I'll see if I can locate Danny. Do you have a telephone number?"

Jacob studied the number on the piece of paper. "There's a telephone at the top of the stairs, but I don't know the number. I live at 9 Basil Street. With Mr. Teeter."

"Wayne Teeter?" Homer asked.

"That's right."

"He's a regular customer of mine."

"He's the one who said I should come here."

Paul sat down in the barber chair.

"Now, Jacob," Paul urged, "do give me a call. I can show you around town. We can go to a movie or something."

"O-kay." Jacob nodded and stuffed the piece of paper into his front pocket. He pulled out an umbrella, grabbed the mailing envelope, and twisted his KOOL baseball cap back on his head.

His next destination was the Finast grocery store, which Mr. Teeter said was on Center Street past the railroad tracks. The rain kept falling. He shivered and looked down at his soaked sneakers but felt self-possessed and determined. He believed that he had crossed a line by shaving his beard and cutting his hair, that he had moved from indecision to choice, from limbo to action. He had an apartment, a haircut, and a handful of pamphlets on how to drive a car. As he sloshed through a puddle near the railroad tracks, he felt gloriously happy.

Lugging the two plastic parcel bags crammed with packaged food and toiletries, he knocked on Mr. Teeter's door to return his umbrella.

"Hey," Mr. Teeter snarled, "that's not my umbrella." Smoke from his cigarette coiled upward over his frowning face.

"It's not?"

"I loaned you a gray umbrella. This is a black one."

"I must have picked up the wrong one at the barbershop."

"All I know is that it ain't mine," he complained in a harsh voice. Jacob could smell the strong odor of alcohol on his breath.

Just then the front door banged open. A young woman with black hair, giggling and holding a newspaper over her head, stumbled into the foyer.

"Don't *push* me," Jessica shrieked.

CHAPTER 15

"Now tell me, why don't you use a computer?" Sergeant Stuter asked Ray, who was clacking one key at a time on an old Remington typewriter in the crime unit of the state police barracks. "The good state of Pennsylvania spends all this money for a state-of-the-art computer system, and you still use an ancient typewriter."

"A computer with all these little boxes to fill?" Ray complained, adjusting the platen knob to line up a box on the report. "No way!"

On the counter along one wall, Agent Tate set down a bulky black briefcase and snapped it open. Inside was a portable computer. He plugged the cord into a wall socket, typed in a command, and paused, waiting for it to boot up; then he inserted the microcassette from his tape recorder into the computer cassette holder, a floppy disk into a disk drive, and typed in more commands. He waited, glancing at the wall clock. Ray stopped typing. Sergeant Stuter watched, his gray eyes curious. Before long, Agent Tate asked for a printer.

"Back here," Sergeant Stuter directed. "I have a laser printer."

The two men stepped into his office, where Agent Tate inserted the disk into his computer and hit the print command. The printer clicked and hissed and spit out sheets of paper.

"Please don't tell me," Sergeant Stuter began.

"That's right." Agent Tate was glancing through the pages. "The latest in voice transmission."

"You mean to say that computer reads your voice on the tape and transfers it to a disk?"

"You got it."

"That's absolutely amazing! I just can't keep up with all these new advances every other week." Sergeant Stuter tossed his yellow legal pad down on his desk.

Agent Tate sat straight in a desk chair with both wing-tipped shoes flat on the floor and read through his printed notes. Meanwhile, Sergeant Stuter poured two cups of black coffee, set both cups on his blotter, sat down, and unlocked the bottom desk drawer. He selected a manila folder marked AMISH BARN FIRES 5 DEC. 1992, leaned back in his chair, and glanced through it.

"A dead end on the Imperial Chicken Plant," he reported. "Jacob quit a week ago."

Agent Tate looked up from his notes. "He quit?"

Sergeant Stuter nodded. "Happens a lot, according to this Mr. Al Plutus, the supervisor. High turnover. It's a helluva place to work but pretty easy to get a job."

"So he wasn't fired?"

"Not exactly. For the past month, he'd been coming in late, leaving early, calling in sick now and then, till Plutus warned him two weeks ago that he was on probation. So he just stopped coming in altogether. He quit, in a way, before he was fired."

Sergeant Stuter set that report down and searched through a pile of folders in his In Box, removing one marked BARN FIRES/KAUFFMAN. He studied a few pages in it, then handed it to Agent Tate. "Within a three-mile radius of the car wreck, not a suspicious person was found."

"And that includes Amish farms?" Agent Tate was glancing at the search report.

"Correct. They looked within reason," Sergeant Stuter qualified.

"They searched the land but not the buildings?"

"To search the farm buildings and the houses would require a small team to go farm to farm, explaining carefully, and asking permission of each farmer. *I* would have to do it, basically; otherwise it might upset the families. Should I make plans for that?"

Agent Tate looked thoughtfully at the report. "Not now. Not yet. At least we know he's not hurt or passed out somewhere in a field or ditch, but he has to be *somewhere*. I doubt he hitchhiked out of the valley that night. But he *could* be on one of the farms, couldn't he?"

Sergeant Stuter nodded.

"I mean, without the Amish knowing about it, he could be *hiding* in a barn or shed?"

"It's possible."

"Or," Agent Tate continued, "an Amish family or just one member of that family might be hiding him?"

"That's possible too."

"For whatever reason, even if he weren't guilty?"

"Even if he weren't guilty." Sergeant Stuter sipped his coffee. "On the whole, the Amish avoid anything to do with the law. A few years ago . . . I guess back in '87 or '88, there were two hoods, two punks from Lewistown, who were robbing the Amish. Stopping them point-blank in their buggies, at gunpoint, and taking their money. This went on for *weeks* before we found out about it because the Amish didn't want to get involved with the police. Finally, Joe Sudser, who owns a barbershop in Wilton, witnessed a holdup and called in the license plate. When I talked to the Amish about it, they said they were just praying it would stop."

"All by itself?"

"Well, they don't file lawsuits or make legal claims. It's not their way. They trust God to take care of them."

"But do you think they're holding back in this case?"

"Noo-o," Sergeant Stuter answered quickly, "my sense is they're not. They're scared."

"But they *might* be holding back information?"

"We-ell, possibly. You never know for sure. At this point they're more interested in rebuilding their barns than in arresting the arsonist. But this shook them up pretty bad."

"And if it *is* an Amish person who set the fires," Agent Tate speculated, "would they protect that person?"

"We-ell, that's hard to say, too. Yes and no. If the person *is* Amish and makes a full confession before his church and repents, then they would not want that person tried in an English court because he would have already been tried in God's court—and that's more important. The Amish *could* protect him under those circumstances. I just don't know."

Agent Tate nodded, digesting this information and sipping his coffee. "Interesting, very interesting. Now what about that ex-Amish family?"

Sergeant Stuter selected another folder from his In Box marked BARN FIRES/HOBBS. "We-ell, dead end on the John A. Zook family."

"The one that left two years ago?"

"Correct. Millie Winegardener was so shocked and upset that anyone could even *suggest* such an idea, that she was willing to drive down here herself to testify. She can verify that the family was with her the entire night."

"Now, this . . . John A. Zook," Agent Tate read, glancing at the report, "he's shunned?"

Sergeant Stuter nodded.

"And the mother."

"Correct."

"Because they left *after* baptism."

"Correct."

"But not the children."

"Because they were never baptized."

"And Jacob is not shunned because he left *before* baptism."

"Correct."

"I'm getting the hang of this Amish business. But why in the world would this Zook fellow stop in Big Valley if he were shunned?"

"To try, on the sly, to see family and friends. They're still human and miss people. But they have to be careful, more so for the people they're trying to see than for themselves. If the church found out, *those people* could get into trouble. Of course, Millie isn't Amish, so it doesn't make *too* much difference to her, though the Amish will even treat her more distantly for having taken in the shunned Zooks. Anyway, he was hauling some steel rims down to Lancaster, so he just decided to take his family along for the drive. Big Valley is halfway between Pittsburgh and Lancaster."

"And so they just stopped for the night?"

"The wrong night."

Agent Tate returned the report. "Now what about that other Amish boy who left?"

"That's Danny. Daniel A. Yoder. We're going to talk to him tomorrow."

"Good. And the status on the tire tracks?"

"Positive," Sergeant Stuter declared, tossing down a photograph in front of him. "The tire tracks found at Levi M.'s farm match the tires on the car in the field. So it seems we found the vehicle."

"Well, we found a vehicle that was *at* Levi M.'s farm." Agent Tate was studying the black-and-white picture. "But that doesn't necessarily *mean* anything. Where is the car, by the way?"

"Impounded. Out back."

Agent Tate set the photograph down, leaned back in his chair, and thoughtfully surveyed his notes. "Typical profile of an arsonist: white, middle-class, twenty to forty years old. And what do we have so far? A baseball cap, a car, a positive photo ID of tire tracks at one barn site. What's missing though?"

Sergeant Stuter pursed his lips and shrugged.

"Motive," Agent Tate declared. "Or *lack* of motive." He crossed his legs, held his cup in both hands, and explained slowly what he knew about fires. Agent Tate sorted through the six basic scenarios a fire marshal confronts at a fire site: accident, money, cover-up, pyromania, politics, or revenge. In other words, plain old carelessness, insurance scams, hiding another crime (theft, murder), the lust to start and watch fires, civil disobedience, or simple vengeance.

He eliminated the first three: the fires were not accidents, there were no insurance claims, and there was no evidence that other crimes had been committed. The problem with pyromania is that, in most cases, the person starts a blaze to watch it. With so many barns burning at once, the arsonist couldn't really do that. Pyromania would have fit for a series of fires but not for simultaneous ones. The fires *could* be some bizarre form of political or religious statement, but he did not feel comfortable with that angle. That left revenge. The barn fires *seemed* to be some type of revenge, but not against a specific person. These fires were against a *people,* the Nebraska Amish.

"And that's the rub," Agent Tate concluded. "The problem is the Amish. Who would attack the White-Top Amish? Unless you *were* Amish, or you *had been* Amish and had some type of grudge."

"Or if *not* Amish, someone who has had constant contact with them like a farm agent or the milk drivers."

"Or someone who just lives in Big Valley."

"Jessica Smith?"

Agent Tate nodded. "She was lying."

"She was nervous."

"Less nervous than most people, even if they're innocent. She was one cool cookie. But what was most obvious about each interview?"

Sergeant Stuter studied his notes. "Too clear on what they did and when?"

"Exactly. I can repeat it for you now: 'We had pizza and left, oh, at eight and drove to State College. We walked around and had coffee and pie at Carrie's—*that's on Atherton Street*—and Jimmy and Lil went to Hobart's—*that's on East College Avenue*—and we stayed there and Jacob and Jessica drove back to Lewistown.' Much too orchestrated."

"So who are they protecting?"

"Good question."

"Do you think they know where Jacob is?"

"I cannot imagine why they *wouldn't* know where he is."

"But they might *not*."

Agent Tate sipped his coffee. "For some reason, I don't know why, my gut sense is that they don't know where he is."

"So they're telling the truth."

"Partly. A half truth, a quarter, an eighth, a sixteenth. Not the whole truth but part of the truth."

"Who do you think'll crack first?"

Agent Tate uncrossed his legs, set his cup down, and replied without hesitation, "Lil."

Sergeant Stuter underlined her name in his notes.

"Now," Agent Tate added, sitting straight again, "what is this other information about Jimmy and Jessica?"

"Background information on James and Jessica Smith of Harrisville, Pennsylvania," Sergeant Stuter said in an even tone of voice, handing him another folder.

Agent Tate opened the folder and read through the first page. "Is this possible?" He rapidly flipped through the other pages. "Their *father*?"

CHAPTER 16

"I *said* to stop pushing me!" Jessica shrieked again, shaking the wet newspaper down from her head.

Lil stumbled in behind her as a gust of wind blew dark rain inside.

"Omigod, my hair!" Lil cried. "My hair will frazzle for sure!"

Then the two women turned and screamed.

"Omigod, *Wayne*," Lil exclaimed loudly, "you scared the living daylights outta me." She laughed. "How ya doin'?"

Jessica shut the door against the storm.

Mr. Teeter merely took a long drag on his cigarette.

"Can you believe this rain?" Lil griped.

Jacob stood staring at the two women, stamping their feet and shaking their hair like two frisky colts in a summer rainstorm.

"Quite a gully-washer," Jessica observed, looking from Mr. Teeter to Jacob. "And who are *you*?"

"My name's Jac—"

"He's the new tenant upstairs," Mr. Teeter interrupted, "in Bob's old room."

"Jake," Jessica intoned.

"You have that front room? That's super. I'm Lil." She smiled broadly, showing the gums of her teeth.

Jacob nodded.

"He just moved in this morning," Mr. Teeter snarled, snatching the umbrella from Jacob's hand, "and he's returning the *wrong* umbrella to me."

Jacob still stood staring at the two women. Lil, wearing a gray *PENN STATE* sweatshirt and tight blue jeans with zippers along the bottom half of each leg, had shoulder-length blonde hair that was almost white and eyelids smudged with blue eyeshadow. Jessica, the prettier of the two, had thick black hair well past her shoulders, tantalizing eyes, and a small, red-painted mouth. She wore black jeans, a pink blouse, and an oversized white jacket. And she was short, about as tall as his sister Emma, who was only five four.

Just then the door banged open again, and Jimmy, wearing black jeans and a black jean jacket, bounded into the foyer with his long black hair pulled back into a ponytail. He was carrying a brown paper bag.

"Hey-hey, is this a party or is this a party?" he blustered, looking around as he shut the door. The wind howled and whistled.

Mr. Teeter glanced at the brown paper bag with annoyance. Jacob looked curiously at Jimmy's pencil-thin mustache.

"Jimmy," Lil explained, "this here's Jake. He moved into that front room this morning."

"Oh, great! Welcome to the Basil Street Institute."

Jacob stared at Jimmy, not knowing what he meant.

"Oh, get off that," Mr. Teeter protested in a sour voice. He was holding the umbrella loosely by his side, so that it appeared as though he had a tail.

"This is the Basil Street Mental Institute." Jimmy laughed loudly and crazily.

Jacob still didn't know what he was talking about, but he smiled as though he did.

"Don't mind him," Mr. Teeter whispered, a line of smoke coiling upward from his set mouth. "Jimmy's a bit of a card." Then he continued loudly, "That's a great way to welcome someone."

"Oh, c'mon, don't try and tell me Big Bob wasn't nuts." Jimmy spoke to Mr. Teeter and then to Jacob. "He was the one living in your room."

"Big Bob had some problems," Mr. Teeter stated firmly. "But they're none of your business, and don't go spreading rumors."

"Well, it *is* my problem when he starts banging on my wall at three in the morning."

"Well, anyway," Mr. Teeter replied sharply, "he's gone."

"Thank God!" Jimmy exclaimed and turned to Jacob. "You don't bang walls at three in the morning, do you?"

"I haven't yet," Jacob replied, smiling.

Jessica giggled.

"He might have to if you keep up like this," Mr. Teeter gibed, sweeping inside his apartment and shutting the door.

"Welcome to Wayne's World," Jimmy said. "Do you wanna hava beer?"

"Excuse me?"

"A beer," Jimmy repeated, already climbing the narrow stairway with Lil following him. "C'mon up and have a beer with us."

Jessica waited at the foot of the stairway. "Why donja have a beer with us?"

"Sure," Jacob answered. "I just have to put these bags away first."

"He's right at the top of the stairs." She held his eyes for an uneasy moment. "Don't be too long." And she scampered up to the second floor.

That eye connection made Jacob feel uncomfortable but also fascinated and excited him. As he lugged the two plastic bags up the stairs, he thought how easy it was to meet people. He put the Pepsi in the refrigerator, stuffed all the toilet articles into the cabinet over the sink, and dropped two bags of Hartley's Potato Chips and a carton of Kool cigarettes on the bureau. On the desk he set the brown mailing envelope. Then he removed his KOOL baseball cap and examined his haircut in the mirror. Disbelieving, he stared at his short hair and his smooth face. *Now I'm really an Englischer,* he thought with sudden surprise and self-confidence. He washed his face, brushed his teeth, and went to Jimmy's door.

"It's open," Jimmy yelled.

Jacob opened the door and looked in.

"Come on in," Jimmy invited. "We don't bite, or at least I don't. Can't speak for those two."

"Oh, cut it out!" Jessica retorted sharply.

"I brought some potato chips." Jacob showed the bag.

"Hartley's! They're the best, buddy," Jimmy exclaimed, lounging on a sofa the dark-gold color of marigolds. He had his white-stockinged feet propped up on the edge of a coffee table. "The beer's in the fridge. Help yourself."

Jacob dropped the bag of potato chips on the coffee table. On the opposite side of the room, Lil was fiddling with a portable tape player. Jessica, sipping a can of Budweiser, sat curled at the other end of the sofa, her feet tucked up under her. Jacob snapped open a can of beer and sipped it, looking around the room. The same wood paneling. The same type of furniture. The same mirrored cabinet, sink, refrigerator, and TV. The sofa was pushed against the wall beneath two windows with a view of a brick wall. Thumbtacked between the windows was a poster of Jim Morrison. The coffee table was littered with ashtrays, matches, and magazines—*AutoWeek, Car & Mechanic, Sports Illustrated,* and *Auto Show.* Lil turned around as heavy metal music rumbled into the air.

"Jake brought some chips," Jimmy announced, stuffing a handful into his mouth.

"That's nice." Lil glided across the room, sank down next to Jimmy, picked up a can of beer, and sipped it. She rubbed his thigh. Jacob sat down in an armchair and sipped his beer. Then it occurred to him that he had never drunk a beer in the afternoon before. This is great, just to sit in a room and drink a beer in the middle of the day. Lil leaned forward and with her long fingernails picked out a cigarette. She lit it, inhaling deeply. Jacob lit a cigarette.

"Kools," Jimmy remarked, glancing upward at Jacob's KOOL baseball cap. "I shoulda guessed. How can you stand to smoke them?"

Jacob shrugged his shoulders.

"Can I try one?" Jessica asked.

"My little sister'll try anything once," Jimmy said.

"Will you cut it out? For once. Can you?"

Jacob leaned forward, extending the green-and-white pack. "Are yew really his little sister?"

"Unfortunately." She took a cigarette.

He noticed there was a single thin silver band on the pinky of her right hand and a small green-and-red tattoo above the knuckle.

"It's a rose," she sighed.

He glanced up at her tantalizing eyes.

"Everyone wonders what it is." Jessica lit the cigarette, her eyes fastened on his face, and exhaled a long stream of smoke. "It's not too bad."

"Can't stand menthol cigarettes," Jimmy teased, winking.

Jacob noticed that he sometimes blinked, squinted, winked, or rolled his eyes as he talked. Jacob also had the uneasy feeling that he knew this Jimmy, that he had seen him somewhere before or had heard about him. Just then, with narrowed eyes, as though he were having the same thought, Jimmy regarded *him.* Jacob thought he kept glancing at his hands.

"So you moved in this morning?" Lil asked.

"Ye-ah." Jacob carefully pronounced a yeah instead of a *ya.*

"How do you like Wayne?"

"He's okay."

"He's a freaking slumlord," Jimmy declared.

"Oh, come on," Lil objected.

"This place is a hell hole, let me tell you. Remember Big Bob we were talkin' about? Well, Big Bob was five feet tall—I swear, no bigger than that—skinny as a rail and as strong as a bull. It was amazing how strong a little guy like that could be. He was in a fight every weekend at Kelly's. Always gettin' arrested: disturbin' the peace, disorderly conduct, assault, public urination—you name it. And for two weeks, he was yellin' in his room and poundin' on the walls. He was goin' nuts, and he lived here at good ol' Basil Street."

"He wasn't that bad," Lil said, "except for the last coupla weeks."

"And those last coupla weeks was bad enuf."

"Well, he's gone now."

"And good riddance. I think he *was* taken to some mental hospital. Mark was the one who filed a complaint."

"Mark?"

"Mark. Lives next door. Good ol' Wayne didn't do a thing. Good ol' Wayne can't fix a thing. Did the doorknob to the bathroom fall off when he showed you around?"

Jacob nodded.

"And when it fell off, did he say he'd have it fixed 'tomorrow'?"

Jacob nodded again.

"Uh-huh. Told me the exact same thing. *And* Mark *and* Rick. As soon as I save up a little money, I'm outa here. Howdja find this place, anyhow?"

"The *Sentinel.*" Jacob took a drag on his cigarette. "How long have yew been here?"

"Since the end of March. Almost two months. Two months too long." Then Jimmy burped.

"You are so gross," Lil pretended to complain, punching him lightly in the arm.

"Get me another beer, willya?"

Lil stood up. "Anyone else? Jake?"

"I'm all set."

"Jessica?"

"Not yet."

"So where are ya working?" Jimmy asked as Lil handed him another Budweiser.

Jacob hesitated. All three had their eyes on him. He felt sudden discomfort since he hadn't yet planned what he would tell people.

"Well, actually, I'm looking fur a job."

"No shit," Jimmy said. "Do ya know anything about cars?"

"Not really."

" 'Cause I work at the Exxon station downtown, and they're looking for another mechanic. I'm a car mechanic."

"Really?"

"Yup, been workin' there now for a year."

"My own little grease monkey," Lil complimented while punching him again in the arm.

"Are ya lookin' for any special kinda work?"

"Anything, really."

"Well, you can get a job up at the chicken plant in Plainsville. They're always lookin' for people. Mark works there."

"Who?"

"Mark. The guy who lives next door to me. Ya haven't met anyone, have ya?"

Jacob shook his head.

"Well, there're four of us up here. You, me, Mark next door, and Rick Munson, who lives at the *very* end of the hall. Rick works at the McDonald's, over the tracks. But you should talk to Mark. He could probably help you out."

"I will," Jacob agreed, stubbing out his cigarette in an ashtray.

"So what are we gonna do tonight?" Jessica wondered.

"It's Friday," Jimmy reminded her. "Get shit-faced."

"No-o, let's *do* something." Lil's voice was whiny.

"Well, whaddaya wanna do?"

"I wanna see that *Basic Instinct,*" Lil declared.

"Oh, for sure," Jessica responded. "I hear Michael Douglas really goes to town in it. They had to edit scenes out to avoid an X rating."

"No shit," Jimmy grunted. "Sounds good to me."

"Do you want to go to the movies, Jake?" Jessica was smiling.

"Ye-ah," Jacob replied, thinking excitedly that he had never *been* to a movie before.

"What time does it start?" Lil wondered.

"Where's that paper I had?" Jessica looked around the room.

"Over there, on the floor."

Jessica flipped through the wet pages. "Seven fifteen."

"What about supper?" Lil asked.

"Pizza?" Jessica suggested.

"Yeah, pizza at the Original, and then a movie," Jimmy proposed. "But I have to shower and change first."

"You better," Lil laughed. "And while you do that, me and Jessica have to go for a little drive."

"Oh, yeah, for sure," Jimmy said. "Just be careful with reverse, okay?"

"I'm always careful with reverse." Lil uncurled from the sofa as he handed her his car keys. "We'll be back in a half hour or so."

Jessica sprang up, pulling on her oversized white jacket.

Jacob stood up. "I'll be back later then."

"Right-o, Jake-o," Jimmy chanted, finishing his beer. "And have a beer for the road."

"Thanks."

He followed Jessica and Lil and watched them descend the stairway. He kept his eyes fastened on Jessica's bewitching figure.

"See you in an hour," Jessica called back with giggles.

In his room Jacob sat down by his front window. The rain had dwindled to a light mist. He snapped open his for-the-road beer, took a swig, and contemplated Jessica as a surge of contradictory thoughts and emotions battled in his mind. He was sure she liked him, just by the way she kept looking at him. But what did all that *mean*? What should he do? And how much should he tell them? He couldn't keep the Amish secret for long. Eventually, it would have to come out. He heard Jimmy slam shut the door to his room and, a moment later, the swooshing sound of water from the bathroom. He decided to take a shower, too. He sat on the edge of his unmade bed, watched MTV, and thought ecstatically about going to a movie.

After fifteen minutes, he opened his door, listening for sounds in the bathroom. When he heard none and saw the bathroom door open, he pulled a towel from the towel rack on the back of his door and walked down the narrow hallway with soap and a bottle of shampoo. The bathroom was steamed and the mirror fogged up. He closed the door, fastened the latch, and looked around with an intoxicated expression on his face. No more outhouses. No more boiled water. No more galvanized tubs. He could shower like this any time he wanted.

He studied the makeshift arrangement: a shower head rigged above one end of the bathtub, fed by a hose from below, and a curtain encircling the tub and tucked inside. Jacob remembered the one time he used a shower. He had helped with a barn raising in Somerstown and stayed overnight at an Amish house with indoor plumbing. As he showered, luxuriating in the flow of hot water, he wondered, Why is it so worldly to have a shower? The Yellow Tops and Black Tops both have indoor plumbing. Why can't the White Tops?

Back in his room, Jacob dressed in the clothes he wore before his shower. He sat watching TV and smoking cigarettes until he heard the chatter of Jessica and Lil as they climbed the stairs. Jacob waited a moment.

"Come on in," Jimmy roared.

When Jacob stepped into the room, he saw only Jimmy, dressed in black jeans and a red plaid shirt, his black hair damp and loose about his face, slouched on the couch. He was picking at the toenail on one big toe. There was an open can of beer on the coffee table. Then he heard a giggle as Jessica and Lil slinked into the room through a dark doorway.

"Hi," Jessica purred.

Jacob smiled.

"I just can't keep them outa the bedroom," Jimmy joked, pulling on a pair of white socks.

"Will you shut up?" Lil spit out sarcastically as she sashayed to the refrigerator to remove a beer. "D'ya want one?"

"Sure." Jacob snapped it open before sitting down in an armchair.

"You, Jessica?"

Jessica shook her head. "Later. I'm all set."

"You're all set?" Jimmy needled her in disbelief. "Is this *my* little sister? Donja know it's Friday night?"

Jessica regarded him with an even stare and sat down on the sofa, folding her legs up under her.

"Didja roll one?" Jimmy asked.

Lil nodded and curled up next to him.

Jimmy spoke to no one in particular, "Dja wanna burn one before we go out?"

A slight frown creased Jacob's forehead.

"I do," Lil agreed, removing a joint from behind her ear.

"You smoke pot, donja, Jake?" Jimmy invited, eyes squinting and winking, as he leaned forward to pull out a cone of incense from a small box on the coffee table. He lit it and placed the smoking cone in a small clay dish. The sweet-smelling smoke rose in a straight line toward the ceiling. "Can't have Wayne too suspicious, now, can we?"

Noncommittally, Jacob nodded. He had never smoked pot before. Lil placed the joint between her lips and lit it, sucking the smoke greedily. Before he had a chance to think what to do, she handed it to him. He noticed how intently Jimmy watched him, studying his thick fingers as he took the joint. He knew, having heard Ken's tales about pot, that he had to hold the smoke in his lungs for as long as possible. The smoke tasted sharp, sweet, thick. When he reached over to pass the joint to Jessica, he saw the tip of her tongue wet her lower lip. After he finally let the smoke out, he coughed and coughed and coughed.

"Strong stuff, huh?" Jimmy said.

Jacob nodded, feeling the strain on his throat and the rawness in his lungs. With amazement, he watched Jessica let out her smoke without coughing. Noisily, Jimmy inhaled a mouthful. The next time Jacob did not inhale as much and did not cough. He felt a slight dizziness, nothing much, but he was not sure exactly what he was *supposed* to feel. He just enjoyed sitting in the room, smoking cigarettes, drinking beer, trying pot, and knowing that he was going to a movie for the first time in his life. Recklessness blurred his eyes. He thought about what his family would be doing at this exact moment: they would be in the barn milking. I would be pulling on a cow's teat right now. He chuckled. Then he laughed.

"Good stuff, huh?" Jimmy was smiling a toothy smile.

Jessica watched Jacob closely, her eyes moist, her expression amused. Lil passed him the joint, pinched between her long nails.

He stared at those nails. Again he inhaled. The smoke seemed to go straight to his head, prickling the inside of his face, his eyes, and his lips. Those long nails were just like the claws on a panther. When he passed the joint to Jessica, he stared straight into her eyes and thought they looked like the eyes of a wolf—a she-wolf. Then he turned to Jimmy with his shaggy mane of hair and thought he looked like a lion. I'm sitting in a room with a panther, a lion, and a she-wolf. Again he burst out laughing. Jessica, for no apparent reason, laughed, too. Then everyone roared with laughter.

"Oh, god, god, god!" Lil exclaimed, holding her sides. "Ohmigod."

"Where," Jimmy laughed, "did you get this stuff?"

Jacob could not stop laughing. Laughter convulsed him. I must be stoned, he thought giddily, I must be stoned (he knew the expression from Ken). And then a sudden chill settled over him and smothered his laughter as a vision crossed his mind, the vague recollection of a dark dream, of three leaping panthers, of a blocked path.

"Ohmigod!" Lil cried. "We *have* . . . we have to get going or . . . we'll be great, I mean, *late*!" She burst out laughing again.

The four walked to the Original Italian Pizza on West Broad Street in downtown Lewistown. The rain had stopped. The early evening air had a dark, clean, cool scent. The sky, still thick with roiling clouds, glowed with an eerie metallic light. Storefront windows were bright with electricity and neon signs. Cars searched the streets. Horns honked. Voices cried. The city whirled with movement, burst with sound, crackled with energy. And Jacob whirled and burst and crackled along with it. He lifted the visor of his KOOL baseball cap, adjusting it farther back on his forehead, to gaze at the buildings and the people, so many people. His eyes glittered, floated, swirled from sight to sight. He felt alive in an unknown world.

At one corner, where a sullen group of adolescents stood smoking cigarettes and hugging skateboards, he realized that Jimmy and Lil had walked slightly ahead of him and Jessica. He liked that she was at his side and was highly conscious of her being there, that bewitching figure with those tantalizing eyes. Jacob noticed that other men glanced at her and vaguely wondered if he were on a "date." Was this how it happened in the *englisch* world? Is this how the *Englischer* conduct themselves? But, no, that couldn't be since he had not asked her. But she had asked him, hadn't she? No, no, he had only joined them. He had been asked because he happened to be giving Mr. Teeter the umbrella when they ran in from the rain.

In the Original they marched straight to the back and sat down in the last booth. Jacob looked around and thought it looked just the same as the one in Fairville: the same booths, the same menu, the same prices. Lil sat down first, sliding over next to the wall, and Jimmy sat down next to her. Jessica also sat next to the wall, and Jacob sat down next to her.

As soon as Lil lit a cigarette, a thin, ragged waitress with thin, ragged hair appeared, clutching four menus and four napkins, rolled up around a knife and fork. "Hey, Jimmy."

"Hiya, Libby, how's it goin'?"

"Same ol' stuff," she complained, dropping the menus and the napkin-rolled silverware on the table.

"Can I get you'ns anything to drink?"

"A pitcher of beer," Jimmy ordered. "Bud."

Her eyes traveled briefly over Jessica and Jacob. "You of age?"

" 'Course they are," Jimmy declared forcefully. "Waddaya think?"

Libby disappeared without a word.

"Jake, how old are ya?"

"Nineteen," Jacob whispered, somewhat nervously, watching the waitress hand menus to a couple in another booth.

Jimmy rolled his eyes, blinked, winked, and groaned, "Oh, great! I'm out with two minors tonight."

After they finished their pizza and beer, they joined a long movie line winding around the block. This is just like the cows, Jacob thought, chuckling, lining up in the feeding pen to be milked.

Lil remarked in a petulant voice, "I said we should have left earlier or we should have bought the tickets first, before the pizza. Now we won't get in."

"We'll get in," Jimmy reassured her, lighting a cigarette. "They all can't be going to see *Basic Instinct*."

Lil tapped the shoulder of a tall man standing in front of her. "Excuse me, but which movie are you going to see?"

"*Basic Instinct*," he answered.

"You seeee," Lil whined.

"She's worried we might not get in," Jimmy explained, in an apologetic but annoyed voice.

"Oh," the tall man replied dryly, turning back to chat with his girlfriend.

"Why do you *do* things like that?" Jimmy whispered harshly. "Asking stupid questions of strangers."

"It's not stupid. What's the big deal if I ask someone what movie they're going to see?"

"I don't like it," he grumbled angrily, eyes squinting.

Lil fell silent and turned to face the line. The odd lightheadedness that Jacob felt earlier had vanished, replaced by a beery bloatedness. He could still not believe that he actually sat in a public place drinking beer, that he smoked pot, that he was going to see a movie. In an odd way, going to see a movie was more momentous than having smoked pot. Ever since he was a boy, he had heard about movies—the large screens, the thunderous sound, the hundreds of seats, the bright clear colors—but movies were verboten. Not now though, he reflected, not now that I'm an *Englischer*. So this is what the real world is all about!

As the line inched forward, the lights on the marquee were bright and vivid, as if advertising electricity itself. Jacob's excitement increased. A smell of buttered popcorn and cigarette smoke floated in the darkening twilight. Cars and pickup trucks continued to drive by. Adolescent boys, in baggy pants, skateboarded along the sidewalks. People shouted back and forth. To Jacob, the *englisch* world was vibrant and alive and energetic. Jacob gazed at Jessica, at her long dark hair, and smiled at her. She smiled back.

"Oohh, I hope they're not sold out," Lil whined again, looking at her wristwatch.

Jimmy grunted and puffed on his cigarette.

"We'll get in, Lil," Jessica soothed.

As soon as they passed through the thick glass doors into the lobby, Jacob's excitement passed into a new phase—that of accepted reality. He kept rubbing his hands together, putting them into the pockets of his jean jacket, and pulling them out. Jessica watched him with a puzzled frown. Then Lil started rubbing *her* hands together and muttering, "I bet they're sold out. I just bet they are."

The lobby was plastered with movie posters, glittering with harsh light, and swirling with people of all shapes, sizes, and ages. Thick purple ropes guided them. Huge glass cases were crammed with candy, popcorn, and pop. Two teenaged boys were directing people into various hallways, and Jacob noticed that they were dressed in identical black pants, white shirts, and tiny black bow ties.

"Why don't we watch *Sleepwalkers* instead?" Jimmy suggested, pointing at a poster.

Lil turned a stern face toward him. Jacob looked at the poster and saw the same frightful picture he had seen on the billboard when Karen, the taxicab driver, stopped at the end of the ramp.

"Just kidding," Jimmy placated her.

The man behind the counter was stolid and immobile, with a blank and reptilian face. He sat on the stool as if he had been sitting there since puberty. "Yes?"

"Four for *Basic Instinct,*" Jimmy ordered loudly, handing the man a twenty-dollar bill.

"Eighteen dollars," the man said mechanically, pressing a black button that spat out four blue tickets from a metal plate in the counter. He handed the tickets and two dollars to Jimmy. Before Jacob realized that Jimmy had bought him a ticket, he was handing him one.

"How much?" Jacob asked, taking the ticket.

"My treat. Welcome to Basil Street."

"Ooonoo." Jacob pulled out a wad of bills. "Let me settle up."

Jimmy brushed aside his offer of money and handed Jessica her ticket.

"Hey, thanks."

"Hey, thank *you* for the smoky," Jimmy returned, since she and Lil had bought the pot.

Lil was standing in front of a glass counter, examining the shelves of candy.

Jessica stepped next to her. "Do they have any of those Sour Patch Kids?"

"Right there." Lil was tapping the glass with the tip of one long fingernail.

Jimmy strutted over to the popcorn counter while Jacob was stuffing his money back into his front pocket, staring at his ticket. He stumbled into one of the rope posts.

"Hey, Jake," Jessica called, "do you want any candy?"

Jacob looked at her for a baffled moment. "A Snickers bar, maybe."

He was pulling out his money again as Jessica handed the girl behind the counter a five-dollar bill and told him, "Don't worry about it."

Upset, Jacob insisted, "Nooo, please," and thrust a ten-dollar bill at her.

"Don't worry about it." Jessica gathered up the candy. "Just buy me a Coke, and we'll be even steven."

"Okay," Jacob agreed, "that'll settle us up." He looked around for a pop machine, patting his pants pocket to make sure he had change. Then he saw Jimmy with a tall cup of pop and a large tub of popcorn. He stepped over to that counter, stuffing the ticket in his pants pocket.

"Can I help you?"

The thin-faced boy in front of him wore a white shirt and a tiny black bow tie. Jacob thought it so odd that the staff was dressed the same, like the Amish dressing according to their rules, and turned to look at the girls behind the candy counter. They, too, were wearing white shirts and tiny black bow ties.

"Can I *help* you?" the thin-faced boy repeated.

"Do yew all wear the same clothes?"

"Excuse me?"

"Do yew all wear bow ties?"

The boy frowned. "Yeah. We have to."

"Why?"

"Why? I don't know why. We just have to. What can I get you?"

"A Coke. Two Cokes."

"What size?"

"Two Cokes."

"Large, medium, or small?" the thin-faced boy said slowly.

Jacob handed him the ten-dollar bill.

"What *size* do you want?" The boy pointed a thin finger at the wall, where various cups and popcorn tubs were mounted.

Jacob studied the display and decided, "Large."

"Thanks," Jessica chortled as he handed her the Coke.

"C'mon, c'mon," Lil cried, "we'll never find good seats with all these people, and we'll miss the previews. I adore previews, so I know what to see next."

"You see every movie anyway," Jimmy snorted.

"Doesn't matter. I still like to watch em."

Jacob didn't know what a preview was, but he didn't want to miss that either. They followed another set of purple ropes and were confronted by yet another teenager, wearing yet another tiny black bow tie. All of a sudden the outfit amused Jacob. Amish clothes identify the Amish as Amish. It's a tradition, religious symbolism, a sign of obedience to God and rejection of the proud and sinful world. But what could that tiny black bow tie mean? His mind drifted to his mother and others in his family and to their living room, where he knew they were now gathered, discussing him in low, serious voices.

"Ticket."

Jacob blinked and shook his head.

"Ticket, please."

Jacob looked at the boy and then past him to Jessica, Jimmy, and Lil, waiting in front of the center doorway.

"He bought my ticket." Jacob nodded toward Jimmy.

The boy turned to Jimmy. "Do you have his ticket?"

"Nah, he has it. Where's your ticket, Jake-o? I gave it to you."

"Oooo." Jacob remembered, transferred the Coke to his left hand, and pulled the ticket out of his pants pocket. The boy tore it in half and handed back half of it.

"Don't lose it. Next?"

Jacob stared at the torn ticket stub.

"Come *on,* Jake," Lil cried.

Jacob stumbled past the boy, stuffing the torn ticket stub into his pants pocket, and followed them down the corridor. At the end of it stood three sets of double doors with signs over each: CAN'T JUMP, WAYNE'S WORLD, INSTINCT.

"Here we go." Lil walked through the only open set of doors on the left.

In the doorway, Jacob stopped and stared in astonishment at the huge white movie screen, the size of the side of a barn. He let his wonder-struck eyes rise to the ceiling, higher than the top of any hayloft he had ever seen. He gazed at the rows and rows of seats and the heads and heads of people. There must be hundreds of people here, he calculated. And this is only one room! There were other rooms with other movies and other people.

"I told ya we wouldn't get good seats," Lil grumbled.

"Will you shut up!"

Jimmy strutted down the center aisle and stood at the end of a row near the front, where a middle-aged couple sat, and requested, "Could we get by?" The couple stood up, and Jimmy and the others edged their way past.

"Do you want your Snickers now?" Jessica asked as she sat down.

Jacob was counting the seats in his row—fourteen seats from the aisle.

"Jake?"

"Huh?"

"Do you want your Snickers now?" she repeated.

"My what?"

"Your *Snickers* bar."

"*Ya, ya,* okay," he replied, forgetting himself, sinking down.

With a puzzled expression, she handed him the candy bar. Jimmy overheard him and looked him up and down anew. Oblivious to their searching glances, Jacob twisted around in his seat to gaze at the crowd and count the rows. If there are fourteen seats here and twenty-two rows in this section, then that's 308 seats in this section alone. Now that's something!

The lights dimmed. Darkness and quiet settled on the crowd. One or two voices shrieked with laughter. Jessica sipped her Coke and slouched down. The sound system crackled as a block of bright blue light appeared on the screen. Jacob sat back and stared at the words, each letter the size of a broom handle: THIS PREVIEW HAS BEEN APPROVED FOR ALL VIEWING AUDIENCES. I'm actually sitting in a movie theater and watching a movie, he thought, smiling, a sense of adventure and rebellion prickling his skin.

The sound seemed to blast from everywhere as the screen suddenly exploded with color and images. Everything was so big! Faces alone were the size of buggies! Giants marched across the screen. With his head tilted far back, he sat hypnotized, fully immersed in the flashing colors and jumping images. From time to time, sipping her pop, Jessica cast a petulant glance at him. She slouched down more in her seat. Lil tossed a handful of popcorn into her mouth.

"Could I have some?" Jessica asked quietly.

Lil handed the tub of popcorn to her.

"Jake doesn't even know I'm here," Jessica whispered, remembering her earlier comment to Lil about how cute he was.

Lil leaned forward to look over at him. "He knows you're here. He's just a real movie buff, I guess."

When the movie ended, Jimmy stood abruptly to leave. Others stood to leave as well, in a great rising motion of figures and voices.

"So," Lil began, "do you think she's the murderer?"

"Who?" Jessica seemed puzzled as she stood up.

"Katherine."

"The doc was the murderer," Jimmy declared, stretching his back.

"Then why did they show that ice pick at the end?" Lil asked.

"Just to throw you off."

"To throw you *off*?"

"For sure. Just a tease," Jimmy said. "Whadaya think, Jake?"

Jacob sat watching the credits, listening to the music.

"Hey, Jake-o," Jimmy called. "Buddy? Who daya think was the killer?"

"That was *something*," Jacob announced, turning to them.

"For sure. But whodaya think killed everyone?"

"Katherine," Jacob answered.

"You see?" Lil relished her triumph.

When Jacob stood up, he was still holding a full cup of Coke and the Snickers bar. Startled, Jessica, Jimmy, and Lil stared at the Coke.

"Wow!" Lil exclaimed, laughing lightly. "You really *do* get into movies, donja?"

Apologetically, Jacob smiled. "Anyone want a sip?"

All four laughed. Jacob put the Snickers bar in the side pocket of his jean jacket. As they filed out of the theater, he gulped down the watery Coke and tossed the cup into a trash can near the exit.

The night was crisp, cool, dark. The crowd leaving the theater jostled and pushed. They turned toward the center of town. Jacob walked slowly, absorbed by the movie images that surged through his mind.

At the corner of West Broad Street and River Avenue, cars, jeeps, and pickup trucks flowed along, honking, beeping. The sidewalks were crowded with clumps of teenagers. One pickup truck, raised high off the ground on huge wheels, slammed on its brakes at the stoplight and then thundered around the corner with a blast of bass-thumping rap.

"Do you know about the Block?" Jimmy asked, lighting a cigarette. "The major hangout for kids on weekends?"

Peering down the street at a tunnel of parked cars and smoking teenagers, Jacob replied, "No."

"Let's give Jake a tour of the Block, shall we?" Jimmy suggested.

"Anyone's who's anyone goes to the Block," Lil remarked.

They had not gone too far when they saw a big, black, old Monte Carlo parked on the side of the street. The back window was steamed.

"Looks like *they're* having fun." Jimmy put his arm around Lil's shoulder.

"That looks like Paddy's car," Jessica said. "I went to high school with him."

As they approached the car, a sweet voice cried out, "Don't! No! You're tickling me. I'll get out, I swear I will." Just then the door to the driver's side flung open as a young woman, adjusting her giggles and her blouse, spilled out onto the sidewalk. She slammed the door shut and screamed, "No more tickling!"

She turned, startled, and her tone of voice showed embarrassment: "Oh, hi, Jessica, what's up?"

"Hi, Frances," Jessica replied dryly.

The car window rolled down, and a young man, his hair tousled, thrust his head out and pleaded, "I won't tickle anymore, I promise. Who're you talking to?"

"To Jessica Smith, at the moment." Frances pronounced each syllable distinctly.

"Oh, hey, Jessica." His head disappeared.

"Hi, Paddy."

Frances stepped to the rear of the car, lit a cigarette, and told Jessica, "I know what you're thinking, and it's true."

Jacob studied her delicate face in the faint white glow from the streetlight. Her blond hair, cut short and curled, appeared almost golden.

She tossed her head, gazing at the others while continuing to talk directly to Jessica in a mellifluous voice. "I can see your thoughts rolling around like mad, Jessica, I can see it. 'How could she do this to John?' "

Then she turned abruptly to Jacob, as though pleading a case. "You don't know me, and I don't know you, so let me ask you one question: Is it wrong to fall in love?"

Jacob turned his face to Jessica with an expression of needing help, but Jessica merely raised her eyebrows. Slowly and precisely he replied, "I dew not think it is wrong to fall in love."

"D'ya see, Jessica?" Frances crowed triumphantly. "*He* doesn't think it's wrong to fall in love."

"He doesn't know the whole situation," Jessica returned coldly.

"The situation is very simple to explain," Frances defended herself sharply. "I was dating John and met his younger brother Paddy and fell in love with Paddy. There. That's it. Is that so wrong?"

"That must have been a difficult situation," Jacob replied, solemnly. "But, no, it doesn't seem so wrong."

"Well, someone thinks so," Frances screeched, tossing her cigarette to the ground and crushing it out with the heel of her sneaker. "I have to go. Nice talking to you." She climbed back into the front seat of the car.

As they passed the car, Jessica began to explain forcefully, "The situation's not as simple as she makes it out to be. Don't be taken in by that sweet voice and that innocent face. She'd been dating John since he was a sophomore in high school and she was a freshman. Almost three years. *Then* she accepted a pre-engagement ring from him at the beginning of her senior year when he went off to college. In November, two things happened. Brother Paddy, all of a sudden, changed from a nerdy "little brother" into a star junior-varsity basketball player. And John had a car accident and lost the use of his right arm. Two weeks later, Frances dumped John and started dating Paddy. John was totally devastated."

"Ohhh," Lil cried, "that's a terrible story!"

"I told you it wasn't as simple as she made it out to be," Jessica pronounced with a flourish of justification.

"Well, that's enough of the Block for me," Jimmy declared, crossing the street. "Now where to? We can't go to Kelly's. Jake and Jessica would never get in."

"Let's just go back and watch some TV," Lil proposed, glancing meaningfully at Jessica.

"Ah, slum, sweet slum!" Jimmy mocked, unlocking the door to his room.

Lil slinked over to the TV set, flicked it on, and flipped through the channels till she found MTV.

"Anyone for a beer?" Jimmy asked.

"I'll have one," Jacob said.

Sinking into the sofa, Jimmy kicked off his sneakers and propped his white-stockinged feet on the edge of the coffee table. Lil curled up next to him, lightly rubbing his forearm with the tips of her long fingernails. Jacob settled down in an armchair and watched them for an uneasy moment. Jessica shrugged off her jacket and ran her fingers through her dark hair.

"Does anyone want to get high?" Jessica proposed.

"It's Friday night, sis." Jimmy didn't take his eyes from the TV screen.

Jessica sat down on the sofa, plunging her hand in between the cushions, rooting around until she found the film canister. She rolled a thin joint, her fingers moving as nimbly as if she were sewing. Jacob had never seen it done before: she's quite an expert.

"Do you have a light?" she asked, looking hard at him.

Jacob reached into his jeans pocket and pulled out a lighter.

"Here you go."

When she took the lighter from him, their fingertips touched. She smiled at him uncertainly.

"Make sure you light some incense," Jimmy demanded, "cuz I don't want Wayne on my back."

She lit the joint and then lit a cone of incense. As the joint made its way around the room, Jacob kept gazing at Jessica. She had crossed her legs and kept swinging her sneakered foot back and forth. She's very pretty. He shook a cigarette from his pack and lit it.

"Hey, Jake." Jimmy was rattling the empty bag of Hartley's potato chips. "Got any more chips?"

"I have another bag in my room." Jake stood up.

Jessica stood up too. "Can I see your room? I'd like to see what the rest of this place looks like."

In his room he turned on the desk lamp. Its murky light barely reached into the corners. A stale smell of cigarette smoke lingered. On the bed lay the white sheets and a pale blue blanket.

"It's a little small," she observed, "but not too bad." She slipped into the room as if shrugging on her oversized jacket, looked around, and touched the edge of the desk while glancing out the windows. "Everyone has to start somewhere."

Jacob stood just inside the doorway, near the bureau. Scenes from *Basic Instinct* flashed through his mind.

"You haven't even made your bed yet. Let's make it," she suggested, picking up the pale blue blanket. "I'll help you."

Impulsively he blurted out, *"Nay."*

"Neigh? I'm not a mare!" She laughed shrilly.

"I mean no, no, yew don't have to do that." For some reason, it seemed embarrassing and terribly wrong, almost immoral, for a woman he hardly knew, a stranger really, to make his bed. Then it struck him suddenly that he was in his room with her alone.

"Oh, don't worry about it." Her tone was authoritative. "I don't mind. It's no big deal."

Before Jacob could object, she tossed the blanket and the top sheet on the lopsided easy chair. The pillowcases dropped to the mattress. She snapped one out and pulled it over a pillow.

"You've gotta get new pillows." She pulled the other pillowcase over the other pillow. "These things are like pancakes."

Jacob stood in the doorway watching her make his bed, not sure what to do or what to think.

"Come on," she growled, shaking out the fitted sheet. "Don't just stand there. Help me with this."

He took the edge of the sheet and fitted it around two corners of the mattress. Deftly she fitted the corners on the other side and ran her hand over the length of it to smooth it. She pitched the pillows back in place.

"Hand me the other sheet."

Together they pulled and folded and tucked the top sheet.

"Now that blanket."

She stood back to admire their work. "There, now, doesn't that look better? But you have to get a bedspread or a comforter or something."

Jacob gazed at the newly made bed. He stood on one side and she stood on the other. He lifted his eyes to her and then, somehow, on impulse, abruptly, falling into her tantalizing eyes, they were tangled on the bed kissing, kissing as he had never kissed before, certainly not the reluctant and frustrating kisses that Leah had bestowed on him in the buggy before she told him she was too young to start seeing someone. Not kisses like that. Jessica opened her mouth. They turned and pressed and twisted into each other, arms hugging, legs coiling. Jessica pulled at the back of his shirt. He felt her warm palms against the flesh of his back. Then, all of a sudden, Jessica lay back against the pillows, her dark hair tousled, her eyes shiny, moist, hungry. She whispered in a heavy growl, "Do you like me?"

He nodded, breathing heavily.

Then she smiled and purred, "I think you should close the door."

He turned to the open doorway, forgetting that he had not shut it, and obediently jumped up. "What about the potato chips?"

She giggled. "I wouldn't worry about chips." She kicked off her sneakers. "Do you have any condoms?"

Jacob looked startled.

CHAPTER 17

"That's an amazing story," Agent Tate repeated, gazing out the passenger window at the bleak winter landscape, already flooded with darkness. "I wonder if this Jacob Hostetler knew that about his girlfriend?"

"Probably not," Sergeant Stuter replied, his eyes held steady on Route 655. "I doubt Jimmy or Jessica would talk about it, and especially not to someone who used to be Amish."

"Do you think he knew about it, in general?"

"Everyone, in one way or another, knew about it, but it was rarely discussed. After all, it happened twenty-five years ago, before Jacob was born, but I'm sure he heard *something* about it. That type of thing was swept under the rug as an embarrassment to the Amish."

"But it's still a coincidence. In fact, a fascinating coincidence."

Sergeant Stuter turned onto a sinuous road that curved its way toward Stone Mountain Road.

"And he changed his name from Zook to Smith," Agent Tate continued. "Why Smith?"

"No apparent reason. Standard English name."

"So Jesse J. Zook became Jesse J. Smith in 1967."

"Correct."

"And this was after he was excommunicated?"

"Basically. After he got paroled, he went back to his family for a few months. They wanted him to make a full confession and return to the church, but he refused because he felt justified in having burned down his uncle's barn. This went on for months, yet he stubbornly refused to confess before the church. Only then did the church officially excommunicate him. He left and changed his name."

"Why did the family take him back?"

"He set the fire on angry impulse, and the Amish are a forgiving people."

"But why did he stay in the valley?"

"Think about a young Amish boy, not too smart, not knowing much about the outside world, not having marketable skills besides dairy farming; he doesn't have too many options. Initially, he moved to Lewistown. Only later, five years or so later, after he married, did he return to the valley. I guess he felt enough time had gone by. He got a job with a construction company and basically stayed with that all these years."

Sergeant Stuter turned onto Stone Mountain Road, driving slowly past a Black-Top horse and buggy, its red lights flashing.

"And this John D. Zook, his uncle, was really mean?"

"Taunted Jesse all the time. Called him stupid, dumb, jackass, fool. Said he couldn't do this right or that right, that he didn't know how to clean the manure gutters, that he took too long to milk a cow. This went on for months and months until Jesse just had too much."

"But it was just the barn?"

"It happened in June, and the cows had already been turned out to pasture. If he had killed livestock, he would have spent more time in jail."

"And this was done during the day!" Agent Tate noted with amazement.

"Broad daylight. I'll never forget it. Jesse didn't seem to care if he was caught or not. He showed up to work, the uncle made a remark, and Jesse snapped. He stalked into the barn and set the hayloft on fire, stalked out, climbed into his buggy, drove home. Just like that."

"And only spent four months in jail?"

"Two years would have been the maximum sentence, but his lawyer and a psychiatrist managed to get him paroled early due to his being Amish. Special circumstances. They argued that he needed the family and cultural support and could not function properly outside the Amish community."

Sergeant Stuter peered at the darkness and the passing barbwire fence.

"And he was a White Top?"

"Correct," Sergeant Stuter answered, slowing down as they

passed a mailbox and milk stand. He made a sharp turn into the Hostetler farm lane. The police cruiser, rising and falling, bounced and shuddered in the narrow farm lane, between open fields wrinkled with the stubble of cut corn and the emptiness of winter.

"But he doesn't see his family?"

"No-oo, not really. Maybe he *sees* them once in awhile in town, but he has nothing to do with them. After the excommunication, the Amish had to shun him. And that included his family."

"Rather hard."

"I don't think it was too hard on *him*, except that he used to be close to one of his sisters. I don't know which one."

"Where is she now?"

"She married. She's somewhere in the valley, I guess."

Sergeant Stuter parked, facing the farmhouse. He cut the headlights, and the beams of light crumbled in the darkness. The downstairs windows were rectangles of white light. The front door opened almost immediately, letting a wedge of light tumble onto the front porch. Isaac D., with heads bobbing behind him, peered uncertainly into the thick night.

"Isaac, it's Sergeant Stuter," he called loudly.

Isaac D. pulled at his beard, turning to talk to someone inside.

"You can still smell it," Sergeant Stuter remarked, sniffing. The night air, chilled with the fragrance of snow, still carried a trace of ash and burned flesh.

As Agent Tate walked toward the farmhouse, he whispered, "So Jimmy and Jessica, technically, have Amish relatives."

"Scads of them," Sergeant Stuter confirmed. "And I bet they haven't seen a one."

"Do you think they know about all this?"

"I can't imagine why not."

"Absolutely fascinating!"

Isaac D. held the door open for them. "Not tew cold out, is it?"

"Not too bad, Isaac," Sergeant Stuter replied, stepping into the kitchen. "A fairly mild night."

"*Ya*, it was not tew bad in the barn," Isaac D. chatted. "They say it might snow. I don't know."

Sergeant Stuter agreed with him. "Now, Isaac, have you met Agent Tate? Of the FBI?"

"*Ya*, this morning, with Ezra S." Isaac D. steered them into the living room. Inside, Abraham C. sat reading *Die Botschaft*. He rattled the newspaper as he closed it. Then he tilted back his head with its great mane of white hair, his beard thrust forward, and peered through his spectacles at the two men with a searching intensity.

"Sergeant Stuter," Isaac D. explained and then introduced Agent Tate.

In response, Abraham C. merely folded his arms across his chest, hands under his armpits, and steadied his gaze.

"They're here to talk about the fires," Isaac D. explained in Pennsylvania German. "Is that acceptable?"

Abraham C. nodded his head in assent.

Isaac D. adjusted his gold wire-rimmed spectacles and dragged two chairs across the floor. "Sit down. Yew have many questions?"

"Just a few," Sergeant Stuter answered. "Is Rebekah here?"

Isaac D. called his wife and adjusted the flame on the kerosene lamp. Rebekah, the sharp features of her face softened in the lamplight, appeared in the doorway, wiping her hands on a cloth. She sat on a bench near her husband, her blue eyes sharp points of concern.

"I know this is difficult," Sergeant Stuter began, in accord with the officers' unwritten agreement that he guide most of the questions with the Amish. "But do any of you know where Jacob is?"

Isaac D. pulled at his beard. "*Nay*."

"He's in Lewistown," Rebekah said.

"He's not at his apartment. And he hasn't been there since Saturday afternoon," said Sergeant Stuter.

She directed her pointed gaze at him. "Then we dew not know where he is."

Isaac D. murmured something to her in Pennsylvania German, but too low for Sergeant Stuter to make it out. Rebekah dropped her eyes to her hands, folded in her lap.

"We dew not know," Isaac D. repeated.

"He is not on the farm anywhere?"

"*Nay*."

"Have you heard anything about where he *might* be?"

Isaac D. glanced around the room and declared in a quiet voice, "He could not have burned down those barns."

"But we have to find him to know that," Sergeant Stuter stated, looking from him to his wife to his father.

The front door slammed shut. Esle stood in the doorway, pulling off his straw hat. Sergeant Stuter spoke to him in Pennsylvania German. With a sullen expression, Esle sat down next to his mother. His legs were apart, his clumsy work shoes planted squarely on the bare floor, his body leaning forward with elbows on thighs. He stared at the floor. He held a flashlight loosely in his soiled hands. A faint odor of cow manure clung to his clothes. Agent Tate watched him closely, noting the flashlight.

"When was the last time you saw him?" Sergeant Stuter asked no one in particular.

"We haven't," Isaac D. responded.

"We have talked to him, though," Rebekah volunteered, "on the phone."

"When was that?" Agent Tate quizzed.

Isaac D. turned to Rebekah for help. She shrugged. Abraham C. tilted his head toward them. "Ooo," Isaac D. speculated, "must have been tew weeks ago. We used to call him each week once we found out where he was."

"What did you talk about?" Sergeant Stuter continued.

Isaac D. pursed his lips and glanced at the ceiling. "Haw he was. Was he eating goot? Chust things like that."

"Und that we pray fur him to come home," Rebekah added. "That he *knows* he can come home anytime."

"Did he sound okay?"

Isaac D. and Rebekah both nodded.

"Nothing out of the ordinary?"

"*Nay*, not reel-ly. I think he was chust tired from work. He said he did not like his job that much anymore."

Sergeant Stuter and Agent Tate exchanged brief glances.

"But other than that, nothing?"

"Nothing."

Agent Tate looked at the young man. "And you, Esle, how did he sound to you?"

Esle gripped the flashlight and shook his head.

With his eyes locked on Esle, Agent Tate persisted, "Would you have any idea where Jacob is?"

Esle moved his head in such a manner that it could have been a yes or a no.

Isaac D. quickly spoke for him. "He does not know. No one knows."

Then Abraham C. stirred in his chair and announced, "I spoke to Jacob on Friday."

"This past Friday?" Agent Tate asked, turning his eyes from the grandson to the grandfather.

Abraham C. nodded.

"Did he say anything unusual?"

"Living in the *englisch* world, everything he said was unusual."

Sergeant Stuter suppressed a smile. "But did he say anything *especially* unusual? Or did he sound strange?"

Abraham C. tilted his head further back and considered. "He did not sound goot."

"In what way?"

"He said he quit his job."

Agent Tate straightened in his chair, listening intently.

"Did he say why?" Sergeant Stuter pressed.

Abraham C. shook his head slightly. "Chust that he was tired of the chickens *un* the factory."

"What else did you talk about?"

Abraham C. fixed his pale blue eyes upon the men. "Faith."

"Pardon me?" Agent Tate was leaning forward.

"Faith," he repeated.

Agent Tate leaned back and studied this ancient man's face.

Sergeant Stuter persisted. "You talked about the Amish faith—"

"*Nay*," Abraham C. interrupted. "We talked about faith. In God. In Jesus Christ."

Sergeant Stuter considered this a moment. "Was he having some type of spiritual crisis?"

"An Amish in the *englisch* world *is* in spiritual crisis."

"But why were you talking about faith?"

"I told him that in his beginning is his end."

"What do you mean 'is his end'? The end of his being Amish?"

"In the beginning is the end."

Sergeant Stuter studied his expression. "Is this some type of parable, Abraham?"

He simply repeated the phrase.

"But was it a *specific* problem that he was having?"

Abraham C. shrugged.

"Was he thinking of coming back? Of doing something?"

Abraham C. shrugged again. Sergeant Stuter felt his back stiffen when Abraham C. started shrugging. It was a sign that he had had enough and would answer no more questions.

As Isaac D. walked the two men to the police cruiser, he held a flashlight, shining its beam down on the ground. An owl hooted.

"*Danki*," Sergeant Stuter told him as he opened the car door. "I know it's difficult to talk about Jacob."

Isaac D. jerked the light around on the ground. "I dew not think Jacob could have burned down the barns."

Sergeant Stuter, even in the darkness, could see the anguished expression on his face. "I hope not, Isaac."

Isaac D. pressed his lips together and turned away, the light from the flashlight skittering along the cold ground.

"Who *was* that old man?" Agent Tate asked as he climbed into the police cruiser.

"That was Bishop Hostetler, Jacob's grandfather."

"What a *presence!*"

"A powerful presence."

As Sergeant Stuter started the engine, Agent Tate inquired, "Now, why did Esle have a flashlight when he came in?"

"For the barn. To check on the heifers, the horses. To toss hay down from the loft."

"They don't use lanterns?"

"Yes, they do. Sometimes it's just easier to shine a flashlight into the stalls. It's fairly common. And safe."

"I didn't know they could use flashlights at all. Isn't that a form of electricity?"

"Battery-powered. As long as it's not electricity from public utility lines, it's acceptable."

"Why is that?"

"The Amish think there's some mysterious connection with the outside world if they use electric power from the high lines. It's a real as well as a symbolic attachment to the English world that they don't want. Batteries are self-contained and separate. The same with diesel- or gas-powered machinery. It's self-contained. The same type of logic follows the use of telephones—a connection with the outside world that they don't want."

"It's *all* very mysterious," Agent Tate observed as he clicked on his tape recorder and then clicked it off. "And by the way, that Esle is hiding something. His body language shouted it." Then he clicked on his tape recorder again as the police cruiser rumbled up the dark farm lane.

CHAPTER 18

When Jacob woke late Saturday morning, Jessica was gone. He sat up in bed and looked around his room, not sure if what had happened last night *had* happened or if he had dreamed it. A headache curled inside his head. His eyes were itchy and his throat was sore. He drank a glassful of water and watched TV and then decided to have lunch at the McDonald's he had seen yesterday afternoon across the street from the Finast. When he glanced out the window, the sky was clouded and cold-looking. He dressed and combed his hair and pulled on his jean jacket.

As he walked along Downe Avenue, the sidewalks were wet and muddy and the smell of the Juniata River, a damp brown odor, pricked his nose. When he started to cross the railroad tracks, a huge black dog, barking, snapping, and snorting, jumped out of nowhere. It rammed its paws in the mud and thrust its boxlike head forward, eyes red and fangs bared, and jerked its head from side to side so rapidly Jacob thought he saw three heads instead of one. It growled menacingly. Jacob stood still. Its body twitched. When Jacob did not move, the dog backed up a few steps and dropped its head into a bowl of slimy dog food, slobbering and growling and gulping. Then he saw that the dog was chained to a stake in front of an abandoned building. Keeping a wary eye on the dog, he crossed to the other side.

Inside McDonald's a shrill noise assaulted his ears. In the far corner, a clump of children, jumping up and down, howled, "Happy Birthday to you! Happy Birthday to you!" Empty hamburger wrappers stirred on the floor. In the center sat a plump boy, a silver-colored cone fastened on his head by an elastic string. As soon as the song ended, he ripped open a bright red package. The sky groaned, rumbled, ripped open—a torrential downpour beat against the earth. The children pressed their faces against the plate glass to watch.

Jacob studied the menu board at the counter and ordered an Extra Value Meal # 3.

"What kind of pop?"

"Coke."

"Do you want a Batman cup for just a quarter?"

"A what?"

"A Batman cup." The girl waved at the display.

"Oh, okay."

All over the restaurant were posters of the movie *Batman Returns*. Jacob sat down to eat his meal, amused at the image on his plastic cup, a muscular man in cowl and cape. The children squealed, shrieked. As he ate his Quarter Pounder, he looked around the room and observed that most diners seemed overweight—the men, the women, and the children. Two laughing women, each the size of a heifer, sat at a table, cramming french fries into their dainty mouths. A big man with sagging jowls munched, open mouthed, on a cheeseburger. Children screamed with delight when a mother handed out cookies.

Then a huge man, not so much holding a tray as embracing it, slowly waddled past him, muttering, "I hate the rain, the rain, I hate the rain." He squeezed his girth into a nearby booth. Jacob could not believe his size, surely weighing over three hundred pounds. He wore a tight white shirt, underarms stained yellow with sweat. His head rolled above the collar on a neckless torso of bulging fat folds that settled, finally, on top of a great bloated belly. Jacob could think only of the swollen udder of a cow as the man unwrapped a Big Mac and bit into it. Shredded lettuce fell to his shirt.

Jacob flicked his eyes away and saw Daniel A. Yoder, clutching a tray of food with one hand, slump down in a seat by the far window. A sudden tightness knotted his chest. Did he want to talk to him? He hardly knew Danny. When Paul suggested that he talk to Danny, it had seemed like a good idea, but now he wasn't so sure. What would he say? He had always heard that Danny was a real mischief-maker and an odd bird. Apparently no one was that surprised when he left the Amish last fall.

The children were marching back and forth in the restaurant, playing some game. The plump boy sporting the silver-colored cone clapped his pudgy hands and shouted, "Cake, cake, cake!"

Munching on a french fry, Danny turned to watch their antics, but his eyes settled on Jacob with a vague look of recognition. For a long moment, he stared at Jacob, turned back to his french fries, then again toward Jacob. When Jacob nodded slightly, an expression of utter astonishment stretched across Danny's face as he stood up and strutted past the stamping children. He was still tall and thin, with a narrow face and a sharp, beaky nose. He wore a black T-shirt, worn blue jeans, and a pair of pointy-toed black cowboy boots with three-inch heels, which made him appear taller and thinner in his long-legged strut.

"Jacob Hostetler?"

"Ya, ya, wie geht's?" Jacob explained that he had left the Amish.

"I coulda guessed *that*!" Danny replied in English, motioning at Jacob's hair and face. "Chust look at yew! Haw the hell are yew? I *can't* believe it! Bishop Hostetler's grandson? Un-bee-*lee*-vable."

Jacob just stared at him. It was apparent Danny didn't want to speak German.

"Let me get my stuff. Bee right back."

When he sat down, his dark blue eyes flashed with mischief. "So ven did yew leave?"

"Friday. Friday morning."

"Chust *this* Friday? Yesterday?"

Jacob nodded.

"Hooo-eee," he whistled. "A babe in the vootz."

Jacob smiled uncertainly and sipped his Coke, already disliking Danny's thick accent. It would have been better to speak German.

"Is it not *great*?" Danny emphatically said in a conspiratorial tone of voice. "Yew can do whatever yew want. No more rules. Yew can eat at McDonald's if yew want: no more family meals un no more prayers. Yew can wear what yew want, go where yew want, watch TV, listen to the radio, go to the moofies, have a telephone in your room, party all night long." His eyes had a gluttonous glaze. "No more straw hats, no more smelly cows, no more cold buggies. I drive a pickup truck naw."

"Do yew?" Jacob showed sudden interest.

"Fur shure, a silver '85 Dodge pickup," Danny teased, aware of his sudden interest. "Have yew applied fur a driving license?"

"Yesterday I picked up the forms and booklets."

Danny laughed. "That soon?"

Jacob nodded, smiling. "I like to drive."

"Ven did yew ever drive?"

"I used to drive Gary Schippe's van around the church parking lots," Jacob bragged. "He's an *englisch* friend of mine in Fairville."

"Vell, prit-tee soon you'll be able to drive a van or truck or car anywhere yew want to. Not chust in parking lots."

Jacob nodded again.

"Where are yew staying?" Danny stuffed his last few french fries into his thin-lipped mouth.

"At 9 Basil Street."

"Chust around the corner?"

Jacob nodded, once again, aware that he kept nodding to minimize talk. "Ye-ah, I have a room right next to a guy named Jimmy."

"Jimmy *Smith*?" Danny was still munching his french fries.

"Long black hair—"

"Vurks as a car mechanic?"

Jacob nodded and realized that he didn't even know Jimmy's last name—nor Jessica's.

"I know him," Danny confided, as though turning something over in his mind. "He's a *true* par-tee animal. Him and Lil. Have yew met Lil?"

Jacob nodded.

"Un his little sister?"

Jacob nodded again and smiled.

"Aaahhh, have yew? Nice, huh?"

Jacob pursed his lips. "She's very nice."

Danny studied his face. "Haw much do yew know abawt Jimmy?"

Jacob wasn't sure what the question meant. "Not much. Where he works. His girlfriend. His sister. I only met them last night. He sure likes cars, though. His room is filled with car magazines."

Danny tilted his head thoughtfully, as though he were about to say something, and then changed his mind. "Have yew partied with him?"

Jacob made a face to indicate that he had.

"Fur shure." Danny smiled and shook a cigarette from his pack, offering one to Jacob. "Those three are *true* par-tee animals. I can hardly keep up with them myself."

"How did *yew* meet them?"

"Awn the Block. Yew know abawt the Block?"

Jacob lit his cigarette. "Fur sure."

"Vell, fur being here only . . . what? Twenty-four hours? Yew shure seem to know the party scene prit-tee vell." He took a long drag on his cigarette. "Do yew have a job yet?"

"Not yet, but Jimmy said there's a guy down the hall who works at some chicken plant."

"I vurked there."

"Did yew?"

"Mmmm, it's not tew bad, but not tew goot either. I vurked there abawt tew months before I got this roofing job. I make eight dollars an hour naw. Un I'd rather be on a roof with shingles than in a big room with dead chickens."

"Well, I need *some* kind of job."

"Un they always need people. It's a job. It's o-kay."

Jacob dragged on his cigarette, his voice hushed with smoke and seriousness. "Why did yew leave?"

Danny stared at him abstractly for a few seconds and said, "Cowboy boots."

"What?"

"Cowboy boots," he repeated, raising his foot and showing him the pointy-tipped, three-inch-heeled boots.

"Cowboy boots?" Jacob was dumbfounded.

"Cowboy boots," Danny declared, bitterly. "Amish can't have cowboy boots. Because I *had* cowboy boots, I could not be baptized."

"I don't understand," Jacob innocently responded as he stubbed out his cigarette.

"I vent through the whole baptism thing, the entire *die Gemee nooch geh*, yew know what I mean. All spring un all summer, I sat un listened abawt haw I had to make a choice, to join the church, to abide by the *Addning*, to follow the rules—the whole hog! I don't know what I was thinking. I chust sat there, yew know. Then, tew weeks before baptism, I got these cowboy boots. Ven my father found awt, he was so provoked. Before I knew it, the bishop was talking to me, telling me that cowboy boots were not part of Amish dress, that the boots showed a mind still filled with indecision un defiance, so I could not be baptized. I was still partying, tew, ven I could, and I think the bishop got wind of that as well."

Danny sighed a long sigh and took one last drag on his cigarette before stubbing it out. "Then it got cold, un I would watch cars go by, thinking that they have heat un I have cold, so I decided to leave. I wanted to leave before, but yew don't know haw to do it or have the strength until it chust happens. I got up one morning, milked the cows, had breakfast, un left." Danny slumped back.

Jacob pondered his story. "So yew left because yew could not have cowboy boots."

"Fur shure," he chuckled. "Un I'm damn glad I *did* leave. I wouldn't go back fur nothing."

"But what about your family? Don't yew miss them? Don't they try to get yew to come back?"

"I miss them," he agreed, with a catch in his voice, "but not enough to go back to being Amish. They still *want* me to go back. At first, I couldn't deal with it—the whole-hog guilt trip from the entire family: aunts, cousins, second cousins, yew name it—I didn't want to see or talk to any of them fur the first coupla months. But they were always callin' as soon as they found awt I had a phone. They've eased off a little naw, but there's still that come-back-naw-all-is-forgiven tone in their voices. Un I see them, tew."

"Yew do?"

"Fur shure, abawt once a week. I'm not shunned. I wasn't baptized, thank Gawd."

Jacob nodded thoughtfully. "That's one reason I left now, tew. I was supposed to start classes tomorrow. I feel bad enough that I stood up and *said* I was going to join."

Danny studied his face intently. "Yew feel bad chust fur *saying* yew were going to join?"

Surprised at the question, Jacob studied *his* face intently. "*Ya*, I felt like a liar because I knew deep down that I didn't want to."

"Didn't bother me," Danny stated nonchalantly and let his gaze drift to the rain outside. "I don't know what I was thinking while the classes went awn. I chust went along with the old routine. Then I saw these cowboy boots in Super Shoes and bought them. 'No baptism,' they said, so I left. Un I have no regrets. I'm glad I left."

Jacob perceived an angry undertone to his words. The conversation had started to spiral downward for him a while ago and now hit bottom. He could not believe that the reason Danny left the Amish was that he wanted to have a pair of black cowboy boots. He knew the boots were merely a sign of his unhappiness with Amish dress and the *Addning*, but he wondered how deeply Danny understood that. For all of Jacob's discontent and restlessness, he still recognized the spiritual value of the Amish: the deep faith that resonated beneath the rules about straw hats and the buggies and the fieldwork.

"Can yew believe this rain?" Danny remarked. "Tew much."

Jacob had another question for Danny. "Are yew going to any church now?"

His eyes dulled. His face turned wooden. "*Nay*."

Jacob had touched a sensitive spot. He did not pursue it.

Danny glanced at his wristwatch. "Uh-oh, gotta go. Do yew have a phone number?"

"There's a phone. I don't know it yet."

"I don't have a . . . chust a minute."

He strutted to the counter and returned with a napkin, inked with numbers. "That's my phone. Yew call anytime yew want. Fur shure?"

Jacob took the napkin. The children screamed. The huge man burped. The rain fell hard.

Then Danny advised, "I would watch that Jimmy, okay? Un his little sister."

"What do yew mean?"

"Chust be careful."

Jacob watched him as he strutted out of the McDonald's into the rain, his pointy-toed, three-inch-heeled cowboy boots singing on the white-tiled floor.

After the shrieking children and the huge man and the disappointing conversation with Danny, Jacob wandered downtown, filled with french fries and Coke and the distinct thought that his life had now changed forever. There could be no changing course now that he had started this journey. The torrential downpour stopped as suddenly as it began, leaving a cool, damp texture to the air. The afternoon smelled of rain and streets and remembered lust. At the intersection of River Avenue and West Broad Street, he stood and watched the afternoon shoppers, with glazed consumer eyes, strolling and pushing past one another along the sidewalks, in and out of stores. Cars crawled in the streets. The sound of voices, the sight of bright jackets and colorful shirts, the feeling of solid concrete beneath his feet—these all appealed to him. This is my new home, he realized, gazing at the swirling circles of the city itself.

Jacob joined the racing shoppers. He bought a blue short-sleeved shirt and a white T-shirt. He crossed the street to Downtown Books. After searching through the shelves, he finally decided to buy the thickest book available in the section marked Fiction: *Moby-Dick*, by Herman Melville—a Signet Classic, 543 pages of small print, only $2.95. He read that short first sentence, crisp and cunning, with an adventurous sensation: "Call me Jacob."

Back in his room, he dumped the shopping bags on his bed, turned on the TV, and opened both windows halfway. A breeze skittered inside. The afternoon light, stained with rain, held the room. He ripped open the package with the blue short-sleeved shirt, tried it on, and then tore the wrappings off the white T-shirt and tried that on. With a Pepsi and the *Pennsylvania Driver's Manual*, he flumped down in his lopsided easy chair.

MTV danced and sang. He lit a cigarette and settled into the cushions, relishing the menthol taste, and let his eyes focus on the TV screen. Watching TV and smoking a cigarette—two simple pleasures denied him when he was Amish. *Was* Amish, he repeated, thinking already in the past tense. In a curious way, the Amish seemed altogether far away and remote. Is this what happened to Danny? But what now was the *meaning* of lolling in a chair, smoking a cigarette, watching TV? He flicked his ashes into an ashtray and flicked those questions away.

For a while he read the driving manual and then remembered the novel and picked it up. He studied the picture of the whale and the clinging men on the cover, skimmed the extracts in the beginning, and then sank into the first chapter called "Loomings." As he lit another cigarette, ready to start the second chapter, there was a loud rap-rap-rap on his door.

"It's open."

Jimmy stepped in with a wicked grin. "So," he asked, eyes winking, "how was it last night? Have a good time?"

Jacob smiled ambiguously, not sure whether he meant partying or Jessica, and said nothing.

"That good, huh?" Jimmy laughed, looking around the room, glancing at the Paula Abdul video on MTV. As Jimmy sat down on the bed, facing him, Jacob just kept smiling and wedged the driver's manual into the cushion.

"So she was pretty good, huh?" he asked again.

Jessica. "Ve-ry nice," Jacob answered, a certain satisfaction evident in his voice but also a measure of reserve. Such matters were rarely discussed among the Amish and certainly not bragged about; besides, he hardly knew Jimmy.

"Y'know," Jimmy began, lighting a cigarette, eyes squinting, "she's my little sister and all but, hey, I can't tell her what ta do. I mean, she's eighteen and all, and she's been doin' whatever she wanted to fer years now."

All of a sudden it struck Jacob with remembered force that Jessica was Jimmy's sister. It had been mentioned fleetingly, and Jacob acknowledged it, but she seemed more a friend to Lil than a sister to Jimmy. Jacob blushed. "If yew don't want me to see her—"

"What?" Jimmy interrupted. "I don't care if ya see her. She's her own boss, lemme tell ya. It's not *my* decision." Then he lowered his voice. His eyes twitched. "Just be careful, if ya know what I mean."

Puzzled, Jacob frowned.

"Ya know," he laughed. "Wrap that puppy."

"Oh, ye-ah," Jacob replied, still not sure what he meant.

"Hey, whaddaya readin'?"

Jacob held up the novel.

"Nah, I don't mean that. What's the mag?"

Jacob stammered.

Jimmy reached over and grabbed the thick booklet. "A driving manual? What the hell happened? Get a DUI?" Jimmy shuddered at the memory of sitting through three weeks of classes at the police barracks to review the manual and to watch movies of car accidents.

Not sure what to say, Jacob just stared at him. His skin prickled.

Then Jimmy's twitching eyes narrowed with triumph. "You mean to tell me you don't have a driver's license and you're nineteen years old?" His eyes narrowed more, as if he were reading small print. "And you don't have a job. And you have a nice new haircut. And you have an accent, though you try to hide it—*yaaaahhh*." Then, indicating the crowning piece of evidence, he declared, "And you have farmer's hands."

Jacob felt his face stiffen.

"Y'know, I kept lookin' at yer hands last night," Jimmy continued, a veritable Sherlock Holmes, puffing on his cigarette dramatically. "Ever since we smoked that pot, passing the joint back and forth, I kept thinking I've only seen those types of hands on farmers—thick, strong, red fingers. And then last night at the movies, when Lil said you were *so* into the movie, that you must be a *real* movie buff, I just wondered. But I bet you've never *been* to a movie before, have ya? Am I right?"

Meekly Jacob nodded his head. He felt the same way when Esle caught him driving Gary's van.

"I knew it!" he exclaimed. "I just *knew* it. You're Amish, right?"

Jacob nodded again.

"So you just up and left?" he asked excitedly.

"Yesterday morning," he admitted.

"Hot *damn*, no kidding! I just *knew* it, but Lil, y'know Lil, she wouldn't believe it, even after I tole her everything I kept thinking about, puttin' two and two together. That's after you took off with Jessica."

Jacob sat glumly, leaning farther back into the cushions as all his visions of now being an *Englischer* crumbled into abject pretension.

"Well, welcome to the *real* world," Jimmy pronounced with emphasis, the heat of anger in his words. "This here is the real world, Jake, not that cow-farm-Amish bull crap in the valley. You're lucky ya left, that's all there is to it, that's all I can say. The Amish are *dinosaurs*."

Jacob, startled at the sudden harsh tone of his voice, stared at him.

"I mean, like this is the twentieth century, y'know. It's the '90s, man, and they still don't watch TV or listen to stereos or go to movies." He took a long drag on his cigarette, eyes twitching and blinking, and sneered with disdain, "And those *freak*-ing buggies. Hogging the road. Slowing you down. Crapping all the way. Just cuz for some stupid reason they can't drive cars. They're *whacked-out* people. Behind the times, *way* behind the times, so *far* behind the times that they don't know what the times are! And you're damn lucky you left, that's all I can say."

Jacob listened to this outburst, unsure how to react or what to say. Then that baffling warning from Danny crossed his mind.

On impulse, Jimmy volunteered, "I'm gonna have to hook you up with Danny. He wised up and left six months ago. Did you know Danny Yoder?"

"I just saw him."

"What's that?"

"I just talked to him in McDonald's."

Jimmy stubbed out his cigarette. "Just now? You're kiddin' me?"

"A couple hours ago. I went there to eat."

"Hot damn! There's luck for ya. So whad he say? He's as happy as a clam, isn't he?"

"I suppose," Jacob replied quietly.

"You suppose?" Jimmy showed surprise as he lit another cigarette, eyes squinting. "What were you anyway? A Yella Top?"

"White Top."

His face clouded, blackened. "They are the *worst*! They use freakin' outhouses! Primitive as black-and-white TV! Man-oh-man, the White Tops. You're one lucky bastard for having left."

Jimmy heard someone thudding up the stairs and stood up to see who it was. "Hey, Mark, how's it goin'? You meet Jake yet?"

A young man as slender as a fence post strolled into the room. Jimmy introduced them and explained that Mark worked at the chicken plant and that Jacob was searching for a job. Mark agreed to take him for a job interview on Monday.

"Great," Jimmy announced and clapped his hands. "Now, let's go have a beer."

Saturday followed a pattern like the previous day. Jacob drank beer that afternoon with Jimmy and Mark, watched TV, and after awhile Mark left. Although Jimmy said nothing more about the Amish, Jacob kept mulling over that angry outburst. Do people think that about the Amish? Late in the afternoon, Lil and Jessica arrived. Jessica wore tight white jeans and had large silver hoops dangling from her ears. He could not take his eyes off her bewitching figure, and he could smell the cool-scented perfume splashed on her skin. That night the four of them drank beer, smoked pot, and drove to State College for pizza. And once again, Jacob and Jessica went to his room.

Nightmarish images of church Sunday splintered his mind. The congregation, drinking beer, smoking cigarettes, and eating french fries, sat on benches arranged in circles. The preacher stood dead-center and delivered his sermon: the Amish should abandon their ways, the Amish were backward, the Amish should go out into the world. The preacher started to laugh. His beard fell off. His hair lengthened and turned black. Then his eyes twitched and winked and squinted and his face split into three.

Jacob woke late Sunday morning to a clouded day. In his chest his heart tightened with remorse. What had he done? How could he have left? He rolled over on a pillow and thought that Jessica was still in bed with him—but she had left at midnight. He reached for his wristwatch and saw it was nine. The service would have started. A sense of loss stippled his thoughts as he lay, staring at the ceiling, and debated what to do on a Sunday morning if he *weren't* going to services. A habit had long been established, and this Sunday would have been the start of his baptismal classes. What should he do?

In Jacob was stored a spiritual depth of faith in God. He did not think he could *not* worship in some form. Jacob knew that many Amish who left the church joined the Mennonites. He had hoped Danny Yoder could help him but was shocked to discover that Danny had turned to nothing. Nothing! How could that be? His chance meeting and his entire conversation with Danny had soured in his mind. He could not talk to him. He could not confide in him. He could not trust him. But who could he talk to? Certainly not Jimmy. Not Lil. Jessica?

He turned over. What a frightful dream. He clutched a pillow in his arms. His thoughts turned over. Images of the farm and his family, the cows and the barn flashed through his mind. His breath was heavy and thick. A thin layer of sweat stained his skin. The room smelled of cigarette smoke and remorse. He ran his hand over his jaw, still surprised to feel the stubble on his chin instead of his thin beard. I really *have* left. I am no longer Amish. But is it as simple as shaving your beard and using electricity?

Finally he slipped out of bed and automatically turned on the TV. With bleary eyes, he gazed at the flickering images and listened to the skittering sounds before pulling on his jeans and lumbering down the hall to the bathroom. Back in his room, he splashed cold water on his face and sat down to stare out the window. He lit a cigarette. He read the second chapter of *Moby-Dick*. There was a light rap on his door before Paul stepped in and said, "Hi."

Jacob, startled but pleased, asked how he got in the building.

"I was about to ring the buzzer when someone leaving opened the front door and told me where your room was. He was pretty skinny."

"Oh, that must have been Mark."

Paul was dressed in a dark blue blazer, a white shirt, and a loosened tie with splotches of color that vaguely resembled wildflowers. In one hand he held up a white Dunkin' Donuts bag and in the other a gray umbrella.

"I'm so glad to see *that*," Jacob laughed.

"The donuts or the umbrella?"

Jacob smiled. "Both, really, but I borrowed the umbrella from my landlord, and he's been snippy with me ever since. Thanks."

Jacob apologized for his room as he pulled the covers up on his bed and pitched empty Pepsi cans into the trash. He pulled out the desk chair, so Paul could have the lopsided easy chair. After Jacob ate two donuts and drank some coffee, he felt much better.

Paul noticed Jacob glancing at his tie and said, "Church."

"What church is that?"

"St. Peter's Roman Catholic Church, just up the street here."

"So you're a Catholic?"

Paul chuckled. "All Italians are Catholics."

Jacob nodded and glanced out the window. "Today was a church Sunday fur me, tew. The first day of instruction."

"Instruction?"

"Fur baptism," Jacob added quietly. "That's the main reason I left."

"I don't understand."

He explained the entire procedure.

Sympathetically, Paul listened to him. "So you're having doubts about having left?"

Jacob did not answer and removed a cigarette from his pack. He held the pack out toward Paul.

"No thanks, don't smoke. Do the Amish smoke?"

"Some dew. Different church groups have their own rules. My grandfather doesn't smoke and neither does my father, so I'm expected not to smoke," Jacob answered and lit a cigarette. He returned to Paul's earlier question. "It's weird, but I'd thought about leaving fur years. Oo-oo, not really in any set way at first. Just the usual thoughts about driving a car, watching TV. Not till last year did I seriously think about it. As the time fur baptism drew nearer and nearer, my thoughts of leaving grew bigger and bigger. The last few months were torture to me. Then it was time."

"To declare your intention," Paul reflected.

"Fur shure. I had to make a *choice*. Either I had to join the Amish or leave the Amish. So I thought and plotted and turned ideas around, struggling with indecision. But I did not want to stumble into baptism, only to leave later and be shunned. If I *were* to leave the Amish, it had to be *before* baptism. But now that I've left, now that I'm *here*, in the world, I can hardly believe it. I sometimes *don't* believe it."

Paul listened to this admission. "So you mean you're *not* shunned for leaving?"

"If yew leave before yew take the vows, then you're not shunned."

"So what are you?"

"We-ell," Jacob sighed, stubbing out his cigarette, "you're not quite anything: you're not Amish, but you're not *not* Amish. You're still part of your family, but not. It's a difficult situation, and your family always hopes you'll give up this foolishness and return, take your vows, and live the Amish life. More than anything else, it's just plain uncomfortable."

"But you can return?"

"Fur shure, even those shunned can return if they make a full confession, repent, and agree to mend their ways."

"So," Paul clarified his understanding, "even though you left, you could go back."

Jacob nodded. "And don't think fur a moment my family won't *try* to get me back."

"How's that?"

"Whenever someone leaves, the family pressure is *so* intense. Every single person in your family will try to reason with yew and convince yew that your decision to leave was wrong. I'm just waiting fur the storm. I know it's coming. After all, my grandfather's a bishop."

"You're kidding!"

Jacob shook his head. "And a very good bishop, tew. Much respected in the valley."

"And that makes it more difficult?"

Jacob nodded.

"I wonder if Danny Yoder went through all this."

"I saw him."

"You did?"

"Yesterday afternoon at McDonald's. By chance."

"So how'd that go?"

Jacob glanced out the window with a distracted look. "Not tew well."

"Why's that?"

"We're tew different people. I don't think the same way he does. Just because he's Amish or *was* Amish doesn't mean that we should get along."

"Different personalities."

Jacob agreed.

"Yeah, I can see that. People say Danny's kinda wild."

Jacob nodded again, absentmindedly, following his own line of thought. "But now that I've left, I wonder, . . . question, . . . think. At least I've changed the outside. Yew saw that."

"That I did," Paul agreed emphatically. "I don't think I'll ever forget it, watching an Amishman have his hair cut off. But what *do* you think now that you're in the world? What have you done?"

"We-ell," Jacob replied, his eyes widening, "I went to the movies Friday night."

"And you've never been to the movies before?"

"Never."

"And?"

"Ab-so-lute-ly incredible."

"What did you see?"

Jacob thought a moment. "The one with the ice pick."

Paul laughed. "*Basic Instinct* was your first movie?"

Jacob looked at him puzzled.

"I mean, it's a pretty violent movie and pretty sexy," Paul explained, "even for me."

"It *was* sexy," Jacob admitted.

"So that was your first movie," Paul mused, shaking his head. "How old *are* you?"

"Nineteen."

Still shaking his head, Paul simply stared at him. "I can't imagine *not* having seen a movie. It's been such a normal part of my life, like having a TV or a radio. It's just *been* there, all the time. I have no idea what it would be like to go to a movie for the first time as an adult. It boggles the mind."

"It's considered tew worldly," Jacob reported simply.

Paul noticed the book. "What's that you're reading?"

Jacob held up the novel.

"*Moby-Dick*?"

Jacob asked innocently, "Have yew heard of it?"

Paul laughed. "Every American kid who graduates from high school knows *Moby-Dick*. They probably haven't *read* it, but they know what it is. It's a masterpiece in American literature."

"That's what it says on the back cover. Besides, yew get the most pages fur your money."

Again, Paul laughed. Jacob did not think what he said was that funny—only practical—but he smiled and chuckled anyway. Briefly Jacob discussed what he had read.

"I read it my junior year," Paul remarked. "I can't remember details that clearly."

"Junior year?"

"In prep school."

Jacob did not understand.

"It's like a public high school but private." Paul started to explain and then remembered something about Amish education. "Oh, that's right, the Amish don't go to school after—"

"After the eighth grade," Jacob finished. "Then we have what is called a vocational school. Until we're fifteen, we write a diary about our work around the farm, what we're doing and learning about dairy farming. Then we turn that in to the teacher once a week."

"But no formal schooling, then, after eighth grade?"

Jacob shook his head. "There was a Supreme Court ruling on that."

"But what if someone *wanted* to go to high school? Could they?"

"No."

"Why not?"

"The Amish idea, the argument in the lawsuit, is that a person doesn't need education beyond the eighth grade to be an Amish farmer. Yew don't need to know higher mathematics or science, but yew need to know how to plow and plant the fields, how to care fur sick cows, and how to thresh wheat."

"But what if someone wants to learn other—"

"Oo-oo, yew read on your own," Jacob interrupted. "That's what I did. I've read things I shouldn't have. Yew can teach yourself." There was a decided touch of self-confidence in his voice because he knew he had read many good books under the guidance of Mrs. Dwan.

"Where do you get the books?"

"The library in town," Jacob reported matter-of-factly. "I used to go every Wednesday, when I went to the auction. All yew need is a dictionary to look up words yew don't know."

"That's pretty impressive."

"I used to read a book a week," Jacob said with pride. "Sometimes tew in the winter when there was less work to do."

"And no one minded?"

"We-ell, my parents would sometimes look at the book and say I should spend more time reading the Bible or *Martyrs Mirror*."

"What's that last one?"

"*Martyrs Mirror*. It's a big, thick book, over a thousand pages of stories about the persecution of Anabaptists in Europe: burnings at the stake, dungeons, torture, murder—things like that."

"When was this?"

"During the Protestant Reformation."

"And what's an Ana—"

"Anabaptist. That means 'rebaptizer.' The Anabaptists left the Catholic church because they rejected *infant* baptism and believed in *adult* baptism for those choosing to follow Christ's teachings. They were called rebaptizers because the early followers had already been baptized as infants. One of our leaders was Menno Simons, who joined Anabaptists about ten years after their start."

"And the name *Mennonite* comes from Menno Simons."

Jacob nodded. "Every Amish household has the *Martyrs Mirror* and the writings of Menno Simons." He lit another cigarette. "And the Bible, of course, and the prayer book."

"Then where does the word *Amish* come from?"

"Jacob Ammann. About a century and a half *after* Menno Simons. Ammann wanted the Swiss Anabaptists to practice stricter shunning and excommunication for backslidden members. That was the main thing. He also wanted them to hold communion twice a year instead of once, and to have foot washing be part of the communion service. And also to practice stricter shunning and excommunication."

"Hey, hey, Jacob," Paul protested. "Slow down. You have communion once a year?"

"Twice."

"That's the body and blood of Christ. The Lord's Supper."

Jacob nodded.

"Now what's the washing part?"

"Foot washing."

Paul screwed up his face. "Actually washing feet?"

"Fur shure."

"I don't get that."

"Foot washing is considered a sign of true humility," Jacob explained, exhaling a plume of smoke. "In the Gospel of John, Jesus stooped to wash the feet of his disciples and said that if *he* washed *their* feet, then they should wash one another's feet. It's done twice a year, at each communion."

"And you use tubs?"

Jacob nodded. "Small tubs and water and towels."

"Now what was the last thing?"

"Shunning and excommunication."

"That it should be stricter?"

"Exactly. Not just withholding communion. Ammann said they should avoid having anything to do with backsliders and not even eat with them. You see, each Amish church has rules for Christian living, and those who break that *Addning* threaten the Amish community. If someone is excommunicated, then that person must be avoided, shunned. It's called the *Meiding*."

"Why would someone be excommunicated?"

"For leaving, breaking your vow in baptism. Buying an automobile. Preaching false doctrine."

"A wife would have to shun her husband?"

"Fur shure. Spiritual love is much more important than earthly love."

"Now, Jacob, you're *not* shunned because you left before you were baptized, but if you *had been* baptized and left, then you would be shunned."

"That's right. That's a serious offense."

"There are different levels of offense?"

"Fur shure. It's minor to be caught drinking or breaking the dress code. Fur something like that, a preacher would talk to that person, and he could make an apology at church, and that would be that. The Amish don't want to lose church members, so they're patient on most things. But fur something serious, like buying a car or leaving the church, excommunication and shunning is automatic. To be accepted back, that person has to go make a big confession, kneel before the entire church, and repent."

"It sounds like Knox Academy, where I went to school," Paul said thoughtfully. "Protecting a small community. There were certain minor rules that if you broke, you had some type of mild punishment. But if you broke a major rule, then you could be expelled, kicked out. It's similar to that, in a way."

Jacob agreed but then requested, "No more about the Amish. My head is swimming."

"Okay, okay. All I wanted to do was say hello and return that umbrella, not have a deep conversation about Amish culture. But, Jacob, you explain things very well, very clearly. You know quite a bit."

Jacob shook his head. "Any Amishman could tell yew the same thing."

"So clearly the history of Menno Simons and Jacob Ammann? The Supreme Court decision?"

"It's just history."

Paul shook his head. "You talk like a teacher, the way you explain something. Or even a preacher."

Jacob laughed at that. "A good preacher *I* would be."

For a critical moment, Paul studied Jacob's face and then glanced down at his wristwatch. "Well, I've gotta get going. I have to be back at school tonight, and I need to study this afternoon. I have finals this week."

"Finals?"

"Final exams. Major tests on everything I learned this semester. But I'll be back next weekend."

After Paul left, Jacob realized he had forgotten to go downstairs to get Paul's umbrella from Mr. Teeter.

CHAPTER 19

Careful not to scrape the bottom of his police cruiser, Sergeant Stuter turned slowly out of the Hostetler farm lane onto Stone Mountain Road. As soon as Agent Tate clicked off his tape recorder, Sergeant Stuter suggested that they stop for a quick supper. "I could at least use a cup of coffee, and Irma doesn't expect us till 7:30 or so."

The Fairville Restaurant was part diner and part pool hall. Green and pink neon signs blazed in the wide windows, advertising Old Milwaukee and Genesee Beer. In one corner a jukebox, all chrome and flash, slapped a twangy Western tune around the dark-paneled rooms and the cracked linoleum floors. A sign stapled over one door stated PENN STATE PROUD. Two long-haired men, both in red plaid shirts, were playing pool at one of four pool tables.

Sergeant Stuter and Agent Tate squeezed into one of the narrow booths along one wall, pulled out the menus wedged between the ketchup bottle and napkin holder, and studied them.

"Hey, Sarge."

"Hi, Meggy, how're you?"

"Just dandy, dandy. Busy on the barn fires?"

"I'm always busy. You know that."

"Any new developments?"

"Only what you read in the papers."

"Yeah, right."

Both men ordered cheeseburgers, chili, and black coffee. After the waitress left, Sergeant Stuter asked, "So you think Esle is hiding something?"

"Absolutely. Wouldn't look at either one of us. Head down. Didn't want to answer any of the questions. Did not even pay attention to any of the questions, as if we weren't there."

"He's upset."

"About Jacob?"

"Jacob. The fires. Eli. He was quite close to the boy. He had to help prepare his body for the viewing. I know Esle, and that must have been very hard on him. Don't forget that Jacob is his twin brother. If Jacob *did* start those fires, then he would be responsible for little Eli's death."

Agent Tate nodded and sipped his coffee. "But he knows something he doesn't want anyone else to know or thinks something he doesn't want anyone else to know."

"Perhaps. But my sense is that he's just plain upset and frightened. Esle's a good boy."

"I'm not saying he's *not* a good boy, merely that he knows something."

Meggy served the food. Sergeant Stuter peppered his chili. Agent Tate poured ketchup on his cheeseburger. For a few minutes, the two men quietly ate their suppers.

Finally, wiping his mouth with a napkin, Agent Tate suggested, "How would you like to have that Abraham as a father or a grandfather?"

Sergeant Stuter shrugged. "I'd be honored. I'd consider myself lucky. He's an extremely effective bishop here in the valley."

"He appears stern. Almost unyielding."

"On certain matters he *is* stern and he *is* unyielding. But in addition to that, he has a huge heart."

"Intimidating."

"That he is."

"I mean, he hardly spoke. His mere *presence* was intimidating. I had the same feeling with him that I had when I met Archbishop Seamus Rooney in Boston for the first time—the presence of a highly religious person."

Sergeant Stuter agreed entirely.

"And how long has Abraham been a bishop?"

"Oh-h, about twenty-five or thirty years, I guess."

"And that's his job?"

Sergeant Stuter laughed. "No, not at all. He runs that small harness shop behind the barn now, but he was a dairy farmer his entire life until Isaac D. took over the farm, and that was only a few years ago. If you're a bishop or a preacher, it's just additional duties and responsibilities."

"What does an Amish bishop do exactly?"

As Agent Tate sipped his coffee, Sergeant Stuter explained that as a bishop, Abraham C. is considered the authoritative leader of his church district. Similar to any priest or minister in other religions, he carries out the observance of communion and baptism and officiates at marriages and funerals. After the ministers and the congregation process an issue, he announces disciplinary action against those who violate the *Ordnung*. When necessary, he is responsible for excommunicating members of the church as well as restoring the church's blessing on those who confess their sins and repent. A bishop also preaches on church Sundays, in turn with the preachers, and at special times. And he must find opportunities to visit from family to family and give general spiritual support and counsel.

"That sounds like a full-time job from *my* perspective," Agent Tate remarked.

"Most Amishmen don't care for such responsibility."

"And is it for life?"

"For life. The position is willed by God for life, yes."

"And what did Jacob think about his grandfather?"

Sergeant Stuter considered this question for a meditative moment. "Jacob, oddly enough, of *all* his family, is most *like* his grandfather."

CHAPTER 20

After that first eventful weekend, Jacob settled into the *englisch* way of life with relative ease. Day chased day with endless and unremitting activity so he didn't have time to brood over lingering doubts about leaving the Amish. On Monday, Mark drove him in his beat-up, fender-rusted car to the Imperial Chicken Plant in Plainsville to meet his boss.

Al Plutus, the general manager and day supervisor, constantly clucked his tongue and raced around the floor, checking work progress, shouting orders, calculating profits, and examining the plastic-wrapped chicken parts. After a few pertinent questions, he hired Jacob to start work on Tuesday morning on the day shift, 8:00 a.m. to 4:00 p.m., at $4.25 an hour. Mark, who worked the night shift, said it was too bad he was hired for the day shift because they could have driven to work together and shared the cost of gas. Jacob shrugged.

He took a commuter bus back to Lewistown, watching the mountainous landscape roll past, glittering with new green. Jacob marveled that within such a few days he actually had a job. His face was creased with concentration while mentally adding and multiplying: if he worked forty hours a week, he would make $170, which would be $680 a month. Then, subtracting the $175 he paid for rent and $14 for cable, that left him $491—a good deal of money to him. He imagined movies he could see, pizzas he could eat, beer he could drink. Almost half a thousand dollars to spend each month seemed perfectly fine! Maybe he would even be able to repay some of the $200 his mother had loaned him, money set aside for Esle's new shotgun.

Then he let money thoughts drop from his mind, the details anyway, for the general satisfaction that he would indeed have enough income to take care of himself. Jacob stretched his legs out in the aisle. He felt a comforting sensation of independence, prosperity, and confidence. The bus bumped into downtown Lewistown and dropped him off. He checked his wristwatch to see how long the ride had been.

Tuesday morning Jacob woke, dressed, packed a simple lunch in his aluminum lunch pail, and caught the commuter bus for his first day on the job. While waiting at the bus stop, just up the street from his apartment building, he bought *The Sentinel* at a newspaper stand.

He climbed on the bus and dropped his coins into the fare box. The bus jerked to a stop two more times, gathering more people before turning onto the highway for the twenty-minute drive. With curiosity and camaraderie, he observed his fellow commuters, each one self-contained and quiet, reading a newspaper, looking out the window, or listening to music with a headset. The landscape shimmered in a cool green light. The crowded smells of cologne and diesel fuel pleased him. The rhythm of the bus lulled him into contentment. In the newspaper he read with interest about Bill Clinton, who was leading in the race for the Democratic Presidential nomination, and President George Bush, who was touring the aftermath of the Los Angeles riots.

From time to time, the fact that he was not Amish seized him—a rush of freedom, choice, and limitless possibilities. Not a straw hat but a KOOL baseball cap, not brown broadfall pants but jeans, not *Die Botschaft* but *The Sentinel*. He turned the page and scrutinized the merchandise on sale in Kmart: alarm clocks, radios, electric razors, stereo systems. Now he realized that he could buy these items, anything he wanted. His face flushed with sudden happiness.

He had done what he had only thought of doing for the past year: he had left the Amish. He had acted. He thought, then he acted. There was something momentous in aligning action with thought, something galvanizing and powerful. As the bus turned the corner into the chicken plant's parking lot, he gazed at the huge square building with the fatalistic impression that now he could not turn back.

The wet warmth of May evolved into the crisp heat of June. Five weeks slipped along in Jacob's life as swiftly as the water of the

Kishacoquillas Creek glided over the smooth white stones in its bed. His new *englisch* life quickly assumed a pattern. He worked, he partied, he watched TV, he studied his driving manual, he bedded Jessica. When Jessica found out that Jacob was from the Amish, that only seemed to intensify her passion. Her tantalizing eyes glistened with corruption.

The Friday he received his first paycheck, Jacob was startled at how much the federal, state, and city taxes reduced the amount, but he still clutched it greedily. After work he opened a checking account at a bank downtown, a rather confusing experience. He scarcely made it to the bank before it closed and the bank clerk, impatient to leave, hurriedly explained everything to him. That night he treated Jimmy, Lil, and Jessica to pizza. How good it felt to have his own checking account and his own money! No longer did he have to turn over every check to his father.

One Saturday night, Danny and Amy, his girlfriend, stopped by to party. Although Danny didn't smoke pot, he drank beer after beer. Jacob, who could drink quite a bit himself, was flabbergasted at how much Danny drank. At one reeling point in the evening, Jimmy made a cutting remark about the Amish. Danny snapped back with a comment that shut Jimmy up for the rest of the night. Jacob didn't catch what Danny had said.

Jacob saw Paul only once, by chance one Sunday morning at Dunkin' Donuts. Paul had moved back to town after finishing his finals, but he was busy, too busy, working in his father's law office. He did promise to stop by to visit as soon as he could. When he asked Jacob if he had finished reading *Moby-Dick*, Jacob had to admit that he wasn't reading much more than the newspaper. Too many good programs on TV.

One Saturday night, Gary Schippe drove to Basil Street with Shem, Jonas, and Gideon for a night on the town. Proudly, Jacob showed his friends his room and the *Pennsylvania Driver's Manual*.

Then, one Friday night in June, Jacob received a telephone call he would never forget; it would alter his *englisch* life irrevocably. As usual, he rode the commuter bus back into town when he finished work. He did not stop at McDonald's to eat supper because he would be having pizza with Jessica later that night. His room was stifling hot, so he turned on a fan and opened both windows wide. He showered and sat down with a beer to watch *Star Trek* on channel 43.

When he first saw the program, he laughed at the alien outfits, yet thought uneasily that the Amish, too, dressed in strange attire. Perhaps that's how some *Englischer* perceive the Amish in the fields and in the stores and at the Wednesday auction. Then he remembered his first impression of the ushers at the movie theater in their white shirts and black bow ties. He considered the uniforms in McDonald's restaurant. Jacob noticed that Jimmy dressed the same way almost all the time: sneakers, jeans, and a T-shirt. The *Englischer* seem to have their own dress code, in a looser kind of way than the Amish, but a dress code nonetheless.

Jacob had barely plopped down to watch *Star Trek* when the shrill ring of the telephone sounded in the hall. He jumped up and dashed to answer it.

"Hello?"

"*Ya*, is Jacob Hostetler there?"

Jacob jerked the receiver from his ear and stared at it as if he had just seen a copperhead. There was no mistaking the firm timbre of his grandfather's voice, even though he had never heard it on a telephone before. Fangs sank into his stomach.

"*Ya*," Jacob replied, softly.

"Jacob?" Abraham C. shouted. "Is that yew?"

"*Ya, Grossdaadi*."

The dreaded telephone call had finally happened. Ever since Jacob left, he had been anticipating this call; he was merely surprised that his grandfather had not called earlier. There was a moment's silence, and he could sense the gathering power of his grandfather at the other end of the line. A dish clattered in the background, and he knew his grandfather must be calling from Irma's farmhouse, where his family usually went to make calls.

Speaking Pennsylvania German, Abraham C. began: "You know you still have a family, Jacob, a home." His voice was firm but compassionate, a tonal balance of emotional and rational appeal, that of a grandfather and a bishop. He clearly knew how intelligent his grandson was, how insightful his mind, how vivid his imagination, how retentive his memory. He had hoped, with God's blessing, that Jacob would become, in due time, a preacher, so he could devote that sharp mind to the Bible, to the church, and to the Amish. "And your family misses you." Slowly and distinctly: "Very much."

Jacob listened to his words intently. In his consciousness, his grandfather loomed almost as an abstract figure, that huge, intimidating presence of faith. He had always toyed with the idea that his grandfather's faith had bent his figure with its weight, that no man could bear such a burden. That set face, surrounded by that white hair and that silver beard, reflected the burning presence of God.

"*Ya,* I know," Jacob answered quietly. "I miss everyone, too."

Until he heard his grandfather's voice, he had not realized how much he *did* miss his family—his twin brother's burly figure, his mother's tender glances, his father's sly humor, his little brother's face. At his grandfather's first word, it seemed as though his family had risen before his eyes again. Just speaking Pennsylvania German made him yearn for the family.

"And you know you can come back," Abraham C. said decisively. "Our arms are open."

"*Ya.*"

There was another pause. He heard, suddenly, a bark and a shush, and knew for sure that his grandfather was at Irma's. Briefly Jacob smiled, picturing Irma's bold blue eyes, watching and listening without appearing to do so as she busied herself at the sink.

"Our arms are open," Abraham C. repeated. "You have strayed, but not far, and you can just come back to the right path. You know that."

"*Ya,* I know," Jacob repeated, knowing that his grandfather meant he was not shunned since he had not been baptized.

"Remember," Abraham C. intoned, "it's your destiny to be Amish. You, more than any other I know. The closer a thing approaches perfection, its pleasure or its pain will be more keen. Your struggle, Jacob, is the Amish struggle."

Jacob's face slowly tightened and his dark blue eyes hardened at the words. "*Nay, Grossdaadi,* my struggle is *my* struggle."

"You must look beyond the immediate," his grandfather counseled. He had planned this conversation with his grandson. The first voice Jacob heard from the Amish would not be angry or condemnatory, but patient and forgiving. He wanted his grandson back home. He knew he had to engage his intellect. His grandson would not respond to anger or to guilt but to reason. That was his manner, his nature, his heart.

Abraham C. repeated, "You must look beyond the immediate."

"But first I must see what is before me," Jacob challenged.

"The smoke and the shadows," his grandfather retorted, as though speaking from the top of a mountain. "You must look past the smoke and the shadows."

Jacob turned the words over in his mind and then, to change the conversation, asked, "How is everyone?"

"They are the same."

Jacob sighed. "Did Daniel finish making that fishing pole?"

"He did."

Jacob and his grandfather discussed various matters about the farm and the family. Jacob then paused. "Is Esle very upset with me?"

"He does not discuss it," his grandfather replied. "Now I must go. God bless you, Jacob." He abruptly banged down the telephone because he was not accustomed to using it. The line disconnected and a hum replaced his voice.

Jacob sank heavily into his lopsided easy chair, staring impassively at the flickering *Star Trek* images on TV as the conversation was spinning in his mind. *Your destiny to be Amish. Look past the smoke and the shadows. The closer a thing approaches perfection, its pleasure or its pain will be more keen.* How he wished that his grandfather had simply scolded him, shouted, condemned! But he knew his grandfather well and his methods even better, employing tactics or strategies to fit the person. Someone responds to simple scolding, another does not. One person listens to reason, another reacts to family emotion. His grandfather was a master of mediation.

That's why his sermons were so effective, because he appealed to many levels with his many words. For that, Jacob had to admire and respect his grandfather. He was indeed an excellent bishop. But he knew, too, that such praise was not appropriate for the Amish, because it smacked of pride. Anything that hinted of pride was viewed with disfavor; after all, pride was the reason Satan plummeted from heaven and fell so heavily and so far.

Yet the words of Abraham C. kept spinning and swirling through Jacob's mind. He knew now, all too strongly, why he had dreaded the first contact with his family. *Look past the smoke and the shadows. Look beyond the immediate. Your struggle is the Amish struggle.*

CHAPTER 21

"Woof, woof, woof."

When Sergeant Stuter parked his car in the circular drive of the Valley View Farm, Kirby was barking and trotting back and forth in front of a former milk house. It was built in 1909 but converted in 1979 into an all-purpose shed, used to store a riding lawn mower, shovels and hoes, garden supplies, and other tools for the yard. Next to that stood an unused dairy barn with a gambrel roof, now merely an architectural splendor, set against the edge of the dark forest high on the slope of Stone Mountain, and often photographed by passing tourists. On a utility pole, a floodlight lit the drive and the side yard.

"Woof, woof, woof."

"Kirby, shush, shush now," Irma shouted as she banged through the door in the breezeway, wiping her hands on a dishcloth.

"Kirby, stop that," Sergeant Stuter said to the dog. "You know me."

Kirby stopped barking. Sergeant Stuter patted his bushy black-and-white head.

"How old is he now, Irma?"

"Going on fourteen years."

Agent Tate turned to admire the evening view of the valley from the drive. "What a beautiful sight from up here."

Sergeant Stuter introduced Irma Keiser to Agent Tate, and they went inside the farmhouse, Irma leading the way and banging once again through the door into the breezeway. They passed through her kitchen, cluttered with pans and plates and pots and spicy smells.

In the living room, Irma commanded, "Now you two sit down. I just have to add the celery to my soup, and I'll be right with you. Do you want some coffee?"

"I'll have some, thanks," Agent Tate responded.

Sergeant Stuter declined. "You don't know what the Amish say about Irma's coffee."

"Oo-ooo, now, Henry."

He grinned. "The Keiser coffee will put a beard on your chin."

She reprimanded him with a sharp look. "Now, it's not *that* strong. Would you like cream or sugar?"

"Black, thank you."

She spun around and whirled into the kitchen.

Sergeant Stuter said in a loud voice, "Whatever you're cooking sure smells good."

"An old family recipe for chicken soup," she called back. In the flick of a moment, she reappeared in the living room with a mug of coffee. "I have to cater a retirement lunch Wednesday afternoon for Cal Maxwell at the IGA."

"Cal's retiring?"

"After forty-seven years, I'd retire too."

"I thought *you* retired from the catering business."

"We-ell," she sighed, sinking into a wing chair, "I should have told Betty no, but you know how it is."

Sergeant Stuter shifted in his seat to shift the conversation. "Now, Irma, would you mind telling us about Saturday night?"

"You mean what I saw. The car?"

"Correct."

"We-ell." Irma settled back in the wing chair, her bold blue eyes bright and animated. "I was up late that night, polishing flatware and washing plates to get ready for this retirement lunch. My sister called earlier, and we talked and talked, you know how she is, so I completely forgot about taking Kirby for a walk that afternoon. When he started moping around with his head down, I gave in and decided I would take him for a quick walk just to the stop sign and back."

"Which stop sign?" Agent Tate asked.

"The one down here at the T-section, at Reigle Creek Road."

Agent Tate nodded and sipped his coffee.

"It wasn't too cold. In fact, it was prit-ty mild for a December night. Anyway, off we go. A little past eleven. All the way to the stop sign. Not a soul in sight. Not a car on the road." She leaned forward.

"But on the way back, headlights flashed behind me. And you know how I do, Henry. I called for Kirby to get to the side of the road, to stay on the side until the car drove by. Well, strangely, the car never *did* drive by—not at first. I turned around, wondering if I'd seen headlights at all, and that's when I could just make out a car parked on the other side of the stop sign. Teenagers, I figured, and continued on my way. Then, just as I turned to walk up the drive, this black car comes roaring, I mean *roaring,* past me. I prit-ty near thought the tailwind was going to pull me down."

"Is this the car?" Agent Tate removed a black-and-white photograph from an envelope and handed it to her. "Or was it a car *like* that?"

Irma studied the photograph a moment. "Sure looks like it."

"Now, what time did this car drive past you?"

"Oo-ooo, must have been around eleven thirty or so. It takes about ten minutes to the sign and ten minutes back."

"Could you see anyone in the car?"

Irma pursed her lips and shook her head. "Noo-oo. Drove by too fast."

Agent Tate, disappointed, slumped back in his chair.

"But I did see *this.*" She pulled a piece of paper from her apron pocket and handed it to Agent Tate.

"A grocery list?"

"No no, the other side."

Agent Tate read numbers scratched in pencil. "Is this the license plate?"

"I always memorize the plates of cars that drive too fast to turn them in to Nat Carrie. He's the town cop."

Agent Tate handed the grocery list to Sergeant Stuter. It showed GFJ 107, the letters and numbers on Jacob Hostetler's license plate.

CHAPTER 22

Standing in the middle of the hay wagon Saturday afternoon, Esle thrust a three-pronged pitchfork into a pile of loose hay, pulled off his straw hat, and ran his thick fingers through his brick-red hair. His shirt sleeves were rolled to his elbows. Sweat dotted his face. The day was dusty, dry, drowsy, the temperature humming over eight-five degrees. His hairy forearms and rust-colored beard were spattered with hayseed. He ran his hands along his forearms, rubbing out the clinging bits of chaff, then twisted his wrists to examine his tight arm muscles. Work in the open fields invigorated his spirit, and once again he felt that summer strength creep into his arms and back and shoulders.

Sam, frowning and red-faced, knelt on one knee to adjust the breeching straps on one of the draft horses. Seth, handsome and tanned, sat on a pile of hay at the front of the hay wagon, holding the reins and shouting advice that was not heeded.

In the front field, under a clear sky, the three boys were haying to bring in the mixed clover and timothy hay. The first cutting of alfalfa had been in early June, and two weeks later, like clockwork, the mixed clover and timothy hay were ready to be cut. All month the weather had been a blessing of good rain and good sunshine.

Esle turned to look at the opposite field, a wide ribbon of bright copper that ran alongside the road. The wheat, too, would soon have to be cut and shocked. How the vibrant colors of the landscape affected him! He shifted his eyes to the daisies and chicory blossoms sprinkled along the shoulders of the road, dizzy points of colors, stunning whites, brilliant blues. Esle turned back to the front field and let his eyes drift over the few remaining windrows, long golden lines of dried hay, and estimated that this one last load of hay should finish it.

So far this afternoon, they already had hauled nine hayloads. The boys started right after dinner, at noon, and it was now close to three thirty. They would have to hurry to finish before supper at four thirty because he didn't want to go back to the fields or to the hayloft after the evening milking. He was hoping to hunt that night for possum or raccoon. Since there was no church tomorrow, he could hunt on Saturday night and then visit Judith as well.

Not since he killed that spring gobbler had he gone hunting. The spring plowing and planting kept him busy, and the two-hundred-dollar incident with Jacob had soured his attitude, just like good milk left out in the sun. His thoughts boiled with spite. That money helped Jacob run away and set up a place in the city. Already seven weeks had gone by, but Jacob had still not sent a card or a letter; he had not in any way communicated with his family. Only their grandfather had talked to him so far, and even then *he* had to make the first call. Esle knew such thoughts were ungenerous and unkind and certainly not worthy of him, especially since he had been attending instruction classes for baptism, but he couldn't help the brief, bitter indulgence.

"*Gut, gut*, come on now," Esle shouted at Sam, stamping his foot. "I want to finish this before supper."

"*Ya, ya, ya*," Sam called as he yanked once more on the straps and slapped the side of the draft horse in a friendly manner. He jumped up on the hay wagon.

"O-kay?" Seth asked in English.

"*Ya, ya*, o-kay," Sam called back, grabbing his pitchfork.

Seth clucked his tongue and shook the reins, and the three draft horses plodded forward. The hay wagon lurched slightly as Esle put the hay loader in gear. It was a ground-driven apparatus as wide as the wagonbed and attached at its rear, jolting along behind at a forty-five-degree-tilt toward the wagon. From a distance, the hay loader resembled a bulky creature attacking and chewing the wagon.

As Seth guided the horses over a windrow, the tines of a rotating cylinder at ground level caught and whipped the hay onto the incline. Other moving arms and prongs dragged the hay as high as a full load would be, then dumped it on the wagon bed. As the hay dropped, Sam forked it to the front of the wagon, where Else spread it carefully and evenly in layers to keep the wagon balanced, so it wouldn't tip over. Then Sam stacked hay in the back, too. Sweat ran down their brows.

"Phew!" Sam exclaimed, spreading the hay. "It's so *hot*."

"At least it's dry."

"Sometimes," Sam ventured, dark circles of sweat staining his shirt under each armpit, "I wish I could just take off my shirt when it is so hot, I do." All three boys were wearing the traditional white shirts, brown pants, work shoes, and straw hats.

Esle spat off the side of the wagon. "Soon you'll start sounding like Jacob. It's not our way."

Sam looked at him, grunted some response, and continued to spread the hay. "Don't you miss him?"

Esle hesitated. "It's not my duty to miss Jacob."

"Oo-ooo, he *is* your twin brother," Sam said emphatically. "I miss him. I miss seeing him in the corner reading one of his library books. I even miss his complaining. Just imagine how he'd be groaning right now about the heat and the dust and the hayseed. But he always did the work, you have to say that, no matter *how* much he whined and moaned, he always did the work. I really do miss him!"

"I wonder how much he misses *us*." Esle commented coldly. "He can't miss us that much, can he? He hasn't written a letter or sent word with anyone. If *Grossdaadi* hadn't called him, we still wouldn't know what was going on."

Sam nodded sadly at this observation.

"Esle!" a young voice yelled from the corner of the field. "Sam! Seth!"

They turned. With a hand clapped on his straw hat, Eli Yoder was rushing barefoot toward the hay wagon. He had long strong legs and unusually big feet for his age, and he fairly stumbled as he ran. His pant legs were well above his ankles; he was growing out of his clothes. His corn-blond hair was almost white from the sun, and his skin a reddish-brown. He hopped up on the wagon, breathless, and scrambled up the mound of hay.

"Well, well, Eli," Esle greeted him, spreading hay to the side. "*Wie geht's?*"

"She . . . she had . . . it," he gasped, his blue eyes wide with excitement, "yesterday. . . . She done . . . had it after . . . supper."

"Had what?" Sam asked.

Seth turned around. "What's that?"

"King!"

"King?" Esle echoed.

"Peggy . . . had a . . . had a . . . colt after supper, and it's . . . it's *my* colt, and I named . . . named him King."

"Oooo!" Esle responded, understanding now.

Seth pulled the reins and shouted "Haw" to turn the horses to the left. Eli was gulping water from a plastic jug.

"And you said the colt was Becky's?" Esle asked with a mischievous smile. Becky was Eli's eight-year old sister.

Eli spat out a mouthful of water and shouted, "*NAY*!" and then explained in his usual rapid-fire speech. "*Daadi* and *Mamm* said *I* was to take care of him and train him. His name is King. I named him. He's a chestnut-brown colt with a white diamond on his face."

With a sudden motion, Eli wiped his face with a handkerchief he had stuffed in the pocket of his broadfall pants. His movements were so quick and jerky, it seemed as if he had pulled the handkerchief out of the air like a magician.

"Here, Sam, let me do some spreading," Eli demanded, stuffing the handkerchief back in his pants. "I was spreading hay yesterday with Joseph and Enos, I was."

Sam glanced at Esle, who nodded okay. Eli gripped the pitchfork dramatically and started to spread the tumbling hay. Sam clambered up to the front of the wagon to watch, wiping his own face now with a rag.

"Phew!" Eli exclaimed almost immediately. "It is so *hot*."

Esle and Sam laughed. Eli stared at them a moment and then laughed, too, though he was not sure why. As Esle spread the hay and watched Eli, he thought how energetic that ten-year-old was—always willing to help, to learn, to listen. Sometimes, though, he was just a tad too exuberant and simply got underfoot. Other times he would start a chore with excessive enthusiasm only to leave it half-finished as he pursued some other activity that captured his attention. And he seemed to be everywhere at once, at the Hostetlers, at the Yoders, at the Speichers, at the Fosters, at Irma's—always helping out, doing some chore, asking questions. Esle wondered just how much help he was on his *own* farm. Nonetheless, he welcomed those wide bright eyes and enjoyed that rapid-fire speech. Eli talked as though he had to get the words out quickly so he wouldn't forget what he was saying.

"A little more to this side, Eli," Sam instructed.

Dutifully Eli spread more hay to that side with a tight-lipped smile on his face.

After the wagon was loaded, Esle jumped down to unfasten the hay loader, which was abandoned at the edge of the field, a forlorn metal hulk. The draft horses, their coats dark with sweat, lumbered down the farm lane as Eli chattered nonstop about the newborn colt. The sun flattened into a pale white disk. The leaves of the black walnut trees, silver with dust, did not stir at all. Flies droned in loopy, clumsy circles. The afternoon had settled into heat and silence and stillness.

In the farmyard, Daniel and Hannah stood on the front porch. Eli waved to them and shouted, "I have a new colt! His name is King!" Daniel just blinked his eyes as he clutched a white puppy in his arms.

Seth pulled back sharply on the reins and called, "Whoa." The hay wagon jerked to a stop near the barn, before the slight rise of the barn bank leading to the threshing floor.

"Why are we stopping here?" Eli wondered.

"To let the horses rest a bit before they haul us up the hill," Esle explained as he watched the heaving sides of the horses. "They've been working hard all day."

Rebekah, barefoot, her angular face flushed with heat, stepped onto the front porch and called, "four thirty still?"

"*Ya*," Esle called back, pulling out his chrome-plated pocket watch. They could easily unload this hay before supper.

Rebekah patted Daniel on the head and, noticing Eli, called out again, "Eli, are you staying for supper?"

Esle asked him, "Do you want supper?"

"If it's not any trouble. Dad knew I was coming over, so they won't worry about me."

"*Ya*, he'll stay."

Rebekah nodded, shooed away some flies around her head, and stepped back inside the summer kitchen.

"O-kay," Esle said in English to Seth.

Seth slackened the reins, clucked his tongue, and commanded, "Giddap." The haywagon lurched forward as the horses strained up the incline to the back of the barn. Seth guided the team of horses directly onto the threshing floor.

"Phew-wee, it sure is hot in here," Eli complained loudly. "Must be a hundred degrees or more."

Esle and Sam, remembering their earlier conversation about Jacob's complaints, smiled at each other.

"Can't you smell that?" Esle sniffed. "That clover fills the hayloft with a faint sweet fragrance."

"I can't smell a thing but dust and heat," Sam declared, shaking his head and climbing over the wooden rails into the haymow with his pitchfork. He spread more hay up against the walls. "Just dust and heat and a few old cobwebs."

Seth unhitched the horses and instructed Eli to take two horses down to the stalls and water them. "We'll use Teddy for the hay."

By the time Esle and Seth finished fastening the thick pulley rope to the horse, Eli came bounding back up the incline.

"I'll help with that," Eli announced, pulling on one of the ropes to tighten it.

The horse impatiently stamped his feet.

"Now, are you sure you can drive the horse right?" Esle asked Eli.

"Of course I can," he answered confidently. "I've done it thousands of times."

Seth climbed up on the wagon. Standing near the barn door, Esle fiddled with some knots and pulled on a trigger rope that released a grapple hook from the roof of the barn into the load of loose hay.

"It looks just like a great big old spider dropping down like that," Eli remarked.

As often as Eli had seen a grapple hook, it still fascinated him. It was a farm tool with four metal claws that initially dangled loose but gripped the hay tight when whisked back up to the hay carrier, a wheeled device attached to a metal track running under the roof ridge the entire length of the barn. Seth spread each claw as wide as possible, stamping the hooked ends deep into the hay. As soon as he finished, he moved to the side and nodded.

"Now watch," Eli told Esle, "how it'll grip that hay just like the claw of a hawk." He clucked his tongue and shouted "Giddap!" and the hooves pounded and the ropes creaked and the pulley wrenched the grapple hook upward, clutching a good three hundred pounds of loose hay. The clawed mound of hay was jerked straight off the wagon. The grapple hook slammed up and latched into the hay carrier, which rolled along toward the side of the barn until Esle pulled a trip rope and dropped the hay into the mow. The entire procedure from start to finish required only a few seconds.

Eli turned the horse around and brought him back to the barn door. Esle tugged on the trip rope to bring the grapple hook clattering back with the hay carrier until it was again above the wagon. As the dust settled, Sam spread the hay evenly in the mow, Esle let the claws drop again, and Seth set them to bite into the hay.

After they unloaded the hay, Seth and Eli led the horse back to the water trough and then to his stall. Esle and Sam walked to the farmhouse, where they washed their hands, forearms, faces, and necks with good cold mountain water in the metal sink. Since Rebekah had thumbtacked craft paper over every window to keep out the sunlight, the kitchen was fairly comfortable. The Nebraska Amish were not allowed to have screens of any kind, but the upper sashes were open a few inches to let the air circulate. She had also thumbtacked flypaper to the ceiling in front of the window, a dangling and sticky dark ribbon, now dotted with flies.

After a few minutes, Seth clumped in with barefoot Eli trailing after him. Eli looked straight at Hannah, who was also ten years old, and announced that he had a new colt named King.

"You already told us that," she responded, making a face. "Besides, we have a new puppy."

Eli ignored her remark and stared at the dead flies on the flypaper. "They look just like raisins, don't they?"

Hannah tittered.

Rebekah chuckled. "That Eli does have an imagination, now, doesn't he?"

With a glimmer in his eye, Isaac D. said solemnly, "Let's just hope we don't have raisin bread for supper."

Everyone laughed and sat down at the table. Isaac D. and Esle faced each other at opposite ends of the table. Eli plopped down next to Esle, where Jacob used to sit. Rebekah and the girls set the table with food from the summer kitchen: a chicken potpie, a bowl of string beans, pickled red beets with onions, creamed lettuce, bread and butter, and pitchers of mountain-cold water. Just before Isaac D. bowed his head for grace, Rebekah glanced at Eli, sitting in Jacob's chair, and felt a sudden pinch in her chest. Then she tightly closed her eyes and bowed her head.

As Isaac D. questioned Esle about the hay and the wheat, Rebekah gazed at Eli in an odd way, almost as though time had slipped backward and Jacob was once again a ten-year old boy. She waved a fly from the bread before passing it to Hannah. Jacob once had corn-blond hair like that, she remembered, but then his hair darkened over the years. Could that mean something? Do the heart and the mind darken as well?

Toward the end of supper, Esle turned to Eli. "Do you want to go hunting with me and Seth tonight?"

"*Ya*, I would." His eyes brightened with adventure and then abruptly dimmed. "But I have to ask *Daadi* first."

"When you go home to milk, ask him then. We aren't going till dusk, anyway."

"What are we hunting for?" Eli's eyes darted toward Hannah.

"Possum, raccoon, skunk."

"Peee-yew, no skunk."

Hannah giggled despite herself.

Isaac D. said, "Jonas H. had a cow with milk fever, penned up along the wood line, where he used to go to give her a bottle of that liquid treatment in the veins." He glanced meaningfully around the table and in a low voice continued. "One night while he was up there, he heard a stomping and a screaming and a scratching until finally, scared out of his wits, he threw down the bottle and backed down the lane, for fear of being attacked . . . by a panther."

"A *panther*," Eli sang, stealing a glance at Hannah.

"*Ya*, just like a cat but the size of a calf," Isaac D. explained, "with a long tail and sharp claws."

"Probably just a coon," Esle murmured in disbelief.

"They say panthers are coming back, though," Sam remarked.

Esle grunted. Isaac D. grew quiet and bowed his head. Stillness descended over the table. All the others bowed their heads to return thanks in silent prayer.

Eli dashed home. The Hostetler men clapped their straw hats back on and headed to the barn for the evening milking. Rebekah and the girls cleared the table, washed the dishes, and then joined the men in the barn.

After the chores were done, the family began to settle down for the night. Sam disappeared into the washhouse to take a bath. Hannah and Daniel played a game in the front yard with the white puppy. Sarah, the grandmother, sat rocking on the front porch, watching the children play. Esle and Seth sat on the porch, legs dangling off the edge, and inspected the shotgun. Isaac D. and Abraham C. stood talking near the buggy shed. Rebekah and Emma picked string beans in the vegetable garden.

From across the front field, the sound of rattling wheels cut into their quiet evening. Ezra S. and Lydia drove their buggy into the barnyard with Eli, Becky, and Levi piled in back. Eli hopped out of the back quick as a weasel and dashed over to Esle and Seth. As Ezra S. and Lydia climbed down, Isaac D. and Abraham C. ambled over.

"I hear Eli's hunting panthers tonight," Ezra S. told Isaac D.

Esle laughed. Abraham C. knitted his brow. From the vegetable garden, Rebekah called hello and then whispered to Emma to get some homemade root beer.

"Possum is more like it," Esle declared.

"We-ell, Jonas H. said he saw a panther just the other week," Ezra S. reported seriously.

Isaac D. agreed. "I heard that Wednesday in the sale barn."

"It was probably just a big old raccoon," Esle countered.

"I don't know," Lydia added. "They say panthers are coming back."

"Well, I'll be especially careful tonight," Esle offered in a mock-serious tone of voice.

During this entire exchange, Eli watched with open-mouthed curiosity.

"Maybe Eli shouldn't go," Lydia suggested.

"*Mamm!*" Eli cried.

"Don't worry," Esle reassured her. "I'll keep a close eye on him."

Lydia nodded doubtfully.

Levi and Becky were playing with Daniel and Hannah and the little white puppy. Chairs were set on the front porch, and Emma poured glasses of homemade root beer.

Esle told Ezra S. that he or Seth would walk Eli home afterward. Then the boys waved and marched up the farm lane straight for Stone Mountain. Esle, with a purposeful gait, carried the shotgun. Eli held a flashlight with great self-importance, while Seth had a burlap bag slung over his shoulder and another flashlight in his hand.

The sun had dipped behind the edge of the mountain in streaks of gold and crimson. The quarter moon, bold and strong and silver, emerged in the pale sky as the twilight absorbed the summer heat and failing light. The scent of wild roses and fresh-mown fields wafted over the roads, farm lanes, and footpaths. In the pastures, tiger lilies closed their faces.

Eli clutched the flashlight and stumbled along behind Esle and Seth, looking all around and lagging behind, then skipping to catch up. "We should have daylight for a little while yet, because this week has the longest days in the whole year. The *Almanac* says the days are fifteen hours long!"

"Fifteen hours?" Esle quizzed.

"Mm-hhmm," Eli confirmed, with authority, scrutinizing the colorful sky. "Those streaks look like pheasant feathers."

"And the grapple hook looked like a spider. The flies looked like raisins. Everything looks like something else to you, doesn't it?"

"But those streaks *do* look like feathers, don't they?"

Esle agreed. "And what about the moon? What does the moon look like?"

Eli received this question as a challenge and stopped and stared at the moon. He shook his head, turned around, and skipped to catch up. "I don't know. I don't look at something and think what it looks like. It just comes to me, just pops into my head like a jackrabbit."

Else laughed. "The jackrabbit is good enough."

Eli frowned, though, visibly upset that he couldn't think of something about the moon, and then asked, his voice full of tense eagerness, "Do you think we'll shoot a panther tonight?"

"*Nay,*" Esle replied emphatically. "There are no panthers in the valley."

"But what about Jonas H.?"

"It was probably a coon, like I said, or some other animal—a wounded deer or a dog or something."

"What about a bear?" Eli suggested hopefully.

"Not in the valley. No one has seen a bear for years and years."

"Oh," he responded in a small voice.

There was no mistaking the disappointment in his voice. Eli fell silent until they reached the road. Perhaps I'm being too hard on him,

Esle thought, spoiling the fun of a ten-year-old boy who wants to be in the woods hunting panthers and bears, not possums and raccoons.

A woof-woof-woof disturbed the quiet.

"Kirby," Eli called when he saw the English sheepdog barking at a huge crow perched on a telephone line. "Kir-beee!"

In her usual brisk manner, Irma marched up the road swinging her arms. "Come on, Kirby. If you've seen one crow, you've seen them all."

"Evening, Irma," Esle greeted her.

"*Gut-n-Owed* (good evening), Esle," Irma returned, "Seth, Eli." She slowed down just a bit. "Going for a little coon hunting tonight?"

"Coon, possum, whatever we can get," answered Esle.

"We-ell, try to get a few woodchucks," Irma requested. "One of them got into my garden the other day and ate a whole row of lettuce."

Headlights flashed in the distance. Irma spun around. "Kirby! Kirby, to the side, to the side, boy! Car!" The dog scooted into a field just as a pickup truck thundered by. "Just *look* how fast that truck is going." She squinted and peered down the road. "TW6. That's an easy one to remember."

"You saw the license plate?" Eli asked, surprised.

"That I did! And I'll be calling it in to Corporal Carrie, too." Kirby trotted at her side. "Good luck tonight." She waved and continued her walk along the road.

Esle glanced down at Eli's small face, knotted in frustration. "You know, I wonder if there might be something in the cave."

Eli skipped ahead. "What's that? What cave?"

"I never told you about the Stone Mountain cave?"

"*Nay*," Eli responded, his voice swelling again with adventure. "A real cave like the cave over in Sinking Valley?"

"Just like that one."

"But they say that one goes on for miles and miles and miles."

"No one knows how big *this* cave is, but it's pretty big."

"Can we go in it?"

Esle considered this request. "Well, I guess we can take a look inside."

Eli's eyes flashed with derring-do as he chattered on, completely forgetting about panthers and bears. "How deep *is* it? How dark? Is it reel-ly scary? Is it like the one in *Mandie and the Abandoned Mine*?"

When they reached the pipeline clearing, they climbed through the barbwire fence and scrabbled past bramble bushes. A herd of cows stood in a side pasture and eyed them uneasily. One cow let out a prolonged moo.

"Now, we might see a possum on the way," Esle advised, "so we have to be quiet."

Eli nodded and snapped his mouth shut in a significant way. Twenty minutes later, they reached the flat and stopped to look at the receding landscape. The failing light had whirled into shadows and blurred outlines. The valley was a plate of pale twilight with burning points of lights here and there in farmhouses. The Hostetler farm, almost directly below them, was a miniature scene: the tiny farmhouse, the cornfields sweeping out behind the barn, the wide ribbons of wheat and alfalfa and oats. Well beyond the farm shone the Reigle Creek Pond, a bright irregular shape in the dark fields. At the first faltering of light, the birds had been cheeping and chirping, but now their frantic song began to taper off as they settled for the night.

"Sure is pretty," Eli said. "Look at the pond shining like that. Just like a mirror."

"Have you thought about the moon yet?"

Eli lifted his eyes to the bright quarter moon and whispered, "*Nay*."

"You will, though, something real good."

They stood a while longer, listening to the birdsong and admiring the view. Then Esle plunged into the darkness of the woods. "This way."

After a few minutes, he stopped abruptly and turned, then turned again. He scrambled up a slight slope, gave Seth the shotgun, and asked him for his flashlight. When he turned it on, the beam sliced the darkness. He played the light over some tree trunks and an outcrop of rock. "There it is."

"Where?" Eli was straining his eyes at the trees and rock. He turned on his own flashlight, playing the beam on the outcrop, and stepped closer. "Where?"

Esle trained his flashlight on a dark shadow. "That's it. Right there. Hidden."

"Where?"

A distant animal cry wrenched the darkness.

"What was *that*?" Eli whispered, his beam of light dropping to the ground.

Esle tilted his head and tried to listen to the sound as it faded. "I'm not sure. Too far away. Might have been a screech owl."

"Or a *panther*!" Eli suggested, hardly containing his excitement.

Esle shook his head and turned his attention back to the cave. He stepped closer to the dark shadow, holding the flashlight beam on it, and motioned for Eli.

"Now, follow me," Esle instructed, crouching down, "and stay next to me, okay?"

"Okay."

As Esle crouched to enter the cave, he vividly recalled the afternoon his father had taken him and Jacob to see it the first time—they were eight years old, the ideal age for such an outing. Seth followed directly behind Eli. The moist, chilly air gave them goose bumps. Inside the narrow entrance, the cave enlarged. Esle stood straight.

"Now be careful," Esle warned Eli, "because it's slippery and uneven, right here on this ledge. There's a jagged dip in the rock, about two feet deep. Here's a plank of wood to step on."

Esle walked across the plank, a yard long and a foot wide, and turned to shine the light for Eli as he crossed.

"Look down there!" Esle played the beam of light on a hole, about the size of a window, that seemed to go deep inside the mountain. "That's called a *streamway*"—he said the word in English—"and it goes down and down and down, how far no one knows. Maybe all the way to Irma's farm!"

Eli shone his own beam of light into the streamway, craning his head, staring into its slippery depths. "No one's been down there?"

Esle shrugged his shoulders. "Can't say no one. But you need long ropes and special equipment for going down there, like those hats with flashlights on top of them."

Eli's flashlight went out.

Esle turned his light on him. "What's wrong?

"Don't know." Eli tightened the end of the flashlight and the beam of light reappeared. "Bad connection."

Seth set the shotgun against a rock and dropped the burlap bag. Both Esle and Eli beamed their lights on the plank for him.

"Now, be careful, Seth," Eli said solicitously. "There's a *streamway* right there."

Esle turned and walked a few feet into a chamber the size of a small shed, about ten feet high and ten feet wide. He wheeled the light all about, illuminating smooth limestone draperies. The interior was damp and cool and smelled of darkness and secrets.

Eli stood speechless as he let his beam of light glide along the walls. He ran his fingers over the smooth limestone. "It looks just like a towel." His eyes wandered to a dark passageway, like a closet door. "Where does that go?"

Without a word Esle stepped into it. Seth and Eli followed. The way was narrow, and Esle and Seth had to crouch again before it opened into another high, long, tunnel-like space with a slippery angled edge to it, as though walking in a room with a tilted floor.

"Look up here," Esle directed, shining his light upward on a black spot on the angled pitch.

"What's that?"

"A bat."

Eli gazed at the small, upside-down creature.

"What do bats eat?"

"Insects. Like a bird."

"How can they see in here when it's so dark?"

"They have real good ears, and they screech as they fly and *hear* their way through the cave. Somehow they listen to the sound and follow the echoes."

Eli listened to this explanation with sheer wonder.

Esle pointed his beam of light down the side, showing other streamways that seemed to dip and turn into the very bowels of the mountain. "You wouldn't want to slip down there, because we might never find you again."

"But I wonder what's *down* there?" Eli was extremely curious.

"Well, don't you ever try to find out unless you're with someone," Esle warned firmly. "And I mean with an adult."

"*Ya*, I know."

The tilted room narrowed into another passageway, only three feet high. All three squeezed through. On the other side, however, the passage expanded into an enchanted chamber the size of a haymow, adorned with columns and draperies, stalactites and stalagmites, flowstone and crystal pools.

Eli let out a prolonged "Oo-ooohhhh!" weaving his flashlight all around.

"You don't see something like this in a cornfield." Esle smiled at Eli's delight. This had always been his favorite part of the cave.

Pointing his beam of light at a stalagmite, Eli exclaimed, "Look at that one! It looks like a shock of wheat, doesn't it?"

"Sure does," Esle agreed, his flashlight beam crisscrossing Eli's, and added, "Jacob used to say this cave looked like the inside of someone's mind. He said that the first time we were in here, just about your age."

"The inside of someone's mind," Eli repeated, thinking about that image.

Eli's face, burning with wonder and astonishment, reminded Esle of Jacob. Never would he forget Jacob's comment, even though he was only eight years old when he heard it. The interior of a cave does, in some ways, resemble the interior of a person's mind: the various rooms and chambers, the passageways from one to another, the surprises in each, the rock and limestone formations. The same way you would follow an idea or explore a thought or feeling. With pleasure, Esle watched Eli move about the huge chamber, examining everything.

"Eli," Esle suggested, "turn off your flashlight for a minute."

"Why?"

"Just do it."

Eli turned off his flashlight. Then Esle turned off his. The black was so black it seemed invasive. When Eli put his hand in front of his face, he could not even see his fingers. He could see nothing at all. Esle turned the flashlight back on.

"It was blacker than closing your eyes," Eli whispered, his voice bright with excitement. "Darker than sleep."

"I don't think you'll *ever* be in such darkness again," Esle declared, underscoring the singular experience upon Eli's young mind.

Esle pulled out his pocket watch and said that they had to be going if they wanted to do any hunting at all that night. It was already well past nine. Eli's face registered a slight flash of disappointment, but not much, since the cave was fully satisfying. As far as he was concerned, the three of them could go back to the farm now. The cave, the limestone formations, and the darkness were even *better* than hunting for a panther.

As they made their way back, Esle cautioned Eli, as his father had cautioned him, never to go into the cave without an adult because the streamways could be dangerous. "If you want to explore, explore only with an adult along." Esle had heeded his father's advice and returned only with adults. The cave never seemed to end, no matter how far they went. There always seemed to be another streamway or another crawl space or another passageway that led deeper into the mountain. Some local people claimed that the cave had over ten miles of passages and chambers and streamways.

Back at the entrance, Esle played his light on the plank and crossed over. Then he turned the light for Eli to cross.

"Can I take something from here, a rock or something to remember?" Eli asked.

"Well, just take something from right around here."

Eli shined his light around until he found a smooth white stone. But just as he bent to pick it up, his flashlight went out again. He shook the flashlight and tightened the end, but the light wouldn't come back on.

"Batteries dead?" Esle called, shining his light on him.

"*Nay*, can't be," Eli replied, shaking the flashlight. "The light dims when the batteries go bad."

"Just be careful on the plank."

Esle turned his light on the stone. Eli picked it up and stuffed it in his pocket. As he crossed the plank, he slipped and screamed, but Esle grabbed him. The flashlight tumbled down the streamway. Eli, puffing and panting, sat down.

"I *said* to be careful."

"I . . . I dropped the . . . flashlight." Eli's heart was pounding.

Esle shone the light around the immediate area but couldn't find it. "Must have gone straight down that *streamway*." He held the beam of light on the hole. "Better that than *you*."

Eli stared at the dark hole and then up at Esle with fear alive in his face. "I almost fell down that hole!"

"Now, I didn't say you *almost* fell down that hole," Esle corrected, thinking immediately of Lydia, Eli's mother, and his comment that he would take care of Eli. "I said it was better that the *flashlight* fell down that hole than *you* falling down that hole."

"Did you see that, Seth?" Eli asked as Seth stepped across the plank.

Seth nodded.

"I almost fell down that hole, didn't I?"

Esle sighed.

"Esle grabbed you before anything could happen," Seth placidly assured him. "You have to be careful in a cave."

The woods were dark now. Eli looked straight up past the pine and oak trees at the night sky, embroidered with the pattern of stars. The topmost branches trembled in a light wind. A twig snapped, and Esle shined the beam of light through the tree trunks.

"Let's move down this side a little bit," Esle guided them. "There's a good place where—"

There was a sudden animal cry, similar to the one earlier, only more clear and distinct. Esle listened to the dark night absorb the sound.

"Was *that* an owl?" Eli wondered.

"Sshhh."

"Didn't sound like an owl."

"It must have been an owl," Esle stated unconvincingly.

Eli pressed his lips together as his eyes opened wide with curiosity and fright.

"Well, come on," Esle urged, dismissing the sound, his shoulders hunched in impatience. "I want to get at least one coon tonight."

In front of the wheat field, Seth said he would walk Eli back home. As Seth and Eli tramped down the road, Esle went down the dark farm lane with his shotgun and the empty burlap bag. On a shelf near the front door, Esle felt in the darkness for a box of matches and lit the kerosene lamp. The house was quiet because everyone else was already asleep, except Sam, who had gone out to run around with his buddies. Esle wondered idly whether Sam had a sweetheart.

Esle carried the kerosene lamp to the washhouse, where Sam had left the large galvanized tub next to the kettle stove. There was a bar of soap and a bottle of shampoo still on the floor. He filled the tub with six buckets of cold water, stripped off his clothes, and eased himself into the tub, the water rising up almost to his chest. He closed his eyes and relaxed, relishing the cold water, the end of the work day, and the tautness of his back muscles.

His mind drifted over the day. His thoughts turned to that eerie animal cry, but he could not place the sound and could not believe it might have been a panther or a bobcat. Yet he knew that long ago the mountains were filled with them until highways and trucks and sawmills drove them away. Then his mind turned to Judith, the walk down the dark road to the Yoder farm, Judith, for a couple of hours tonight, Judith.

CHAPTER 23

Sergeant Stuter, stunned by the information Irma had penciled on the back of the grocery list, drove down the long sloping drive back to the road. The tires crunched on the gravel as Agent Tate murmured into his tape recorder. At the bottom of the drive, he clicked it off and said, "That was a piece of good luck."

"An unbelievable piece of luck," Sergeant Stuter agreed, turning onto the road. "Positive identification that places Jacob's car at the crime scene twenty minutes or so before the Yoder barn fire was called in."

Agent Tate nodded and then, shifting his thought, asked, "Irma Keiser is a Mennonite?"

"Correct."

"Aren't the Amish related to the Mennonites?"

"Correct. Amish are part of the Mennonite church family. The Amish broke away from other Mennonites and formed their own church because they wanted stricter church rules." A few seconds later, Sergeant Stuter turned onto a macadamized driveway. "The name *Mennonite* links them with their spiritual leader Menno Simons, a Dutch reformer who broke from the Catholic church to become an Anabaptist. Most Mennonites who are not Amish take full advantage of modern technology. But the two groups have the same basic beliefs."

Sergeant Stuter parked his car in front of a buggy shed converted into a two-car garage. The renovated Amish farmhouse blazed with electricity on the slope of the mountain, somewhat below the forest line. Next to the side entrance, the porch light glowed.

"Are the Fosters Mennonites, too?"

"Oh no, they're Presbyterians and . . . well, they've been married a long time."

"And this woman, Mrs. Foster, called in the first fire?"

"Lizzy was the first one to call in a fire, but the Yoder barn was probably one of the last barns to go up."

Agent Tate turned to look at the valley. From the driveway at the corner of the house, through an opening of trees at the T-intersection, there was a perfect view of the Yoder farm.

"Good eve-ning, good eve-ning, Henry," Lizzy sang from the doorway.

"Hello, Lizzy," Sergeant Stuter called.

"Come in, come in," Lizzy invited, opening the storm door wide. "Do come in."

As Agent Tate wiped his wingtip shoes, he read the welcome mat: One Nice Person and One Mean Person Live Here.

"You'll have to figure that one out, detective," she said, smiling and extending a thin powder-white hand. "I'm Lizzy Foster."

"How do you do, ma'am," Agent Tate replied politely. "Special Agent Michael Tate."

"And this is my husband, Dennis."

Dennis grunted a good evening.

Behind her eyeglasses, Lizzy widened her eyes and lifted an eyebrow to indicate that the answer to the doormat was apparent. She escorted them like a hostess into the living room.

"Well, well, now, let's go in here. It's much more comfortable, and I've prepared *tea*." She emphasized the word *tea* as if that were the sole reason they were there and added, "Lapsang souchong."

Sergeant Stuter and Agent Tate sat on the floral-patterned sofa while Lizzy fussed with the teacups and tea and served them. "Cream or lemon?"

Dennis sank into an easy chair, rubbing a hand through his hair and scratching his ear.

"I heard, ma'am," Agent Tate began, "that you were the first person to call in a fire."

Sergeant Stuter thought, Where is all this ma'am business coming from? He listened with amazement to the conversational tone of Agent Tate's voice to accommodate tea talk and to flatter Lizzy.

"Oh, yes! Look, here's the *Centre Daily Times*," Lizzy replied excitedly, turning to a side table and placing a folded newspaper in front of him. "That's the view of the Yoder farm from our front porch with a quote of mine beneath it."

"I noticed that wonderful view from your driveway."

"It *is* a lovely view of the valley, isn't it? Especially in the spring, with all the wildflowers and new leaves on the trees and the Amish working in the fields. Just breathtaking! And you should see the Yoder apple orchard in May."

"It must be spectacular."

"Oh, it *is,* it *is,*" she agreed and daintily sipped her tea.

"And you were on the front porch the night of the fires?"

"Oh, ye-es, I was. Wasn't that awful, just awful, what happened to our good Amish neighbors? And poor little Eli!" Her eyes glistened.

"That was quite, quite awful," Agent Tate echoed. "That's why Sergeant Stuter and I are trying to piece together that night as best we can to figure out who set those fires."

"Oh yes, yes."

"And were you on your porch that night?"

Her eyes gleamed as she said with noted satisfaction, "I was reading."

"That late?"

"I usually read every night until midnight. I can't fall asleep before midnight."

"And you, Mr. Foster? Were you up, too?"

"Hah!" Lizzy exclaimed.

"No-o," mumbled Dennis. "By then, I was in bed fast asleep."

"He can't stay *awake* past nine, never mind *read.*"

"Now, that's not true, Lizzy," Dennis defended himself. "I usually go to bed around ten."

"But you're nodding off in your chair at nine every night, every single night," she declared and nodded her head once for emphasis.

Agent Tate smiled broadly and shot a quick glance at Sergeant Stuter, who had an I-told-you-so look on his face.

"You were reading on the front porch?" Agent Tate guided her back to the night of the fires. "Not in this nice room?"

"Oh, well, yes, this is nice, but the front porch is a lovely place to read as well. I have a wonderful wing chair out there and a superb reading lamp. It's quite comfortable and warm. We have thermal glass, you know, put in for the winter and had heat put out there too. I grow plants and herbs there all year."

"Humph," Dennis muttered.

Lizzy frowned at him and sipped her tea.

"And that's where you saw the barn fire?"

"Right from the front porch. Usually, you can't see a thing at night with the reading lamp on, but that *fire*." She shook her head. "I could even *hear* it." She shuddered as she described the entire incident, having repeated the story countless times over the past two days with more and more polished detail.

"Was there anything else that night? Did you happen to see a car or anything?"

She lifted her eyebrows, "*I* didn't, but Irma did." She sipped her tea, then added in a whisper of intrigue, "I'm sure she told you *that*."

"Yes, ma'am, she did. But you didn't see a car or hear anything?"

"I didn't see a *car*, but I did see *some*thing unusual. Very unusual, now that I've had a day or two to think about it. Though I doubt it has much to do with the barn fires."

Sergeant Stuter and Agent Tate both pricked up their ears. Agent Tate, against all instinct, even sat up and leaned toward her.

"Well, ma'am, even so, we'd appreciate hearing it."

"Well," Lizzy reported in a hushed tone, "at exactly 10:30 I set my book down. I know it was 10:30 because I glanced at my watch." She held up her thin wrist with the digital wristwatch. "I was reading *The Narrative of Arthur Gordon Pym of Nantucket*, by Edgar Allan Poe, with all those strange incidents on his journey, especially the very odd ending with that mysterious white figure. It's really an *inward* journey, a quest novel. But, anyway, I set the book down to rest my eyes for a moment when I remembered we were having a lunar eclipse this Wednesday, so I decided to take a quick step outside to look at the moon. We have quite a wonderful night sky here in Big Valley. It was a mild night, if you remember, Henry. Not too cold at all for December. Well, the sky was beautiful, and the moon, a half moon, was a lovely white. So I stood there for a while admiring the view when, all of a sudden," she paused for effect, "I saw Esle walking along the road toward the Yoder house."

Dennis harumphed. Agent Tate narrowed his eyes. Sergeant Stuter remarked, "He must have a sweetheart."

"Oh, he does, that he does. Judith Yoder."

"Judith Yoder?" Agent Tate repeated.

"The Yoder's eighteen-year-old daughter. A lovely girl, lovely."

"So he must've been going to see her," Sergeant Stuter stated.

Lizzy shook her head slowly no.

Agent Tate glanced at Sergeant Stuter, not sure where this was going.

"There's nothing unusual about that, Lizzy," Sergeant Stuter observed.

"It is," Lizzy insisted dramatically, "when there's church the next day."

Sergeant Stuter leaned forward. "That's right. Church was to be held yesterday *at* the Yoders."

Lizzy nodded significantly. Agent Tate, puzzled, looked from one to the other.

"The night before a church Sunday, young people can't go out," Sergeant Stuter explained.

"So Esle shouldn't have been out that night?"

"Correct."

"*That's* what's so unusual," Lizzy agreed. "At the time, I didn't give it a thought. Only later on did it occur to me that he shouldn't have been there."

"So he must have been at the Yoders when the fires broke out."

Again Lizzy shook her head slowly no. "We saw him running down the road *back* to the Yoders afterward, isn't that right, Dennis?"

"That's right," Dennis confirmed.

"You saw him running *to* the Yoders the night of the fires," Sergeant Stuter reflected, "*after* you saw him walking over there earlier?"

Lizzy slowly nodded her head yes. "He was walking over to the Yoders at 10:30 and then running over to the Yoders about midnight, isn't that right, Dennis?"

"That's right," Dennis said. "We were standing at the edge of the lawn watching the fire and all the goings-on when Esle ran by."

"At that point, Irma was with us, too," Lizzy added.

"Could it have been someone else?" Agent Tate asked.

Lizzy firmly shook her head no.

"You're *sure* it was Esle?" Sergeant Stuter quizzed her.

"Of course I am, Henry. Even though I'm seventy-seven, I can still *see*. Besides, I'd know Esle's walk anywhere."

Then Agent Tate dropped a simple question. "How do you know he was walking to the Yoders?"

Lizzy hesitated. "Well, I just assumed that's where he was going. There's not much else down that way. If he wasn't going to the Yoders, then what was Esle doing out Saturday night around ten thirty?"

Agent Tate replied, "We'll have to ask Esle that."

CHAPTER 24

One Friday afternoon in July, when the temperature simmered at ninety degrees and the humidity stood at a sopping 98 percent, the air conditioner on the commuter bus shorted out. Jacob undid another button on his blue short-sleeved shirt, flapped the front a moment to cool himself, and then propped his head against the window. With his head jostling against the glass, he gazed listlessly at the passing landscape.

The summer green had reached an intense peak, but thick haze dulled its vibrant color. Horns honked and beeped in the rush-hour traffic as the bus approached city limits. The smells of exhaust fumes roiled in the air. His eyelids drooped and shut. The heat and the smell and the noise burrowed into his head. Did he have any aspirin left in his room? He would have to buy another bottle when he bought another fan. His fan had been smashed to pieces on the sidewalk when Jessica accidentally knocked it out the window.

Jacob sat hollow and exhausted. Now he knew the meaning of TGIF because the factory work proved to be so monotonous. On Friday afternoon he could not *wait* for his shift to end, so he could have two days free from its drudgery. At the planing mill, he used to build sheds or assemble trellises or hammer together picnic tables. At least he *made* things, objects he himself pounded together, things he could see and touch. Afterward, he possessed some sense of accomplishment. But at the chicken factory, all he did all morning and all afternoon was separate chicken parts on conveyor belts—separate and separate, separate, separate and separate—how much more of that could he do?

The smell, too, started to disturb him, not the sweet scent of pine or hemlock, but the dead odor of chicken flesh. And the men he worked with were crude and vulgar and guffawed at off-color jokes he did not think funny. He had endured this for over two months. Is it possible? Had that much time already vanished? All that time, and what had he done? In the morning, he woke, dressed, climbed on the bus to go to work. After work, he stopped at McDonald's. In his room, he studied the driving manual and watched TV. On weekends, he partied and went to the movies and played miniature golf and drank beer and smoked pot and got together with Jessica.

He sat limp, his aluminum lunch pail on his lap with his paycheck inside. No longer did he have to rush to the bank before it closed on payday because he now had a twenty-four-hour banking card, which he could not at first figure out until Jessica patiently explained how to use his secret code and follow the electronic instructions. Jessica. Jessica Smith. He had seen her every weekend. Sometimes during the week. But this weekend, abruptly and for some unclear reason, she had decided to visit her aunt in Harrisburg.

Days and nights were consumed with thoughts of Jessica. Jimmy's little sister. But he didn't know how to classify his feelings for her. Did he dare describe these impassioned thoughts as love? Clearly she was a good-looking girl with that black hair and those tantalizing eyes and that bewitching figure. But she swore too often, partied too much, and laughed too shrill. They never seemed to talk about anything—just ate pizza, listened to music, and went to the movies. He was never sure what she *thought*—about the world, about him, about the Amish, about him having been Amish. Jimmy, of course, boomingly denounced the Amish every chance he could and seemed to take perverse pleasure in partying with Jacob, as if he were proving a point or confirming a theory.

A line of sweat dribbled down Jacob's temple. He wiped it away with his fingers and sat up straight, stiff, adjusting his KOOL baseball cap on his head. Jacob stared past the heads in front of him at the oncoming highway. The heads all seemed to sag and wilt, like overripe wheat buckling under its own weight. Wheat fields. He wondered if tonight he would get another telephone call from his family. After his grandfather had called that one night, two weeks passed before he received another call, again on a Friday night, but that time from his grandfather as well as his grandmother. On the next Friday, he spoke to his father, mother, and Sam, but not to Esle, who was working in the fields. Then the family called again last Friday, and he spoke with his mother, Seth, Emma, Hannah, and Daniel, but again not to Esle, who was working in the barn. The family always called at six thirty, after the evening milking and before the other chores.

Jacob knew Esle must still be upset about the two hundred dollars. He wanted to repay him and intended to repay him but hadn't yet saved that much money. Jacob's original plans to earn enough money to live on and to buy things dissolved as soon as small costs appeared out of nowhere, like mosquitoes. His money went for beer, pizza, McDonald's, movies, clothes, bus fare, food for lunches, and laundry costs. Everything seemed to *cost* something in the *englisch* world. Whenever he bought a tomato or a head of lettuce to make a sandwich for work, he thought about the vegetable garden next to the farmhouse.

He reminded himself that Esle must also be upset that his twin left the Amish. Though he did not consider his brother a thinker, he did recognize that Esle was a deeply religious person who embraced the mystery of God's natural world through labor and wonder. Still, he wished Esle would speak to him. After all, he *is* my twin brother.

In an odd way, Jacob enjoyed talking to his family. The conversations certainly didn't last long, but it was good to hear the familiar voices—the squeaky intensity of little Daniel, the subdued tone of Emma, the laconic hello of Seth. He did miss his family but could not yet go back to visit. They kept asking him to visit, and he kept saying that he would come soon, but he hadn't. He wasn't sure why, except that he had a hunch, a deep and dull and obscure ache, that the time was not yet right for a visit home. Did he fear their reaction to his short haircut and clean-shaven face? Did he have qualms about wearing *englisch* clothes in their presence? Did he cringe at the thought that he would not want to leave? Despite everything he enjoyed in the *englisch* world, he was still startled at how much he missed the farm, the fields, the fragrance of fresh-mown hay, the soft glow of a kerosene lamp.

The commuter bus swerved around a curve and jerked to a stop downtown. Half the riders left the bus and, like automatons, lumbered into the haze of the city. He lifted his eyes to the leaden sky, hoping a sudden storm would crack the heat and drench the buildings and streets and sidewalks with cool rain. Country heat seemed much more tolerable than city heat.

Jacob trudged to the ATM to deposit his check and then trudged downtown to buy a bottle of aspirin and a fan at Mercer's Discount Department Store, only looking forward to the air-conditioning. When he pushed open the glass door, the store whirled with shoppers, pushing into each other, bumping, grabbing. A banner fluttered above the crowd: ONE DAY SUMMER SALE—HALF PRICE. Shopping carts banged together.

He pushed his way past a knot of people and saw Danny Yoder sitting at the deli counter with a friend. Jacob hadn't seen him for a couple of weeks and did not particularly want to see him now. He never felt comfortable with Danny. There was something insincere about him, something deceitful. The few times that he and Jimmy were together, Danny would join right in and make fun of the Amish, except for that night when he had snapped at Jimmy. Jacob wondered how Danny could scoff so easily and eagerly at the Amish, then decided that he didn't think seriously or deeply enough about the issues.

When Jacob saw Danny, his mind envisioned two strange animals, warily circling each other. It was strange, too, how they both acquired different names in the *englisch* world: Daniel became Danny and Jacob became Jake—another face, another image, another facade.

Before Jacob could escape into the crowd of shoppers, Danny noticed him and waved him over. He wore a tight green T-shirt with a pack of cigarettes bulging in the front pocket.

"Hey, Jake, haw's it goin'?"

"A little hot and tired today. The air conditioner broke down on the bus."

"Yew should've been on a roof poundin' nails if yew want hot, let me tell yew," Danny griped in a voice that topped all complaints. "But sit down un have a Coke or somethin'. Do yew know Porter, here?"

Jacob shook his head and plunked down on the stool. "How d'ya do?"

"Not that great," Porter announced, his face pushed out of shape with impatience, "because I should be on my way to State College instead of sitting here in this dump."

"He's waitin' fur a friend."

"He won't be a friend for long, let me tell you. It's already four thirty." He glanced at a gold wristwatch. A star sapphire glimmered on his ring finger.

The waitress ambled over. Jacob decided to have supper while he was there and ordered a turkey sandwich, potato salad, and a root beer.

"Oh, here's the coupon shopper now," Porter announced, his eyes clamped on a curly-haired man shoving his way through the crowd and clutching a plastic shopping bag to his chest. When he reached the counter, Porter tackled him, "Don't you know it's already four thirty?"

"So what?"

"I wanted to be at State College at FIVE."

"So we'll get there at SIX," Jason answered. "Look at all these great tapes I got, only $2.99 each." He plunked the bag down on the counter, opened it, and peered inside with tight-fisted eyes. "Singles only cost $2.99."

"Who cares?" Porter snorted in contempt as he stood up, his spendthrift attitude swelling his chest. "If I like a tape, I don't care what it costs."

"Well, I care what it costs," Jason cried, his chest thrust forward with miserly pride. "I'm not going to spend any more money on tapes than I have to."

"Everyone doesn't spend an eternity searching through newspapers for sales."

"Everyone doesn't drive around in a BMW and toss Daddy's money out the window."

"How do you want to get to State College? On cheap skates?"

With that pun, Porter marched toward the front door, stiff-legged, shoulders hunched up in his white silk shirt.

"Well, see you guys around," Jason said. Clutching the plastic shopping bag to his chest again, he followed Porter to the front of the store.

The waitress slid a plate of turkey sandwich and potato salad in front of Jacob. When he looked at the food, he longed for Amish cooking.

"That cra-azy Porter," Danny remarked. "He's spoiled rotten. His father's some big businessman in town. Gave him a BMW with an awesome stereo system. Un his friend Jason there is as cheap as yew can get. Won't spend a dime if he doesn't have to."

Jacob bit into his sandwich, suddenly weary of Danny's acquaintances.

"Wurk tough?"

"Not tough," Jacob replied carefully. "*Leidig* (disagreeable). Boring. It's not the planing mill, and it's certainly not the farm."

"Nah," Danny snorted, lighting a cigarette, "the chicken plant shure ain't that. It got to be a drag. But yew don't have to stay there forever, y'know." He blew out a long stream of smoke. "Pays the rent, buys the booze. That's what's important."

Jacob chewed his food as he pondered that comment and watched him take another drag on his cigarette. The way Danny smoked annoyed him, but he didn't know why.

"I haven't seen yew around lately," Danny said.

Jacob shrugged his shoulders.

"Haw's Jimmy doin'?"

"The same."

An exaggerated leer distorted his face. "Un haw's Jessica?"

"The same," Jacob replied impassively. "She went to visit an aunt in Harrisburg."

"So-o yew're solo tonight, eh?" He jabbed him in the ribs knowingly. "Yew shure can get a bit more from an *englisch* girl than an Amish girl. Chust another goot reason fur leavin'."

"But don't yew ever miss . . . I mean, don't yew miss *anything*?"

Danny exhaled smoke slowly. "Havin' second thoughts, Jake?"

"I don't know."

"I don't miss the Amish at all," Danny declared firmly. "Not. At. All. Shure, I miss mam un dad, the brothers un sisters. But I *see* them. I go un see them every couple weeks. Have yew been back to visit yet?"

Jacob shook his head. "Not yet. With my haircut and jeans and my grandfather being a bishop and all."

"Ye-ah. Yew'll get over that prit-tee soon. Prit-tee soon it won't make a difference. It's normal to miss your folks. But do I miss gettin' up at five in the morning to milk cows? To drive a buggy in winter un freeze? To *not* watch TV or listen to tunes? No. I don't miss any of that at all. Nothing could get me to go back."

"But what about church?" Jacob asked on impulse.

Danny stared intensely at him before he stubbed out his cigarette.

"Are yew havin' some kind of religious probe-lem?"

"No, not really." Jacob nonchalantly chewed on a bite of potato salad. "I just think about church from time to time. After all, that's the whole point, isn't it?"

"But yew don't have to be Amish to go to church!" Danny argued forcefully as he lit another cigarette. "Look around. Look at the Mennonites or, fur that matter, the Black-car Amish. Not using electricity or driving a car has nothin' to do with religion. Look at haw many Christians there are around yew who are *not* Amish."

Jacob stared at his plate, at the half-eaten sandwich. "I don't know. I just don't know. The peculiar people and all that."

"Ver-ree peculiar."

"It's . . . just that," Jacob stammered, displeased that he stumbled into this conversation in the first place but with a sudden need to talk. "It's just that the Amish way of life is *itself* a form of worship. It's like praying or worshiping all the time. Do yew know what I mean?"

"Milkin' a cow half-asleep at five in the morning shure don't strike me as being a prayer. Un neither does driving a buggy in the dead of winter."

Jacob realized that trying to explore this idea with Danny was futile. After all, Danny left the Amish for a pair of cowboy boots. The two sat silent. The conversation had died, as though the mere mention of the words *church, worship,* and *prayer* had embarrassed them.

"We-ell, I have to get goin'," Danny said, finally. "Big date tonight with my woman. See yew later. Un Jake, have yew tried a Mennonite service?"

Jacob shook his head.

"Maybe yew should check that awt."

"Maybe."

With his long-legged strut and his black cowboy boots, Danny shouldered his way through the shoppers to the front of the department store. Jacob was relieved he had gone. As he finished the last bite of his turkey sandwich, he suddenly thought of his mother barbecuing slabs of beef on a grill. He glanced at his wristwatch, paid for his food, and hustled into the crowd to buy a bottle of aspirin and a fan.

As soon as he unlocked the front door, he heard Jimmy's laugh cannonading down the narrow stairway. At the top of the stairs, Jimmy straddled a chair tilted back against the wall, wearing a black tank top, scratching his beer belly, and chortling on the telephone. He muttered, "Hey, Jake-o," and continued his cackling conversation.

Fumbling with his shopping bag, Jacob pulled out his keys and dropped them twice before he unlocked his door. He left it open so air could circulate and opened both windows as wide as possible. He set the fan on the bureau. The blades sputtered and rapidly revolved, spinning shivers of air into the hot room. He swallowed two aspirin, snapped on the TV, kicked off his sneakers, pulled off his shirt, and flopped into his lopsided easy chair. The conversation with Danny disturbed him, and the sound of Jimmy's hooting laughter in the hall further unsettled him. He pulled off his socks, stretched his toes, and stared abstractedly at the screen. A local TV commentator summed up the evening news, just before *Star Trek* began. His family would call at six thirty—probably.

He lit a cigarette. The ashtray was crammed with cigarette butts. Wrinkled shirts and soiled socks were dumped in a pile on the floor. The garbage pail was stuffed with pop cans and beer cans and McDonald's wrappers. The sheets and pillows were twisted into a lump on the bed. How had his room become so messy? But he could not muster up energy to change it. He flicked an ash on the mound of butts.

Jacob watched *Star Trek* with half interest, irked with the silly costumes and aimless dialogue. He constantly checked his wristwatch as the minute hand ticked toward six thirty. *Still* Jimmy yammered on the telephone. Who in the world could he be talking to? If Jacob's family *did* try to call, the line would be busy. They would wait five or ten minutes, try again, and then return to the farm.

For some reason, Jacob longed to hear his mother's voice. Maybe even Esle would talk to him this time. He stood up, annoyed, and stepped into the hall. Jimmy roared as the minute hand kept ticking. For forty-five minutes he had been talking. Maneuvering past Jimmy's bare feet, Jacob huffed to the bathroom. A moment later, he stopped in front of Jimmy, who was picking at one big toenail.

"Hold on a sec. Hey, Jake-o, buddy, how 'bout getting me a cold brewski from the fridge? And help yourself, too."

"I think I'm getting a call at six thirty."

"Hold on a sec. What's that?"

"A call. I'm supposed to get a call at six thirty."

"Jessica's down in Harrisburg."

"No. From my folks, I think."

"Oh. For sure, I'll be off in a sec. How 'bout grabbin' me a beer?"

Jacob snatched a beer from Jimmy's refrigerator, shoved it into his paw, and stomped back to his room. Standing in the doorway, he watched the minute hand move: 6:30. 6:35. 6:38. 6:39. 6:40. Jimmy at last shouted good-bye and slammed the receiver down.

"Hey, Jake-o," he called, thumping down the hall. "Sure is hot, ain't it? That was an old buddy of mine who moved over to Sinking Valley. I haven't talked to him in over a year. Man-o-man, he's gonna have a phone bill when that one goes through. Hey, no beer?"

"Not right now." Jacob was listening for the telephone to ring.

"So whaddya gonna do with your old lady outta town?"

Jacob shrugged.

"Well, Lil and I're goin' fer pizza at seven if you want some."

"I think I'll pass tonight."

Jimmy snickered. "Feelin' a little blue without the woman?"

"Ye-ah, I guess so."

Just then the telephone rang. Jacob bolted down the hall.

"Hello? Uh-huh, just a minute. Jimmy, it's Nathan."

"What? Again?"

It was past six forty-five. Closing his door, Jacob consoled himself with the thought that they probably hadn't even tried to call. He flopped down on his bed and lit a cigarette. He didn't know what he wanted to do that night. His skin glistened with heat and frustration. The fan twirled the cigarette smoke around the room. Through the windows, he listened to the fragmented sounds of the city: the honking horns, the loud voices, the bursts of music from passing cars, the thudding footsteps. The sounds seemed hard and harsh and sad in comparison to the sounds of the farm he now remembered: the rattle of buggy wheels, the neighing of a horse, the wind rushing and sweeping through a field of wheat.

"Hey, Jacob!"

He thrust his head out the window and saw Paul standing on the sidewalk, dressed in white shorts and a gold polo shirt, holding a knapsack.

"Let's get out of this heat and go swimming," Paul yelled up at him.

"Where?"

"At the Community Park on the river. It's just down—"

"The place across from Dunkin' Donuts?"

"That's it."

As they walked down Loew Avenue, Paul wanted to know if Jacob had finished reading *Moby-Dick*.

"No, not yet," Jacob admitted guiltily. "I haven't been reading as much as I used to. It's odd. I thought I would have more time to read, but I'm actually reading *less* now."

"Too much TV?"

"Maybe."

"How far have you read?"

"Up to the part about the whale being white. The whiteness of the whale. I got dizzy just reading that chapter, never mind thinking about it."

"Dr. Renierg, a professor of mine, says that chapter 42 might be the most important chapter written in American literature."

"And the whale is not just a whale, is it?"

Paul smiled, his eyes bright and clear. "It is and it isn't. Enter the world of symbols. Enter the world of ambiguity."

Until they reached the Community Park, the two discussed *Moby-Dick* with the enthusiasm of an undergraduate seminar on the nineteenth-century American novel. Across a baseball diamond and a wide field, the park buildings and the pool area appeared in a wavering haze, surrounded by a chain-link fence. The steps down the side of the hill were boarded off for repairs, so they had to stumble down the grassy bank and journey across the marshy field. The ground was spongy, and at one point the grass was black and slimy.

After paying a dollar, they spread their towels near the pool, jumped in to cool off, and returned to their towels. All around them near-naked people, boys and girls, men and women, old and young, fat and muscled and emaciated, cavorted around the pool, leaping into the water, splashing, shouting, burbling. Beyond the immediate area of the pool, near the Cyclone fence and the marshy field, other people lolled on towels or lounge chairs, sluggish, napping, idle, gobbling ice-cream sandwiches or slurping down pop. Jacob looked around and thought that all the voices and faces and gestures had some element of anger or spite. The weather was too hot, too humid, too uncomfortable. The pool itself seemed to bubble with discomfort. The lifeguard, his face flushed with heat and wrath, whistled furiously at children racing along the edge of the pool.

"So how have things been going?" Paul finally asked.

"O-kay, I guess."

"Just okay?"

"We-ell, I'm very tired today. The air conditioner broke on the bus, and it's hot, and I just finished another forty-hour week at Imperial."

"How's that going?"

Jacob let out a weary sigh. "Boring, dull, terrible. But it pays the rent."

"So it serves a purpose," Paul reasoned. "You don't have to work there the rest of your life."

"Where am I going to work, then, fur the rest of my life?"

"Are you concerned about that?"

"Sometimes," Jacob admitted, uneasily, but willing to talk since Paul seemed wise and intelligent. He was a Penn State student, after all, and showed more empathy for what Jacob was feeling and thinking than anyone else he had met in Lewistown.

"Have you been talking to Danny Yoder?"

Jacob laughed. "Cowboy boots? I just saw him earlier at Mercer's. I don't really like him, if yew want to know the truth. His reasons for leaving were so weird."

"But he left because there were too many rules, and he wanted to drive a car and go to the movies. I thought that's why you left, too?"

"It is," Jacob agreed, "and it isn't." His thoughts were becoming blurred and confused. "Those things were on the surface. They're easy to understand. But since I left, I mean, one morning, all of a sudden, I woke up on Basil Street in an entirely different world. Now I'm wondering how I got there. I've been looking at everything in a new way."

Paul asked for elaboration as Jacob's eyes narrowed in concentration. "My grandfather, the one who's a bishop, told me the first night he called that my struggle was the Amish struggle, that I must look beyond the immediate, look past the smoke and the shadows."

Paul pondered that a moment. "Well, to look beyond the immediate means to look toward the future, doesn't it?"

"And toward the past," Jacob added quickly. "Once my grandfather named four types of time."

"Four?"

"*Ya*. The past, the present, the future, and the eternal. He said the Amish exist in eternal time because the Amish are pilgrims, constructively using time on earth, engaged in a journey, till they meet God face-to-face."

"So, to look beyond the immediate means to look toward eternity."

"Not only eternity but the past, tew. The sense of ancestry. Amish history. We're continuing a tradition that has existed for hundreds of years and has endured many trials and hardships—but has survived. And, of course, there's the Bible and the entire Christian tradition."

"But there are many forms of Christianity."

"And that ties into the shadows business," Jacob explained. "The Amish believe they are a chosen people. The true light of Christ's love shines on the Amish while everyone else is merely in the shadows of that plain and simple belief. All the others are in the shadows."

Paul puzzled over this view of life and then nodded.

"We-ell, at least I think that's what it means," Jacob confessed. "But it could also mean that here on earth we're mere shadows, and that in our soul is Christ's true light. Or maybe that the earthly world is a shadow compared to true light of Christ or the radiance of heaven—to which the believer travels, after life's moment on earth. Here we deal with the past and the present and the future, and yet we yearn for release into eternity, to be with God."

"And so ordinary time is a shadow, and we should not confuse it with eternity."

"Fur shure."

"And the smoke? To look past the smoke?"

"We-ell, when Moses discovered the burning bush, he stared at the fire, not at the smoke fading into the desert sky."

"Your grandfather seems like a wise man."

"He is that," Jacob affirmed with satisfaction. "I've always been a little afraid of him, in a good way though. I mean, he *is* a bishop and well-respected, but just to be with him is to be aware of solid faith. His faith is like a great tree with roots growing deep in the earth and with branches spreading far into the sky. He knows who he is and what he's doing."

"And you'd like to be like him?"

Jacob hesitated. He pondered that simple question with humility and marked interest. "I don't know if I ever thought about that. I mean, I don't think I could ever have the type of faith he has. Or the conviction. And not just in the Amish way of life but in Jesus Christ."

"Don't you have faith?"

Jacob shrugged his shoulders.

"Don't you think faith is something developed?" Paul challenged. "It's not something you can go out and buy somewhere in a department store. It's not a *thing* made to order."

Jacob mulled over that comment. "But it just seems that some people have more faith than others."

"But how do they get that?"

Jacob shrugged.

"Do you think your grandfather was just born with great faith?" Paul pursued. "I don't think so. I think faith is developed. Faith is nurtured. It's something a person must consciously choose to strengthen and cultivate, and then that faith will mature."

Jacob shrugged again. "I don't know. We're taught to believe in Jesus Christ as our Savior. We're taught to believe in God. That's a given in the Amish world."

"But your choice to believe is a decision. Isn't that the purpose of your baptism? To make a conscious *choice* in that given faith?"

Jacob agreed. "But some people lose faith. I think Danny Yoder lost his faith."

"In the Amish?"

"*Nay*, in Christ. Or maybe he never had any faith."

"He told you that?"

"We-ell, not really. But when I started talking about church and all, he got uncomfortable and suggested I should go to a Mennonite service. But he didn't say that he was going or that we could go together."

"So, that doesn't necessarily mean he lost faith in Christ. Maybe he just doesn't need an organized church."

"But how can faith work without a church?"

"Maybe he reads the Bible on his own and prays."

"I doubt it."

"And you? *Are* you going to try a Mennonite worship service?"

Jacob sighed. "I don't know about that."

"But you're feeling lost without some kind of church worship?"

"*Not rooted* might be a better term. I don't know how to explain it. I left the Amish because I wanted to drive a car and watch TV and smoke cigarettes. I wanted to leave the Amish rules but not necessarily the Amish faith, though I didn't realize it at the time. It's not possible to dew that. The Amish faith is the Amish rule, and the Amish rule is the Amish faith. And now I don't have either."

"Couldn't you attend a Mennonite service to see how that goes? Isn't the worship similar?"

"Not reel-ly. The Amish don't go to a *church*—a special place—to worship. *We* are the church, God's people. We hold services in our homes, you know. The home is the special place for families to gather and worship God. It's so odd to have a building devoted solely to services, as if God were only there, inside, and nowhere else."

"It's odd for me to think about that, being a Catholic and all, because we build huge churches to worship in. But, Jacob, in the Old Testament, God demanded that a tabernacle be built for him."

"*Ya*, that's true," Jacob admitted, thoughtfully. "But that's not our way."

"Worship is like a habit."

"It's what you're used tew."

"So you couldn't just attend church with the Amish once in a while?"

"Noo-o, it's not right for someone to attend church only when he wants tew. You need to put your heart into it and live in obedience."

"So you have a dilemma."

Jacob nodded. "Yeah. I don't know what to dew. It's as though I lost something inside. I never questioned the truth of the Bible or the teachings of Christ. After all, the core of Amish belief *is* the New Testament. And my grandfather's favorite book is John. He often used to say, whenever he saw me reading some book, to be shure to balance *that* book by reading a chapter in John."

"And did you?"

"I have read John many times." Jacob smiled. "Many times."

"So your struggle is the Amish struggle," Paul confirmed quietly.

Jacob examined the calm, friendly face of his Catholic friend and did not answer.

"Meaning," Paul continued, "that what you are going through *now* is something that every Amish person has gone through, though not in such an extreme way."

"Maybe. Not all desire to leave. It's normal to question the rules, I suppose, though few admit to *that*. Some question the rules less than others. My twin brother, for example. I doubt he ever once truly questioned the Amish way of life. He's perfectly content with the farm life and the church rules. Some Amish have thoughts and doubts and then pray and dismiss them as unworthy.

"The time fur most reflection is just before baptism. As the elders tell yew, it's better *not* to make a vow than to make a vow and break it. Some do though. There was an entire White-Top family—the John A. Zook family, husband and wife and five children—who up and left the Amish two years ago. One day they just packed up their belongings and left. That shook up quite a few people. Naturally, they were shunned. The time to leave is before baptism."

"How many *do* leave?"

"Before baptism?"

Paul nodded.

"O-oo, not tew many up here. Maybe 5 percent. It's a little higher with the Black Tops and Yellow Tops. Every few years an Amish boy will leave."

"No girls?"

"Almost always boys. Very few girls. Everyone is taught to be obedient, and the girls submit to the rules better than the boys."

Jacob and Paul both fell into silence, absorbed with their own thoughts. But the children continued to howl, dash about, splash, and scream. Twilight veiled the park as the sky blurred and darkened. Jacob gazed upward and then directed his vision to the children, the men and women, the angry faces, the sullen faces, the vindictive faces. He muttered, "Dark, dark, dark."

"What's that?"

"I said it's getting dark."

CHAPTER 25

Lizzy stood waving as they climbed back into the cruiser.

"We have to talk to Esle," Agent Tate said.

"Not now."

"Why not now?"

"Too late."

Agent Tate glanced at his wristwatch. "It's only nine."

"Amish farmers get up at five. By now they'll be in bed or getting into bed."

"But we have to talk to him."

"It'll have to wait."

Agent Tate groaned. "Well then, we'll talk to him first thing tomorrow morning."

Sergeant Stuter started the engine. "Not tomorrow either."

Incredulously, Agent Tate stared at him. "Why not?"

"Eli's funeral," Sergeant Stuter answered. "It would not be a good idea on the day of a funeral. The families must be left alone. We pushed it today with the viewing."

Agent Tate groaned again. "When then?"

"Wednesday."

Agent Tate fell silent, organizing his thoughts, and then clicked on his tape recorder. Sergeant Stuter turned onto Stone Mountain Road and drove back toward Route 655, puzzled by Esle's behavior the night of the fires. Perhaps Lizzy just saw some other Amishman loping along in the dark. Then again, there weren't many farms out that way. As Sergeant Stuter turned onto Route 655 to drive back to Bantam, Agent Tate clicked off his tape recorder.

"Tomorrow," Agent Tate declared, "if we don't find out where Jacob is, we put out an APB on him, and we get a search warrant for his room on Basil Street."

Sergeant Stuter nodded in agreement.

"Also, we've matched tire tracks near the stop sign at Yoder's barn with the tires on Jacob's car. Let's just plant it in the news that we have a clue. Maybe that'll frighten the arsonist and smoke him out."

Again, Sergeant Stuter nodded, this time with a grin.

"And tomorrow we're going to have another talk," Agent Tate said, his eyes going hard, "a slightly stronger talk, with Lillian Leach."

Jimmy had a clean and powerful break and sent the balls clacking and clicking across the smooth green felt. But he missed his first shot, swore under his breath, and stood to the side. He angrily chalked the tip of his cue, his eyes blinking wildly. His opponent studied the pattern of balls, moving his head from side to side, sauntering slowly around the entire pool table before deciding on a shot.

In a side booth with half a mug of draft beer in front of her, Lil sat alone, staring out the window past the Old Milwaukee neon sign at the street, the parked cars, the passing cars. Dead flies littered the sill. Her vigilant eyes kept returning to a man slouched in a car parked across the street. She was distracted, momentarily, by a fly twitching on its back. Lil lit a cigarette and began ticking her long fingernails on the tabletop. She listened without interest to the clack of pool balls and the murmur of the distant TV set, mounted high over the bar.

On Monday night, few people frequented the Bantam Pool Hall. Two pool tables stood in the middle of a large room with booths running along two walls. The bar stretched along one end with a few Monday-night regulars lounging on the stools, drinking, cracking jokes, watching TV. In another booth sat a couple, young and tense, whispering intently to each other. The bartender wiped glasses and set them on shelves.

At 10:30, the station carried a local CBS News update. Lil heard the word *Amish* and jerked around to face the TV set. The men at the bar lifted their heads. Jimmy's pool partner stopped playing to watch the newscast.

"Hey, whaddaya doin'?" Jimmy complained, holding the cue out to his side.

"Shhhh, I wanna hear this."

The screen filled with black letters THE AMISH BARN FIRES superimposed over the image of a burning barn. Denny Bronson, a local man who worked for CBS, was the only person who managed to film the fires, at Ezra S. Yoder's barn and at Moses C. Hostetler's barn. The letters then faded for more footage of the fires, followed by Sandra Kapalton, wearing a trench coat and a solemn face, who stood in front of a burned-down barn. In a low voice she reported, once again, on the tragedy of the barn fires, the loss of property and livestock, the shocking and senseless death of Eli Yoder, the progress that day with the community cleanup effort. She announced that the FBI, who joined forces with the state police this morning, had discovered an important clue in their investigation of the arson case but could not yet reveal what that was. The broadcast ended.

Lil stubbed out her cigarette and lit another one. Jimmy, eyes winking and squinting, made a bad shot and swore loudly. The young couple returned to their intent whispers.

"The news of the century for Big Valley," one of the regulars at the bar remarked.

Another one agreed. "That's for sure."

"I wonder what the FBI found?"

"Did you see all them highfalutin' TV reporters swarmin' round in the valley?"

"Someone said Geraldo is coming up here to do a program, but he'll have trouble getting the Amish to talk. Diane Sawyer is coming, too."

"No kiddin'."

"That's what they say."

"Well, it *is* a tragedy."

"Sure is. And that poor little Amish boy dying, tryin' to save his colt."

"Ain't that somethin'? Runnin' into a burning barn to save a colt!"

"How could anyone kill all those animals? That's what I want to know. I mean, what's the point?"

"Sick mind, sick, sick, sick!"

"How much damage did they say?"

"Over a million and a half dollars!"

"Whew. You wouldn't think those old barns were worth that much."

"It's all them cows and horses, too."

"That's right."

"Those Belgian draft horses cost a pretty penny."

"They say an Amish boy did it, one of 'em that left the Amish."

"For sure. They found his car in a field, but they can't find *him*."

"How could he do that to his own people?"

"He'll be put in jail, for sure."

"Well, he *killed* someone!"

"That was an accident."

"It's still killing someone, accident or not."

"They don't call that murder, though. What do they call it?"

"Manslaughter."

"Yeah, that's it. Manslaughter."

"He'll be put away for quite a stretch."

"Can't hide long from the FBI."

"Yeah, the FBI will find him, for sure."

Lil abruptly stood up and yanked on her jean jacket. Jimmy was in the middle of a shot and looked up. "Whe're ya goin'?"

She hurried to the door. "Out."

"Hey, wait!" Jimmy slammed his cue on the rail.

Lil had already banged through the front door and was hurrying toward her silver pickup truck when Jimmy caught up with her.

"Whe're ya goin'? C'mon now."

"Home!" she snapped.

"Are you gonna let a TV clip spook you?"

"That's not *it*, Jimmy."

"What is it then?"

"You don't get it, do you?"

"That Agent Tate? He freak you out?"

"What do you *think*?" she screeched, fumbling in her purse for her keys. "There's probably someone in the bar watching us. Or watching us out here. Do you know there's been a guy sitting in his car out front for the past twenty minutes?"

"Don't freak out on me, Lil, not now. Just come back in for a beer and relax."

"Relax!" she shouted.

"Shhhh."

"*How* can I relax? *How*?" she cried. "I can't take much more of this. I just can't."

"Not here." He was trying to keep his voice calm although he seethed with anger. "Everything's under control."

She bit her lower lip and gripped her keys. "I'm going home."

He watched her quick, angry, determined gait. She yanked open the door to her pickup truck, clambered inside, revved the engine, and rocketed out of the parking lot into the street. He shook his head in disgust, spun on his heel, and scrambled into his car.

Lil flashed down the street, recklessly driving through a light a moment after it turned red. A driver braked and honked his horn long and loud at her. She drove past the Sheetz convenience store where she worked but didn't turn to look at it. She drove past the street where she lived without a glance. Her face was set, grim, brittle. Tears had smeared her mascara, and she kept wiping her eyes with her knuckle. The voice of Sandra Kapalton on the TV set and the voices of the men at the bar were spinning and darting in her mind. She kept squinting, as if she were trying to stare at the voices in her head. Lil snapped on the radio, hoping the music would drown out the voices in her mind.

She braked and accelerated hard, shifted gears, and kept glancing in her rearview mirror. The mascara stung her teary eyes, and she kept wiping them with her knuckle. When she swerved onto Route 655, she saw headlights in the rearview mirror and soared into the valley well over the speed limit. Ignoring the solid yellow center line and blaring horns, she passed cars and trucks and motorcycles.

Lil did not slow down when she saw in the far distance, just before the bend, flashing red lights. As she swerved to pass the horse and buggy, Lil glanced in the rearview mirror just as her pickup truck shook, tipped, flew off the road into a field, and flipped over twice before it crashed to a stop with the cab on the bottom.

CHAPTER 26

The first day of August was the first Saturday of the month and not a church weekend. Just past ten that night, Esle, freshly bathed and wearing a clean shirt, hastened up the farm lane with a flashlight. Though he had combed his hair and brushed his beard, he threaded his fingers through his damp beard once more. His step was light and buoyant since he was going to visit Judith.

During the summer months, when field labor was at its peak, Esle had little chance of seeing Judith except once a week: at church on Sunday and at the singing later that night, or the following week on Saturday night. He might see her during the week at the Wednesday auction or in an occasional neighborly visit, but it was almost impossible to spare time in the growing season, with the work in the fields.

As Esle passed the wheat field, his eyes surveyed the stubble; the wheat had been threshed that week, a good harvest, with over a hundred bushels from each of the four acres. His back ached from the heavy work that afternoon, the last of the threshing, but he had swallowed two aspirins earlier before he bathed. He did not dash to the chiropractor with every little ache and pain like Gideon Speicher. A few aches were worth it when a good harvest was pulled in. The entire round of farming never ceased to flourish in his mind as a providential miracle—plowing, planting, weeding, cutting, harvesting—a simple but rewarding act of human creation, in cooperation with God.

The Amish clearly dress and keep the garden, he thought, as commanded in Genesis. The past Sunday his baptismal instruction class had touched on that. Esle felt a sudden surge of gratitude that for hundreds and even thousands of years, farming had existed and would continue to exist until the day of judgment. To tend the land is to labor for the Lord. What greater work could there be than that?

His work shoes kicked up a little dust as he walked. He stopped and took a deep breath of fresh country air, filling his chest with the dark summer night. Breezes, silken and fragrant with the smell of wildflowers and cut alfalfa, purled through the cornfields and the clover and the oats. He considered the difference in air from season to season: in summer, soft and warm; in fall, crisp and dry; in winter, sharp and hard; in spring, smooth and moist. Colors also changed: the white fields of winter melted into the rainbow riot of spring, into the deep green of summer, into the red and orange and yellow and brown of autumn. And men, too, changed from season to season, year to year. He looked up at the black sky, studded with thousands and thousands of bright silver stars—nails of light hammered into eternity. The waxing moon was a mere sliver of silver. Vaguely he wondered if Eli had yet thought of a likeness for the moon.

When he reached the end of the farm lane, he heard the distinct clip-clop, clip-clop of a horse and buggy on the road. He waited a moment until it drove past and recognized Enoch Zook, driving over to court Deborah, Judith's older sister. Esle chuckled slightly. The Yoder household will be filled with men calling tonight. Most of their friends knew that Enoch and Deborah were serious, so serious that the community was waiting for the engagement to be announced any church Sunday now so they could plan for a fall wedding. No one had been too surprised when Ezra S. bought turkeys at the auction last month.

The strong feelings Esle had about Judith were becoming more powerful and vigorous; once again he questioned his own thoughts about marriage. The same fall after baptism? Too soon. Much too soon. He would have to work for at least two more years before he could even entertain the idea of taking a wife. Esle stood next to the milk stand to watch the white-topped buggy disappear in the distant darkness. The sound of the hooves faded into silence. He was thankful he could just walk the short distance to the farm, only fifteen minutes at a brisk pace.

When he hiked past Irma's Valley View Farm, he looked up past the sloping, well-manicured lawn at the farmhouse. Every window in the two-story structure was lit, illuminating the wide front porch. Irma always kept wicker furniture out there so her guests could sit and enjoy the view. A couple sat there now, bobbing back and forth in rocking chairs. He always thought it an odd occupation, putting up these tourist folks. But at least it was not like the Lancaster Amish, who can hardly turn their heads without seeing tourists wandering all about.

Esle had been up to Irma's house just a few Friday nights ago, when his mother convinced him to talk to Jacob on the telephone. Though there was so much fieldwork to be done, he went along since he was the only one who had not yet talked to Jacob. It was important, his mother insisted, that Jacob know the *entire* family still thought about him and loved him and wanted him to come home. So after the evening milking, Esle and his mother and Daniel and Hannah, trooped up to Irma's. The result was a busy signal. "Maybe it's off the hook," his mother suggested. "It has never been bissy before. I don't understand why it's bissy."

Irma banged a few pans around and said, "But it might not be *him* on the phone. After all, he shares it with three other people." His mother looked surprised; she had not even considered that possibility. From six thirty to six forty-five, they tried calling three more times. Finally, they had to leave to finish the evening chores.

The last few weeks before Jacob left still thumped around in Esle's mind. He had shrugged off all Jacob's complaints and had never given them much attention. Now the thought that churned in his conscience, from time to time, was whether or not he *should* have given more weight to certain warning signals and somehow stopped Jacob from leaving. The matter of the two hundred dollars had dwindled inside him, from resentment to merely a bitter taste.

Esle increased his pace, as though trying to outwalk his thoughts about his twin brother. He turned his eyes and his mind to the opposite field, where rows and rows of corn, six feet tall and tasseled, whispered in the summer dark. He heard a rustling noise in the first few rows and debated whether it was a porcupine or a possum or a skunk. A little further down the road, he saw Lizzy sitting in a cone of light on her front porch, surrounded by various plants and flowers, reading. She always seemed to be reading, just like Jacob in the evenings.

In the short distance, at the junction of the T intersection where Reigle Creek Road ran straight into Stone Mountain Road, he saw the twinkling glow of the streetlight mounted high on a utility pole. Moths and beetles and midges darted and danced and died in its pale light. Rammed in the bank at the side of the road stood a stop sign, surrounded by a profusion of carefully tended flowers Irma planted years ago: gladioli, tiger lilies, zinnias, bells of Ireland, daylilies, chrysanthemums, daisies, marigolds. When Esle once asked her why she planted the flowers, she said it was in memory of the yield sign that used to be there. Three years ago the local ordinance changed yield signs to stop signs on many back-country roads. She was irritated and thought that a foolish waste of time, energy, and money. Now she was supposed to *stop* before turning onto Stone Mountain Road.

Under the artificial light, the stalks and leaves and petals looked pallid and unreal, drained of their bright sunlit colors. Then, trusting the goodwill of his neighbor, Esle bent down and picked two red chrysanthemums, two daisies, and two daylilies. As he arranged the flowers into a haphazard bouquet, a high shrill animal scream rent the night. He listened carefully as the cry melted into the stillness of the mountain. The same cry he heard that night they explored the cave. Certainly not a screech owl. Was it possible a panther *was* roaming Stone Mountain?

Inspecting the dark edge of the woods and mulling over that eerie cry, he continued his walk to the Yoder farm, the bouquet of flowers in one hand and the flashlight in the other. He passed the apple orchard and turned into the farm lane.

Peering through the darkness, he saw Enoch's horse and buggy tied by the buggy shed near the barn's south side. The Yoder barn stood solid and huge in the night. He could hear the horses stamping and moving in their stalls, and the sound emerged as if the massive structure itself was breathing. When he opened the gate through the picket fence, the hinges seemed to squeak unnaturally loudly. He left the gate open and strode toward the silent farmhouse. Since Deborah and Judith shared a bedroom, he wondered whether Enoch and Deborah were circumspectly courting there, following an old custom, or had gone somewhere else. That always made it a bit complicated since both couples could not be in the same room together if they wanted privacy. By virtue of their imminent engagement and inevitable marriage, Enoch and Deborah had prior claim to the room.

He crept toward the back of the farmhouse, nearly tripping twice. When he stood beneath Deborah and Judith's bedroom, he pointed the flashlight at the second-story window and turned it on. The bright beam shot through the panes. He moved it around for a few seconds and switched it off. The window opened as Deborah called down quietly, "She'll be down in a minute." The window closed.

After that one blast of light, Esle waited a moment for his eyes to readjust to the darkness and then made his way to the front porch. There he stood gazing at the barn and the rig tied outside under cover of night, the symbol of a household besieged by a suitor.

Behind him, the front door opened soundlessly, and Judith appeared barefoot at his side, wearing a dark blue dress without the apron. She adjusted her white cap. Her thick auburn hair had recently been brushed and braided and pinned to the back of her head. She peered at his profile with her shimmering eyes.

"Enoch is upstairs," she whispered.

"I know," he responded, turning to her.

"Shall we walk to the tree?"

He nodded and smiled. She smiled, too, shyly. On the way out of the yard, he closed the gate and winced again at the squeaking hinges. When they reached the south side of the barn, he remembered the flowers.

"These are for you." He held up the flowers for her to see.

"What's that?" she asked, squinting. "Flowers?" She took them from him.

"I picked them from Irma's stop sign."

"She will not mind?"

"*Nay*, I'm sure not."

"They're nice."

They strolled past Enoch's buggy. The horse whinnied and turned its head to them. At the far edge of the buggy shed stood a magnificent black walnut tree. They sat under its great spreading branches, he with his back against the trunk and she with her legs curled up under her. Judith examined the flowers again and raised them to her face to inhale their perfume.

Esle fiddled with his flashlight and set it on the ground. "I wish we were inside."

"Enoch is there," she repeated in a matter-of-fact voice. "Besides, it's nice out here. Warm. Quiet. And look at the stars. It's nice."

He agreed. "And you are nice."

Judith turned her face from the stars to his face and then lowered her eyes to her lap as she fussed with the flowers.

"Will Enoch and Deborah marry this fall?"

She answered playfully, "I don't know."

"But you must have some idea. Enoch is now twenty-three years old, and his father is ready to give him some land to farm. It's time for them to marry."

She glanced at him. "So you could be inside?"

At first he did not respond, and then a timid smile played along his mouth. "*Ya*, so I could be inside."

She fussed again with the flowers. "I thought so."

Esle had first asked her in April if she wanted a ride home after the singing. Late in May, he again asked her if he could drive her home. Since then, he had come over every other Saturday night all summer, five times in all. Judith had been surprised at the sudden interest but secretly pleased. She thought highly of the Hostetler family and especially of Esle, known as a hard worker and a good farmer. He knew how to plow, how to treat the animals, how to repair broken wagon wheels. He was a sober, religious, steadfast Amishman, someone whom she could admire and respect and with whom she could rear a family.

Rearranging the flowers on her lap, she declared demurely, "I'm glad you would like to be inside."

Esle moved closer to Judith. She did not stir or say anything. He fumbled for her hand, and she let him take it. Hand-holding was nothing unusual; since June she had already allowed Esle to hold her hand on the Saturday nights he visited. All they had done was to hold hands and to speak gently to each other. She *would* have allowed him to kiss her in July if he had wanted to, but he had not made the attempt. No matter, she thought, all in good time. But now he held her hand tightly, firmly stroking her palm with his thick, rough thumb. With her free hand, she continued to touch the petals.

"I think it would be nice to be inside," he said as softly as he could, edging closer to her.

A gentle breeze fluttered through the dark summer air and sighed in the high branches of the tree. She lifted her eyes. He leaned forward and kissed her gently on the cheek. When she did not resist, he kissed her lightly on the mouth. Then he kissed her again, and the flowers fell from her lap.

CHAPTER 27

Lil was dead. Sergeant Stuter and Agent Tate stood in the cold field as paramedics walked the stretcher with her body on it to the ambulance parked on the side of Route 655. On the opposite side of the road stood a yellow-topped buggy. Joseph Swarey, who had witnessed the accident, had his hand on the neck of his horse to calm him and was talking to a police officer. Two wreckers were in the field as workers looped thick chains around the crumpled chassis in an attempt to right the pickup truck. Police and newspaper photographers were taking pictures.

Sergeant Stuter shook his head. "She must have been driving out to see Jessica."

When Agent Tate turned to him, he saw the flashing red-and-white lights of the ambulance reflected in his glasses. His eyes and his voice were cold. "Or she was going to see Jacob. Tomorrow morning, first thing, an APB goes out on Jacob Hostetler, and we get that search warrant for Basil Street."

The following day, the sky, dense with clouds the color of ash and pearl, dropped to the top of the mountains. The scent of snow purified the air. The morning was mild, temperate, and still. The funeral for Eli Yoder was held Tuesday morning at nine.

Earlier, Isaac D. and Esle had carried the coffin from the washhouse to the *Kammer*, set it on a bench, and placed the lid upright in a corner of the room. The strong smell of pine scented the room as the two men carefully placed Eli inside the box.

Ezra S. asked Karl Eckard to have the cleanup crew wait until the family drove to the cemetery before the noisy machines and shouting workmen began. Cars, trucks, vans, buggies, and construction equipment were parked in the front field and the back pasture and along Stone Mountain Road. A cement truck, its huge barrel spinning, stood where the milk house had been. Men, in baseball caps and straw hats and black hats, milled about the site, talking and sipping coffee.

Ezra S. and Lydia decided that the funeral would be only for the immediate family and close neighbors, their own congregation. They were fearful that Eli's death had already attracted too much attention. Horses with white-topped buggies were tied along a makeshift hitching rail in the barnyard. Three Amishmen, black felt hats pressed down on their heads, stood in their Sunday best, observing the crowd and the vehicles. One of the men glanced at his pocket watch, and they entered the farmhouse, first wiping their feet on the rumpled piece of dark fabric tossed in front of the door.

Inside, partitions had been removed and benches were placed throughout the living room and the *Kammer*, where Eli now rested in the plain pine box, with a white sheet draped over its sides. Ezra S., Lydia, and their children sat stiff on two benches facing the coffin. Seated behind them were other members of the Yoder family. The Hostetler family was there. In that room, every adult and every child sat perfectly quiet and motionless.

Abraham C. stood and removed his black felt hat. The other men removed their hats. He placed his hat carefully on the seat of the chair and turned to face the rows of faces, eyes lifted to him in dignified silence. He sighed. He looked down at the floor and then up at the ceiling, and when he spoke he raised his prophetic voice deep from the dark desert of his soul.

"Faith," he proclaimed, closing his eyes to capture the words. " 'Now faith is the substance of things hoped for, the evidence of things not seen.' Faith. 'Through faith we understand that the worlds were framed by the word of God, so that things which are seen were not made of things which do appear.' Faith."

He opened his eyes and he opened his arms, palms upward. "If ever faith were commanded, if ever faith were challenged, it is now, as we are faced by the sudden death of this child, this ten-year-old boy, one of God's precious children."

He paused. He hesitated. He gathered words, his mind fixed on the image of Eli. He knew, in the tradition of Amish funerals, that he should simply call upon the living to live a better and more righteous life, that he should warn the living that they too could be called by God at any moment, that he should not mention the person's name. Yet an intense inspiration urged him to draw upon Eli's life and to use Eli's name to enrich his sermon.

His pale blue eyes were steady and clear. "Our very own Eli Yoder has been called home. And we don't know why. He has been called to everlasting life. And we can't know why. It is not for us to *know* why, but to have *faith* that this is the way of our Lord, and to accept it with *Gelassenheit* (yieldedness to God). 'The evidence of things not seen.' We must not question and cannot question. It is difficult to understand why someone so young and so tender and so early in his earthly life would be returned to the throne of heaven. We must have faith. Before God, we are sojourners and strangers, as were our fathers. King David certainly spoke the truth: 'Our days on the earth *are* as a shadow, and there is none abiding.' Faith."

He paused again and gradually returned to a traditional sermon. For close to an hour, he exhorted the people to live in Christ and to receive his blessings. When he closed his sermon, he picked up the Bible and read from John: "Verily, verily, I say unto you, the one who hears my word, and believes on him that sent me, has everlasting life, and shall not come into condemnation; but is passed from death unto life."

The bishop flipped to Revelation and read about the one who sat on the great white throne to judge, with the book of life. His voice quavered on these last few lines. Lydia sat still, her back straight, her face somber, her hands in her lap, resting on the swelling of new life. Ezra S., his eyes flat and grave, listened with his head slightly bowed. After Abraham C. closed the Bible, everyone knelt for prayer.

Daniel S. Zook, the preacher with the copper-colored beard, stood for the benediction. Everyone rose, and the congregation was dismissed. There was no singing; as they filed out of the *Kammer*, Daniel S. read a hymn, one of the saddest hymns in the German language, "Gute Nacht, mein liebe Kinder (Good night, my beloved children)."

In the kitchen, a traditional light meal was served before the ride to the cemetery. Rebekah and Fronnie, one of Lydia's sisters-in-law, distributed sweet bread with slices of longhorn cheese. Isaac D. and

Sam carried around trays with two short-stemmed glasses and a bottle of red wine which had been watered down and sweetened with sugar.

Lydia drank a small glass of red wine and gazed at the faces of her family and her neighbors, all of whom were eating slices of sweet bread and cheese and drinking wine. She quietly sighed at the simple human activity of sharing food and drink and expected any moment to see Eli with his corn-blond hair dashing across the room. Lydia reached out to place her hand on the edge of the table, steadying herself while wrenching groans tightened her chest. She heard someone say, "Lydia?" but she closed her eyes and slightly shook her head to indicate that she was managing.

The coffin was placed in the living room for the final viewing. Ezra S., Lydia, and the children stood behind the pine box as everyone else moved in slow, silent rotation past the figure shrouded in white, murmuring in their hearts a final prayer and casting their tear-tinted eyes upon the boy one final time.

The four pallbearers, older cousins of Eli, helped Hosea M. screw shut the lid and then carried the coffin outside to the hearse, a one-horse spring wagon. Esle, his face drained of expression, sat on the seat, holding the reins with gloved hands and staring at the mane of the horse. The horse shook its head and nickered.

The moment the coffin was borne out of the farmhouse, the men milling about the equipment and the burned-down barn stopped and turned. Every man removed his baseball cap or his straw hat or his black felt hat. No one moved. No one spoke.

Ezra S. and Lydia and the little ones, Levi and Becky, climbed into a buggy directly behind the spring wagon while the rest of the family climbed into the next two. Everyone else trudged through the snow-scented morning to their respective buggies. From the side of the road, newspaper photographers took pictures discreetly.

Esle snapped the reins of the horse, and the spring wagon bumped forward, jolting its way up the deeply rutted farm lane. It was followed by a dipping, tilting line of white-topped buggies. White-knuckled hands gripped the corner buggy posts. Esle turned the spring wagon onto Stone Mountain Road and pulled back on the reins to keep the horse plodding at a slow pace. The hooves of the horses clopped heavily on the road. The sound of the many clopping hooves echoed loudly and distinctly in the still morning air.

Lydia tightened the black scarf around her head and stared straight ahead at the spring wagon and the pine box trembling in its bed. She listened to the rhythmic clopping of the hooves. The sound of the clopping hooves burrowed deeply into her being, the same way the steady drone of the Singer Sewing Machine had pierced her heart. But the sound of the clopping hooves seemed to stamp down sorrow as though Eli were being borne along on a steady stream of sound, carried along effortlessly. The road dipped and rose and curved along the base of the mountain as the funeral procession pushed forward on this four-mile journey to the Nebraska Amish cemetery, located in neighboring Greenville township.

The sky had embraced the valley. Clouds as solid as the mountains themselves hid the tops of both ranges. The morning light seemed to breathe and then, all at once, the air filled with snow. The snow, at first, did not fall but simply appeared, as if tiny crystalline flakes blossomed from the light itself. And then the snow fell, fluttered and fell, and touched the spring wagon and the buggies and the faces of solemn sorrow.

Lydia lifted her face and felt the snowflakes touch her eyes.

The Nebraska Amish cemetery, just off the side of the road, was a parceled section of land set off from the surrounding fields by a weathered split-wood rail fence—an acre of land exposed to the sun and the sky and the moon, with no flowers, no shrubs, no trees. The grass was an uneven surface of winter-brown tufts. The sandstone and granite markers, simple square slabs rounded at the top, a foot or two high, were leaning forward or tilted back, some straight, lining the cemetery in irregular rows. Nothing more adorned a headstone than an etched name, a birth date, and a death date. Near the gate stood a small tin shed for the tools.

Esle steered the spring wagon to the gate. The horses immediately behind were tied to the fence railing. Other drivers stood their horses on the side of the road or loosely secured the tie rope to the barbwire fence along the field. The four pallbearers quickly appeared at the end of the spring wagon as Esle dismounted. The Yoder family stood in a loose knot next to the gate as everyone else filed into the cemetery. In the far distance, a yellow van stood out from the cars parked along the road. Local CBS reporters were videotaping the procession while the newspaper reporters snapped photographs.

The family and other mourners gathered next to the open grave, a deep, raw hole in the earth, with a great mound of dirt next to it. Meanwhile, the pallbearers lifted the pine box from the bed of the spring wagon and carried it into the cemetery. Snow, falling softly, silently, sifted into the valley, the fields, the cemetery. The snow, soft and silent, fell into the dark grave.

Wooden poles had been placed lengthwise over the grave, and two long straps were laid across them. The pallbearers settled the coffin on the wooden poles, and then each one lifted an end of a strap while other mourners removed the poles. They gently lowered the coffin into a rough wooden box lining the grave and then pulled the straps back up. One of the pallbearers eased himself into the grave and laid wide boards across the larger box. With that done, the pallbearers shoveled dirt back into the opening.

At the first hollow thud of earth against wood, the muscles of Lydia's face tightened. Judith cried out. Thud upon thud. Esle regarded the shovelfuls of soil through eyes cratered by loss. Ezra S. gazed into the pit with eyes hard as stones. The family wept. The family sobbed. The soft snow fell. The shovelfuls of dirt fell. The snow filtered softly into the open grave, and the swirling snow softened Lydia's face as she recognized that Eli was being buried in both snow and soil, both sky and earth.

Once the grave was filled, Abraham C. presided over a short graveside service and enjoined the mourners to say the Lord's Prayer deep within their hearts. The men removed their snow-powdered hats. Each man and each woman and each child bowed a head in silence. In silence, the soft snow fell. The snow, soft and silent, covered the grave, touched the bowed heads, outlined the edges of headstones, and dusted the open fields and the winding roads and the huddled farms.

The mourners, one by one, and in twos and threes, drifted from the gravesite. Horses stamped the snow-covered road. Wheels clattered and rolled into the muffled distance. Ezra S. and Lydia were the last to leave. Husband and wife stood silent in the softly falling snow. Father and mother stood silent, gazing at the snow-concealed grave, listening to the snow-soft silence fill the world. The two figures stood silent in the falling snow, falling softly, silently, purifying their hearts with everlasting silence and *Gelassenheit.*

CHAPTER 28

In the middle of August, on Saturday morning, Jacob, Jimmy, and Jessica drove around to used-car dealerships and knocked on doors at addresses listed in the classified ads Jacob had circled in red. Finally, in midafternoon at Phil's Auto Sales on Route 22, Jacob saw the car he wanted: a 1982 black Grand Prix. It spoke to him and called to him, as Jimmy said a car must do.

Two Saturdays earlier, Jessica had taken Jacob to the motor vehicle department to apply for his driver's license. Jacob had studied the *Pennsylvania Driver's Manual* diligently all summer and had practiced parking and turns with Jessica in her father's Honda Civic. So he easily passed the written test and the road test, using the Honda. When he returned that afternoon, he waved his driver's license with pride in front of Jimmy.

All that night, he kept pulling it out of his wallet: to study the lamination, to scrutinize the dates and figures, to examine his photograph. He had never seen a picture of himself before. He gazed at the solemn expression, the clean-shaven face, the short hair, the ears that looked like handles on a milk pail. At one point, staring at his license, he felt an ascending chill that he now could not return to the Amish. With this rite of initiation, he had passed as decisively into the *englisch* world as though baptized into it. Indeed, all summer the driver's manual and Jessica had instructed him for driving in place of the Bible and the Amish ministers instructing him for baptism.

When Jacob first saw the black car, priced on the windshield at nine hundred dollars, he walked around it, enthralled by the polished black exterior, the sleek shape, the glistening chrome detail. He opened the front door to sit in the driver's seat.

Phil Gyas, the owner and manager, a thin, red-faced man, came wheeling out of the front office and shouted, "Hey, you, what d'ya think you're doing over there?"

"I want to buy a car."

"Well, well, well, you've come to the right place, my boy. A beautiful car, isn't it?"

With his eyes Jacob caressed the dashboard, the gauges, the radio and stereo system, the speedometer and odometer. He ran his hands lightly over the steering wheel and then gripped the stick shift.

"A beautiful car, don't you think?" Phil continued as Jimmy and Jessica strolled over. "A great buy."

For a good five minutes, Jimmy inspected the car from end to end, especially the motor, yanking up the hood, checking the oil, and prodding the engine. He slammed the hood shut with a satisfied grin and said they'd have to take it for a drive.

"That engine purrs like a kitten, let me tell you," Phil declared.

Jimmy opened all four doors and rolled all the windows up and down.

"Hey, c'mon, do you think I'd sell a car with broken windows? Huh?"

Jimmy opened the trunk to check for the spare tire and jack and found a plastic bag filled with flares. There must have been a dozen or more of the red spiked sticks.

"Hey, what can I say?" Phil shrugged. "The guy was afraid of getting a flat."

There was a crack along the seam of the driver's seat, another small crack in the dashboard near the glove compartment, and a little body rot on the right rear quarter panel. But, all in all, Jimmy pronounced the ten-year-old car to be in "pritty good shape." He expressed some suspicion about the mileage, which Phil brushed off. "What? What? Fifty-eight thousand is fifty-eight thousand!"

They drove the car around, up and down the street while Jimmy listened to the engine. Then the radio hummed. The stereo system blared. In the long run, Jimmy decided, even if Jacob ran it for only a year or two, he'd get his money's worth. Phil sat Jacob down to work out a deal. He'd only managed to save $150 and thought, with regret and misgiving, about Esle and the shotgun fund; he'd have to take care of that later. Since he had a steady job, some savings, and a clean driving record, Phil worked out all the details with ease: the insurance, the short-term loan, the monthly payments. Jacob signed this paper and that paper and tried to keep the dollar figures straight in his head. Within two hours, he owned a black 1982 Grand Prix.

When Phil dropped the car keys into Jacob's palm, he gripped them as if they were a talisman or a charm. The keys to a car! I own a car. He kept repeating those words as he emerged from the office and beheld the black car parked in the lot, gleaming black and bright, with Jessica leaning against the hood and smoking a cigarette. To Jacob, the car and Jessica resembled one of those calendar photos in the Exxon station where Jimmy worked: she had her hand resting on the glossy fender with her black hair pulled back loosely in a ponytail, her tight red T-shirt, and the rolled cuffs of her white jean shorts prominently displaying her smooth tanned legs.

"Mind if I hitch a ride, big boy?" Jessica asked, tossing her cigarette to the ground.

"No-o probe-lem." Jacob smiled as he swaggered past the front of the car, examining its grill and headlights.

"Hey, Jake-o, I'll meetja back at Basil Street," Jimmy called from the window of his Camaro before roaring out of the lot.

When Jacob sat in the driver's seat, he adjusted the rearview mirror and the side mirrors and fastidiously fastened the seat belt over his lap and chest. He gripped the steering wheel and marveled at the dashboard. "I can't believe this."

"Well, believe it, Jake," Jessica snorted. "You're in the *real* world now."

"We-ell," he said meditatively, "I'm in the *englisch* world now."

"*This* is the world, Jake." Her eyes sharp, her voice pointed. "Don't start any of that stuff about the spiritual world of the Amish. You can be spiritual and drive a car, too, for godssake. The Amish are just plain weird and backward. Backward people. Just keep repeating that to yourself: *backward, backward, backward!*"

Her clawing tone did not affect him that much that afternoon. He was much too excited about the car to be offended by her remarks. Jacob imagined showing the car to Gary. He won't believe it when I drive up to the Original in my own car. When he started the engine, it rumbled and throbbed. He shook his head in disbelief that he could bring this huge beast alive with the turn of a key. He shifted into first gear, let the clutch up slowly, pressed down on the gas pedal, and plunged into a world he could not change.

The rest of the afternoon, Jacob drove his car all around, and that night they celebrated. Jimmy and Jessica bought a case of Coors Light, Jacob's favorite, and set it on the coffee table with a new issue of *Car and Driver* on top of it.

Jimmy reminded him, "All this means, Jake-o, is yer gonna have ta pay an extra twenty bucks a month fer a parking space out back."

"I wish I didn't have to work today," Lil remarked, curled up next to Jimmy on the sofa, "so I coulda been with you'ns. I'm really happy fer you, Jake."

Everyone snapped open a Coors Light.

"Here's to Jake's new car and his new driving career!" Jessica cried.

Raising his can of beer as a toast, Jimmy intoned, "Welcome to the *real* world."

Jacob hesitated before lifting his can of beer because Jessica had used the same phrase earlier, insinuating that the Amish do not live in the real world. What is the real world, anyhow?

Jimmy continued, "You've finally entered the twentieth century."

"I guess so."

"You *guess* so?" Jimmy was surprised. "You *know* so, man. Owning a car is every teenager's dream. Now you own a car—a coupla years late, maybe, but no matter. You've got a set of wheels, you've got a woman, you've got a can of beer in yer hand. What more could you want? *This* is the real world. Be glad you're part of it now and not part of the dinosaur world, that tribe that clogs up the roads with their freakin' buggies."

"Ah-men!" Jessica exclaimed.

Jacob knew it was useless to try to discuss the Amish with either Jimmy or Jessica. Most people he met expressed interest in the lifestyle, religious beliefs, and simplicity of the Amish world. But never had he met anyone who criticized the Amish as much as they did. He drank his beer, ignoring their comments.

Jacob drove everyone to the Original for pizza even though it was within walking distance. He also wheeled around the Block, the music turned loud, before parking the car directly in front of the pizzeria so he could see it through the window.

"You have competition, now, babe," Jimmy teased Jessica.

"Oh, great!"

That evening, instead of pulling out his driver's license every half hour, Jacob kept removing the keys from his pocket to stare at them and jangle them. The sensation of owning a car, surprisingly, was similar to feelings he had at sixteen when he and Esle were given their own buggy to drive: excitement, maturity, trust.

Since Jacob wanted to be in his car all the time, they decided to go to the Bantam Drive-in for a double-feature night of horror. Two Wes Craven movies were playing: his recently released *People Under the Stairs* and his classic *Nightmare on Elm Street*. Back at Basil Street, they packed the rest of the Coors Light on ice in an Igloo cooler, stashed it in the trunk, and headed out to the drive-in.

At this point, Jacob felt a little "buzzed" and somewhat concerned about his driving, but Jimmy always drove drunk and stoned, so he assumed he had to learn to do the same. He adjusted his KOOL baseball cap, gripped the steering wheel, and with studied concentration cruised down the road.

"Turn there, past that sign," Jimmy directed. "And be real careful cuz the road's narrow and real twisted."

Jacob had never been to a drive-in. To watch a movie in a car and to drink beer with a girl seemed to link the best possible elements in the *englisch* world. When he turned the final sharp bend, he saw in the short distance a series of booths, with lights burning on top of each one, forming a gated wall. Directly behind that, in the distance, the top of a mammoth white screen stood against a sky soaked in blood-red clouds.

At the center booth, Jacob stopped to wait behind a convertible with its top down. Coiled inside it were four young women with dark and long and wild hair. There seemed to be some trouble between the attendant in the booth and the driver of the car, whose hair spread in a savage mass of ropes like horned snakes. The creature in the passenger seat, her face etched with fury, sprang up and started hissing and gesticulating.

"What is *up* with those gorgons?" Jessica complained. "Back up and pull over to the next booth."

The sky rolled and thundered. Lil said the news had not once mentioned rain all afternoon. After they were admitted, Jacob bumped his car over the uneven, dusty surface. Throughout an open field, cars were strewn and scattered, isolated, music murmuring, teenagers entombed within. After he parked his Grand Prix on a mound facing the movie screen, he peered through the windshield at it, once again, in disbelief at its size. It seemed as though an entire acre of white space had been nailed up against the sky. "Does the whole screen fill with the picture?"

"The *whole* screen," Jessica replied, lighting a cigarette, kicking off her shoes, and angling her back against the door.

"But doesn't the sound disturb the people in front?"

"Whaddaya mean?" Jimmy asked from the back seat.

Jacob faltered. "We-ell, it must be pretty loud to reach all the cars."

Jessica laughed shrilly while Jimmy and Lil hooted. Their laughter clawed Jacob's ears, as a touch of rancor crept into his eyes.

"Just turn the radio to 1140 on the AM dial," Jessica snickered.

Most of the time, Jacob was amused by his unfamiliarity with the *englisch* world, but he did not like to be ridiculed. So often, with these three, he was confronted by something foreign to his upbringing. Once again, they made him and the Amish seem to be stupid. Resentment soured his mouth.

"Man-o-man," Jimmy chuckled, "yer lucky ya left when ya did. Now, let's get that beer outta the trunk and into the back seat."

Jimmy passed a can of beer to Jacob, who snapped it open and drank it quickly.

"Hey, Jake-o, take it easy. The movie hasn't even started yet."

"TGIS," Jacob recited, snapping open another can of beer.

"TGIS?"

"Thank God It's Saturday."

Jessica giggled uneasily.

In back, Lil twisted about, pushing her feet against the cooler. "I don't know if I'm going to like this. It's a little cramped for four whole hours."

Jimmy said peevishly, "We don't havta watch both movies. I didn't want to come anyway."

Jacob adjusted the radio dial when the movie started and then drank four beers in a half hour.

"Geez, Jake, whaddaya tryin' to do?" Jessica was still sipping her second beer. "Drink for the whole Amish country?"

At ten, loosely holding another beer, Jacob sat gazing at the windshield, his eyes glazed and disengaged. He sat, without drinking, holding the can of beer, till the movie ended.

"What a dumb movie *that* was," Jimmy declared as the intermission began.

"I dunno," Lil responded, snuggling comfortably against him. "I liked how he helped her."

"And how did *you* like it, Jake?" Jessica asked cuttingly.

Jake didn't respond.

Jessica turned around to the back seat. "He's completely out of it, Jimmy. Look at him."

Lil sat upright when Jimmy leaned forward.

"Hey, buddy," Jimmy called out, shaking his shoulder. "How're ya doin'?"

"Oo-oo, *ya,*" Jake murmured. "*Was?*"

"Oh, lord, now he's talkin' Dutch," Jessica griped, lighting a cigarette.

"Jake-o, buddy," Jimmy continued.

"No-o probe-lem," Jake said. "No-o probe-lem."

"That's right, buddy," Jimmy laughed, imitating his accent, "No-o-o-o probe-lem."

Jacob's eyes snapped back into focus, losing that faraway glaze, and focused on Jessica's face.

She wrinkled her nose. "You're drunk!"

"Oo-o-o no-o," Jake slurred slowly. "Just buzzzzed a leeettle."

"Buzzed a little, yeah!"

"I'm gonna get some popcorn," Lil decided, straightening up. "Does anyone want some? Candy?"

"I'll take some popcorn," Jessica requested, turning to face Lil. "Just a small one without butter. I have to do *some*thing up here."

Lil clambered over the cooler to get out of the car.

"Another beer, Jessica?" Jimmy suggested.

She nodded.

"Could I have one?" Jake asked.

Jessica, her voice hard as iron, declared, "No, you've had enough already."

"Oh, c'mon, let him have one. He's celebrating his car."

"The way he's drinking, he won't have one to celebrate with after tonight."

"I can . . . drive . . . o-kay."

"*Ya* fur shure," Jessica mocked.

"I can. No-o probe-lem."

"Sure ya can, buddy. Here ya go."

Jacob snatched the can of beer and drank it down.

"Do you see that?" she moaned, deeply annoyed. "He's drinkin' like it's pop."

Jimmy whispered across the front seat. "One of us can drive home. He's never had a car before. He's never even had a driver's license before, for godssake. Let him party hearty!"

Jacob caught the last of this. "*Ya*, let me par-tee har-tee."

Lil climbed back into the car with two tubs of popcorn and passed one to Jessica. Jacob snapped open another beer and drank it down as the next movie started. Then he drank another beer. His eyes glazed over again with that faraway look. His head fell back, and his baseball cap tumbled into the back seat.

Jessica frowned, turning around. "Now he's asleep."

"Passed out, you mean," Jimmy declared. "Just watch the movie. Let him sleep it off."

Jessica let out a disgusted sound and hunched down in her seat to watch the movie. When Jacob started to snore, she shook his arm roughly. He muttered, "No-o probe-lem," and slumped against the door. After ten minutes, Jessica started to whine about having seen the movie before, and Jimmy said he would drive home. With little difficulty, they shifted Jacob's slumbering figure over to the passenger side of the front seat. Jessica, irritated and affronted, climbed in back with Lil. Jimmy zoomed through the exit and turned back onto the narrow road, twisted in tight curves. Within a few minutes, the headlights illuminated the orange slow-moving triangle attached to the rear of a Nebraska Amish buggy.

"Damn!" Jimmy cried, slowing down to five miles an hour. "What the hell are they doin' out here, anyway?"

"They must live in Wilton," Lil suggested matter-of-factly.

Jimmy flashed the headlights high and low and leaned on the horn. On the narrow road, the buggy couldn't move closer to the shoulder.

Jessica scowled. "Just pass it."

"Freakin' conchies," he muttered fiercely under his breath. "They shouldn't let them on the roads if they don't want to drive cars."

He pressed down hard on the accelerator and jerked around the horse and buggy, leaning on the horn the entire time. The driver talked soothingly to his horse to keep it from getting spooked as he heard someone yelling words he could not understand.

"Dinosaurs! Fossils!" Jimmy screamed as he thundered past. "You have one less now, hah!"

After he reached the main drag, he started in on the Amish again. "Should be off the roads. Slowin' everyone down. It's one thing if *they* want to go slow, but they don't have no right to slow everyone else down. There should be some law against that."

"C'mon, Jimmy," Lil quietly soothed him.

"Hey, Jessica," he said, grinning, "remember that Halloween night when we burned down them corn shocks? The whole field dotted with fires! Had to call the fire department and everything."

Jessica said nothing. She lit a cigarette.

CHAPTER 29

On Tuesday morning Mr. Teeter, a cigarette clamped in the corner of his thick lips, stood in the front door of his apartment building, reading the search warrant. "I just knew he was trouble the first time I laid eyes on him, I did. So he's the one who burned down all them Amish barns, huh?"

"Have you seen him at all this weekend?" Agent Tate asked.

"Nope," Mr. Teeter replied, handing the search warrant back to him. "I haven't seen him and haven't heard him since Saturday afternoon."

"Heard him?"

"His room's right over my living room. I can hear him clumping around."

As he unlocked Jacob's door, he added, "He always paid his rent on time, though, that much I'll say." He coughed and hacked. "I really gotta give up smoking, I tell ya." When he pushed opened the door, he gasped, "Hoo-boy, look at this!"

Sergeant Stuter and Agent Tate were hit by the strong stale odor of cigarette smoke and dirty clothes. Pop cans, beer cans, and whiskey bottles were scattered on the desk and floor. One can of beer had spilled and dried. Ashtrays spilled over with cigarette butts and ashes. The trash can overflowed. Empty Kool packs, candy wrappers, and McDonald's cups and paper bags were everywhere. Clothes were piled on the floor and the desk chair. The bed was unmade. The lopsided chair was even more lopsided.

"Look at this mess!" Mr. Teeter wheezed, shaking his sizable head. "And look at that. Pulled the book right out from under that chair."

"Not usually like this?" Agent Tate asked.

Mr. Teeter crushed his cigarette out in an overflowing ashtray. "Why, no, not at all. He was always pretty clean for a guy. I can't believe this."

"It looks like he didn't clean this room for days," Sergeant Stuter remarked.

"For weeks," Mr. Teeter complained. "And you wonder why I have to take a security deposit. I'm surprised at this, very surprised."

The ringing of Mr. Teeter's phone bounced up the stairway. "Gotta get that. Just close the door when you leave. I'll lock it later."

Agent Tate moved to a stack of books on the bureau and picked up the *Pennsylvania Driver's Manual*. "What does this say?" Something in German had been scrawled on the cover: *Meine Unterweisung auf die englisch Welt.*

Sergeant Stuter studied the handwritten words. "My instruction for the English world."

Agent Tate, shaking his head, laid the pamphlet down and looked through the other books. A copy of *Moby-Dick*. "Here's that Stephen King novel." He showed Sergeant Stuter the copy of *Fear and Trembling*. "Do you know anything about this author, Søren Kierkegaard?"

"Not really."

Agent Tate nodded and set the book down. A copy of *Walden*. A copy of *The Old Man and the Sea*. Other books. The Bible. Its black cover was oddly indented. When he opened it, he saw that many passages were underlined or flagged. Out of idle curiosity, he flipped to Revelation and checked some marked lines: "I saw seven golden candlesticks. . . . He had in his right hand seven stars. . . . When he had opened the seventh seal . . ."

Holding the Bible open in his hand, Agent Tate remarked, "In Revelation there are seven seals, and in Big Valley seven barns were set on fire."

"But only six burned."

"Seven candlesticks, seven stars, seven seals, seven barns. Any connection, do you think?"

Sergeant Stuter answered with a shrug.

Agent Tate then read out loud from Revelation 9:2. "He opened the bottomless pit; and there arose a smoke out of the pit, as the smoke of a great furnace; and the sun and the air were darkened by reason of the smoke of the pit."

He closed the Bible and opened the closet door. From the top shelf, he pulled down a crumpled IGA grocery bag and dumped its contents on the unmade bed—brown broadfall pants, white shirt, straw hat, and black work shoes. "Couldn't get rid of his Amish clothes, I guess. Now why do they dress like this anyway?"

Sergeant Stuter stared at the heap of abandoned clothes. "It's a language. What you wear tells who you are, what you do, how you live. My blue uniform and badge announce that I am a law enforcement agent. Think of a doctor dressed in white. Think of a lawyer dressed in dark sober suits. The same basic idea. The clothes are simple, plain, modest, good for work on a farm. The Nebraska Amish always wear white shirts and have white hatbands."

"And the other groups have the black hatbands?"

"Correct. The Black Tops and the Yellow Tops have black hatbands and colored shirts."

"And some have black pants with a single suspender. Why just one?"

"Two are considered worldly excess. One is enough."

Agent Tate turned the straw hat over in his hands. "It's something right out of the past."

"Some say the eighteenth century. The Amish basically kept the dress of their peasant ancestors in Europe. There are many small differences, though, that most people just don't notice but are very important to the Amish—the color of the hatband, or even the *width* of the hatband or the hat's brim. There are a lot of small details not caught by the average tourist."

"Well, they don't have to waste time deciding what to wear each day."

"Correct. On a day-to-day basis, they give little thought to vanity or variety of clothes."

"Similar to a nun, you know, married to Christ and all that."

"Quite similar. Her outfit identifies her; it's a symbol. Same with the Roman collar on priests and ministers. It's a sign of living a religious life."

"And it's the same thing with the haircuts and the beards?"

"Symbols as well. They all help to separate the Amish from the rest of the world. It's a statement that they have committed themselves to the Amish community and to Christ."

"So Jacob hid his Amish clothes, cut his hair, and shaved his beard, so he could become like the outside world?"

"In appearance, anyway."

Agent Tate rubbed his chin and pondered this for a moment. He laid the straw hat on the bed, squatted down, and opened the refrigerator. "Nothing in here but a six-pack of Coors Light." He glanced out the window, the glass stained with smoke. "Well, apparently he hasn't been here since Saturday. No indication that he was. But this mess here," gesturing at the room, "this isn't from a lazy weekend. This stuff has been piling up for weeks. Jacob stopped taking care of his room."

Sergeant Stuter surveyed the room once more. "I'd say Jacob stopped taking care of *himself*."

CHAPTER 30

On Sunday, Esle woke at five to a sky that rumbled and flashed. He sniffed the air, dark with thunder and rain and new beginnings. On that September morning he would be baptized into the Amish church. He knew, as he lay there listening to the chaotic sky, that he would remember every moment of this day.

Yesterday, those preparing for baptism met with the preachers for one final meeting. At that time, the young people were given their last opportunity to "turn back" if they did not feel they were ready to take the vow of baptism. None had. Each young man present was also asked to promise that he would accept the duties of being a preacher if chosen. Esle doubted that he had the ability to preach well, but if God called him to that ministry, then he would obey that divine command.

He turned his head toward his brother's empty bed and the bright blue, light blue, dark blue pattern of his quilt—Jacob's ladder. His own quilt pattern was called turkey tracks. A sadness, heavy and complicated, rumbled within him as he brooded over his brother and his absence.

Esle sat up and placed his bare feet on the cool hardwood floor. He lit the kerosene lamp, transforming the dark room to a watercolor of pale light. The sky coiled and cracked and rain fell in abundance. He stretched his arms over his head, rubbed his eyes, and got dressed. Even on the day of his baptism, he still had to tend the cows. But his every activity that day, no matter how ordinary or familiar, carried additional meaning and greater significance.

When Esle passed through the kitchen, Seth sat at the table sipping a cup of instant coffee to wake up. As he hurried across the barnyard, the cows placidly stood in the warm rain. Sam was already in the cow stables, tossing feed into the troughs.

After breakfast, the rain stopped, the sky cleared, and the sun poured fresh light into the morning air. Esle stood at the kitchen sink and washed his face, neck, and hands and combed his brick-red hair and rust-colored beard. The night before, he had taken a long hot bath and scrubbed himself extra clean. Upstairs he changed into his best Sunday clothes: white shirt, brown trousers laced up in back, black socks and shoes, a gray *Mütze* (frock coat), and a plain-crown black felt hat with a wide brim.

The barnyard of Moses C. Hostetler's farm was jammed with white-topped buggies. Samuel, Stephen, and Levi, the three sons of Moses C., were acting as hostlers, unhitching horses and putting them to stable.

"The preachers are here already, Esle," Levi remarked, grabbing the horse's bridle. "And there's that bishop from over in Sinking Valley." A bishop and a preacher from the neighboring valley were attending the special service.

"*Gut,*" Esle replied, stepping out of the buggy.

As he crossed the barnyard, he scanned the group of young women, all clad in dark blue dresses and black caps, gathered on the front porch. But he could not find Judith. In the kitchen, he saw her whispering with Rachel and Deborah in the far corner of the room, heads bowed, solemn and quiet. When she lifted her shimmering blue eyes, she caught sight of him, and a faint smile played on her lips. He nodded slightly before she turned back to her younger sister.

Then Esle saw his father and mother, with radiant faces, talking to Ezra S. and Lydia. When his mother turned to him, her eyes brightened, but he noticed a twinkling of sadness as the absence of Jacob passed like a cloud-shadow over her sharp-angled face. Esle stood serene and self-possessed near the front door as he watched various people enter, engage in chitchat about the weather and the crops, and then nod meaningfully in his direction.

At nine, the *Vorsinger* announced the first hymn. The men removed their black hats. As the voices swelled with glorious sound, the bishops, preachers, and deacon retired to an upstairs room along with the baptismal applicants for one last time. With grave, pensive faces, Esle, Judith, Rachel, and three other boys followed the ordained men. The singing to Esle seemed particularly moving and melodious as he mounted the stairs.

In the upstairs room, the applicants sat before the elders and listened with sharp attention and slightly bowed heads to their final admonition and counsel: the importance of the vow of baptism as well as the difficulties and the rewards of a Christian life of service and humility within the Amish community. As the ordained men urged and cautioned the six young people, their wise voices were punctuated and underscored the entire time by the singing vibrating through the rooms downstairs.

With keen regard Esle listened when his grandfather Abraham C., the bishop, spoke in a firm and strong voice: "This morning when you are baptized into the Amish church, you begin your true spiritual journey on this earth with one decisive act, a bold and courageous choice, to take a vow you must uphold the rest of your life. God and the congregation will be witnesses to your vow. It is a decision for Christ and the church, a promise to cling to the godly world of the Amish and to avoid the evil of the *englisch* world. The path is straight. The path is narrow. The path is difficult. But this is the true way.

"You now end one life and begin a new life. Dress according to the *Addning*. Avoid worldly amusements, the games, the dances, and the music. Do not swear. Do not boast. Do not gossip. Do not drink. Do not carouse. And above all, do not yield to the lust of the flesh. Your words should always be modest, your conduct considerate and kind. Bear in mind the golden rule which Jesus set forth: Do unto others as you would have them do unto you. Tell the truth; never must your word be questioned. Let your speech shine with light for others to see.

"The rewards you shall reap are beyond your imagination. Your *new* life begins this morning with baptism. There is no turning back. There is no looking back. There can be no change from the course you take today. This is a moment that will alter the entire shape of your life. Be dedicated to the Amish way, to your church, and to Jesus Christ, our Lord and Savior." Abraham C. fell silent.

The young people were then dismissed to return to the places reserved for them, one bench for the two sisters and one for the four young men, just behind the preachers' chairs. The six applicants went downstairs, bearing the burden of counsel on their shoulders, and stepped with slow, sure steps down the center aisle. Old Man Sam sat at his usual spot in his rocking chair. The mothers dandled infants on their laps. Then the bishops, preachers, and deacon entered.

The service followed the same order as on any other church Sunday. After the hymns and the periods of silence, Stephen D. Hostetler preached first, touching upon the solemnity of the occasion. John D. Yoder, the deacon, read from Scripture, Matthew 13 and John 15.

As John D. read, Esle could hardly concentrate on the words and simply stared at the deacon's copper-colored beard. There was something about fields and mustard seeds and tares, but he could not absorb the meaning. All at once, the deep responsibility and absoluteness of this vow burst before his eyes with startling reality. He had never questioned entering the Amish church or taking the vow of baptism, but the intense *reality* of the day itself and the actual ceremony filled him with sudden awe and fearful wonder. Next, John D. read from John, but Esle did not hear a word. His grandfather would soon preach the main sermon, to be followed by the sacred ceremony of baptism.

Abraham C. stood. Everyone seemed especially attentive, not only for the pleasure of his sermon but also from knowing that this morning their bishop would baptize one of his own grandsons into the Amish world, thus fulfilling, in a true way, his respected name as the "grandfather of faith." For that, they rejoiced. But everyone also knew that one *other* grandson, one of the twins, had left the Amish that spring: one lost to the *englisch* world, one found by the Amish. There was an odd, lopsided emotion in the room because Jacob's absence was a palpable presence. The older members knew the sermon would resonate with additional, painful meaning as Abraham C. spoke about how the Amish must abstain from the ways of the outside world.

Abraham C. stood still, stood straight. He removed his spectacles and with a white handkerchief rubbed the lenses clean. After he secured the end pieces to his ears and fixed the frame in place, his patient blue eyes alighted on the bowed head of each applicant, one by one, as if merely through the intensity of his gaze he could instill faith into each one. His intense gaze then traveled over the congregation. He held his hands waist-high and touched his fingertips together before spreading his arms.

"In John," he began, in a hushed voice, "Jesus says, 'I am the vine, you *are* the branches. The one who abides in me, and I in that one, the same brings forth much fruit: for without me you can do nothing. If one does not abide in me, that one is cast forth as a branch, and is withered; and men gather them, and cast *them* into the fire, and they are burned.' " He paused so the words could resonate within the minds of the congregation and especially within the minds of the applicants. Then he said in a booming voice, "Do not wither and be cast into the fire!"

Again he paused and then repeated, softly but emphatically, looking directly at the row of applicants, "Do not wither and be cast into the fire. Do not mistake the world for heaven. Do not mistake the temporal for the eternal. Do not mistake the body for the soul. Do not mistake the smoke for the fire. The pilgrimage you begin today is a difficult one, but one also filled with extraordinary rewards and spiritual riches. As God never abandoned his Son, so, too, will the Amish never abandon a single member of the church *as long as the rules and the regulations are followed*. Be mindful of the *Addning*.

"I remind you of the fate of the children of Israel when Moses descended from Mount Sinai with the two stone tablets and found that they had forsaken God, were worshiping the golden calf, and were running wild. The true path is narrow and strait, but the rules and expectations of the Amish are unmistakable, straightforward, direct, clear, and plain. The journey is indeed dark and difficult, but the light of God is bright and reassuring. Do not wither and be cast into the fire. Be attached to Christ, as a branch is to the vine. Together let us be a vigorous vine in the Amish faith."

For an hour, Abraham C. instructed and warned everyone present about the temptations of the world, the spiritual dignity of the Amish, duties of the young people starting on the path of Christ, and the continued inspection of behavior for those who have already started.

For the entire sermon, Esle kept his head bowed and listened—or only half-listened—to his grandfather's words as excitement teased his mind. He kept his eyes on the hardwood floor, on the lines of the boards, on a dark knot in the wood. Every now and then, his eyes shifted to his feet, where he noticed a scuff on the tip of his left shoe.

Abraham C. repeated one last time as he concluded his sermon, "Do not wither and be cast into the fire." Then he paused again and drew in a deep, reverential breath. "Today, we have the ceremony of baptism. We have gathered here six young people who have expressed their faith in God, who have promised to obey the rules of the church, who have requested baptism, and who now wish to be received into our fellowship. If there is anyone who believes that any of the applicants should not be allowed to enter the church, let him or her speak now. No other complaint shall be entertained after this time." He carefully surveyed the gathered members of the church. "There seems to be no objection. Let us prepare for baptism."

The deacon walked out of the room. A soft breeze stirred the air, fragrant with chrysanthemums and turning leaves and the rain-fresh morning.

In a commanding voice, Abraham C. pronounced, "The vow you are about to take is not made to the preachers *nor* to the church. The vow you are about to take is made to God alone, with all of us as witnesses. If it is still your desire to become members of the body of Christ, then kneel."

The six applicants kneeled. The deacon returned with a small pail of water and a tin cup. Esle was oddly aware that his knee had covered the dark knot on the floor when he knelt down. The wood was hard against his knees. Esle kept his head bowed low.

Bishop Abraham C. Hostetler, his own grandfather, stood in front of him. "Can you confess that Jesus Christ is the Son of God?"

"I confess that Jesus Christ is the Son of God."

"Are you willing to walk with Christ and his church and to remain faithful through life and until death?"

"*Ya.*"

"Are you willing, by the help and grace of God, to *renounce* the world, the devil, your own flesh and blood, and be *obedient* only to God and to his church?"

"*Ya.*"

Then Abraham C. stood in front of the next boy and asked him the same three questions. The last to be questioned was Judith. To the members of the church, Abraham C. said, "Please rise."

While everyone else in the room stood to pray, the six applicants remained kneeling, with bowed heads.

"O almighty God and dear merciful Father!" Abraham C. intoned from *Die ernsthafte Christenpflicht*, "you knew from eternity that created humanity would not remain in its innocent state but would come to a Fall. Not only that, but you knew they would load upon themselves the just blame for their punishment. You (who love your creation) have also from eternity provided for humanity in the fullness of time. You did not spare your only Son, but sent him and gave him up on behalf of humanity, so that all who believe in him should not perish but have everlasting life. You let such love and grace be proclaimed and offered to humanity through your holy gospel. By this same message, you commanded that all who accept and believe the gospel are to submit to baptism in the name of Jesus. . . ."

After the prayer was concluded, the congregation sat down. Abraham C., John D., the deacon, and Hannah, the deacon's wife, proceeded with the rite of baptism. Esle's heart was pounding, like a horse kicking in its stall, pommeling the inside of his chest. His stomach ached and his rib cage tightened. He was barely aware of how they baptized the first young man.

Soon Abraham C. and John D. stood before him, and his grandfather placed his ancient palms gently but firmly on his grandson's head. "Esle Hostetler, upon your faith, which you have confessed before God and these many witnesses, you are baptized in the name of the Father, the Son, and the Holy Spirit. Amen."

As Abraham C. said each name of the Godhead, the deacon poured a bit of water through the bishop's loosely cupped hands. Esle felt the water drip on his scalp and dribble down his face, around his ears and along his neck. He could not tell if the water was cold or hot or warm or how much water had been used. All he knew was that then and there in that concentrated moment he was transfigured into an adult with responsibilities, a full-fledged member of the Amish church, a true Christian. His hooves-beating heart subsided at once when he heard the words of faith. His rearing heart steadied and settled in the presence of his grandfather's faith and love. With this simple act, his life had changed forever. He would be a fruitful branch, attached to the vine. He would not wither. He would not be cast into the fire.

They baptized the other two boys and then stood before Rachel. Hannah, the deacon's wife, stepped forward, untied the strings to Rachel's black cap, and removed it. Abraham C. placed his hands upon her head and repeated the ceremony. Then Judith.

Finally, Abraham C. came to Esle in a second round, clasped his hand, and said, "In the name of the Lord and the church, we extend to you the hand of fellowship. Rise up." Abraham C. kissed his grandson on the lips with the holy kiss, a symbol of love and fellowship between believers as commanded in Scripture. He gave the same handclasp and words of welcome to the others just baptized and greeted each young man with the holy kiss. Hannah bestowed the holy kiss upon the young women. Rachel's pretty face was streaked with tears. Judith's shimmering blue eyes were moist and radiant. Esle felt a stinging sensation in his nose and eyes. A single tear slipped down his cheek. He quickly wiped it away with his knuckle.

Now Abraham C. asked the six to be seated again. He implored the congregation to be helpful to these new members and exhorted the newly baptized, one last time, to be faithful to the church and to the ministry. Abraham C. read from Romans 6. As he concluded the reading, his voice rose in majestic tones. "But now being made free from sin, and become servants to God, you have your fruit unto holiness, and the end everlasting life. For the wages of sin *is* death; but the gift of God *is* eternal life through Jesus Christ, our Lord."

Abraham C., visibly moved and visibly tired, sat down and folded his hands in his lap. The other preachers gave a brief commentary. After that, everyone knelt for prayer and a short benediction. The congregation sang a final hymn and, after four hours, the baptismal service ended.

Esle stood on the front porch, his eyes sweeping over the brown fields and the blue skies. Rebekah came up to him and, with her penetrating blue eyes, gazed with beaming satisfaction at her son. Sam and Seth and other youth crowded around him with joyous congratulations. Rebekah, though, turning to the far fields, sighed as a flicker of sharp sadness betrayed her thoughts: only half her heart was pleased that day.

All afternoon was a glorious celebration, although the afternoon activities remained the same: talk and the customary meal—the traditional white bean soup, homemade bread and butter, apple butter, white or green pickles, apple *Schnitz* moon pies, coffee, tea, and water. Conversation centered on the baptismal ceremony, the new members of the church, the affirmation of the Amish lifestyle, and the spiritual rewards. Virtually every man in the district clapped Esle on the shoulder, gave him the right hand of fellowship, and wished him well on taking the vow. Some men joked that he could soon be married.

Esle rode home with Sam and Seth late that afternoon for supper and the evening milking. Afterward, Esle stood in the barnyard and looked up at Stone Mountain. The setting sun, a great saucer of red-yellow light, hung just above the dark crest of the mountain range. How huge the sun appeared to him. He turned to Jacks Mountain and saw the full moon, a perfect cream-white disc, already floating in a crisp clean sky.

Esle asked Sam, "You're going to the singing, aren't you?"

"*Ya*, I'm going to take *Daadi's* buggy."

"I'm going to the Uni-Mart before I go over. Do you want anything?"

"Buy me some Pepsi."

When Esle drove his buggy into the parking lot, he saw the Zook's buggy tied to the hitching rail and Gary Schippe's metallic-green van parked directly in front of the Original. Next to the van was a black car he had never seen before. If Shem and Jonas were here, then Gideon must not be far behind. He wondered idly why they weren't at the singing yet. They must be up to some monkey business, he thought sadly, hoping that these Amish boys would settle down and take their vows, too. Otherwise, their flirting with the world would send them down the same path as Jacob. He pulled at his rust-colored beard and settled his black hat more firmly on his head.

After he tied his horse, he noticed that a clutch of onlookers had suddenly formed around the black car. Gary stood slouched, in a white nylon jacket and jeans, smoking a cigarette. Johnnie stood outside, as well, in his sauce-stained apron, his head held high and bobbing up and down like a rooster as he examined the black car. Jonas was there, dressed in his church clothes but not wearing his black hat. He was looking at the black car with his arms folded across his chest as though he were pronouncing judgment on some farm issue.

A rather attractive girl, with long dark hair pulled back into a ponytail, wearing a dark red jacket, leaned against the front fender and stared off into the distance as though she had been born bored. Shem, a cigarette dangling from the corner of his mouth, was opening the door on the driver's side. Someone sat in the driver's seat.

"Al-loo, Shem and Jonas," Esle called as he walked past them, touching the brim of his black hat.

Shem dropped his cigarette and crushed it with his boot as a guilty expression crossed his face. Jonas's eyes registered alarm as he unfolded his arms and dropped them to his side.

"Going to the singing tonight, I hope?" Esle asked.

"*Ya*, we'll be there."

Esle noticed that the girl was staring at him in an odd, amused manner, almost as though she knew him. Then he saw someone vaguely familiar, wearing a white baseball cap, climb out of the driver's seat and look over at him with an expression of surprised pleasure and embarrassment. Esle's reaction was difficult to trace because his emotions flowed easily and rapidly from elation and pleasure to disappointment and displeasure and, finally, to resentment and discomfort.

All these thoughts and feelings altered Esle's expression so quickly that Jacob could not discern one from the other and stood helplessly among his friends. Esle could not move and felt suspended, as though grappling hooks had suddenly hoisted him off the ground. In the dying light of a September afternoon, Jacob approached his twin brother.

"*Wie geht's?*" Jacob asked in a quiet voice, standing before him.

"Jacob." Esle finally replied, in a flat voice, seething with emotion but devoid of meaning.

"Do not be angry with me."

"It is now well beyond anger." Esle looked into his brother's face.

"You, more than anyone else, knew that I had to leave."

"I would have stopped you. I would have *tried* to stop you."

"And that is why I could not tell you."

There was an awkward pause. Although they could not hear, everyone at the black car had their eyes fastened on the two brothers.

"That's my car," Jacob explained in a tight voice, to break the silence. "I bought it a month ago. And that's Jessica—Jessica Smith."

Esle, his face besieged with emotions, shifted his eyes to the black car and the girl. Until that moment, *Jacob having left* had existed as an abstraction, as though he had not actually left but had been in the hospital for an extended recovery or had gone to visit relatives in another state; almost as though it did not exist except through intermittent telephone reports from week to week. In a sense, it was not *real* for him. However, now he was confronted with the concrete facts of Jacob's haircut, his clothes, his car, his girl. Esle had to acknowledge that his twin brother had been swallowed by the *englisch* serpent.

"Would you like to see the car?" Jacob asked in a feeble voice. "There's a radio in it and everything."

Esle looked with abhorrence at the black car, a visible symbol of worldly temptation, a black image that ripped and scarred the surface of his memory. In a firm voice he answered, "*Nay*."

Jacob, his head bowed, nodded.

"That is not your life," Esle declared.

Jacob looked up at him, exploring his face.

"That is not your life, Jacob," Esle repeated. "That is mere distraction."

He responded weakly, "But it *is* my life now."

"*Nay*. *Nay*. Your life is Amish. It will be always Amish. Your soul is Amish. With all your brains, you should see that. All *that* is distraction from your true purpose."

"What do you mean?" Jacob demanded. "What *is* my true purpose?"

"To seek God."

The words stunned Jacob. He could not speak, overwhelmed at the simplicity of the truth.

"And to seek his righteousness," Esle added.

A long moment passed, an eternity, before Jacob asked, "Are you going to the singing now?"

"*Ya*, just picking up some Pepsi and snacks."

"Where is it?"

"At Moses C.'s."

"Oh."

"I was baptized today."

Jacob stared at the space between their faces, as though the words were floating there between them in the evening air. He realized, with forceful suddenness, that he also would have been baptized that morning if he had not left in the spring—a spring that seemed so long ago. He said nothing, wrestling with words and meaning and knowing how futile words were for the solemnity of the occasion.

Esle gazed curiously into his eyes, as though searching for something. "You have Grandfather's eyes. The color is darker, maybe, and deeper, but still the same."

Jacob glanced down and his shoulders drooped. "But you have Grandfather's faith," he said.

"I have the simplicity of Grandfather's faith, but you could have the complexity of Grandfather's faith."

The words, again, stunned Jacob.

"I must go," Esle said gently as he departed.

Jacob stood in the parking lot, watching his twin brother march away into the twilight, on the day of his baptism, bearing the divine weight of that decision like a mighty shield in one hand and in the other an angelic sword. His figure was armored in light. Jacob felt cataclysmic loss.

CHAPTER 31

Sergeant Stuter and Agent Tate found Danny Yoder on Tuesday morning, clinging to the edge of a roof on an old Victorian house on the south side of town.

"Hey, Yoder!" his boss shouted.

"Ye-ah?"

"Some gentlemen here to see you."

Danny glanced down at Sergeant Stuter and Agent Tate standing on the front lawn and accidentally dropped his hammer. The three men watched the hammer bounce on the withered brown grass. Danny slipped down the ladder and picked up his hammer.

After introductions, Agent Tate said, "Just a few words, Mr. Yoder."

"This abawt Jake?" Danny rocked from side to side on his feet, shifting his weight, folding his arms across his chest, and unfolding them.

"This is about Jake."

"I don't know nothin'. I haven't even *seen* him since . . . since last month, no, since October."

"Do you know where he is now?"

Danny vigorously shook his head no.

"Are you sure about that?"

"Fur shure."

"Where were you Saturday night at midnight?"

A shocked expression galvanized his face. "Here in town. With Amy, my girlfriend, at my place."

"Where is that?"

"Twenty-seven Westbrook Drive."

"Is Jake Hostetler in your apartment?"

"No. No way. What are yew sayin'?"

"When, exactly, was the last time you saw him?"

"Like I said. Over a month ago. He chust gave me a ride up the street."

"And you haven't seen him since?"

Danny shook his head. "Chust that time."

"How did he seem to you?"

"I don't understand."

"Was he happy? Sad? What did you talk about?"

Eyeing both men nervously, Danny shifted his weight again. "I don't think he was tew happy."

"Why?"

"He didn't like his job."

"At the Imperial Chicken Plant?"

"Ye-ah. Hated it, he said."

"That all?"

"He was kinda . . . confused, I think."

"Confused?"

"Livin' here. In the city."

Sergeant Stuter spoke to him in Pennsylvania German. "You mean living here in the *englisch* world and not adjusting well to its ways?"

Danny, his eyes flat, scanned Sergeant Stuter's face and nodded. "He always talked abawt the Amish."

"In what way?" Agent Tate asked.

"Missin' his family. Missin' church. I couldn't always understand what he was gettin' at."

"Did he drink or use drugs?"

Danny glanced at Sergeant Stuter's silver badge. "He drank."

"How much?"

"Don't know fur shure. But ven yew can't do something and then yew can, yew go a little crazy. I think he was drinkin' tew much, with vurk un all. He had a six-pack in his car ven he gave me that ride."

"Was he drinking it?"

"Not right then. It was chust there on the front seat. But he didn't look goot. Bad. Reel tired. Chust like things were gettin' to be tew much. Talked abawt quittin' his job, but I said it don't look goot ven yew want to get another one."

"Did you know he quit his job?"

"No."

"A week ago."

"I haven't seen him."

Agent Tate looked directly at Danny. "Do you know where Jacob might be?"

Danny folded his arms across his chest. "With Jimmy and Jessica? He's seein' Jessica. I don't know. Or with his friend Paul?"

"Paul?"

"Ye-ah, Paul . . . Paul Virila, Vagila, I dunno, some E-talian name. His dad's a lawyer here in town."

"Paul Virgilia," Sergeant Stuter supplied.

"Ye-ah, that's it. Paul Virgilia. He's a guy at college. At Penn State."

"And Paul and Jake are good friends?"

"I think so."

"Is this Paul in town now?"

"I don't know. I don't know him reel-ly. He's likely over at Penn State." He shrugged and blinked and turned his eyes upward. "We-ell, I'll bee. They *said* it was gonna snow."

Sergeant Stuter and Agent Tate both looked up at the gray sky and the falling snow, falling softly, silently.

CHAPTER 32

Baptism was not complete without communion. Esle was eager for this Sunday church and pleased to be wearing his gray *Mütze*. He briskly drove his horse and buggy along the road with Sam sitting next to him and Seth crouched in back. His eyes were flooded with the eloquence of mid-October: fields shorn and stubbled from harvest, mountains fiery and elevated with color, pastures trampled and worn from summer. He inhaled the sharp, crisp air. The trees and leaves saturated his senses with the gold and orange and copper tones of the autumn landscape. Needles of the pines had already solidified into a deeper, richer, darker green. Esle, within himself, deep within himself, through the mystery and wonder of baptism, had also changed, and with the forthcoming ceremony of communion—the consummation of his baptism—he again would change.

Four weeks had gone by since his baptism. At the intervening church Sunday, members met for *Attnungsgemee*, the preparatory service. It was a time of purification, of spiritual housecleaning, when members were expected to voice their agreement or disagreement with the *Addning*, the rules. Differences had to be settled, faults exposed and confessed, and peace and agreement established within the community. Nothing must be left standing to hinder any member receiving communion. The sermons that day lasted longer as the preachers proclaimed their opinions on the rules and the discipline and acts that are forbidden. Every member had to affirm unity with the Amish church and the Amish way.

In those four weeks, with the fragrance of ripening pears and apples, Esle plowed fields to plant barley and wheat. In the fall landscape, under clear autumn skies, he rode the one-bottom plow behind four straining draft horses and thought he plowed straighter furrows and drilled neater rows than before. He felt immersed in happiness. All that summer, the rain was good, the sunshine strong, the harvest plentiful. All that summer, he had labored both in the fields and in the instructional classes for baptism. All that summer, a resolve, strong and keen, flourished as he saw more and more of Judith. The summer and the harvest and the baptism and the imminent communion filled him with joy and bliss and a sense of now being part of a complete world, a world whole, integrated and magnificent, melting into a great cosmos, dissolving into the greater glory of God.

As Esle approached Solomon E. Hostetler's farm, his scalp tingled. His toes felt pinched in his black shoes, though he had worn this same pair for countless Sundays. Last night, he had carefully scrubbed his toes and feet and clipped his thick toenails. The early morning air was cool and sharp and alive with color and faith. White-topped buggies lined the side field. Solomon E.'s boys were walking the horses to the stable or to the pasture. It was 7:45. This Sunday, church started at eight rather than nine and did not end till four or four thirty in the afternoon. For the Amish, the communion service was among the most meaningful of observances to reinforce their commitment to Christ and the church. Esle's eyes dimmed only once, briefly, when he considered his sole loss that year—his twin brother Jacob.

Inside, familiar faces and smiles and conversation about crops and good weather built invisible bridges throughout the rooms. Many women were seated on the benches in the *Kammer*. Old Man Sam leaned back in his rocking chair. Judith was in the kitchen, chatting with her sisters. When Esle turned in her direction, she let one long meaningful glance butterfly across the room to settle its delicate wings upon his face. All were in their usual places on the numerous benches. Once Esle sat down, he was conscious of those by whom he sat. On his left was Joseph, Judith's older brother, and on his right was Enoch, who was courting Judith's older sister. Before the first high-pitched note of the hymn sounded, he glanced at their shoes as he thought of the foot washing to come.

A time of silence followed the first hymn. Two guest preachers had joined his grandfather and the other preachers in the *Abrot* and would give spiritual and emotional support for the longer sermons required for communion. When they returned, singing ceased. Esle sat erect, his shoulders squared, and listened attentively to each word.

The first preacher was young Daniel S., with his copper-colored beard. In the *Aafang* he spoke about the special fellowship of the Amish and the need to observe the discipline of the church's rules and regulations, no matter how difficult that might be. Then Stephen D. delivered the first main sermon. He took a deep breath before beginning. Throughout his message, he quoted passages from the Old Testament, starting with Genesis and the Creation and the Fall of humankind, the curse and condition of sin, the forces of good and evil that battled humanity throughout early history. As he recounted biblical stories, selected to symbolize the eventual coming of the Messiah, he commented at length on each of them before concluding with the children of Israel searching for the Promised Land.

Communion sermons were taxing, but Stephen D. spoke with power and with emotion until the noon hour. Then Abraham C., as bishop, stood to preach the main sermon that continued the narrative of the Old and New Testaments, ending with *das Leiden Christi* (the suffering of Christ), the historical climax of the crucifixion.

The entire time Esle sat erect and attentive but was slightly embarrassed, now and then, when his stomach gurgled and growled. The noon hour had passed, and he watched as several persons rose quietly and slipped into the kitchen for a light snack. Esle was determined, however, not to eat anything until the breaking of bread.

Abraham C. had delivered this sermon for many years and neatly ended it at 3:00 in the afternoon, at the moment of Christ's death, for the breaking of bread and the drinking of wine, the symbolic body and blood of Jesus Christ. While he was nearing the end of his sermon, two preachers left the room and returned with a loaf of bread wrapped in a white cloth and a pitcher of red wine, which they placed on a small table. While they cut the bread into long sticks, Abraham C. recounted the origin of the bread, sowing, growing, harvesting, milling. He spoke of the wine, the growth of the grapes, having them pruned, and the need of the wine and all members to be purified.

When Abraham C. had finished preaching, the deacon handed him a stick of bread, and the congregation rose for prayer. Esle stood tall. After the prayer, all remained standing while the bishop and one of the ministers distributed morsels of bread to the members, row by row, bench by bench, first to the men and then to the women.

When his grandfather stood before him, Esle looked at the small, crumbly piece of white bread and felt the sky and the earth tremble as he bowed his knees in reverence to his Creator before taking the morsel into his mouth and slowly chewing and swallowing it. He sat down with total serenity in his heart, bridged to the earth, to the skies, to the Amish, to his Lord and Savior Jesus Christ. The red wine, in a common cup, was then passed to each member, and each took a sip.

After Abraham C. served all the church members, Stephen D. read from John about Christ washing the feet of his disciples: "Jesus rose from supper and laid aside his garments. He took a towel and girded himself. After that he poured water into a basin, and began to wash the disciples' feet, and to wipe them with the towel with which he was girded. . . . If I then, your Lord and Master, have washed your feet, you also ought to wash one another's feet. For I have given you an example, that you should do as I have done to you. Verily, verily, I say unto you, The servant is not greater than his lord; neither is the one sent greater than the one who sent him."

After Stephen D. read this account, Abraham C. urged everyone not to be partial but to wash the feet of the nearest person. Foot washing was to show humility, willingness to serve each other, and a resolve to seek daily cleansing from Christ. The closing hymn was "Vo'm Hertzen will ich singen (From the heart I will sing)." As the congregation sang, the other ministers and the deacon left the room and returned with wooden pails of water and white towels. The women retired to the kitchen to wash feet while the men remained in the main room.

Esle turned to Joseph. He thought it fitting that he should wash the feet of Judith's older brother. The hymn resounded through the farmhouse and the fields and the mountains. The pair removed their shoes and socks and in their turn went to a wooden pail of water. Joseph sat down and lifted one foot over the pail, and then the other. Esle, to show utmost humility, did not kneel but stooped to wash Joseph's feet by lifting water with his hands and pouring it over his feet. Then he toweled them dry, and they exchanged positions. Once they had washed each other's feet, they clasped hands and exchanged the holy kiss.

Joseph, who was older, said, "The Lord be with us." With deep solemnity, Esle responded, "Amen, in peace."

CHAPTER 33

Late Tuesday morning, Sergeant Stuter and Agent Tate drove through the mountainous landscape to Pennsylvania State University at State College. They had just talked to Paul's father, a prominent tax lawyer in Lewistown, who told them his son was at school. The snow veiled with white the roads and fields and mountains and trees. But the heavy gray skies grew light and pale, and the soft falling snow was dissolving in the morning air.

Sergeant Stuter pressed down on the accelerator for the steep incline through the Seven Mountains. "Do you think he actually might be all the way out here?"

"Well, let's put it this way," Agent Tate replied, fiddling with his tape recorder, "Jacob Hostetler has to be *some*where. And I'm going to find out where that somewhere is."

They found Paul that afternoon on one of the wrestling mats in the Greenberg Sports Complex. His dark hair was pushed back and his face flushed as he jogged over to the bleachers with a white towel draped around his shoulders.

"Coach said you wanted to speak to me?"

"A few minutes, Mr. Virgilia." Agent Tate went through the usual introductions and explanations. "Is Jacob Hostetler anywhere on this campus?"

Paul looked directly into the faces of the two detectives. "No."

"Do you know where he might be?"

Paul sat on one of the lower bleachers and wiped his face with the towel. "I saw him two weekends ago, during the Thanksgiving break, but I haven't *seen* him since then, and I haven't *talked* to him since then. I have no idea where he might be if he's not at his own place."

Agent Tate sighed and looked across the gym floor at two wrestlers, circling each other and bobbing from side to side.

"Do you really think Jacob set those barns on fire?" Paul challenged the two men.

"At this point, we don't *know* who set the fires, though we have some clues," Agent Tate replied. "We found Jacob's car in a field near Fairville, but we haven't found Jacob. And we need to find him."

"To find out what happened?"

"At least to find out why his car was in the field. But you were a pretty good friend of his. What did he seem like when you last saw him? What was he doing?"

A great thump shook the floor. The two wrestlers were now twisting and grappling on the mat. Paul watched their moves and countermoves a moment, weighing his response. "I was really concerned about him."

"In what way?"

"Well, on a simple level, I was concerned that he was drinking so much."

"Was this the last time you saw him?"

"At Thanksgiving. I had gone over to see him Saturday afternoon, just to talk and go out for a meal at Bob Evans. I remember I was upset about what he did for Thanksgiving."

"What did he do?"

"Nothing. That's what bothered me. The Amish apparently don't really celebrate Thanksgiving the way everyone else does, but I was still upset that he couldn't be with his family for the day." He wiped his face again. "I mean, *I* would have been upset to be alone, though it didn't seem to bother him. If I had known, I would have invited him over to have dinner with my family. Anyway, we walked back to his apartment, but his isolation on Thanksgiving disturbed me. It seemed to set the tone for the night because everything was . . . I don't know . . . gloomy."

"Gloomy?"

"Well, first, there was the solo Thanksgiving. Then two kids were having a fight outside his apartment building, and the police had to break it up. And Jacob told me about a suicide in the valley, and that he and his girlfriend were on the outs. Jacob couldn't stand to be around one of Jessica's friends who didn't believe in God, so Jessica was mad at him. He was drinking beer after beer. The whole night was just gloomy and morbid. And Jacob didn't look good, didn't look happy. He seemed lost, lost and isolated. By the time I left, he was pretty drunk. Jacob just seemed to be in trouble, as if the new world he was in was getting to be too much for him to handle. And then he had a big surprise."

"A surprise?"

"Well, I don't know if it's true or not, but he said he found out that Jimmy and Jessica, his friend and his girlfriend, were Amish, or that their *father* used to be Amish."

Agent Tate traded a glance with Sergeant Stuter. "How did he find that out?"

"Danny Yoder, another Amish boy who left, told him."

"How did he feel about that?"

"Well, when he told me, he was really upset. He felt betrayed that they hadn't said anything to him about it."

"What happened when he told them he knew?"

"Well, he hadn't told them. I don't know if he confronted them with it later on or not. It seemed like he couldn't trust anyone. And she was his so-called girlfriend."

"But he trusted you?"

Paul paused. "Yeah, I suppose he did."

"Was there anyone else he trusted? Did he trust Danny Yoder?"

"Oh, no! Certainly not him. He didn't get along with him at all." Paul paused again. "But he did have a friend in Fairville that he used to party with before he left. I think he taught Jacob how to drive a car, too."

"What's his name?"

"I know his first name—Gary."

"Gary Schippe?" Sergeant Stuter supplied.

"That's it."

CHAPTER 34

Late Thursday afternoon in mid-October, Jacob saw Danny Yoder strut out of McDonald's in his pointy-toed three-inch-heeled cowboy boots just as he was pulling out of the drive-through lane with a Big Mac, a large fries, and a large Coke. He had finished work and drove back to Lewistown on the highway, gazing absentmindedly at the turning leaves and the surging swamp of traffic. On the way, Jacob had also stopped at a package store where the clerk would would sell him beer, no questions asked.

"Hey, Jake," Danny called, hurrying over to his car window. "Amy has my truck. Can yew give me a ride chust around the corner, up to Farinat's Hardware?"

Jacob nodded. Danny strutted around the front of the car, nodding his head admiringly before climbing in. How Danny made Jacob's skin smoke and sizzle! He had only seen Danny a couple of times around the Block since he had last talked to him in Mercer's Department Store—Jacob had come from work that hot day on that miserable bus ride and had just started to dislike the work at Imperial. Now, however, he definitely loathed the chicken factory: the same routine, the foul air, the endless moving belt of chicken parts, the unceasing boredom.

"Hey, dude, long time no see," Danny said. "Haw's this baby been treatin' yew?"

Jacob turned the corner onto River Avenue. "Pretty good."

"Fur shure. It's a nice car, reel-ly nice." He saw the six-pack of Coors Light in the middle of the front seat, next to the aluminum lunch pail. "Chust off vurk? Haw's that goin'?"

"The only good thing I can say is that I can drive there instead of taking the bus," Jacob responded.

As the car bumped over the railroad crossing, Danny studied Jacob's tired face. "It gets to yew, don't it?"

"I'd like to quit."

"Haw long have yew been there naw?"

"Four and a half months."

"Wait till yew vurk fur six months before yew quit. It don't look goot if yew quit naw."

"Look good fur what?"

"To get hired somewhere else," Danny explained, his thin eyebrows raised in condescension. "No place wants to hire someone who's gonna leave after a few months."

"I don't know if I can put up with it fur another tew months."

"Yew'll chust have to," Danny insisted arrogantly. "Pull over there, in that space."

Jacob parked the car across the street from the cemetery. "Do yew smell something?"

"It's that dumpster behind the Chinese restaurant," Danny noted and then returned to the work topic. "But if yew want to keep your hirin' status goot, yew have to put up with it a little longer. Chust tune it awt or something. Yew don't drink at vurk, do yew?"

"*Nay*," Jacob swiftly replied.

"That might help yew. Quite a few dew. I did fur a while."

"I'd never be able to work if I were drinking," Jacob declared. As he let the idea tumble through his brain, it didn't seem such a bad idea. "As it is, I've been late—"

"Yew've been late?"

"Well, since I had a car, I thought I could sleep a little longer and just didn't figure the time that well. All the traffic."

"It's not goot to be late."

"It was only a few times."

"And were yew partyin' the night before?"

Jacob paused, pondering that question, since it seemed he did party every night or, at least, he *drank* every night. "Well, I wouldn't call it partying, but I do have a few beers each night."

"Haw many's a few?"

Jacob shrugged and turned to the cemetery. He always found it odd that there was a cemetery right downtown. Every time he saw it, he had an uneasy feeling. It was so unlike Amish cemeteries with their simple wood fences and plain slabs of stone. This cemetery had imposing stone posts, a black iron fence, huge headstones of various shapes and sizes, and tall dark trees. In the center was a marble figure as large as a man, with great wings stretched out like a hawk.

Jacob turned back to Danny, the cemetery reflected in his eyes. He sniffed. The rotten smell from the dumpster seemed stronger.

"I don't know how many I have. A few."

"Whoo-ee, dude! Yew gotta cool the party scene durin' the week. Same thing happened to me, till I kept my drinkin' to the weekends. Jimmy's havin' a bad effect on yew."

"Oh-h, I don't think so."

"Un what abawt Jessica?"

"What about her?"

"Haw's that goin'?"

"It's going."

Danny studied Jacob's face. "I chust don't know abawt those tew."

"What don't yew know?"

"I'd chust be careful, that's all."

"Yew said that before. Why?" Jacob asked.

"We-ell, I'd chust be careful cuz they hate the Amish so much, yew know."

"I just never talk about the Amish anymore when I'm with them."

"Have yew ever wondered vhy they're mad at the Amish?"

"No-o, not really," Jacob answered evasively.

"Yew mean to tell me yew don't know yet?"

"Don't know what yet?"

Danny looked hard at Jacob and asked in a puzzled voice, "Yew don't know that their father was Amish?"

The words appeared between them, rigid and haughty, as though kneeling on the front seat between them. Jacob sat in stunned silence.

"Believe it or nawt, their dad left the Amish abawt twenty-five years ago. I thought yew would have found awt by naw. It was some bad scene, tew. Excommunication, shunnin', the whole hog."

"From the valley?"

Danny nodded gravely, now enjoying the role of informant. "The Amish buried it. Totally. They never talked abawt it."

"It was that bad?"

"Prit-tee bad."

"I wonder what it was?" Jacob flipped through his memory for some past incident. Most of the terrible things were never openly discussed: suicide, adultery, insanity, domestic violence.

"I never could figure it awt," Danny admitted.

"And he stayed in the valley?"

"Nawt at first. But eventually he moved back. Don't reel-ly know."

"But their last name is Smith."

"Their father changed it."

"I just can't believe this."

"Well, don't tell Jimmy *I* tole yew. That's nawt something he tells *anyone*—I found awt by mistake vun night ven he was trippin' on acid. It sort of chust came awt. I don't know if he even remembers that he tole me."

"But didn't yew say something to him one night that upset him?"

Danny smiled. "Fur shure, he's always so uppity. So I ribbed him, 'Who knows, *everyvun* in this area might be related to the Amish.' "

"But they don't even look German."

"Their mom's Italian. They take after her. The dark hair, dark skin, dark eyes."

"Do yew know what group?"

"Not shure, but it must be the White Tops. They're the vuns he always screams about."

"None of this makes any sense," Jacob summed up.

"We-ell, like I said," Danny emphasized, lighting a cigarette and climbing out of the car, "don't say I said anything. I don't need Jimmy Smith hasslin' me."

Jacob glanced at the marble angel with the outstretched wings. "You're safe," he promised. "I won't say a word."

CHAPTER 35

The two detectives spent the rest of the afternoon in State College at the FBI office, Agent Tate's home base, reviewing material. That evening they returned to Big Valley to interview Gary Schippe and corroborate the pizzeria story of the night of the fires. Sergeant Stuter and Agent Tate first drove to Johnnie's Original Italian Pizza in Fairville.

During the afternoon, the sky had cleared and the snow had melted, turning the roads damp and the fields muddy. The evening air was unusually mild and soothing for early December. Stars punctured the sky. As they drove into the parking lot of the Original and the Uni-Mart, a yellow-topped buggy backed up from the hitching rail and rattled out. A single car stood parked in front of the Uni-Mart.

"Hey, hey, hey, Sarge, pretty busy, I bet," Johnnie called out the moment Sergeant Stuter and Agent Tate entered his pizzeria. "Still no word on Jacob, huh? He's hidin' out in some Amish barn, I betja. Do you want a nice hot stromboli tonight?"

When Sergeant Stuter introduced Agent Tate, Johnnie's eyes narrowed as he pointed the remote control, like a laser gun, at the TV screen to mute the sound. "So this is about Jacob, huh? Officially, huh?"

"Officially," Sergeant Stuter affirmed. "Did you see him the night of the fires?"

Johnnie looked from one to the other and nodded his head significantly. "Sure did, early on, all of 'em."

"All of whom?" Agent Tate asked.

"There was that Jessica Smith from up in Harrisville with Jimmy, her brother. And there was Jacob. And there was another girl, too, a blond, bleached blond, ya know what I mean. She was with Jimmy."

"That would be Lil."

"Yeah, yeah, that's it. Lil."

"What time were they here?"

Johnnie pressed his lips together and moved his mouth from side to side histrionically before answering. "Hmmmm, I'd say about seven. Yeah, I'm pretty sure it was seven cuz *The Wheel of Fortune* was on. Hey, how 'bout that Vanna White, makin' all that money for what? Turnin' cubes around!"

"How long did they stay?"

Johnnie shrugged, rolling his eyes upward. "They had a pizza. To cook it . . . eat it . . . about an hour."

"Then they left?"

"Then they left."

"All together?"

"They all came in together, and they all left together."

Agent Tate's eyes wavered for a second, then focused on Johnnie again. "Was there anything unusual that night?"

Johnnie watched him closely, knowing he had information they needed. He adopted a character attitude from the TV program *Murder, She Wrote*. "With Jacob?"

"With any of them?"

Johnnie pursed his lips and nodded his head in large arcs. "I'd say there was sumthin' just a little unusual." He leaned against the counter. "Jacob and that Jessica had a big fight."

"A fight?"

"Not hittin', nuthin' like that. But Jacob was real mad and shouting, and I had other customers in here. I've never seen him like that."

"What was the fight about?"

"I shouldn't know, ya know what I mean, but I overhear things sometimes, a word here and there. They were sittin' right at that table, ya know what I mean."

Agent Tate assured him, "I know what you mean. But what was it about?"

Johnnie leaned farther forward on the counter. "Abortion."

"Abortion?"

Johnnie gave one long and knowing nod. "Uh-huh."

"Jessica?"

He kept nodding his head.

"Recently?"

Johnnie straightened and gave a shrug.

"Jacob's child?"

Again Johnnie shrugged and held his hands up. "That I don't know, but he was real, real upset. I don't think I've ever seen him like that. He was always a leettle crazy, ya know what I mean, in a good way, though, a fun way. But that night, hey, hey, hey, he was *real mad*."

"Then they left?"

"Pretty soon after that, they left."

"Johnnie," Sergeant Stuter fished, "have you heard anything at all about where Jacob might be? Local gossip?"

Johnnie shook his head. "Amish barns. Families hiding him. Hitchhiked out of the state. Disguised as an Amish woman. You name it, I heard it."

"What about Gary Schippe?"

Johnnie lifted his eyebrows and twisted his middle finger about his forefinger. "Best buddies, those two. Long time. Always in here on Saturdays hangin' out. Foolin' around." He tilted his head back and made a drinking gesture. "Out to party, know what I mean?"

"Would Gary be home now, do you think?"

Johnnie's eyes lit up. "Hey, hey, I just thought of sumthing. The kids used ta go to a hunter's cabin in the mountain sometimes. To party."

"Do you know which one?"

He moved his lips up and down and around. "I think . . . the name's Freedman."

"Oh, sure. Martin Freedman. Gentleman hunter. He hasn't used that for years."

Johnnie shrugged his shoulders again. "At least it hasn't been used for huntin'."

"Is that on Stone Mountain?" Agent Tate asked.

"Yup, next township over."

CHAPTER 36

On Saturday afternoon, two days after Thanksgiving, Paul visited Jacob to ask him out for a meal at Bob Evans. Later, as they strolled back to his apartment, the evening settled in the streets, eroded by streetlights and shattered by headlights.

When they reached the intersection at Basil Street, a frenzy of racing and stumbling teenagers boiled in the street near his rooming house. Mr. Teeter stood outside like a chained bull, visibly infuriated and biting his knuckles.

"Right in front of my windows, they start!" Mr. Teeter bellowed. "They broke one on me last week, the lowlife scum! Right here, pushing and fighting and shouting!"

"What happened?" Paul asked.

"Does it matter? Someone tried to steal something. One of those damned radio boxes! I'd smash every single one!"

"Someone tried to steal a radio?"

"I called the police, you can bet on that!"

Near his feet, Jacob noticed a streak of blood on the sidewalk and then, suddenly, heard horses' hooves clattering on the street. His mind snapped back to the valley, not trusting his ears, not believing the sound. Two mounted policemen galloped past them. In the rush and movement and shadows, each man-and-horse combination resembled a single animal.

One policeman dismounted, raised a nightstick, and pushed aside a few taunting adolescents. There, on the sidewalk, under the pale cone of the streetlight, one stocky teenaged boy with coal-black hair sat astride another stocky teenaged boy with white-blond hair, smashing his fist into the boy's bloody face. The officer began dragging the dark-haired boy off. "Break it up! Break it up!"

At that instant, the boy with the bloody face sat up, his eyes bruised and half-closed, and spat a mouthful of blood into the face of his adversary. A police cruiser shot down the street like an arrow. "Everyone outta here! This isn't a show!"

The spectators scattered up and down the street and alleys. The two boys, bloody and screaming and swearing, were handcuffed and forced into the back of the cruiser. The mounted policemen clip-clopped into the darkness as the flashing blue lights of the police cruiser vanished.

"Right here they start!" Mr. Teeter bellowed. "The lowlife scum. They should all be thrown in jail, sent away to reform school!"

Jacob and Paul stepped over the streak of blood and took refuge inside, while Mr. Teeter raged outside on the sidewalk.

When Jacob threw open the door to his room, Paul saw jeans and T-shirts tossed on the backs of chairs and on the floor. Like precious knickknacks, McDonald's soda cups, empty and half-empty, and cans of Coors Light were arranged on the desk, on the top of the TV, on the windowsills. The waste basket overflowed with crumpled beer cans and empty cigarette packs. Ashtrays flowered with cigarette butts in the ashes. One had tipped over onto the shag rug next to the lopsided easy chair. Books were stacked on the bureau. Sheets and blankets were tangled into an odd-shaped lump at the foot of the bed. Both pillows were on the floor.

In the room was a smell of smoke and wreckage and soundless renunciation.

"What a mess," Jacob remarked flatly, not at all embarrassed, merely stating a fact. "I really need to clean this room."

Paul said nothing, but his face registered surprise at the disorder.

At the window, there was a flurry and a flutter and a scratching of wings and shrill bird sounds. Jacob banged on the windowsill. "Pigeons. They're making a mess. They must be nesting up above."

Jacob picked up some of the clothes and tossed them in a corner. He threw the bed covers up. Paul, dressed in a blue sweater and khaki pants, pulled off his white nylon parka and sat down in the desk chair.

"Do yew want a beer?" Jacob asked.

"Just one."

Jacob flopped down in his lopsided easy chair, snapped open his can of beer, and lit a cigarette. "Seems like a fight happens every other night."

"There's a bar down the street, isn't there?"

Jacob nodded. "But it's not just that. Other things, other fights. People stealing, vandalizing. It's unbelievable."

"No vandalizing among the Amish?" Paul used a mock-serious voice.

Jacob shook his head as a distant expression washed over his face. "No, no vandalism or stealing or fighting . . ."

"But?"

"But there are some sad things," Jacob admitted, as a memory bubbled to the surface of his consciousness.

"Such as?"

"Such as depression, insanity, suicide."

"Suicide?"

Jacob nodded his head slowly, taking a long drag on his cigarette.

"I didn't think that happened among the Amish," Paul said quietly.

"Not often. Hardly ever, but it does happen. The Amish, after all, are human beings and not perfect. They strive fur perfection, spiritual perfection, but they get sad like everyone else, and they get happy like everyone else. Maybe not over the same things, but the basic feelings are the same."

"Were there any suicides in Big Valley?"

Jacob's eyes seemed to age. "Someone committed suicide when I was a boy, when I was six years old."

"Someone you knew?"

Jacob stared at the line of smoke rising from his cigarette. "Not reel-ly. A neighbor's sister."

"Would you rather not talk about it?"

"No, I don't mind. I was just remembering what happened. I mean, what happened to *me*, when I was a child. My parents didn't tell me anything because I was so little, except that it was a 'sad death.' Even now I don't know much about it, but I *dew* remember the day it happened. It was in the fall, but it was a warm twilight when we drove over to see the Yoders, the neighbors up the road. Lydia Yoder's only sister, Ruth, had killed herself, over in Wilton. The two sisters had been very close, since they were the only two girls in a family of boys."

Jacob paused to crush out his cigarette. "After we tied the horse to their fence, our parents told Esle and me to play in the front yard. They climbed the front steps to go inside. Esle started fiddling around with some newborn puppies in a cardboard box, but I wandered off toward the apple orchard near the house. I don't know why I did. I think all the apples had already been picked.

"What I remember most and what I will never forget about that night is the moment I reached the edge of the orchard. I heard plaintive weeping, distinct sobs and cries, and I thought the trees were weeping. I thought the trees were weeping. Then I saw Lydia, her hands to her face, under a tree, moaning and wailing. As I turned to leave, I saw my mother hurrying through the backyard to the orchard, to the trees, to Lydia. It's an odd memory, but for an instant, a solitary moment, I really thought the trees were weeping."

Thoughtful silence claimed the room for a minute.

"Why did she commit suicide?"

"Why does anyone? She was depressed. She might have had some chemical imbalance they talk about today. And her marriage was childless."

"Childless?"

"Her husband was sterile. Had mumps as a boy. Without children, an Amish woman often feels useless because childrearing is such an important part of Amish life. I think the husband at first blamed her for not having children, and that was hard on her. Then when he found out that he was the problem, he thought he was cursed or something, and that made life even worse."

"How did she do it?"

"Shotgun."

Paul grimaced.

"That," Jacob observed, "was apparently the only way she could think to leave her problems. Amish life can sometimes be hard on women. Do you want another beer?"

"No thanks. Speaking of women, how're things going with Jessica?"

He snorted. "On and off, off and on. We stopped seeing each other at the end of October, but she came over last night and," he shrugged, "who knows?"

"What happened?"

Jacob took a long pull from his beer. "Too much, too much. We got into a disagreement."

"A disagreement?"

"Ye-ah, because of Cyn . . . Cynthia . . . something, someone she works with. Remember how hot it was at the end of October? A reel-ly humid Indian summer?"

Paul nodded.

"Well, Jessica wanted to go up to Lake Crete fur a picnic, which was fine with me, except that Cyn was going along. When we got there, it seemed like everyone else had the same idea. The parking lot was jammed with cars. Families huddled around picnic tables. Grills smoking. Radios blasting. On the curve of the beach, bodies were stretched out on the hot sand, burning in the last blast of summer sun.

"Jessica tossed down the blanket, and there we were, crowded among all the other half-naked souls. I sat and stared at the blazing red leaves of the maples and sumacs that wreathed the lake. Once in a while, a leaf would drop like a flake of fire. The surface of the water was so calm and still that it mirrored the color and looked like a lake of fire or a lake of blood.

"Then Cyn asked me if I was really Amish. I said I *used* to be, but she couldn't believe it and went on to say she couldn't believe that anyone, in this day and age, could be so religious. When I questioned her about that, she shrugged and said she didn't believe in any kind of organized religion and didn't believe in Jesus Christ. I asked her whether she believed in God, and she said she didn't believe in God either.

"All that time, Jessica just lay there sunning herself. I watched a leaf drop and, all of a sudden, I did not want to sit next to Cyn or to talk to her or to be in her company. So I said I wanted to go. And Jessica was reel-ly angry because we had just arrived. But we *did* leave, and then she didn't talk to me fur weeks."

"So it made you uncomfortable to be with a nonbeliever?"

Jacob finished drinking his beer. "I don't know why, but it did. I mean, not to believe in *God*?"

"You're being exposed to quite a bit out here in the English world."

"Fur shure."

"But Jessica finally came over last night?"

"To make up. What a strange, tense time it was with her. But it was great when she stopped seeing me."

"Why?"

"I had a chance to read again."

"To read?"

"*Ya*. I had more time. I didn't realize how much time I used to spend with her and Jimmy and Lil. Every now and then, Jimmy used to knock on my door and say, 'What's goin' on between yew and my sister ain't got nothin' to do with me, Jake-o. We're still buddies.' But I just told him I wanted some time alone, and he'd shrug and leave."

"But what about TV and movies?"

Jacob made a face. "I forgot how much I liked to read. I was sick of watching TV and going to the movies. Stupid shows, dumb stories. They don't make yew *think*. All they do is distract. There's no *meaning* behind any of it."

Jacob stood up and got another beer. "A damp, drizzly November in my soul."

"So you finally finished *Moby-Dick*?"

"Fur shure, and other books too."

"What other books?"

"The Bible, fur one." Jacob stumbled over to the bureau. From the stack of books, he pulled out a thick black volume and held it up. "Dew you see this?"

"Yes."

"Do yew know where this was?"

Paul, a bit confused, shook his head.

"Under the chair."

"Excuse me?"

"Mr. Teeter used a *Bible* to prop up the back leg of that chair. I've been sitting on the Bible fur months now and never even knew it. Can yew believe that?"

Paul had no response, merely accepting the outstretched Bible to examine the dent in its cover. Then he flipped it open and glanced through it, noticing various passages marked and underlined. "At least it didn't damage the pages."

"At least."

"Which books do you like the most?"

Jacob sat down. "The prophets: Ezekiel, Isaiah, Jeremiah, Daniel.

Then I like John and Matthew, and there are some wild images in Revelation."

Paul read a couple underlined sentences he chose at random from Jermiah: "But *his word* was in mine heart as a burning fire shut up in my bones. . . . And the land shall tremble and sorrow."

Paul closed the Bible, set it on the bureau, and looked over the other books. "This is an impressive reading list. *Fear and Trembling*?"

"Have yew read it?"

"I've read some of it. He's an existentialist Christian."

"A what?"

"It's a type of philosophy. Existentialism. I had a survey class in philosophy last spring."

"What's existentialism?"

Paul laughed. "I can't really explain it, but it has something to do with a person not *being* something already but *becoming* something through action and choice and free will."

Jacob knitted his eyebrows as he listened.

"It's that one is not *born* with meaning but *creates* meaning through the choices he makes. Conscious decisions. A person creates what he is or *who* he is through what he does and what he chooses to do. . . . I'm not being that clear. Existence precedes essence—that's the catchphrase for all of it."

"So it's not so much *what* we dew as what we *choose* to dew that makes meaning in our lives," Jacob reflected.

Paul nodded.

"And that means," Jacob continued, "that if yew just *dew* things without *thinking* about what yew dew, then your life *doesn't* have meaning."

"Sounds good to me."

"Yes, that's what he writes about. That entire book, which was very hard fur me to read, discusses faith, the paradox of faith, but that faith gives meaning to your life and to your actions."

"I haven't read the book, so you have the advantage here."

Jacob laughed. "Then we'll have to save this until you read it."

"Is that an assignment? I'm used to those! I can talk about *Moby-Dick* or Hemingway, but not Kierkegaard."

"The paradox of faith," Jacob murmured. He lit another cigarette.

"Have you talked to your grandfather lately?"

Jacob nodded and then coughed in a cloud of smoke.

"Are you okay?"

Jacob coughed one last time and stood up. "Fur shure."

Paul was concerned. "In general, though, how have you been feeling?"

"O-kay. Do yew want 'nother beer?" Jacob's speech was starting to slur.

"Another beer? Jacob, how much are you going to drink tonight?"

Jacob, red-faced from coughing, just stared at him.

"It's only seven thirty, and you've had . . . what? Five or six beers already?"

"It's Saturday night," Jacob defended himself.

"How much have you been partying?"

Jacob slumped back down in his lopsided chair with another can of beer and smiled grimly. "Oo-oo-oo, not tew much, Paul, reel-lee."

A moment of silence ensued, both pursuing their own thoughts.

Finally Paul asked, "How's that job at the chicken place going?"

"I'm on pro-ba-tion."

"For what?"

"Ab-sen-tee-ism," Jacob admitted, slowly, remembering the exact words. "Tar-di-ness."

"What's going on?"

"I couldn't get awake in the mornings, and when I did, I felt bad and couldn't get out of bed or just got out of bed too late."

Paul was silent, his face was marked with confusion and concern, and he just looked at him.

Then suddenly Jacob announced fiercely, "Did you know that Jimmy and Jessica have Amish connections?"

"What?"

"Amish!" Jacob repeated, watching the astonishment pop into Paul's face.

"How are they related to the Amish?"

"Their father was Amish. Can yew believe that?"

"But he left the church?"

"He was excommunicated. I don't know why."

"Did they tell you this?"

"Danny told me, back in October."

"And that makes you angry?"

Jacob's fierce tone wilted. "*Ya,* it does. Why didn't they tell me about it, considering the circumstances?"

"What did they say when you *did* tell them?"

"I never did."

"So you don't know if it's true. Maybe Danny just said they were Amish as a joke or something."

Jacob had not considered that Danny might say it as a joke. "I don't think so. I think he's telling the truth. Why would he joke around like that?"

"Why not?"

"No-oo," Jacob replied slowly, pondering the possibility. "He wasn't joking."

"Then why don't you say something to her? After all, you're seeing each other."

In an unconvincing tone, Jacob stated, "I will. Sometime soon. But it makes yew think about what they say about the Amish. The dinosaur stuff and being backward and all that. It makes me wonder if I'll be like that."

Paul was amazed that Jacob would even imagine such a destiny for himself. "I doubt that you'll be like that."

"It just makes me wonder, that's all."

Jacob stood up for another beer. "Do yew want one *now*?"

With apprehension, Paul studied his red-rimmed eyes and staggering steps.

CHAPTER 37

In the night air, even more mild and soothing than earlier, Sergeant Stuter and Agent Tate drove along Stone Mountain Road into Harrisville. As soon as Agent Tate clicked off his tape recorder, he rolled down his window a few inches.

"Is the weather usually this unpredictable in the valley?"

"As unpredictable as everything else so far."

"True, true," Agent Tate assented. "But an abortion. What do the Amish think about abortion?"

Sergeant Stuter glanced over at him and quipped, "What does the pope think about abortion?"

Agent Tate thought for a few moments and then assessed the findings. "First, Jacob finds out that Jimmy and Jessica's father used to be Amish, but they never told him, as far as we know. Second, he finds out that his girlfriend aborted a child, which may or may not have been his. So he was twice betrayed."

"Twice deceived."

"But why turn against your own?"

"The Amish do not turn their anger outward. It is turned inward."

"So in his confusion, he blamed himself. Somehow he failed."

"Correct."

"So he had to punish himself?"

"Could be, somehow."

"But the punishment was symbolic, setting the barns on fire?"

Sergeant Stuter shrugged as he turned off Stone Mountain Road and started to climb into the mountain range along Peachey Lane.

Agent Tate peered past his profile, the bald head, the glasses, the fixed expression, into the gathering view of the valley, a bowl of light and darkness. "Is this cabin far?"

"Well, it's up in the mountain, a little above the flat."

"Too far for someone to walk?"

"Not at all. Jacob could have climbed up there that night," Sergeant Stuter said, guessing his thought. "It's quite a walk though."

Agent Tate commented dryly, "Not under the circumstances."

"Then again, a ride up there in a van would have been easier."

"Much easier," Agent Tate agreed. "Something else I don't understand is why Jacob would take up with the likes of Jimmy and Jessica when he had met someone like Paul. He was a sincere and sensitive young man. He was being straightforward the entire time."

"Comes from a good family. A good Roman Catholic family, I might add. But I don't think Jacob thought like that. Besides, Jimmy and Jessica were just *there*, in his backyard, while Paul was away at school most of the time."

"Now, who is this Gary Schippe?"

"Local boy. Not a bad sort. Still in high school, technical program. Plans on being a car mechanic, I think. Normal teenager: loud music, girls, beer."

Sergeant Stuter stopped the car at the entrance to a dirt road.

"This it?" asked Agent Tate.

"This is it."

Casting his eyes up the narrow road at the ruts, rocks, and crooked branches, Agent Tate assured Stuter, "The FBI will reimburse all damage to state vehicles in pursuit of this suspect."

"I certainly hope so." Sergeant Stuter pressed the accelerator and crept up the rough mountain road. When they turned a bend and reached a clearing, Sergeant Stuter cut the headlights. A metallic-green van was parked under a tree. Rock music vibrated the glowing cabin windows.

"Do you think they saw the headlights?"

"Might have," Sergeant Stuter replied.

"But they certainly didn't *hear* us."

The two detectives stole toward the cabin, Agent Tate moving with the swiftness of a fox. They moved toward a window and looked inside.

CHAPTER 38

Early Saturday night in December, Jacob sat in his lopsided easy chair, sipping a beer, smoking a cigarette, staring at the shadows and the emptiness in his room. The plumbing in the walls groaned. Down the hall, someone turned on the shower, and the muffled rush of water echoed and plunged into his thoughts just as the phone rang.

The voice on the phone asked for Mark. Just before he knocked on the door, Mark jerked it open and charged out, bumping into him.

"Sorry, Jake, gotta jet."

"You have a phone call."

"Oh, not now!"

The water rumbled and roared, and Jacob, noticing that Jimmy's door was ajar, guessed that he must be in the bathroom. Mark bolted down the hall, snatched up the receiver, and before anyone could have said anything, declared, "I can't talk now."

Jacob stood near the top of the stairs, listening to the humming rush of water and watching Mark stretch the cord from the phone base toward the stairway. "I can't talk now." He stopped. "No." He stepped down the stairs, stretching the long curly black cord after him. "I can't talk." Step by step. "No." Down he went, pulling and lengthening and unwinding the cord over the banister into the well of the stairway. "Okay. Okay. No. G'bye. Hey, Jake, pull this back up, willya?"

The downstairs door slammed shut. Jacob shook his head and smiled at Mark's maneuver as he examined the phone cord stretched taut across the hall, over the banister, down into the foyer. When he started to pull up the cord, almost as though he were fishing, he felt resistance. He tugged at it, and the cord, by itself, elevated miraculously from the murky stairwell until, with the black receiver hooked in his hand, emerged the figure of Mr. Teeter. His impassive face, drained of all emotion, appeared almost calm and innocent. Clad in a tank top that revealed his bulky torso, his hairy armpits, and his forearms with an arabesque of tattoos, he lurched up the stairs with the curly cord of the receiver as though dragging a tail tipped with a stinger.

"Oh, hullo, Jacob, didn't know you were up here. Look what that Mark did, can you believe it?"

With a great gasp he reached the top and slapped the receiver back into place. The whirling sound of water vibrated the upstairs. Downstairs, the doorbell buzzed. Mr. Teeter spun around and peered down into the foyer as into an abyss. "The phone, the door—won't I have a moment of peace tonight?" His words were sharp and forked, tiny scorpions twitching in the air.

"That might be Jessica," Jacob said.

Mr. Teeter descended the stairs. Jacob followed him, settling his eyes on his enormous shoulders, hunched up about his thick neck. The doorbell buzzed and chirred and whined with mounting insistence.

"Awright!" Mr. Teeter yelled. "Awright!"

When he flung open the door for Jessica, frumped with impatience and clutching a newspaper, Mr. Teeter shot into his apartment like a shaft from a bowstring.

"Well, it is about time!" Jessica bitched. She pulled her purse from her shoulder and lightly slapped Jacob on the arm with its whiplike strap, purring in a whorish voice, "So? Have a nice time last night?"

Gazing at her tantalizing eyes, the color of iron in the dark light, and receiving her bantering words, he felt a vast landscape of craggy cliffs open within him. "*Ya*, nice."

"*Yah?* What are you doing, talking Dutch now? Well, I don't mind," she cooed. "You can talk any way you want to."

A disagreeable odor crinkled the air.

"Pee-yew!" Jessica exclaimed. "What *is* that?"

Jacob sniffed and scrunched up his nose.

"Smells like dog—" With a glance down, she cried, "Ohmigod!"

She yanked the front door open and rushed outside to scrape the bottom of her sneaker on the curb. "Can you believe that! Can't people clean up after their dogs? They shouldn't have 'em if they can't take care of 'em."

Inside, grumbling and complaining, Jessica kicked off her sneakers outside his door. She hopped on the bed and fell back, her legs dangling off the edge and her toes twitching and moving as though flames were dancing across the soles of her feet. "Y'know, I'm gonna try and get Lil a job where I work. I think a good word here and there can loosen up the boss easy. I made it a point, y'know, of donating twenty bucks to the United Way to look good. I think I could help her get a job there, huh, donja?" Her voice writhed with animation. "Yeah. I think I could help her out."

Before he could answer, he noticed she had a new gold chain wrapped around her neck. She flipped over on her elbows and spread out a tabloid paper.

"Now, look here, Jake," she read, "in the year 2000, they say New York City is gonna be taken over by space aliens."

She turned to him, twisting her head over her left shoulder, and from where Jacob stood, it had the eerie effect of her head spun around to face backward. "From Pluto. Of all places. Can you believe that? Space aliens in New York? I don't think so. But I *do* believe in UFOs." She turned back to the tabloid. "But *not* that they're gonna take over. We'd beat 'em in a war."

Jacob felt as though a stone bridge had crumbled and fallen between them. He on one side, she on the other. Was it possible he had spent so much time with this person?

She flipped through more pages, and then, bored, flung it to the floor and turned over, stretching her arms out straight at her sides and asking in a voice thick as pitch, "Isn't Jimmy out of the shower yet?"

Jacob could still hear water humming like a beehive. "Not yet."

She sighed and played with her new gold chain. "Do you like this?" Jacob nodded without comment.

"I got a good deal on this. Listen to what I did." She tittered and her voice, like a pitchfork, poked the air. "I took back an old gold necklace I had with a broken clasp. I mean, I had it fer years, and I tole the sales clerk that I had just bought it but lost the receipt, and they replaced it with a brand-new one. Wasn't that *clever*?" The last word bubbled on her lips.

Jacob stared at her. "Not tew clever."

Her eyes became hooded, and her voice turned slow, heavy, leaden. "And why not? Oh, excuse me, it's not *honest*."

"Well, Jessica, it *isn't* honest."

"Aw, c'mon, all the stores rip ya off in the first place," she hissed, coiling upward to a sitting position on the bed. Her eyes turned to ash. Her voice sharpened and bit the air challengingly. "Wanna know how I got the first gold chain with the broken clasp?"

"No, not reel-ly."

"I stole it," she declared triumphantly, unclasping the gold chain and dragging it over her neck and shoulders and arms. "Any clerk that thinks I'd pay two hundred bucks fer a gold necklace is sorely mistaken. So I just stole it."

Jacob watched her, his thoughts tumbling and falling and trying to rise. Her figure darkened and crumbled before him, like a phoenix, then re-formed as some hideous unknown creature. He wondered why she was saying this, doing this, troubling him.

Jessica let the gold chain slip through her fingers, setting it against her dark skin. She admired it and laughed in a smoldering tone. "How's *that* for honesty, Mr. Amish?" She reclasped the gold chain around her neck. "Before you condemn it, you should try it. You can get quite a lot of nice things with sticky fingers, Jake."

"I don't need this kind of advice."

She snickered. Her words fell from her mouth, mutilated and amputated and ripped apart. "Well, other people *like* my advice. Birds of sticky feathers flock together. How d'ya think Lil gets all her fingernail polish these days? And how d'ya think Jimmy gets so many magazines, huh? Don't be so naive."

Jacob listened to her words, false and vicious, plunge into an abyss inside his mind that swirled with pained voices and punished figures and tortured shrieks. *Who is this person before me?*

"If you're going to get *anywhere* in this world, ya gotta lie, ya gotta cheat, and ya gotta swindle. It's the only way, Jake, lemme tell ya. Lie, cheat, swindle. And ya can rule the kingdom."

Her voice seemed to echo in his room as from a deep and miserable pit. The plumbing in the walls groaned as the shower was turned off. Jacob still stood in the doorway, not sure whether to enter or to retreat.

Jessica flopped back on the pillows and looked at him seductively. She lit a cigarette and sent puffs of smoke into the air. "Hey, Jake, let's cool it. Just get me a beer, huh? It *is* Saturday night."

CHAPTER 39

When Sergeant Stuter and Agent Tate looked in the window, they saw Gary Schippe, Ken Heller, and two giggling teenaged girls. On an apple crate in front of a lumpy sofa were scattered plastic cups, a bottle of ginger ale, and a bottle of sloe gin. Both girls were smoking cigarettes on the sofa. Near the sofa stood a Coleman space heater.

When the music faded, Ken pressed the stop button on the portable stereo to flip the cassette. At that moment, the detectives rapped decisively on the door. The laughter inside stopped abruptly, as though someone pressed a stop button on their voices.

"Gary Schippe, open the door. It's Sergeant Stuter, and you are not going to get in trouble for being here."

After some surprised shushing, the door opened and a wedge of light fell on Agent Tate's black wingtip shoes. A visibly shaken Gary stood in the doorway.

"Am I in trouble, Sarge? Lucy said we could use this place. You can ask her."

Agent Tate introduced himself. "Mr. Schippe, I want to know who is in this cabin."

"Just me, Ken, Pam, and Helen."

"Is Jacob Hostetler here?"

Gary stared in astonishment at the question. "N-no, no."

"Do you know where he is?"

"No, I don't."

"Has he been here?"

Gary turned with a baffled expression to Sergeant Stuter. "Sarge?"

"Answer the question."

He hesitated. "I dunno. He might have been."

"What do you mean, he might have been?"

"I came up here last Friday night, and when we came up here again tonight, I found empty beer cans and a pack of cigarettes that weren't mine."

Agent Tate raised his eyebrows and waited for Gary to explain further.

"The cans were Coors Light, and the cigarettes were Kools. Jacob drank Coors and smoked Kools. That's why it might have been him."

"But it could have happened any time between Friday night and tonight?"

Gary bit his lower lip and nodded agreement.

"Do you mind if we look around?"

"Sarge?"

"We do not see any alcohol, okay?"

Gary nodded meekly. The two girls cowered in the corner of the lumpy sofa. Ken stood stiffly near the window. In the kitchen, Gary showed them the empty beer cans and the cigarette pack in the garbage pail. "They were lying around, so I just tossed 'em in there."

"Any food wrappers?"

Gary shook his head no.

"But here's a Marlboro pack."

"I smoke that brand. It might be mine."

"But you're not sure?"

"Not sure."

"So someone else might have been here?"

"Could be."

"Who else knows about this cabin?"

"Well, Lucy does. Lucy Freedman. It's her uncle's place. A few other Amish kids I know. Jacob does. That's about it. It's a pretty secret place."

Sergeant Stuter and Agent Tate searched all through the cabin. Jacob *had* to have been there at some point after Friday night. The puzzle remained. When had he been there? And why? Did it have anything to do with the fires?

CHAPTER 40

At 11:30 p.m. on Saturday night, December 5, 1992, Bob glanced at the wall clock as Dave, carrying a Wendy's bag and a cup of coffee, pushed open the door of the Lewistown Dispatcher's Office in the basement of the municipal building on River Avenue. Dave came to replace Bob for the twelve-to-eight shift and always came in a half hour early to shoot the breeze.

Bob leaned back in his chair. "Hey, Dave."

"Allo, allo, allo," Dave returned, setting his cup of coffee and paper bag on top of a file cabinet.

"Hi, Dave," Tami said without looking up, writing some figures on a sheet of paper at her desk.

Greg, staring at the telephone computer screen, grunted a greeting from his desk.

"Busy tonight?" Dave asked, hanging his denim jacket in the closet.

"The usual," Bob replied, stretching his arms over his head. "Cold out?"

"Nah, not really. Just a little nippy when the breeze comes up."

The dispatcher's quarters, a four-room space filled with state-of-the-art equipment, was buried beneath the offices, archives, deeds, court rooms, and legal libraries of the Lewistown Municipal Building. The main room, where the dispatchers were located, had five Motorola telephone computers and three radio ones, complete with computerized emergency communications access. Along one wall were reel-to-reel tapes, each reel the size of a bicycle tire, encased in two tall imposing black cabinets. The tapes circled slowly since every telephone call or radio call that entered this office was recorded. The room crooned and flashed and spun with computerized gadgets.

Bob leaned farther back in his desk chair—the newfangled type with the lower-back adjustment lever—and rolled away from his work area, Operations Position Four. He and Dave always manned the same desk. Two computer screens, one for the telephone and one for the radio, pulsed an incandescent blue with letters, numbers, and access codes in white and red and green. All local fire, police, and ambulance services were hooked up through computers with PEMA (Pennsylvania Emergency Management Agency), NOAA (National Ocean Aeronautics Agency), and ECOMM (Emergency Communications).

Bob adjusted his telephone headset, a thin band set on his head. The speaker was an extension, thinner than the band itself and fixed an inch from his mouth. Idly, he watched Dave sip his coffee and open the food bag. A distinct odor of french fries filled the air.

Dave asked, teasingly, "Do you want a french fry, Tami?"

"Yuck!" Tami glanced up for a moment. "I don't know how you eat that junk." Tami took aerobics classes at the Y four times a week and ran every other day. She watched her diet with a precision that bordered on obsession.

Bob smiled broadly. He was a young man in his early twenties who saw the world through a pair of glasses tinted with the color of civic duty. He had worked as a dispatcher, volunteered as a fire fighter, raised funds for the ambulance and police departments, and attended church every Sunday at the Bantam Presbyterian Church.

At 11:38 p.m., just as Dave stuffed more french fries into his mouth, the 911 line sounded on the computer screen.

"Nine-one-one emergency," Bob answered.

"There's a *fire!*" an elderly woman's voice said. "A fire in the Amish!"

"What is the location, ma'am?"

Dave and Tami and Greg pricked up their ears—fires were a major emergency call.

"Stone Mountain Road. This is Mrs. Foster . . . Lizzy Foster . . . on Stone Mountain Road."

"What township, ma'am?"

"In Fairville. It's in *Fairville*. It's Ezra S.'s *barn!*"

Bob pressed a button on his keyboard to trip the computerized fire siren for the Fairville Fire Department and the Greenville Fire Department. He then typed in Stone Mountain Road.

Tami had already clicked into the radio dispatcher's wavelength, speaking distinctly into her microphone to send out information over the scanner system: "Structure fire in Fairville Township, Stone Mountain Road."

"Can you be more specific on that location, ma'am?" asked Bob.

In a breathless and frightened voice, Lizzy Foster blurted out, "The corner of Reigle Creek and Stone Mountain Road. It's Ezra S. Yoder's barn! An Amish *barn*."

Fingers tapped rapidly along the keyboard.

"Are you sure, ma'am? Can you be more specific?"

Lizzy cried impatiently, "It's a *fire!*"

"Can you check to see if it *is* a barn and not a house?"

"I don't want to take the *time* to do that. It's a fire—"

"The fire department has already been dispatched," Bob reassured her in a professional voice. "I want to know whether other fire departments should be alerted, ma'am."

At 11:41 p.m., the 911 line sounded again, jumping over to Tami's line. "Nine-one-one emergency."

"A barn fire!" a man's voice boomed. "An Amish barn is burning!"

"What is the location, sir?"

"Dry Run Road. It's the Hostetler barn near Patch Lane."

With baffled expressions, Tami, Bob, Dave, and Greg looked at each other. Bob breathed a silent prayer.

"Sir, are you *sure*—"

"The Hostetler barn on Dry Run Road in Greenville Township is burning. I can *see* it."

Her fingers flew across the keyboard, typing in information for the Wilton Fire Department. Dave discarded his coffee and french fries and sat down at an Operations Desk.

At 11:45 p.m., the 911 line sounded again. Dave took the call.

"The Zook barn is burning," a woman's voice cried, "on Orchard Lane."

"What township, ma'am?"

"Wilton. It's in Wilton."

"Are you sure it's a barn, ma'am?"

"Oh-h yes, yes."

Dave studied the computerized graph system of available fire departments nearest that location and saw empty boxes. The fire departments in that area had already been dispatched to another fire. He covered his headset speaker and declared, "We're in *big* trouble."

Andy arrived for work and strolled in to replace Tami. He stepped into a buzzing, beeping, talking, crackling room of confounded voices. The radio traffic, in a short time, scattered over the valley with sudden intensity.

Andy asked Greg, "What's going on here?"

"Three fires. All Amish barns."

"*Three?*" Andy exclaimed incredulously. "Are you sure they're *different* fires?"

At 11:47 p.m., the 911 line sounded again. Greg took the call.

"There's a fire on Orchard Lane," the man said.

"The Zook barn? in Wilton Township?"

"Yes."

"Sir, that's been reported—"

"There's *two* barns burning on Orchard Lane!" the man shouted.

Andy stared at Greg, who gathered up the information and typed it into the computer.

At 11:55 p.m., the 911 line sounded again.

"This cannot be happening," Bob groaned.

"There's an Amish barn burning on Meetinghouse Road."

"Is that in Wilton Township?"

The dispatcher's office was a confusion of noise. Firefighters and ambulance drivers called to verify a fire's location because they could see another fire as they were going to their assigned blaze. Concerned voices, baffled and distraught, traveled back and forth over the radio waves. Never had there been so much radio traffic in the valley as the dispatchers tried to assign appropriate fire-fighting equipment to various locations. Bob stayed on past his shift to help coordinate response to the catastrophe.

They had sent the Wilton Fire Department to Greenville to fight a fire because the Greenville Fire Department had been dispatched to Fairville to fight a fire before they had sent the Bantam Fire Department to Wilton. The noise in the office did not stop. The last call came at 12:40 a.m., reporting that another Amish barn was burning on Route 655 in Harrisville Township. When other callers described fires that had already been reported, the dispatchers had to be absolutely sure that they were not talking about new fires before they ended contact.

Six Amish barns were burning simultaneously Saturday night. Near midnight, Tami sent a request for Life Star, the medical emergency helicopter, to fly to Stone Mountain Road: a young Amish boy was badly injured trying to rescue a colt.

Wiping his forehead and rubbing his temples, Bob worried incessantly that there would be more casualties since there was so much confusion, so much noise, so much panic. Only toward dawn, as everything seemed somewhat under control, did Bob have time to wish he had been in the valley fighting one of the barn fires rather than tied to his desk.

CHAPTER 41

Leaving the line of cars still creeping along the road to stare at the burned-down barns, Sergeant Stuter and Agent Tate drove down the Yoder farm lane on Wednesday morning. Esle was at the Yoder farm helping the men clear the area to pour the cement for the barn floor. A Greyhound bus from Lancaster County stood parked along the snow-damp front field. From the road, one man, rather stout and red-faced, used a camcorder to record the devastation. Sergeant Stuter repressed his disgust and shook his head with tightened lips.

Next to a black-topped buggy, Isaac D. and another Amishman stood talking and gazing at the back pasture, with its raw red mound of dirt visible where the dead animals had been buried. Ezra S., sawing planks with Esle in the pasture lane, had plunged into work with vigor to have moments of forgetfulness. When Esle saw the police cruiser park in the barnyard, he dropped his eyes to the saw and pushed the wood along. Their beards and sleeves were flecked with sawdust.

Sergeant Stuter greeted Ezra S. and Esle, "*Gut mya.*"

Ezra S. said his good mornings to him and to Agent Tate.

In Pennsylvania German, Sergeant Stuter explained, "We'd like to have a word with Esle if you could spare him for a few minutes."

Ezra S. pulled at his beard and nodded. Esle stared at the sawdust piled at his feet.

"Let's just walk over here." Sergeant Stuter indicated an area in the pasture lane away from the noise of the saw and the bustle of men hauling planks and timber.

Esle pulled his straw hat down a bit and kept his eyes on the ground.

Sergeant Stuter began the interview in English so Agent Tate could follow it. "Do you know where Jacob is?"

Esle looked up at both men with alarm. "*Nay*."

"Do you have any idea where he *might* be?"

"He is with the *Englischer* now."

Agent Tate, his eyes hard and impatient, used a clipped voice: "Mr. Hostetler, do you know what the English phrase 'obstruction of justice' means?"

Esle lowered his eyes and shook his head.

"It means that if you *know* something about a crime and do not tell the police, you can get into trouble for holding back that information."

Esle's face registered confusion. Sergeant Stuter then explained what it meant in Pennsylvania German. Slowly Esle nodded his head, his eyes glazed with sudden suspicion.

"Where were you on Saturday night?" Agent Tate asked.

Defensively, Esle responded, "I'm a farmer. I was at home. On the farm."

Sergeant Stuter persisted. "Did you go out at all on Saturday night after evening chores?"

Esle dropped his eyes and said nothing. He shifted his weight from one foot to the other.

Agent Tate glanced at Sergeant Stuter and signaled him to push Esle for an answer.

"Esle," Sergeant Stuter stated slowly, "we know you were out Saturday night because someone saw you."

Esle looked up with surprise.

"We need to know what you were doing out on Saturday night?"

Esle bit his lower lip and turned his hurt eyes to the burial mound in the back pasture.

"It was a church night, Esle," Sergeant Stuter reminded him.

"*Ya, ya,* I know," Esle agreed quickly, not moving his eyes from the back pasture. "Who must know this?"

Agent Tate said, "It depends on what it is."

Esle voice tightened. "I dew not want to condemn my brother. He *is* my brother. I did not want anyone to know what I saw."

"We will help you however we can," Sergeant Stuter softly assured him.

Esle hesitated for a long moment. "I saw my brother's car."

"Where?"

"Parked near Irma's stop sign."

"Irma's stop sign?" Agent Tate asked.

"I'll explain that later," Sergeant Stuter interposed quickly. "You're saying that you saw Jacob's car parked near the stop sign at the intersection?"

Esle nodded.

"What time?"

"Must have been about eleven fifteen. I'm not shure."

"How did you know it was his car?"

"I saw it before." Esle told them about meeting Jacob at the Fairville Original one Sunday night in September and how shocked he was to see him with that black car. He could not forget that black car.

"Are you sure it was that car?"

"Ya."

"Was anyone in it?" Agent Tate demanded.

"That I don't know. I don't think so."

"Didn't you think it strange that his car was parked there that late at night?"

"I did then. But not now."

"Do you think your brother set those fires?" Agent Tate quizzed.

Esle looked from one to the other and lowered his eyes without answering.

Agent Tate let the question die. "Have you told anyone this?"

"Nay."

Sergeant Stuter continued, "And did you see anything else? Did you actually *see* your brother?"

Esle shook his head no.

Agent Tate knew that Irma Keiser's identification of the car through the license plate number was much stronger in a court of law. So he promised, "You do not have to say anything to anyone, Mr. Hostetler. No one needs to know what you saw that night."

"But, Esle," Sergeant Stuter persisted, "that still doesn't tell us why you were *out* that night?"

Straining to overcome his moral dilemma, Esle quietly confided, "I went to see Judith."

"Judith?"

Esle nodded, embarrassed at this revelation, his face flushing. He stared again at the ground. Sergeant Stuter let a slight smile cross his face before he assumed a serious mien again.

"But it was not a visiting night."

"Nay."

Sergeant Stuter supplied the words for him. "And you should not have gone out that night to see her."

Else merely nodded.

"And you're afraid of being punished?"

"Judith, tew," Esle admitted, "fur my foolishness. She had nothing to dew with it and said that I should go, to go home. I was there only a few minutes. She would not come down. I just wanted to *see* her. I didn't get to see her the past weekend because I had to repair the heifer pen in the barn, and that night I was a little sick with a cold and then slept all the next afternoon. I have never done anything like that before."

"That is something we don't need to tell anyone," Sergeant Stuter told him.

"And you walked over there and back?" Agent Tate asked.

"Ya."

"And that's how you saw the car."

Esle nodded.

Suddenly, Ezra S. and Gideon M., the farmer from next door, were striding down the pasture lane toward them, their faces alive with discovery.

CHAPTER 42

After the evening chores that Saturday night, Ezra S. once again checked the animals in the barn before returning to the farmhouse. The horses stood in their stalls, the sleepy cows were secured at their stanchions, the calves were huddled on fresh bedding in their pen. As he crossed the barnyard, he glanced up past the roof of his farmhouse at the winter night: the column of smoke rising from the chimney and dissolving into the cold sky and silent moon and enduring stars.

The interior of the farmhouse was warm and comfortable since plenty of firewood had been fed into the woodstove. The distinct odor of burning hickory overpowered the fading fragrance of apple *Schnitz* from the baking of moon pies all day for church Sunday. Lydia washed Becky's thick golden hair in the washhouse. Eli, his corn-blond hair dark from a vigorous scrub, looked over Ben's shoulder as he pieced together a picture puzzle on one of the church benches to be used tomorrow. Judith and Rachel cleaned water pitchers and set them on the kitchen table. Joseph sat in the living room, turning the pages of *Die Botschaft*. Enos had gone upstairs to clean his rifle.

In the living room, Ezra S. sat in his wooden swivel desk chair and tried to read an article in *Reader's Digest*, but his thoughts kept sidetracking to Deborah. He was surprised that he still missed her so much, his eldest daughter, his first girl, who had been married almost three weeks ago and was happily established with her husband in her new farmhouse on Tyler Road. Ezra S. could not believe that one of his children was already married. He missed not only her quiet ways about the house but also her strong hands for the milkings.

He read, his thoughts wavered, his eyes drooped. Then, as usual at nine p.m., Ezra S. stood, stretched his arms upward, and stepped into the *Kammer* to prepare for bed. When he crawled into the sheets and blankets, he wore a pair of white wool socks for additional warmth. For a moment, he gazed through the open doorway at the windowpanes in the living room, reflecting the glow of the kerosene lamp, before drifting into a light sleep. At nine thirty, with his wife softly breathing at his side, he sank into a deep slumber. Lydia had kept the *Kammer* door open for better heat, and the house was quiet now except for the occasional stir of a burning log in the woodstove.

From a deep dream of serpentine flames and smothered cries and howling heat, Ezra S. struggled upward to consciousness. He woke with a jolt, snapped up straight with his eyes fixed on the windowpanes, glowing a lurid red, and saw the living room swimming in orange light.

"Fire!" he shouted, hoping, at first, that he was still dreaming. "Fire! The barn is on fire!"

Lydia bolted up next to him and cried, "Oh my!"

He had already hopped out of bed. Pulling on a pair of pants and a shirt, he streaked through the kitchen. "Fire! Fire! Wake up! Wake the children! The house might burn!"

Lydia sprang out of bed. Ezra S. flung open the kitchen door and stood on the front porch, staring in disbelief at the north side of the barn rippling in what looked like a single sheet of roiling fire. He heard the calves crying. Black smoke poured into the cold sky. The horses kicked in their stalls, and the cows mooed piteously. The wood cracked like muffled rifle shots.

His conscious thoughts were submerged in instinctive action and intractable terror. *The animals! I must get the animals out!* He charged across the barnyard, his huge figure hurtling through the red and amber light. Joseph and Enos rushed onto the front porch, their eyes charged with fear.

"The cows!" Ezra S. shouted in a tormented voice. "The calves! The horses!"

When he reached the barn, he somehow managed to slide open the door to the stables before staggering back from the heat. Joseph and Enos raced to their father. In panic, Lydia and the children gathered on the front porch, transfixed by the frenzy of the fire.

Then Prince burst as in a vision from the barn of fire and smoke—the great mane flaming, the leonine head scorched, the eyes blinded—he stamped and reared and galloped straight into a barbwire fence, where he crashed to the ground, tangled in the sharp barbs, writhing, jerking, snorting. Ezra S. hurried to the horse. Joseph and Enos, Lydia and the children watched in helpless fright. Judith burst into tears.

Eli broke from his mother, shouting, "King! King!" and dashed across the barnyard into the wall of fire to save his colt. Lydia cried out and hastened down the steps. Ezra S. plunged into the burning barn after his son. Judith, sobbing, clutched little Levi and Becky to her skirt and dragged them down the steps into the orchard. Rachel grabbed Ben's hand and pulled him after her. Isaiah M. and Annie, the *Grossdaadi* and *Grossmammi*, their faces white and strained, stumbled through the front yard.

The colt darted through the open door and scampered in trembling circles in the barnyard, kicking up its spindly hind legs. Ezra S. rushed from the burning barn with Eli, unconscious, in his arms. The calves were screaming, screaming. Blue-and-white lights flashed in his eyes as Ezra S. laid his injured son on the cold ground. Lydia, her soul shattered in agony, knelt next to her husband and stared fearfully at Eli. In the apple orchard, Judith sobbed and tightened her grip on the children as the terrible sounds rose into the night: the horses kicking in their stalls, the cows lowing, the calves screaming. The terrifying sounds rose with the trembling fire and the surging smoke into the cold sky.

A police cruiser, its siren blaring and its lights flashing, jerked to a stop at the front gate near the orchard. A police officer, talking into a portable radio, hurried over to Ezra S., Lydia, and Eli. Joseph and Enos stood helplessly behind their parents. Prince, tangled in the barbwire fence, snorted and shuddered. The police officer marched over to the horse and shot it, once, in the head.

Rachel pressed her hands against her ears and cried out.

Other whining sirens joined the crackling fire and animal cries. The red-and-white lights and screaming siren of a fire truck bounced down the farm lane. Men clad in bulky jackets and black boots scrambled off the vehicle, uncoiling and dragging a thick yellow hose toward the picket fence. There they turned on the nozzle and directed the powerful force of water on the tin roof of the house to wet it down so it wouldn't catch fire. At the edge of the orchard, Isaiah M. and Annie stood silently, like an elderly Adam and Eve, watching in fascination as the solid arc of water slammed into the farmhouse, three thousand gallons of water per minute.

An ambulance wailed into the barnyard. Lydia remained kneeling next to her limp son as men surrounded him with tubes and cylinders, metal boxes, and a stretcher. Ezra S. stood and watched as the men prodded and poked and examined Eli. A metallic voice crackled over a walkie-talkie.

Another fire truck, a tanker, roared down the farm lane just as the milk house started to burn and the flames licked the base of the concrete silo. The firefighters turned arcs of water on the barn fire to contain the blaze. Men ran back and forth, dragging hoses, hooking hoses, clearing areas, shouting at each other.

Another fire truck, a supply engine, entered the farm lane and parked near the tanker. The supply engine dropped off two portotanks, ready to rush back to the pond to fill each empty tank again with three thousand gallons of water, because there were no fire hydrants in the area.

"Fully engaged," George Dobson, the Fairville fire chief, reported on his radio—no hope of saving the barn. Their effort was to prevent the fire from spreading to other buildings. George was standing next to Ron Hertzle, the assistant fire chief, when sudden soft explosions, odd bursting sounds, followed each other in succession.

"Now whut in the world is that?" asked Ron.

"Cows," George said quietly, not shifting his eyes from the fire.

"Cows?"

"Methane gas," George explained calmly. "All that gas inside their stomachs just heats up, and they explode."

"Well, I'll be!"

There was sudden shouting and running and calling from the front field. George and Ron turned to look.

"There's fire in your barn!" Rudi shouted to Gideon M. "Fire in your barn!"

"Fire in your barn!" Daniel echoed.

Gideon M. turned and stared wild-eyed at the dark presence of his barn and the thin line of smoke. He raced toward his barn.

"Get help," Mahlon T. told his sons as he hurried over.

"There's a fire in Gideon M.'s barn!" Rudi and Daniel shouted, running toward a knot of men who stood next to a pickup truck with a flashing orange light, parked at the end of the farm lane.

"Where?"

"Next door! Next door!"

The men hustled down the road, their black boots slapping the pavement. The boys followed. One man flagged down a Greenville fire truck.

"We might need you here instead," the man shouted, pointing to Gideon M.'s barn.

"What the hell's going on here?" the man in the fire truck asked, watching the men scrambling to the barn, bright beams of flashlights flashing. "I don't know where to go."

"Tell me about it," the other man said. "There's a barn burning here and on Dry Run Road, but the Wilton Fire Department turned up there. We have one attack engine here by mistake cuz we thought the address was wrong, seeing the barn burning and all, so we stopped in. The scanners are going wild."

Gideon M. and Mahlon T. dragged a smoldering bale of hay out into the barnyard; one side of it was entirely black. The firefighters dragged out two more smoking bales.

"Is that it?" one firefighter called to another coming out of the barn with his flashlight trained on the ground.

"That's it," he answered breathlessly.

The men stared at the bales of hay as if searching for the secret of the barn fires. Gideon M. poured a pail of water on the smoldering bales, sending up hissing clouds of steam. Sergeant Stuter stood next to them, dressed in civilian clothes.

Ron ordered, "Two of you take some buckets of water in there where the hay was burning and splash them around. Then stay for a while and watch to make sure it's out. All the rest of us need to get back next door. Come on, boys."

George turned to Gideon M. and Mahlon T. "Don't touch these bales, *sei so gut* (please). They might help us figure out how this devilish thing happened."

"Don't clean this up," Sergeant Stuter directed the Amishmen in Pennsylvania German. "I'll be back later to look at the burned bales and the inside of the barn. If you see anything unusual, let me know."

Gideon M. and Mahlon T. continued staring at the mess of black hay. Rudi and Daniel, Mahlon T.'s sons, huddled together at a distance from their father.

Gideon M. looked over at them and said, *"Danki! Danki, Buwe!* (thanks, boys)."

"You did *gut,*" Mahlon T. told his sons. "Now go home."

Rudi and Daniel nodded and smiled. They had been watching Ezra S.'s burning barn and the fire trucks from the window of their living room across the road when they glanced at Gideon M.'s barn. Through the partly open great door, they saw slithering smoke and sparks. Both had dashed down the lane, shouting and calling for their father and Gideon M.

Sergeant Stuter and the firefighters trotted back next door. The cold night air smelled of burning wood and hay and animal flesh. The barn burned fiercely. Arcs of water thundered into the roaring barn, but the flames thrived and thrashed and twisted higher and brighter and cracked the night.

Fire trucks, ambulances, police cruisers, pickup trucks, cars, and rescue trucks jammed both sides of Stone Mountain Road, the front field and the farm lane. A fire truck swerving into the farm lane had knocked over the milk stand and sent empty milk cans flying. The entire area was a field of flashing red and blue and white and yellow lights. Dark helmeted figures raced back and forth from vehicle to vehicle. Amish figures appeared, on foot or by buggy, to help.

The moment Irma heard the fire siren and saw flashing lights race past her house, she locked Kirby in the breezeway, dashed outside, and saw the great blaze. Watching the play of light and listening to the distant sirens, she walked down her long driveway when Esle, his face stricken with fear, appeared suddenly and startled her. Irma watched him race down the road to the Yoder farm at surprising speed when she noticed Dennis and Lizzy standing at the edge of their lawn. Lizzy stood there in a thin pink bathrobe, her arms folded across her chest as though hugging herself for warmth, while Dennis stood placidly in a tattered, thick blue sweater with his arms at his side.

"Why, Lizzy, you'll catch your death of cold out here like that," Irma remarked, walking over.

"It's not that cold," Lizzy replied and then, as if to make her point, unfolded her arms.

"It's December," Dennis declared, as though Lizzy were in the habit of forgetting what month it was.

"I know it's December," Lizzy responded lightly, "but it's not that cold out."

"Did you see Esle?" Irma asked.

"Oh, yes. You know how close those two families are."

A horse and buggy drove past them with reckless speed, the horse straining at its bit. Irma, Lizzy, and Dennis turned toward the apparition. For an instant, they saw by the light from the fire, in eerie clarity for the dead of night, the terrified face of Deborah. Enoch, her newlywed husband, drove the horse hard. Deborah was hastening home to her family, not knowing whether they were hurt or safe or what buildings were burning.

The three of them stood watching the white top of the buggy glow faintly with reflected firelight before it vanished into the confusion of vehicles, racing figures, flashing lights, and crackling radio sounds. Each pondered the image of Deborah's terrified face, as though all the confused emotions and unknown terrors and maddening panic had converged, suddenly, in the momentary glimpse of the face of a daughter rushing home to her family. More sirens rent the night. The fire flourished, intensified.

"It's only the barn that's burning, isn't it?" Irma asked.

"As far as we know," Lizzy replied.

"Lizzy called in the fire," Dennis reported.

"Did you?"

Sadly Lizzy nodded. "I wish I didn't have to."

A supply engine pulled to a stop in front of them as a firefighter shouted, "Where's the pond? Reigle Creek pond?"

Dennis rushed to the side of the truck and explained, pointing down the road. The truck roared away.

Dennis stepped back onto the lawn. "They're pumping water out of the pond. They say there's more than one barn burning. No one knows how many. Maybe a dozen. The fire stations are going nuts. He said the whole valley, end to end, is burning tonight. There's another barn burning on Dry Run Road. Might be Moses C.'s farm."

In the far distance, past the bright blaze of the Yoder barn fire, the horizon was lit with a fiery glow. Leafless winter trees with their crooked branches and solid trunks, stood out in eerie distinctness in the empty landscape. Then in the opposite direction, the horizon grew pale with light as new siren sounds stretched themselves over the valley darkness. Just then, another fire truck roared past. For most of the night, tankers zoomed back and forth, like thirsty cows lurching to the pond to drink.

Irma shivered. "What is happening? Who's setting these fires?"

"And *why* are they doing it?" Dennis asked. "*Why?*"

Then, among the sirens and radio sounds, a new sound agitated the night. From above, in thick slow waves, a thundering thudding sound like the beating of great dark wings descended. The three looked up and saw the lights of a helicopter. The sound boomed above them with the whop-whop-whop of the rotor blades as the helicopter galloped across the sky. An intense beam of white light then fell from the sky as the searchlight scanned the back fields and pastures behind the Yoder farm buildings.

"That's the Life Star," Irma said.

"Oh, just terrible, terrible." Lizzy hugged herself impulsively. "Someone must be hurt bad."

The helicopter flew back and forth and circled over the back field, its bright beam tracing the ground in great sweeping circles. Then the helicopter steadied and hovered and the spotlight steadied and shortened, as though the beam of light was being driven like a stake into the earth. The helicopter floated down to the back pasture, this modern chariot of wings and light and thunder.

As the bright light passed over the back fields, Lydia, her face drawn and empty and her eyes wet with sorrow and pain, pulled herself from the ground to follow the men bearing Eli on a stretcher down the pasture lane and into the dark field. Ezra S. moved alongside her, past the raging barn, the soaring arcs of water, the terrified animal cries, the dead horse.

The Yoder family stood in the apple orchard. Firefighters handed blankets to the women. Judith, still sobbing, hugged Levi and Becky to herself. Deborah, her face tight with anxiety about Eli, stood near Rachel and Ben. At the edge of the orchard, Enoch murmured with Joseph and Enos, Esle and Isaac D., Sam, Seth, as the men gazed uncomprehendingly at the fire. Isaiah M. and Annie stood silent under a tree. The fire burned in their eyes. In the back pasture, the Life Star helicopter, this great chariot of light and thunder, took Eli up in a whirlwind of smoke into the burning heavens.

Lydia had gone in the helicopter with Eli. Ezra S. returned to the barnyard and stood in sorrow before the raging barn fire. The fire raged and seethed in convulsive fury. Black smoke boiled up into the sky and the moon and the stars. A bottomless pit had rent the surface of the land and swallowed the terrified cries of the animals in its dark throat. The only sound now was the ceaseless rumble of fire as from a great furnace.

All mortal effort was useless against this destructive force. The flames spun themselves around the entire barn like some cocoon until the structure collapsed, with a trumpeting crash, releasing enormous wings of fire that seemed to beat the very sky itself. The old concrete silo eventually cracked and pitched into the flames. The sky and the moon and the stars were darkened by smoke and fire.

And Ezra S. still stood in the barnyard. His mouth tasted of smoke and screams.

CHAPTER 43

When Ezra S. reached Sergeant Stuter and Agent Tate, he said in a breathless voice, "Gideon M. found some kind of fuse this morning."

"A fuse?"

In Pennsylvania German, Gideon M. tried to explain what he had discovered.

"He found some kind of fuse when he was cleaning the horse stall," Sergeant Stuter relayed to Agent Tate. "He figures it fell through a crack in the threshing floor."

Agent Tate asked, "Where the burned bales were pulled out?"

Ezra S. and Gideon M. nodded simultaneously. The men hurried up the pasture lane past the men working on Ezra S.'s new barn floor. In front of Gideon M.'s barn, the blackened bales of hay still stood in a haphazard pile. They walked down alongside the barn to the stables. Inside, Gideon M. moved swiftly past the stanchioned cows.

As he approached the horse stalls, he started talking. "*Ya,* I found it in Billy's stall. In the corner." Billy was a 2,200-pound Percheron, a rugged, powerful, and beautiful gray-brown draft horse. The horse nickered. "To think I could have lost him.

"Easy now," Gideon M. spoke to the horse when he opened the door. He pointed with his shoe to a flare lying in the corner. "That there's the fuse."

"A flare?" Agent Tate's eyes narrowed to slits, his mind racing. "Where was it, exactly?"

"Right there."

While Gideon M. held Billy steady, Agent Tate stepped in and squatted by the flare. "Did you touch it?"

"What's that?" Gideon M. asked, holding the halter.

"Did you touch this fuse?" Agent Tate repeated.

Gideon M. looked at him as though he were slightly daft. "*Nay*, I just found it and walked over to get yew because I thought it might be helpful."

"Yes. This is helpful, all right," Agent Tate assured him. "And this is where you found it?"

"Right there." Gideon M. pointed at the beams of the barn floor above them. "I figured it dropped down through that hole. I've been meaning to fix it."

Above the stall was a long jagged gap where part of a wooden plank had split and fallen through.

"And the threshing floor is right above this?"

"Sure is."

With the others, Agent Tate walked up to the threshing floor. He squatted above the long jagged opening in the barn floor, peering down into the horse's stall. Slowly he stood to gaze at the vast interior of the barn filled with hay.

"The hay bales were burning right here," Gideon M. indicated, standing not far from the jagged hole in the threshing floor.

"Have you told anyone else about that flare?" Agent Tate asked.

"Chust Ezra S.," Gideon M. replied.

"Well, let's not tell anyone else for now, especially not the newspaper reporters, not the radio and TV people."

Gideon M. nodded his head like a conspirator. "Yew figure that was used to start the fires?"

"Could be," Agent Tate said and turned to Sergeant Stuter. "Do you have evidence bags in the cruiser?"

Gideon M. and Ezra S. were puzzled as they watched the officers carefully pick up the fuse and drop it into a big, clear plastic bag, similar to the ones used to wrap moon pies for Wednesday market.

Sitting in the police cruiser, Agent Tate stated, "We should be able to dust that flare for prints. Unbelievable good luck!"

"Do you think the flares were used to set the fires?"

Agent Tate studied the foot-long flare with a spike extending from the base. "That would explain the distance. This is a half-hour flare. Ram one into the wood floor, scatter some hay nearby, set it going at eleven, and by eleven thirty, when it starts to burn the hay, you're miles away. It's almost *ingenious* in its simplicity."

CHAPTER 44

When Jacob reached for his KOOL baseball cap, his fingers gripped emptiness where his visor should have been. He had lost it. But where? When? He found himself walking. He stumbled. *Where am I?* He seemed to have emerged from a deep darkness, a lost time, or a lost timelessness with echoes of rushing footsteps. *Why am I here?* He rubbed his elbow, which hurt and which puzzled him, before he saw the stop sign. He came to an abrupt halt to survey the tangled and shrunken stems, the wreck of fall and frost. He turned toward the apple orchard and the open field and slowly recognized the Yoder farm, Irma's stop sign, Stone Mountain Road.

His head throbbed. His entire body ached. With his fingertips, he rubbed his elbow again and his eyes and his temples. He stamped his foot on the road. *What am I doing here?* His thoughts reeled and jumbled in confusion. Again he started haltingly to walk down the road, attempting to piece together the evening and where he was and how he got where he was. Then the black thought slammed into him and his stomach clutched in nauseating anger. *Jessica, the Original, the abortion.* He stopped and vomited at the side of the road.

On the roadside, he stood heaving. A case of Coors Light, a nickel bag of "skunk" pot, a bottle of Four Roses whiskey. Car doors slamming. Racing through the valley. Jacob had vague memories of drinking beer after beer and shot after shot and smoking toke after toke to forget the abortion. He could not remember anything else. After the pizzeria, the night blurred and then blacked out. He turned to the side of the road and vomited again.

Then he saw Lizzy, reading on the front porch, and remembered how often he had seen her there in a cone of light, a book propped before her. Though he was still drunk and stoned and his head still throbbed and his elbow hurt, his thoughts cleared slowly. How often he had walked this road! He looked out over the empty fields and recalled working the land with his father and his brothers. It all seemed simple and beautiful compared to the dull and monotonous work at the chicken plant. Jacob lifted his eyes to the sky and beheld the moon and the stars and heard the cry of an animal, a distant call from the mountain, that sounded like the screech of an owl but not an owl, and then heard another strange sound behind him, a sudden whooshing sound. He turned and saw a wall of fire in the short distance.

Jacob stared at the trembling flames as though witnessing a sudden whirlwind of fire in a desert, such as Ezekiel had seen while standing on the bank of the river Chebar. When he realized the fire was the Yoder's barn burning, he started running up the lawn to the Fosters' house until he saw Lizzy staring wild-eyed and rushing from the front porch. She saw. She'll call the fire department.

But what can I do now? Then, for some reason, he thought of Paul and wished that he were there with him because Paul would know what to do. Of everyone in the *englisch* world, Paul was the only true friend Jacob had made, someone smart and kind and reasonable. Then the image of Rachel Yoder, her sweetness and her beauty and her faithfulness, flitted like a barn swallow through his mind.

When he turned back to face the whirlwind of fire, deep shame—the drunkenness and the anger and the betrayal—burned inside him. This was what had happened to Jacob Hostetler after he left the Amish. He could not be seen, not like this, drunk, stoned, vomit dribbling down the front of his shirt. All the neighbors would be out for sure. His thoughts and emotions tripped over each other as he stood indecisively in the middle of the lawn.

A fire siren shrieked, a loud and plaintive summons that wrenched the stillness of the valley. A pickup truck, a red light flashing on its dashboard, zipped past him. But I can't just stand here. Out in the open. Without thinking, he ran up past the Fosters' house toward the edge of the woods, stumbled and fell, striking his elbow again. He cried out in pain. The cool blades of the withered grass pressed against his cheek. He struggled to his feet and thought fleetingly that he should just walk to the house, knock on the door, ask if he could use the telephone to call Jimmy or Gary or a taxi. But he couldn't do something like that, not in his condition. Within a day, everyone would know; he would not embarrass his family like that. Besides, how would he explain why he was here in the valley? That he just "woke up" in a drunken stupor on Stone Mountain Road? Where were Jessica and Jimmy and Lil?

He felt sudden abandonment. He stood no where: not in the *englisch* world, not in the Amish world. He hurried to the fence along the backyard, climbed over it, and stood at the base of the mountain at the edge of the woods, in the darkness, thinking sadly that the Yoder's barn was burning and he couldn't do anything to help. He watched, absorbed in the fiery spectacle, wondering if the animals had escaped.

Just then he heard what sounded like a gunshot. Two fire engines, lights flashing and sirens screaming, sped up Reigle Creek Road. He saw cars and pickup trucks and police cruisers zooming up and down. He heard Kirby barking across the side lawn and the faint buzz of voices over scanners and radios. He smelled the night air burning with destruction. Black smoke boiled into the sky. In the far distance, he caught sight of other fire engines moving along Route 655 past the intersection at Reigle Creek Road. Where were they going? To another fire?

Dennis and Lizzy were standing at the edge of their lawn. Irma soon joined them. A white-topped buggy drove swiftly past. Then the Life Star helicopter, its bright beam of light playing over the dark landscape, soared through the valley.

Outside the fence, Jacob walked to the opposite corner of the backyard and saw another fire in the far distance on what must be Dry Run Road. So there *is* another fire. Two barn fires in one night? At the same time? How could that be? He peered farther into the southern horizon at a faint pink glow and wondered if there was yet a third fire. But that's not possible, he reasoned, dismissing the thought. More than two barn fires in one night? In his lifetime, he could remember only four other barn fires in the valley: one from hay combusting, one from a kicked-over lantern, and two from electrical storms. But there did seem to be a glow, and there did seem to be flashing lights farther away.

Jacob decided to climb farther up the side of the mountain for a better view. The rocky ground was covered with dead oak leaves, pine needles, withered beech leaves. He knew this area well since he used to hunt here with his father and Esle. Jacob pushed his way through the trees with his body inclined forward for the ascent. That cave that Esle and I used to explore is up here, too. Never would he forget the afternoon when his father had taken them there the first time. What an adventure that had been for an eight-year-old.

He had not climbed far before he paused, out of breath. Jacob turned around and saw firefighters and Amish people dashing about the Yoder farm. Great arcs of water splashed into the fire. All the figures were animated with helpful actions and purposeful movements. He remembered watching one barn fire as a child: the fire marshal had shouted orders to the firefighters, and the farmers had helped. But what was he doing? Hiding and ashamed, lazy and drunk.

Jacob decided to climb farther up for a better view and had to draw upon his willpower to do so. Here the mountain was steep, but he knew that the climbing would become easier. As he scrambled up the rocky slope, he came to realize that he had become an outsider, a mere observer in the valley, in the valley of the Amish, who were living for eternal reward. He had fallen from that quest. He had left *that* struggle for another struggle in the *englisch* world; it was still a struggle, but with different means and methods and goals, an aimless trip rather than a seeking pilgrimage.

He paused and looked back over the track he had climbed before he continued his ascent. Thoughts of Rachel glimmered and sparkled in his mind as he wished, bereft of reason, that she would pray for him.

Just as Jacob pulled himself up past the steepest part, his thoughts folded and tightened. He forgot why he was scaling the mountain. He gazed at the fiery exhibition, by now a recurrent image each time he turned around. He remembered that he was climbing higher to see whether or not the distant glow was another fire, that he was climbing higher to hide because he was drunk and stoned and ashamed, that he was climbing higher to reach some level of understanding.

Jacob thought of Jessica, Jimmy, Lil. Jimmy with his crude talk, his excessive drinking, his hatred of the Amish. Lil with her dazed eyes, her constant pot-smoking, her gummy smile. Jessica with her greed, her lies, her abortion. His mind boiled with bitterness. What had his life become? What had gone wrong? What could he do? How could he have become friends with Jimmy in the first place? How could he have become so involved with Jessica?

At first, he had thought he was courageous for leaving the Amish, for taking that risk, for summoning up the resolve to act. He had let Jimmy's initial encouragement and Danny's first welcome swell his pride. To what avail? To reach this point? To have friends whose sole purpose was to get drunk on weekends? Paul, with his reason and his intelligence, had said on more than one occasion that things are not always what you think they are—for good or for bad.

Jacob climbed on and again heard that unknown animal cry, a sudden prolonged shriek, only closer and more unnerving. Was it a dog? A wounded dog? Some kind of owl? He was certain it was not a bear. Then his face darkened as he peered in the direction of the cry. *Could it be a panther?* He shook his head at that guess and started to climb again when his sneakers hit something. He lost his balance and tumbled forward. What in the world was *that?* Jacob moved his hands along the ground and felt three steplike timbers, the remains of an old hunter's cabin above the Fosters' house. The long timbers served as a foundation for what once had been a small hut used for deer hunting. Long ago the hut had disappeared, decaying into the mountainside, but the three timbers remained embedded in the rocky soil.

He rubbed his face, smearing dirt on his forehead. When he turned, the tip of a low branch grazed his brow, and he batted the branch away as thoughts of Jessica and the abortion once again clutched at his mind. Never had he felt such anger as when she told him; blind rage seized control of his emotions and weakened his will. His mind withdrew into itself as he realized that he must never again yield to such anger, no matter how justified. The six months he had spent with Jessica imploded, followed by a stillness of extreme sorrow. Finally he decided that he would simply pray for her, and for himself.

Jacob sat down cross-legged on a ledge above the three-timbered foundation to watch. From this height, he could see the full extent of the valley and figure out that the far glow was indeed a third fire because the flashing lights of fire engines dashed toward it. He listened to the sirens, near and far, wailing through the night. Was the entire valley burning? How could that be happening? As he looked at the Yoder barn burning like a great bonfire, he thought about the firefighters, risking their lives to rescue others, and felt humbled before them. He considered the Yoder family and imagined their confused and frightened faces. Ezra S. and the boys were probably helping the firefighters save their other buildings.

He watched the fire and searched the past and the future. The air mingled the glow of the fire and the light of the moon so the woods and the rocks assumed a silvery pink tint. He lit a cigarette and held up the flame from his lighter to look around at the trees. As he smoked, he began to wonder what it was, exactly, that caused him to leave the Amish. He wanted freedom to do what he wanted to do. *What, though, is freedom?*

Jacob felt so tired, so worn-out. His eyelids grew heavy, and he let them fall and kept them shut, as though sewn together with thread. How he used to envy Gary, bobbing around in his van, listening to music, drinking beer, smoking cigarettes. He had been filled with pure envy. Gary was down there, too, somewhere. Sitting on the side of the mountain, Jacob felt that he had climbed above the world to view it, and his mind shifted to the story of Cain, fated to be a fugitive and a wanderer on the face of the earth. Is that now what I have become? A fugitive, a wanderer?

He opened his eyes. The valley continued to burn and smoke. He took a final drag on his cigarette and crushed it out. His mind settled as he thought back to his first day in the city and how he wanted a car, new clothes, a stereo system, money. How he wanted, wanted, wanted! He was swollen with simple greed since there was so much out there that you could use, that you could buy, that you could have. All earthly possessions, evanescent in the eternal realm. And what had come of this desire? Nothing. In fact, the ease with which he possessed material objects diminished their importance accordingly. His grandfather had often told him that the day-to-day struggle for *spiritual* possession was the single greatest possession to strive for and to attain, not material possessions.

How he *thought* he had made the right choice. After all, he had decided to leave of his own free will. He had planned his escape to Lewistown, where he would live a non-Amish life, where he would adopt the ways of the *englisch* world. He knew he could still return to the Amish if he chose to do so. That thought weighed heavily on his mind. As he relived the past few weeks, especially the last week, black smoke obscured the moon. He had done little but smoke and drink and read. His body seemed heavy with sloth. He could not remember being so lazy before. On a farm, there is no time for indolence. Another fire engine zoomed down the road. Back and forth the engines raced. Back and forth the firefighters ran. All that ceaseless activity mocked him.

Jacob uncrossed his legs, stretched out, and leaned back. A rock bit into his shoulders, so he turned over, his face resting against fallen oak leaves that smelled dusty and moldy. How he would like to just go to sleep, but as he lay there, more thoughts kindled in his mind about his life as an *Englischer*.

As he fell into a half-sleep, a dreamlike image stumbled into consciousness, a terrifying cross-eyed woman with sallow skin, deformed feet, and twisted hands. That ugly likeness swiftly changed. The woman, her skin now suffused with pink, her feet and hands unknotted, her eyes uncrossed, turned into Jessica in a wondrous gown, who started to sing a beautiful hymn. Then Paul appeared. And Rachel appeared and asked, "Who *is* that singing?" Paul ripped open the front of Jessica's gown, exposing her rotten belly, which fouled the air with a nauseating stench.

Jacob jerked his head up and blinked a few times. Just then the mountain seemed to tremble. He sat up to face the valley. The fire burned with demonic power. The fire engines still raced back and forth. His stomach contracted in abrupt hunger and emptiness. At the Original, he had lost his appetite and did not eat any pizza, which was unusual for him, for he regularly ate more pizza than anyone else. Indeed, he had grown a belly from junk food and beer because he never burned off calories as he did while working on the farm. He searched the pockets of his jean jacket and discovered a Snickers bar, though he hadn't worn this jacket for some time and could not remember having bought the candy. As he ate it, he thought briefly of the fat people he used to see in McDonald's, gorging themselves on cheeseburgers, french fries, and Cokes.

After eating the candy bar, Jacob fixed his eyes on the burning fire and thought again of Jessica. The first time he saw her. The first time he climbed into bed with her. The first time he saw her strong legs and smooth naked shoulders. How easy it had been to have sex with her that first night. Embarrassed at his shamelessness, he remembered how he had boasted to Gary about it later. Then fondly he thought of Rachel, of her shy beauty. The act of sex is blessed by God through the marriage covenant—that is what he was taught. The act of sex was elevated with meaning in the larger context of marriage and family. What was the meaning of sex with Jessica? Just lust. Sensuality. Sex for the sake of sex.

Jacob shook his head at how fragmented and hollow the *englisch* world appeared to him now. The back of his head started to ache, and he wiped his forehead, feeling the grittiness of dirt on the tips of his fingers. Just then, quite close, that animal cry—a prolonged shrill scream—clawed at his ears and frightened him. That was clearly not an owl or a dog or a raccoon. He sat absolutely still and listened intently. Soon he heard a rustling of dead leaves and then a caterwaul, a distinct catlike noise. All the Amish tales about panthers hurtled into his mind. He had to move, but he couldn't go down to the valley.

The cave! Inside, he could start a small fire and wait till morning. He could get a stick to ward off an attack in that narrow entrance. Jacob could not see the animal and didn't hear the cry any more, so he stood up with extreme slowness, alert to any sound or movement. With a sudden jolt of energy, he scrambled farther up the side of the mountain, along a diagonal, toward the cave. He stumbled, fell, and picked himself up. His lungs burned from running. When he reached the area of the cave, he looked wildly around at the tree trunks and outcrops of rock, trying to locate its mouth. He rushed to one outcrop, but he could not see the cave and rushed to another.

An impatient snarling scream burst from behind him. Jacob turned, stared deep into the darkness of the woods, bent down, and grabbed a thick stick. He stepped sideways toward another outcrop, glancing left and right. When his hand pushed through the dark entrance of the cave, he sighed just as he felt or thought he felt something hit the back of his leg. He cried out and turned and swung the thick stick hard against the night as he lunged into the cave, squirming through the narrow opening on hands and knees, spinning around into a squatting position to brandish the stick before him.

He took one step backward, missed the wooden plank, and lost his footing. As he tried to regain his balance, his leg twisted and his ankle snapped. Jacob lurched sideways, knocked his head hard against the rock, and slipped straight down the streamway.

CHAPTER 45

Sergeant Stuter and Agent Tate sat in the conference room of the Fullertown Planing Mill. Directly across a large table was Jessica, who wore a white blouse with a silver cross dangling from a thin silver chain around her neck. Her eyes were clouded with agitation and distrust. She appeared tired and sleepy. Her long dark hair was loose about her face and shoulders. Clearly nervous, she lit a cigarette and inhaled deeply, as though the nicotine would have a tranquilizing effect.

For a moment, Agent Tate fixed his eyes, bright with irony, on the silver cross.

"I don't know why you're talking ta me again," Jessica began, trying to mask her frightened voice with exasperation.

"We have a few more questions for you, Ms. Smith," Agent Tate said.

"I already tole you I don't know where he is." Her voice was strained but sincere. "I wish I did."

Her words gave pause to Agent Tate. He was so adept at interviewing that he prided himself on interpreting the tone of voice to determine whether or not someone was telling the truth. He concluded that Jessica Smith did not know where Jacob was. However, the events of that fiery night were still jumbled and perplexing, and another piece of the puzzle might reveal the whereabouts of Jacob. He studied her face, boring into her eyes, and had the clear impression that she was amoral and did not care whom she hurt or whom she used or what she did as long as it fitted into her own plans.

"We need to go over the events of Saturday night again," Sergeant Stuter told her.

She shifted her eyes to him. "But why?"

Agent Tate answered in a strong voice, "Because you left out an important detail."

She stared at him, her face panicked and her voice clenched. "That was no one's business but my own."

Agent Tate responded in a hard, clipped tone. "It *is* someone's business, my dear young lady, when you have a ten-year-old boy dead, a twenty-one-year-old woman dead, cows and horses dead, six barns destroyed, and a respected religious community shaken to its foundations. It is *my* business to decide what is and what is not important. It is *my* business to decide what is and what is not significant. It is *my* business to determine 'obstruction of justice' for not answering questions, and that carries a heavy criminal penalty. Do I make myself clear?" Agent Tate spoke with such forcefulness that her face paled. "You told Jacob on Saturday night that you had an abortion."

She nodded slightly.

"And he took it so well that he just went about business as usual."

She sat silent, staring at the tabletop, her eyes flat and without emotion.

"You lied to us, Ms. Smith, and I want you now to tell me the truth. I want you to tell me what Jacob did that night."

She crushed out her cigarette in the glass ashtray, lit another one, and gazed directly and defiantly at the two men. "He just got real, real mad."

"How mad?"

"Very mad."

"And you were at the Original when you told him about the abortion?"

She exhaled a long plume of smoke as that sassy tone returned. "I didn't really *tell* him. I mean, I hadn't *planned* on telling him. I wasn't going to *ever* tell him since it's none of *his* business what I do with *my* body, or anyone else's business, for that matter. I had the abortion back in July and didn't say a thing about it. It just slipped out, so I *had* to tell him. "

"How did it just slip out?"

"Oh, God," Jessica moaned, her voice tight. "Lil and—" She paused as her eyes dimmed with tears. "Lil and I were talking about condoms and birth control and all—Lil had been on the pill—and I said something about my always making sure Jake wore a condom because he's so potent. And Jake, being Jake, asked what I meant by *potent.* And it all . . . just came out from there."

"Was it Jacob's child?"

She looked down thoughtfully, lifting her eyebrows. "It could have been. I'm not sure."

"Did you tell *him* that?"

She nodded.

"And he was angry?"

"Fer sure. I never saw him so mad before. I couldn't remember if I had *ever* seen him mad before. I mean, *really* mad, not just upset or angry, y'know. He said something like 'How could you do that?' He just couldn't believe it. On and on and on. I mean, I didn't want to listen to that, especially when I didn't even plan on telling him. And that's one reason I *didn't* want to tell him because I *knew* he would be like that, being Amish and all . . . or having *been* Amish. I tole him I wasn't even sure it was his kid because I was dating someone just before I met him. He said it didn't matter, I should have had the child, he would have *married* me. Can you believe that? As though marriage would make it all right to have a kid. And I said I was not some Amish baby factory and never would be. And then he just got quiet."

"Got quiet?"

"Just stopped. Just stopped talking about it. The rest of the night was lousy."

"What *did* you do the rest of the night?"

"Well, we drove around and—"

"The four of you?"

"Yeah, the f—" She cut her sentence short and stared dully into his eyes.

"We need the truth, Ms. Smith. Was there only one car that night?"

Her face sharpened under her blunder. She hesitated. "Ye-ah. There was just one car. Jake was driving. Jimmy's car was in the shop."

"That's fine. The truth. That's all."

"Jake just drove around the valley, fast, real fast, all along those back roads. And then he drove to some cabin in the woods."

"Where was that?"

"I dunno. Somewhere on Stone Mountain. One of those hunter's cabins. Jake never talked the whole time. And the rest of us were trying to have a good time, y'know."

"Did he drink that night?"

She paused a moment. "We were all drinking. But Jake drank a lot. I mean, a lot. Beer, whiskey. He always drank quite a bit, but that's all he seemed to be doing, downing one drink after another."

"How long did you stay at the cabin?"

"Maybe an hour. It wasn't much fun, and I wanted to go home. So we did."

"So you went home?"

"Yeah. He just drove me home."

"So you never did go to State College?"

"Nope. Just to the Original and to that cabin."

"And then he took you home, and that was that?"

"And that was that."

"What were Jimmy and Lil doing all this time?"

"They were trying to calm Jake by telling him that abortion was no big deal and that he had to stop thinking Amish."

"That he had to stop thinking Amish?"

"Fer sure. To stop thinking Amish. You'd have thought he'd have more sense by now. I mean, he left six months ago."

"Six months can't wipe out nineteen years of being Amish," Sergeant Stuter observed.

She shrugged and puffed on her cigarette.

"Did he know that you and your brother had Amish grandparents?"

Jessica closed her eyes to slits. She had expected the question. "I don't think so. I never tole him, and I know Jimmy didn't."

Agent Tate nodded. "And you have no idea what he did or where he was going after he dropped you off?"

"He drove Jimmy and Lil back to Lewistown."

"And after that?"

She crushed out her second cigarette in the glass ashtray. "And after that, I just don't know."

CHAPTER 46

Jacob beheld a great ladder, leaning against the side of a great barn, with figures moving along the roof and up and down the ladder. Then in a flash of bright fire, the barn vanished, but the great ladder and the moving figures remained, suspended in a space of incandescence, ascending and descending the ladder, which now reached into the infinite realm of a day-breaking sky. The fragrance of a pure blue morning sweetened the air. The dawn hushed all sound. The bright angelic figures, flowing and floating, climbed up and down the ladder.

He heard Rachel calling for him. And then he heard his mother calling for him. Their soft voices merged in the shimmering dawn. He tried to answer, but his voice did not work. His mouth and his tongue moved, but no sound would come forth. He tried to answer, but his words were cold stones that lay on his tongue. He tried to answer, but the stones slipped down his throat into the cave of his chest, and he coughed and choked.

Jacob choked and coughed and opened his eyes to absolute darkness. He closed his eyes to absolute darkness. He did not know if his eyes were open or shut. On the floor of the cave, he lay crumpled with a bulging bruise on his forehead, where he had banged his head against the wall of the upper chamber after he lost his balance and fell. His right ankle was swollen. His head and his ankle throbbed with violent pain. Together with the pain and the darkness and the panther and losing his balance, his consciousness slowly cleared as he realized he was in the cave, but not where in the cave. When he sat up, his head thumped and drummed. When he tried to stand, his ankle exploded with jolts of pain. He knew he had broken his ankle but also knew he had to alleviate the swelling. Trying not to move his leg at all, fighting the agonizing jolts, he stretched down to untie his sneaker and edged it off with the toes of his other foot.

The cave was cold, damp, dark. With his face veiled in sweat, he shivered. He reached into the top pocket of his jean jacket, pulled out his lighter, and flicked it on. The tiny flame had an almost blinding effect. He blinked and squinted. The chamber was immense. Then he saw a flashlight near his left leg. When he pushed the switch, nothing happened. He shook it and tried again. Finally he unscrewed its end and tightened it and a stream of light appeared. He did not think at all about the flashlight being there, assuming that someone dropped it by accident or left it behind. In the impenetrable darkness, the flashlight had a comforting effect on him, something of the human world that he could grip and hold.

He played the beam of light around the spectacular chamber, as spacious as a haymow, glistening with smooth limestone walls. At the farthest point stood a row of pale columns. One column, the farthest one, almost directly in front of him, had a curiously human shape, a figure wrapped in a flowing white gown. At another angle were a series of stalactites and stalagmites, like an immense mouth of sharp, jagged teeth. Finally he saw, directly above him, the narrow hole.

As he pieced together his memory, he realized that when he lost his balance, he slid down the streamway next to the entrance—the one his father had always warned him about. With a dislocated sense of adventure, he was finally seeing where that much-warned-about streamway led. Since he was near the wall of the chamber, he dragged himself toward it and propped his back up against it. The stick he had picked up the night before had also fallen down the hole.

Jacob shifted the light to another corner of the chamber and noticed, a few yards from him, scattered animal bones and tufts of fur. The sight of the cracked, broken bones filled him with sudden dread, and he turned the beam of light away from them. Fear clutched his body. He cried out. His voice scattered and echoed, faded, dissolved.

Rather than waste the batteries, he switched off the flashlight. Again, that total darkness whirled into him, as panic anchored in his brain. He had to escape. He had to get out of the cave. He had to climb up the streamway. In a desperate movement, he heaved himself over, his ankle screaming in pain, and he slipped into the darkness of his own mind as he lost consciousness.

He heard a blast of powerful thunder and saw a great herd of cattle, oddly marked, circling on the surface of a endless plain. He approached the circling cattle, then saw that the cattle were not animals but cars, hundreds of cars, painted all black or with black rings or with black spots. He saw that the plain was not land but a lake, a winter lake frozen solid. He felt cold terror. The cars drove in violent circles, sliding, skidding, skittering, but never hitting.

Jacob wondered who could drive such cars on such ice with such speed without damage. He peered closely and saw that all the drivers were distorted images of Jimmy and Jessica and Lil, steering in wild and reckless abandon. As soon as he recognized the drivers, the ice trembled and shook and great chains erupted from the ice and looped around the cars, hooked to the bumpers and the hoods and the roofs, yanking the cars to a standstill. The drivers, trapped in the cars, their eyes frosted over, screamed shrilly as he moved through them to the center of the frozen lake, where a towering figure stood encased in ice to its chest. The figure had three heads: one a she-wolf, one a lion, one a leopard. When he stood before it, three gigantic mouths chewed and chomped on the bloody figures of Jessica and Jimmy and Lil, each laughing, screaming, cursing. Then another voice called out to him. And Jacob called out to the voice. And the good voice said to leave this lake of ice, to leave, to leave.

When Jacob woke, his teeth chattered in the cold. The pale gray color of chilled light had wrapped itself around him. Disoriented, he shivered, at last realizing that the chilled light fell from the hole above him. Daylight! That reassured him, somehow, since he could now devise a plan to get out of the cave. But his entire body was stiff, his back and legs were numb, his ankle throbbed. He could hardly move his foot without intense jolts of senseless pain. He was overcome by fright and apprehension about his ankle, his leg, his body. How could a broken bone prevent him from moving, from climbing, from freeing himself?

Tears dimmed his eyes with a sickening sense of futility as he wondered how he would get out—or *if* he would get out. No one knew he was in Fairville, except Jessica and Jimmy and Lil. A fragment of the night torn from his awareness returned to him: footsteps, the slamming of car doors, his fall, the red taillights vanishing. He remembered waking in the back seat of his car. He remembered climbing out and stumbling to the edge of the woods, his bladder full, to relieve himself. He remembered the sound of rushing footsteps, car doors slamming. When he turned, he fell, with the entire weight of the impact hard on his elbow. He staggered up to see taillights, like angry red eyes, shrink in the distance.

It was then that he "woke up," walking on Stone Mountain Road. But did they know he had climbed out of the car in Fairville? Surely, they would turn around to search for him. More of the evening pieced itself together. He drove his car because Jimmy's car was in the shop. They picked up Lil and then Jessica. The Original. The abortion. The deceit. The anger. Jimmy had a case of Coors Light, Lil had a nickel bag of "skunk" pot, Jessica had a bottle of Four Roses. He drank and smoked at the Freedman cabin. He drank and smoked because he did not want to think. Then he couldn't remember anything else.

I must have passed out at the cabin the same way I passed out at the drive-in, and Jimmy was driving me home. But why on Stone Mountain Road? Why were they parked there? Why were they running back to the car? A sudden shudder encased him when he thought of the barn fires. He ripped that thought from his mind and returned to his present torment: no one knew that he had climbed the mountain or that he had fallen into the cave. Again he felt miserably alone and cried out—only to see the cold ghost of his breath and listen to the mocking echo fade within the chamber.

Jacob stared at the semidarkness. His stomach contracted in hunger. If he could get out, he could start a fire with some leaves in the woods to signal for help. But he could hardly move. He would never be found. He would die of exposure and starvation, swallowed in the depths of the mountain. Black fear pulsed through his blood as his eyes closed and hopelessness settled within him. Now he stared at his own inner darkness, the cave of his mind. Never before had he felt so alone. How had all this happened? Why had he climbed the mountain in the first place? For a better view of the valley and the many fires. What had happened that night? He had climbed the mountain to escape his own shame, his own drunkenness, his own anger.

Then he centered his attention on being hurt and trapped in the cave. He wondered what time it was and looked at his wristwatch, but the face had been broken and the hands were frozen at 12:55. Time had stopped. He let his hand drop listlessly to his side. Jacob started to pray, repeating the Lord's Prayer. Since he could do nothing more for himself, he placed his trust in the hands of God. He was amazed that he had not earlier thought of praying. Had he distanced himself so far from the Amish that he had also distanced himself from God? The thought chilled him. He had never ceased to believe in God or in Jesus Christ. Jacob said to his mind, *Be patient.* Patience settled his breath. And he said to his soul, *Be still.* And stillness surged through his veins like a current.

Jacob remembered God's ancient promises: *Now faith is the substance of things hoped for, the evidence of things not seen.* The plain and simple people. In their simplicity and plainness, the Amish had discovered the simple beauty of faith on this earth. The Amish were a living prayer, faith incarnate, in each generation breathing the paradox of eternity in a time-bound place. The Amish life is faith itself, a living testament of devotion to Jesus Christ, their Savior. Jacob contemplated the words of James: *Even so faith, if it has no works, is dead, being alone.*

How alone and how dead had he felt before he started to pray! But now—*Look beyond the immediate.* He reflected upon his immersion in the immediate—immediate pleasure, immediate gratification, immediate sensuality. And now, another type of immediacy confronted him, that of being trapped in a dark, cold cave with a broken ankle and no hope of being rescued. *Look beyond the immediate. Do not confuse the smoke with the fire.* He should have listened more attentively to his grandfather. But he could, at least now, at the end, examine his grandfather's words with care.

Once he saw his grandfather in his shop behind the barn, an open book on the counter, and asked what he was reading. Without glancing up, his grandfather read from Menno Simons: "The night is far spent, the day is at hand; let us therefore cast off the works of darkness, and let us put on the armor of light." The words, especially the manner in which his grandfather had uttered them, had so affected Jacob that he had memorized the sentence. *Cast off the works of darkness. Put on the armor of light.* The armor of light. The Amish armor of light.

And what is my *armor?* he lamented. He was cold and alone and wretched and hungry. His muscles were stiff and sore. His right leg had gone numb, as though pain now were a useless sensation. He rubbed his face and shook his head. His mind was active and restless but peculiar. Never before did he have to handle such pain, such hunger, such cold. Ragged memories, remembered words, and faded images, severed from all sense and notion, without logic or reason, paraded before him and impinged upon his consciousness. *Seek the Lord, and his strength: seek his face evermore.* Seek his face evermore. Evermore seek his face. What *is* the face of God?

The gray light turned dark as various images and words and memories clamored in his ears and eyes. He felt he was losing his mind: *to seek his face evermore, your struggle is the Amish struggle, beyond the immediate faith, the armor of light, look beyond Jesus Christ, the face of God evermore, the struggle evermore, the light.* His head slumped forward as he slipped into voices and darkness.

Jacob heard a soft thud. Or had he dreamed he heard a soft thud? He opened his eyes to pure darkness once again. How long had he been sleeping? *Had* he been sleeping? He was aware of another presence in the cave and rubbed his face and picked the sleep from his eyes. His dry mouth tasted of death. He still held the flashlight loosely in his hand. He switched it on and a cold fright stirred within him. Directly in front of him, a few yards away, the beam of light illuminated two burning eyes. Jacob blinked and shook his head, thinking that he was dreaming or hallucinating, but he did not remove the spotlight from the two eyes—bright, bluish, lustrous—that were fixed upon him.

The bobcat sat hunched, facing him, chewing a rabbit. Snarling sounds of anger checked its movements, its fangs sunk deep into the neck of the rabbit, prepared to defend its meal. The head, large and solid and striped tan and black, had thick and long white cheek whiskers. The rounded ears, set back in rigid defense, were tufted with two distinct white spots. Its strong golden body had spots of black.

Jacob's fingers crept along the soil for the stick and grabbed it. The bobcat hissed and growled and stared into the light. When nothing happened, the guttural sounds dissolved as the bobcat turned its full attention to its food, biting and ripping and gnawing. Jacob watched this night creature devour the rabbit, its jaws working, the blood staining the dirt and reddening its fangs and claws. Fascinated and terrified, he gazed at the feeding creature when he sensed another presence behind the bobcat and rolled his eyes slightly to encompass more of the background. His astonished vision embraced a human figure in white flowing robes. He blinked. Then he remembered the far limestone column that resembled a human figure. His eyes were playing tricks on him, but as he shifted his point of focus from the bobcat to the column back to the bobcat, the flowing white limestone structure seemed to surround the predatory cat with its whiteness.

Finally, the bobcat finished eating, stood up, and lifted its wide head. Its burning eyes stared straight into the light. The bobcat sniffed the air. With cautious steps, it approached the light and seemed to pull the pillar of limestone along with it. Jacob sat perfectly still, one hand holding the flashlight and one hand gripping the stick. His mind, in a few concentrated seconds, wrestled with fear and strangeness for what seemed endless hours of intense anxiety and dread. His mind dodged and turned and spun, but he knew it was best not to antagonize a bobcat. Only if the bobcat attacked *him*, would he then defend himself.

The bobcat stepped closer and stopped, its ears standing straight and alert, and turned its head. Then it moved again and seemed to float with limestone wings along the floor of the cave toward his broken ankle. Jacob held his breath. The bobcat peered at the swollen, stockinged foot and then reached out one paw and tapped it, pulling back swiftly to watch. It touched his foot again and with sudden swiftness darted from the light and bounded up the streamway. Jacob let out a long breath and realized, with humiliation, that he had wet himself.

Hunger tightened its grip. He had never felt such hunger, a sensation not just physical but also spiritual. He licked the damp limestone wall with his dry tongue. His body had gone numb with cold and pain. Only his head throbbed anew. Only his thoughts and hopes stirred within him. He could not remember how long he had been there. Time was lost. He was trapped. He was lost. Then he started to cry because he did not know how much longer he could last. The simple, agonizing, brutal question of survival surfaced in his mind.

He would die in this cave, he realized. And no one knew he was there. Even if someone explored the cave, no one ever went down the streamway. That streamway had been a constant source of speculation and mystery for him as a boy. And now he was in it, in that speculation, in that mystery. And in that mystery he would die. What would everyone think? Where would they guess he had gone? His mind churned with painful longing for the farm, for the room he shared with Esle, for his family, for Rachel, for his grandfather, for the Amish. He would never see them again. Then the voices began anew. *Seek his face evermore. Your struggle is the Amish struggle. The armor of light. Look beyond the immediate. Faith. Jesus Christ. God.*

The voices seemed to go on forever. The hunger slowly relaxed its grip as a curious emptiness, satisfying and replete, emerged within him. He heard sobbing and he heard weeping and he tasted his own tears. His breath became light, shallow, short. The cold penetrated his body and then *became* his body, and the voices continued. He held onto the flashlight with almost absurd happiness and kept the light trained on that distant column, as if this light could somehow save him or help him. The limestone pillar expanded and glowed and grew in the center of his dark mind like a blossoming white rose, like a weeping white tree. *This is death. This is God.* Jacob lowered his head, a slow bow of *Gelassenheit*, submission and humility, and let his eyes close as he drifted into the enfolding snow-white wings of pure white armor.

CHAPTER 47

On Wednesday morning, Lydia Yoder stood on the front porch, watching the men digging and setting forms to pour the concrete barn floor. She noticed a dark brown van lurch into the farm lane and park. Ezra S. and the boys were in the back pasture cutting timber. The girls were in the kitchen baking bread. She wondered idly who this latecomer was and placed her hand around one of the porch posts, prepared to tell whoever it was that Ezra S. was in the back pasture.

A short, stocky, middle-aged man, dressed in jeans and a dark blue jacket, climbed out of the driver's side and stood for a moment, peering intensely at the burned-out area, as though searching for someone or something. He placed his hands on his hips in what she vaguely recognized as a familiar stance. She thought the man sighed or groaned, but then guessed that she imagined it.

Lydia was about to tell him that her husband was in the back pasture when he turned abruptly, and, with a defiant step, tramped toward her and stopped at the gate. With the same searching look, he peered up at her from beneath shaggy eyebrows, his eyes dark and direct, his face compact and set. He placed his hands again on his hips in that familiar stance. For the first time in many years, a name floated into her mind and formed on her tongue as she whispered, "Jesse?"

"Lydia," Jesse J. Smith greeted her tentatively.

Tears filmed her eyes, and she took one step forward, down the front steps toward him, hesitation and confusion controlling her awkward movements. Her hands fluttered aimlessly before she settled them in the pockets of her *Mitzle*. Her brother Jesse was still shunned for his unrepentant behavior. She took one step more and then stopped with sudden rigidity. His face flung her back twenty-five years into the past, when she stood as a girl of nineteen, watching her Uncle John's barn burn. Then she had to suffer the excommunication of her little brother, the first tragedy of her life, the first test of her faith.

She stared at him hard, searching *his* face for some answers to questions she had tried to avoid through her entire adult life. Painful thoughts and images came to the surface of her mind. Her brother, just a year younger than she, had started the fire that destroyed her uncle's barn. It was difficult to sort out everything that had happened. All the charges and accusations. The arrest and the short prison sentence. The eventual excommunication and the bitter words. So many questions unanswered. The blind anger that had burned down their uncle's barn had settled into her brother's mind. He left the house and the Amish without a backward glance.

Lydia had not seen Jesse for years. In the beginning, she caught sight of him occasionally at the auction. But even that diminished over the years until she no longer saw him at all. She could not even say his name. That, too, had disappeared from the family's lips after his excommunication, and he was never discussed, never talked about, never considered, as though by not talking about him and by not mentioning his name, he ceased to exist. He vanished along with his name. A rush of deep sorrow flowed through her as she stared, uncomprehendingly, at her brother. Then her damp gaze turned hard.

She asked quietly, "Why have you come?"

"Lydia—," Jesse began, looking down.

"Yew know the rules of the church," she reminded him calmly.

"You are my sister." Lifting his eyes, he was almost apologetic. "You are my blood and my flesh. You were my favorite sister."

She said nothing.

"I've followed the Amish rules to the letter, Lydia," he stated forcefully, "and you know that. But I cannot always follow the rules."

She leveled her eyes at him. "You cannot stay here."

"I do not plan on staying," Jesse responded sternly. "I came to say how sorry, how very sorry I am about what happened to your little Eli." He glanced over his shoulder at the fire site. "I know what a frightful loss it must be."

Her face softened at his words.

"But I could not go to the funeral," he continued, "and I wanted you to know how terrible I felt and how sorry I am and that I thought about you and your family. I remember how I felt when our Ruth died."

The image of her beloved sister Ruth was pulled into her consciousness—another tragedy, another test of her faith. Ruth committed suicide one bright Monday morning in April when her husband had gone to work at the sawmill. The marriage had been childless. After three years of trying while her husband claimed that something was wrong with her, he finally agreed to see an *englisch* doctor. The exam found him sterile—he had had mumps as an adolescent. For months he was depressed. He sulked and moped, dragging himself about the house, turning bitter. He took no joy in marriage. He went to work, he helped on his father's farm, he went to bed. He rarely spoke.

For four more years, Lydia's sister Ruth suffered this black silence, this cruel condemnation of their marriage. She was devastated that she could not have children. Without children or husbandly companionship, Ruth drifted, lonely and lost, and finally, after seven years of an unhappy marriage, killed herself. When Lydia first found out, she had rushed to the apple orchard to be alone and to sob. For weeks she could hardly speak, and whenever she had a moment alone, she stole into the orchard to cry.

In recent years Lydia had not thought so deeply about Ruth or Jesse. The pain of these two family tragedies burned into Lydia's heart was now joined by the third tragedy, the death of her own son, a further test of her faith. Her eyes were dim with loss and sorrow; her face was drawn and empty.

"Eli is now with God, Jesse," she finally said. "And so is Ruth."

Jesse nodded his head knowingly. "Yes, Lydia, they are both with God."

An awkward loss of words emerged against the noise of saws and the shouts of men.

"You will have a new barn soon," he observed, to break the silence.

"Ya."

"I still can't believe that happened. Still can't believe it."

"No one can. But everyone has been very generous, very helpful."

"That's good."

Lydia nodded.

"Well," he said, abruptly, "I should go."

She wanted him to stay, and she wanted him to go. She wanted him to come inside to meet her other children, and she wanted him to drive away in his van. The expression on her face betrayed her inner conflict.

Jesse gazed at his sister, at her confused expression, at her hesitant stance. "Lydia, you made the right choice with the Amish."

"There was no choice involved," she responded. "I cannot imagine any other life."

In silence, he regarded her figure, dignified and upright in the face of such catastrophic sorrow, in white cap and brown jacket and purple dress—the image of an Amish woman secure in her faith.

"And you?" she asked. "Did you make the right choice?"

He did not expect the question. He hesitated and stammered. "I . . . don't know. I just . . . don't know. I don't know what else I could have done at the time."

In firm simplicity, she declared, "You could have prayed."

He turned his eyes down. "Yes, I could have prayed."

"Please pray for us."

"I will, Lydia."

He turned and walked back to his van.

CHAPTER 48

In the Hostetler kitchen on Wednesday morning, Rebekah was preparing dinner with Emma and Hannah. As she minced an onion, her thoughts kept shifting back to the barn fires, to the suspicions about Jacob, to the mystery about his whereabouts, and to his black car being found in the field: Where *is* Jacob? Where can he be? Has he run away? Is it possible that he set those terrible fires and disappeared?

Her mind churned as she scraped the minced onion from the cutting board into a bowl with ground beef and cracker crumbs. She refused to believe he had set the barn fires. She refused to believe that her son could be responsible for such destruction. Whatever had happened to him in the *englisch* world, a person's basic character could not change that dramatically. Rebekah cracked two eggs against the side of the bowl and added them to the mixture. She poured in some raw milk and mixed it for meat loaf.

Whoever set those fires was evil, she decided. And her son was *not* evil. No matter how far he had removed himself from the Amish, he was not capable of burning those barns. But she still wondered where he could be. Was he staying at the house of one of those local boys he knew? Sergeant Stuter said he had checked, and Jacob was not there. But that doesn't mean, necessarily, that the boys were telling the truth. Sergeant Stuter and that FBI agent also searched through all the barns and sheds in the local area. She heard reports that the police thought the Amish might be hiding him somewhere.

With sharp slaps, she divided the meat into three loaves. When Rebekah opened the oven door, she peered curiously into the dark opening as the heat warmed her face. She grabbed a pot holder from a hook, pulled out the rack, and set the three pans inside the dark recess as the seed of a wild idea started to form in her mind. Absentmindedly, she cleaned the counter and then sat in the living room darning socks for the rest of the morning. At eleven thirty, Rebekah pulled open the oven door to check the meat loaves and didn't move, deep in thought.

Emma and Hannah watched their mother curiously as she stood bent before the oven, staring into it, not moving, not closing the oven door. Then she straightened herself so abruptly that the girls thought she had burned herself.

"The cave!" Rebekah exclaimed. "He's in the cave!"

Without putting on a jacket or closing the oven door, she dashed out of the kitchen, still carrying the pot holders, and rushed out to the barn. The men had just returned from Ezra S.'s place and were unhitching their horse. At first, Isaac D. and Esle dismissed her idea and said they would look after dinner. But Rebekah was so adamant that they agreed to go to the cave immediately.

"He might be hurt," she warned.

Isaac D., Esle, and Rebekah returned to the house. As she removed the meat loaves and set them on the counter, the two men grabbed flashlights, with grumbles of doubt and hunger. Rebekah stood on the front porch and watched Isaac D. and Esle walk stiffly up the farm lane.

"Where's *Daadi* going?" Hannah asked.

"To find Jacob."

When they reached the mouth of the cave, Esle called out loudly, "Jacob?"

Jacob heard his name echoing through the cave and wondered if the bobcat had acquired speech, or if he had cried out in his sleep and was hearing his own voice. That same chilled light enveloped him.

"Jacob?"

Jacob recognized his brother's voice through thick pain and numbness and humiliation. He did not know if he was dreaming or hallucinating or dropping into a deeper level of insanity. Sounds were tricking his ears as the light had tricked his eyes. He could not respond. He had lost his voice. He saw flashes of light in the streamway.

"Jacob?"

That was his father's voice. His brother and his father.

"Jacob?"

Were the voices *real*? He opened his mouth, but could make only a feeble grunting noise. *Here!* he wanted to shout. *Here! I'm here!*

"He's not here," Esle finally declared. "I have no idea what's gotten into *Mamm*."

"She's hopeful," Isaac D. replied. "No one knows where Jacob is."

Jacob gripped the flashlight and snapped the switch, but nothing happened. He shook the flashlight violently before he realized he must have fallen asleep with the light turned on. The batteries were dead.

"Well," Esle said, "at least we can tell *Mamm* we came here. I don't think there's any sense in going inside much more, do you?"

"*Nay*."

Jacob flung the flashlight as hard as he could against the opening of the streamway. The sound clattered in the chamber.

"Did you hear that?" Esle asked.

Jacob threw the stick. A beam of bright light fractured the pale light of the streamway. Jacob threw his sneaker.

CHAPTER 49

For two days, Jacob remained at the Lewistown Municipal Hospital in critical condition, unconscious, his vital signs unsteady. Friday afternoon, however, his mind and his body and his spirit ascended into a deep slumber. He was out of danger.

Now Jacob lay in a private room, linked to monitoring wires and green and clear tubes. His right foot and ankle were embedded in a cast and his forehead wrapped in gauze. He had snapped the lower part of his tibia, contracted an infection, and suffered a mild concussion. Dr. Kray said, though, that he was in pretty good shape, considering the circumstances.

Near the hospital bed, Rebekah sat in a chair reading *Die Botschaft*. She glanced at the wall clock over the door, settled the newspaper on her lap, and gazed at her son with anxiety and hope. "If only you would wake up, Jacob," she said gently.

Isaac D. had stayed at the entrance to the cave while Esle scrambled down the mountain to call 911 at Irma's place. Esle waited for the ambulance. Irma climbed into her silver station wagon to get the rest of the family. She had barely returned before the Fairville Rescue Truck roared up her driveway. Two local volunteers clambered out of the truck, marched to the back of the truck, swung open the large doors, and methodically pulled out the necessary equipment. They had flashlights, ropes, a life-support unit, a rope ladder, and a stokes stretcher—a body-shaped basket into which they would strap Jacob to hoist him safely out of the streamway and carry him to the truck.

The Hostetler family gathered around the rescue truck. Irma stood in her driveway, hands on her hips, and surveyed the scene with wonder. She imagined Dennis and Lizzy standing at their kitchen window and watching all the commotion. She was sure to get a telephone call any minute. Out by the old milk house, Kirby barked at all the excitement.

The men and boys loaded themselves with the equipment and started to climb. Just then Sergeant Stuter and Agent Tate pulled into the driveway.

"Where is he?" Sergeant Stuter asked.

"The cave!" Rebekah exclaimed, pointing at the side of the mountain. "He's in the cave!"

Agent Tate gazed at Stone Mountain with astonishment.

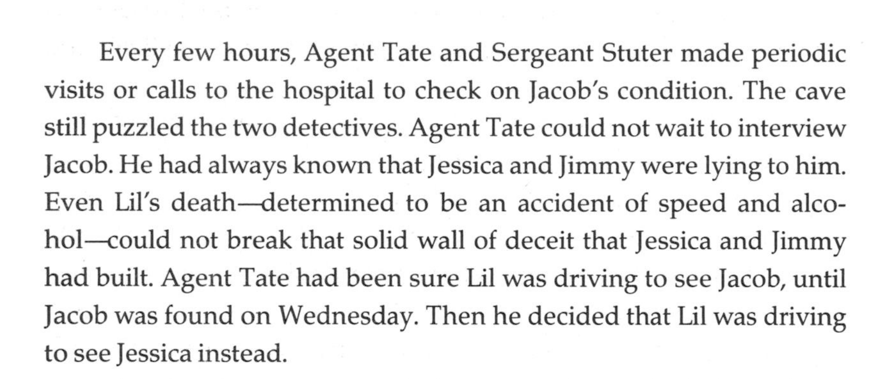

Every few hours, Agent Tate and Sergeant Stuter made periodic visits or calls to the hospital to check on Jacob's condition. The cave still puzzled the two detectives. Agent Tate could not wait to interview Jacob. He had always known that Jessica and Jimmy were lying to him. Even Lil's death—determined to be an accident of speed and alcohol—could not break that solid wall of deceit that Jessica and Jimmy had built. Agent Tate had been sure Lil was driving to see Jacob, until Jacob was found on Wednesday. Then he decided that Lil was driving to see Jessica instead.

Since Jacob was rescued, the brother and sister had plunged into a pit of silence, refusing to answer further questions. On Thursday, Agent Tate had bumped into Jimmy at the nurses' station. He had been trying, unsuccessfully, to see Jacob. Agent Tate banned him from the hospital.

Rebekah folded the newspaper and spoke a little louder, "Wake up, Jacob."

Her husband would soon be here for the night since it was almost six. Rebekah had stayed with Jacob through the first night. After a few hours of sleep, she sat by Jacob during the rest of the day and on the following days. Isaac D. stayed in the room at night. His parents were the only family members allowed to see him until he regained consciousness.

"Wake up, Jacob!" she called intently, as though words alone could give him the necessary strength.

Jacob moved his head slightly.

She gasped, raising her hand to her chest. "Jacob?"

He squinted. The light was so bright, and the voices had started again: How long have I been here? How long? Have I died? The cave won. Jacob heard his mother calling him again. The light. The bright light. The dreams and images returned. Voices and visions. The bobcat wheeled over his head with dark wings in an amber light. He saw himself standing at the edge of a dark chasm. The other side was so far, so distant, so bright. He could never reach it, but he leaped nonetheless, he leaped. To the other side. He was going to turn around to see the dark chasm once again but did not. He would not turn around ever again and started to walk into the other side, into the light, into his mother's voice.

"Jacob?" Rebekah repeated, her voice thick with emotion. "Jacob?"

He turned his head and opened his eyes.

"Mamm?"

She cried softly, "You're safe! You're safe now!"

"Am I alive?" he asked in confusion.

"You are alive," she sobbed with laughter. "You are in the hospital."

"I want to be home," Jacob declared with sudden fervor. He had leaped to the other side. He had seen the image of God. "I want to go home."

Rebekah reached for his hand.

That evening Sergeant Stuter and Agent Tate insisted on seeing Jacob, and Dr. Kray reluctantly allowed a fifteen-minute interview. Agent Tate agreed to the time limit. The mysterious Jacob Hostetler had finally surfaced. All that Agent Tate needed was Jacob's version of Saturday night, which he was sure would be the true version, and his explanation of how he got to the cave.

When the two men entered the room, Isaac D. sat in the chair reading *Die Botschaft* to Jacob, who sat propped up in bed. Isaac D. stopped reading and stood up. Jacob recognized Sergeant Stuter and looked at Agent Tate curiously.

"We need to ask Jacob a few questions," Sergeant Stuter explained. "The doctor said it was okay. But we need to be alone."

Isaac D. put down the newspaper and, as he left the room, whispered to Sergeant Stuter that Jacob did not yet know about Eli's death. "We thought we would wait."

Sergeant Stuter nodded and approached the hospital bed. "This is Agent Michael Tate from the FBI."

Jacob nodded.

"Do you know about the barn fires, Jacob?"

He nodded again.

"We need to know a few things about Saturday night," Agent Tate stated quietly. "Can you answer some questions for us?"

"I think so," Jacob replied.

"How did you end up in the cave, son?" Agent Tate asked.

Briefly, Jacob described how he woke up in the back seat of his car. Then he had to get out to relieve himself because he had been drinking. He continued his story up to the point of lunging into the cave's entrance, fearful of what he thought was a panther.

"You don't remember anything before that?" Agent Tate quizzed.

"The last thing I remember was drinking at Freedman's cabin."

"What happened before that?"

Jacob explained that he was driving his car that night because Jimmy's car was in the shop—something wrong with the starter. He and Jimmy stopped at a package store, bought a case of Coors Light, picked up Lil, and drove to Harrisville for Jessica. They had no specific plans beyond having pizza at the Original and going somewhere to party.

"And while you were at the Original, Jessica gave you some pretty bad news."

"Do yew know?"

Agent Tate nodded.

Jacob sighed heavily. "*Ya,* Jessica let slip that she had an abortion. That was the weekend she told me she'd gone to visit her aunt in Harrisburg."

He had been shocked and galvanized into a rage he had not felt before. Jacob was angry, not only at the abortion itself but also at her deception. He said he got so upset he could not even talk. Even now, he could not adequately describe his feelings, so Agent Tate suggested that he move on to what happened afterward.

"When we got to the cabin?"

"Yes, and before that. Did anything else unusual happen that night?"

Jacob stared at his hands on the white sheets. "*Ya*, there was something else."

After they left the Original, he just drove around the back roads, and Jessica kept pestering him about where they were going. At one point, he had to slow down behind a horse and buggy on Route 655 and couldn't pass it easily because of oncoming traffic. Jimmy went into another fit about the Amish, saying that the state government should *force* them to drive cars. Jacob had heard this line so often before that he confronted them both about their father having been Amish. It didn't seem to faze Jessica at all, but Jimmy fell into a black mood.

"He was surprised that you knew?"

"I think so. I don't think he liked to be reminded about it."

"And then?"

"And then I passed the horse and buggy and drove to the cabin."

"And nothing else happened?"

"Not reel-ly, unless yew mean the flare."

"The flare?" Agent Tate asked, glancing at Sergeant Stuter.

"*Ya*, I was afraid it was going to burn down the porch, but it went out. I hadn't seen one before, burning, that is, until Jimmy used one to light our way to the cabin."

"How's that?"

"Well, it was so dark up there, and when we opened the trunk fur the case of beer, he grabbed a flare. There must've been a dozen of them, stuffed in the corner. They came with the car, yew know. He said, 'Watch this, like magic,' and lit one to guide our way."

"Like magic."

"*Ya*, it was pretty bright."

Jacob remembered little more once they reached the cabin because he drank so much. Next, he was climbing out of the back seat of his car.

"That's enough for now," Agent Tate concluded. "Thank you, Jacob, for your cooperation."

When they stepped into the hall, Sergeant Stuter and Agent Tate said good-night to Isaac D., sitting in a chair outside the room.

"Well, that explains the white baseball cap," Agent Tate observed, opening the door to the police cruiser. "It fell off when he got out of the car."

As Sergeant Stuter drove out of the hospital parking lot, Agent Tate said they should first go to Harrisville to take Jessica down to the station and break her. After that, they would get Jimmy. Then Agent Tate talked quickly into his Sony tape recorder while Sergeant Stuter drove swiftly through the narrow streets of Lewistown toward Big Valley. The December night was cold and clear. The valley was quiet. When they turned into the Smith driveway, Jimmy stood leaning against his black Camaro, parked in front of the garage.

"Well, isn't this convenient!" Agent Tate remarked with sardonic surprise.

A cold wind blew Jimmy's long black hair about his face as he confronted the two men.

"What do you want?" he shouted.

"Answers," Agent Tate replied. "Answers, Jimmy."

"I already tole ya everything I'm gonna tell ya."

"You have a lot more to tell me," Agent Tate snapped. "I want you and your sister to come down to the station to answer a few questions."

Just then, the snap and groan of the automatic garage door cut the conversation. The white-paneled door rose jerkily as it opened to reveal Jessica standing there with two suitcases. She dropped them, staring at the two men with a startled expression on her face; her eyes narrowed like those of a trapped wild cat.

At the state police barracks in Bantam, Agent Tate and Sergeant Stuter escorted Jimmy and Jessica through the building into the outer area of the crime unit. Jimmy and Jessica were questioned separately in the interrogation room, a small nondescript room with a single table and several straight-back chairs.

Agent Tate and Sergeant Stuter finally pieced together a bizarre tale of senseless vindictiveness. At the cabin, Jimmy had sunk into a vile mood, brooding over Jacob's comment about being Amish. He wanted to *do something*, then and there, that night. He sat on the lumpy sofa in the cabin and watched the reddish light of the flare, stabbed into the deck and eventually spluttering out. Then the idea sparked in his mind. *Why not set a few barns on fire the way they had set those corn shocks on fire that Halloween night?* A flare burns for thirty minutes. They could set one, drive away, and be a good half hour from the barn before the flare ignited the hay.

The idea thrilled Jessica, who considered it brilliant and fun. They knew the valley well. They knew it was a church night—Jacob had mentioned it earlier—which meant that the Amish would be asleep and quiet that night. So after Jacob passed out, the other three dumped him in the back seat, then squeezed into the front seat and took off. Lil drove at first. The brother and sister took turns dashing inside a barn, setting a flare, and dashing out. Lil didn't want to have any part of it, but to make sure she wouldn't squeal, they finally convinced her to help set a fire. They said that no one would ever know and assured her that the farmers could get the animals out in time.

First they drove to Wilton. They set three flares going and drove into Greenville to set another one. When they drove to Fairville, two barns were directly next to each other, so Jimmy sent Lil with Jessica while he went to the other one. Jimmy set one flare, but Jessica said she accidentally dropped the flare through a hole in the floor. Jessica was rattled because Lil was excited and upset and just wanted to get out. So Jessica used her cigarette lighter to start a bale of hay on fire. The bale, apparently, was damp and merely smoldered. Jimmy was furious with Jessica for doing that because that might blow their whole cover. They piled into the car in a frenzy, and Jimmy drove like crazy because the barn could go up in a flash. They raced into Harrisville and set one last flare before driving Jessica home.

When Jessica got out of the car, she saw that Jacob wasn't in the back seat. Jimmy exploded. They had no idea where Jacob was and figured that he must have climbed out when Lil was out of the car. So he had to be in Fairville. Jimmy was furious. This was ruining the entire plan. They had to find Jacob, but at that point, fire trucks and police cruisers were already zooming back and forth across the valley. Jimmy took the wheel and drove like a madman down Route 655, not concerned about the police since they would think he was a volunteer firefighter speeding to a burning barn. In Fairville, though, when he took the corner at Reigle Creek Road, he lost control of the car and swerved off into a field. The driveshaft snapped.

Jimmy cursed like a fiend. No one had seen the accident. Neither Jimmy nor Lil were hurt, though Lil was violently upset. Jimmy sputtered and shouted obscenities and walked downtown with Lil in silent tow. From a telephone booth, he phoned Mark, who lived in the room down the hall on Basil Street, and asked him to come and get them. Mark, raising no questions, drove into the valley for them. Meanwhile, the valley erupted into an inferno.

Jacob climbing out of the car had ruined the entire plan, Jimmy said angrily. If Jacob had stayed in the car, Jimmy and Jessica would have never been caught. Never. Never.

That night James Roland Smith and Jessica Marie Smith were arrested and charged with seven counts of first-degree arson and with criminal homicide in the death of Eli Yoder, their first cousin.

CHAPTER 50

At dawn a week later, on Monday morning, a black van drove down the Yoder farm lane and parked near the house. Twelve Amishmen, half wearing straw hats and half wearing black hats, climbed out of the van. Some of the men had nail aprons tied about their waists, and some carried work gloves in their hands. They had traveled an hour from Brush Valley.

Ezra S. greeted them warmly. On the front porch, Lydia had a pot of coffee and styrofoam cups set out on a folding table. A few of the men poured cups of coffee, while the others, straight-backed and purposeful, walked over to a gathering group of Amishmen near a great pile of lumber.

"Not too cold," Ezra S. murmured to one of the men. "As soon as the sun comes up, it'll get warm."

"Once we start working," the man replied, "we'll be warm."

Though the temperature had plunged to thirty-four degrees the night before, Ezra S. knew the *Farmer's Almanac* called for a clear and calm day with temperatures in the fifties. More vans pulled into the barnyard, bringing Amish and *Englischer.* A Greyhound bus parked beside the road, and a line of Amishmen from Lancaster County streamed into the farmyard. A little after seven, the sky lightened in the east, turning the dark sky into colors of deep amethyst and amber and gold. Then the action began. The shouts and the orders and the hauling of beams. The hammering and the pounding. The harsh buzz of table saws. The amazingly coordinated effort.

By seven thirty, the sun had just crested the edge of Jacks Mountain, and the volunteers were working busily to build the Yoder family a new barn. Ezra S. pulled on a pair of work gloves, hauled lumber, set it in place, and hammered nails. He inhaled the rich wood smell of the oak timbers. He lifted beams with pleasure and God-fearing gratitude for all the help that descended on his farm to raise the new barn.

Ezra S. could see his sons working diligently and felt pure happiness spread through his strong body. Isaac D. and his four boys were there. He could see Esle at the far end. As Ezra S. hammered and the framework of the new barn slowly formed, he felt as though he were hammering together the very soul of the Amish. For him, the barn fire was already in the past, forgotten and forgiven, and the task at hand was to build. To build together.

The men swarmed over the new barn site, working industriously and in perfect teamwork. Over two hundred Amishmen and *englisch* volunteers hauled, lifted, pounded, and cut the oak and pine. In the house and on the front porch, almost as many women and girls bustled about, preparing dinner and supplying the workers with cups of coffee and tea and glasses of fresh mountain water.

Part of the gathering, Jacob Hostetler stood, leaning on a pair of wooden crutches, a straw hat jammed far down on his head. His right foot was still encased in a cast with a huge white sock pulled over it to keep his toes warm. Next to him stood Paul Virgilia. Jacob observed the laboring men with an expression of satisfaction. A barn raising is one of the strongest symbols in the Amish community. All toiled together for the common welfare. His eyes glittered with renewed strength and settled faith.

The spiritual wrestling in the cave had transformed Jacob, dramatically and abruptly, dragging to his consciousness the disillusioned thoughts and emotions about the *englisch* way of life that had evolved over the summer. He was no longer enchanted by that worldly lifestyle. What he had been searching for had been before him and within him all the while. He was a child of God who needed spiritual nourishment, and he realized he could not find that anywhere in the world but with his own people, the Amish. In the simplicity and plainness of the Amish, the complexities and anxieties of his spiritual confusion were absorbed.

When Jacob reflected on his earlier plight, he saw that what stood at the center of that distress, no matter how he had cloaked it in desire for money or goods or comfort, was selfish desire. As soon as he abandoned that selfishness for the abiding love of Jesus Christ, for faith in God, for submission to God's commands as defined by his people—all sorrow and all sighing had flown away. With damp eyes, he watched his twin brother climb and help fit two sections of framework together. Esle, after inward struggle, had forgiven him for the lost money and said he would rather have a brother than a new shotgun.

Rebekah, who had just brought out a fresh pot of coffee, paused for a moment and watched the men work before she caught sight of Jacob leaning on his crutches. Her eyes glistened with tears. The day before, her son once again had gone with the family to church. He was back in Amish clothes and letting his hair and beard grow out.

Lydia appeared next to Rebekah and looked at the great wooden skeleton in the clear morning light. "How much they have done already!"

Rebekah nodded.

Lydia's face was solemn and still with renewed faith in God's succor. But the revelation that Jesse's children, her own nephew and niece, were responsible for that dark, fiery night had further challenged her faith with deeper suffering and her heart with the love of Christ. At this point, she seemed so used to tragedy and suffering. When she saw Jacob, her face settled into a gentle expression. How glad she was that the rumors about Jacob were false! She had always refused to believe them. She watched Rachel, her eyes bright, hand Jacob a cup of coffee. "We are so happy that Jacob returned."

Rebekah, her eyes beaming, nodded her head again.

"And that is his *englisch* friend?" Lydia asked.

"*Ya*, the *good* one."

All morning and all afternoon, the men worked hard, stopping only for a brief dinner. The air was thick with the scent of pine and coffee and hope. By midafternoon, the remaining two walls were hoisted into place and the wooden pegs driven in deep. The men then set the corrugated tin roofing in place, piece by piece. By late afternoon, the barn was finished, a monumental structure of pine and oak that stood on the cold winter landscape like a rock, built to last a hundred years or two hundred years or more. Tomorrow, the livestock would arrive.

Jacob stood next to Ezra S., gazed at the new barn, and breathed a silent prayer in joy and *Gelassenheit*.

GLOSSARY

The Amish are bilingual. Among non-Amish, they speak English. Among themselves, they speak Pennsylvania German, a dialect sometimes called Pennsylvania Dutch, for *Deitsch,* meaning "German." Eighteenth- and nineteenth-century immigrants brought the basics of this dialect from the Palatinate of Germany. Here is the pronunciation and definition of some *Deitsch* words and phrases used in this novel.

Abrot (AH-broat)	ministers' counsel before church for prayer and to determine who will preach which sermons
Anfang, Aafang (AH-fahng)	(beginning) introductory sermon
Attnungsgemee (AHT-noongs-ga-may)	preparatory service before communion for church members to agree on rules and regulations
Ausbund (AWZ-boond)	(paragon) official hymnbook, choice lyrics from sixteenth century, tunes by oral tradition
Daadi (DAH-dee)	Dad
danki (DAN-kee)	thank you, thanks
Die Botschaft (dee BOT-shaft)	a weekly newspaper serving Old Order Amish communities

Die ernsthafte Christenpflicht (dee URNST-hafta KRIS-ten-pflikt)	(The earnest Christian's duty) Swiss Anabaptist prayer book from early eighteenth century
die Gemee nooch geh (dee ga-MAY nooh gay)	to follow the church
englisch (ENG-leesh)	(adjective) non-Amish
Englischer (ENG-leesh-er)	non-Amish person(s)
es schwere Deel (es schveer-a DEAL)	(the heavy part) the main sermon
Gelassenheit	yieldedness to God
Grossdaadi (GROSS-dah-dee)	grandfather, grandpa
Grossdaadi Haus (haws)	grandparents' house (retirement home), usually attached to main farmhouse
Grossmammi (GROSS-mah-mee)	grandmother, grandma
gut (goot)	good
gut mya (goot MY-ah)	good morning
gut-n-Owed (GOOT-n-O-vet)	good evening
Kammer (KAH-mer)	parents' bedroom, downstairs
Leid (lyt); *leidig* (LY-tig)	suffering; disagreeable, nasty
Lied (leet)	hymn, song
Mamm (mahm)	Mom
Mantel (MAHN-tl)	gray cape with black edges
Meiding (MY-ding)	shunning

Mitzle (MIT-zl)	short brown jacket for women
Mütze (MOOEE-tza)	frock coat first worn by men on day of baptism
nay (nay)	no
Ordnung, Addning (ATT-ning)	the order, rules, and regulations of the Amish: the principles of belief, baptism, separation from the world as well as clarification of what is forbidden, such as cars, high-line (public) electricity, and much of twentieth-century technology
Schnitz	slices (of apple)
sei so gut (sigh so goot)	please
Überrock (ooee-bur-RAWK)	gray cape overcoat with black buttons
un/und (oon/oond)	and
Vorsinger (FOR-zing-er)	song leader
was? (vahs)	what?
wie geht's? (vee GAYTS)	(how's it going?) how do you do? how are you?
ya (yah)	yes
Zeugnis (ZYG-nis)	testimony or comment on the main sermon

AUTHOR'S NOTE

This is a work of imagination, though loosely based on a historical event. On the night of March 14, 1992, six Amish barns did burn to the ground in Big Valley in central Pennsylvania. This was widely reported in the national media.

At the time, I was chair of the English department at a prep school in Litchfield, Connecticut. One weekend I drove to the valley, five weeks after the fires, to see if I might be interested in writing a novel. I was more than interested; I was enchanted! The following weekend I again drove through the mountains and visited the valley. By then, I realized that I would have to live in Big Valley for an extended period of time to research material for this novel. As soon as school let out in early June, I moved some clothes, a few books, and my computer into a room I rented for the summer at Esther Stuter's Far View Farm, a bed-and-breakfast establishment in Belleville.

That summer no one knew who set the fires or why, although rumors abounded. Out of all the speculation and the facts available at that time, I dreamed up the plot, the characters, the themes, and the incidents I wished to develop. The person responsible for the barn fires was not arrested and convicted until the following year. By then, I had already finished writing the first draft and made no substantive changes.

What captured my imagination more than the barn fires and the search for the arsonist was the Amish themselves. That was the true story, and I wanted to portray their plain and simple lives as accurately and realistically as possible. The barn fires became my vehicle to describe how the Amish were living in the 1990s.

THE AUTHOR

Ted Wojtasik was born and reared in Wallingford, Connecticut. His grandparents, Polish immigrants, ran a successful dairy farm there.

He holds an M.F.A. from Columbia University and is a Ph.D. candidate at the University of South Carolina, specializing in twentieth-century American literature. He is also an instructor of English at the university and received an Elliot Award for Excellence in Teaching in 1995. He has had short stories published in various literary journals. *No Strange Fire* is his first novel.

Ted Wojtasik lived and worked among the Amish for months. He woke at dawn to milk cows, knelt with families for morning prayers, ate in Amish kitchens, pitched hay, rode in buggies, loaded milk cans, attended livestock auctions, watched Amish women bake, roamed through fields of grain, tossed feed into cow troughs, cranked ice-cream freezers, talked with youths who left the Amish and with some who were about to join the church—and much more.

This *Englischer*, Ted Wojtasik, became a trusted friend to the Nebraska Amish of Big Valley, who have the most traditional districts among the Amish in North America. His novel accurately depicts their simple and faithful lifestyle in the complicated 1990s.

Wojtasik has worked as a researcher in the Archives of the National Geographic Society in Washington, D.C.; taught English at the Forman School in Litchfield, Connecticut; and was employed in Aiken, South Carolina, as a private tutor for Barry Goldwater III, grandson of Senator Barry Goldwater.

Ted Wojtasik now lives in Columbia, South Carolina, and is a parishioner at St. Peter's Catholic Church.